Fists of Justice

(Schooled in Magic XII)

Christopher G. Nuttall

Twilight Times Books
Kingsport Tennessee

Fists of justice

This is a work of fiction. All concepts, characters and events portrayed in this book are used fictitiously and any resemblance to real people or events is purely coincidental.

Paladin Timeless Books, an imprint of
Twilight Times Books
P O Box 3340
Kingsport TN 37664
http://twilighttimesbooks.com/

First Printing, November 2017

ISBN: 978-1-60619-326-6

Library of Congress Control Number: 2017958804

Cover art by Brad Fraunfelter

Printed in the United States of America.

Dedication

To George, with many thanks.

Prologue

AS SOON AS SHE WAS SURE HER MOTHER WAS ASLEEP, ALBA PULLED HER WAND OUT OF HER sleeve and tapped it against the anchorstone embedded within her bedroom window. There was a flicker of magic – strong enough for her to feel, but too weak to trigger the house's wards – and the protections unlocked. Opening the window, Alba clambered out and scrambled down the uneven wall until her feet touched the ground.

She glanced up and down the alleyway, then waved her wand again. The window slid closed, stopping a second before the lock could snap shut. Alba allowed herself a moment of relief as she carefully recharged the wand, channeling magic and spells into the wood. She *thought* she'd worked out the spells properly, but accidentally locking herself out of the house would be embarrassing. Her mother would be furious if she caught her daughter outside after nightfall. Alba would be lucky if she wasn't grounded for the next thousand years.

A shape appeared at the far end of the alley. "Alba?"

"Quiet," Alba hissed, as she slipped the wand into her belt. "Mum's wards might notice you!"

She smiled as her boyfriend came into view. They were very different; she was short, with red hair cropped close to her scalp, while Antony was tall, his pale skin contrasting oddly with his dark hair and darker almond eyes. Like many others from the merchant class, his father had been born in Beneficence, but his mother's family hailed from somewhere on the other side of the known world. She didn't hold that against him. Beneficence *lived* by trade. Family connections to distant lands could only come in handy. Besides, he was one of the few boys brave enough to court the daughter of a sorceress. Most young men didn't have the nerve.

"We're going to be late," he muttered, as he took her hand and hurried her down the alleyway. "How far do the wards stretch?"

"I'm not sure," Alba confessed, sourly. She touched her wand, feeling a flicker of the old regret. She'd been born with magic, but not enough to justify her parents paying for a proper magical education. The spells her mother had taught her – and the spells she'd sneaked out of her mother's spellbooks – were all she'd ever had. "I think we'll be safe once we're out of the alley."

"I hope you're right," Antony said. He glanced at his watch. "Vesperian always throws the best parties."

Alba had to smile. "Did your father get the contract?"

"And several hundred notes," Antony added. "We should be sitting pretty for the next few years, at least until Vesperian's Track is completed."

"Good," Alba said. Antony would be first in line to take over his father's business. It would give him a secure base to support a wife, if they got married. Alba's family was wealthy – she could support herself, if necessary – but they'd expect Antony to pay for everything. *And* they should have no grounds to object. Antony might not be a magician, but he could definitely lift Alba up the social scale. "And how much of the negotiation did *you* do?"

"Just a little," Antony said. One of the reasons Alba liked him was that he wasn't as boastful as some of the other young men. "I purchased a few dozen notes for myself, though, at very good rates. They should pay off in a couple of years."

The streets grew more crowded as they made their way towards Starry Light, the wealthiest part of the city. Beneficence never slept, not even late at night. Her heart pounded with excitement. It wasn't something she saw often, considering her mother was a little overprotective. She smiled as she saw a line of dancers making their way down the street, clapping and cheering as they extolled the praises of someone she'd never heard of for guildmaster. Antony pulled her through the crowds, then stopped. There were so many people!

"We'd better go this way," he said, pulling her into another alley. "We don't want to be *too* late."

Alba smiled. There were alleys down in the Lower Depths, her mother had warned her, where anyone foolish enough to enter would never emerge again. She'd never been allowed to visit the area, so she didn't *know* if it was true. But here, with the City Guard patrolling regularly, the alleys were clear. Drunks, beggars and muggers knew better than to tangle with the Guard. The alleyway even smelled better than the street near her house.

Her smile grew wider as they came out of the maze and walked towards the mansion. No one really knew how rich Vesperian actually *was*, but anyone who owned a giant mansion in Beneficence – where space was at a premium – had to be *immensely* rich. To Alba, the line of young men and women entering the mansion, some of the women wearing dresses that revealed far too much, was just icing on the cake. She recognized a number of people who were either wealthy and powerful in their own right, or heirs to great wealth and power. A handful surrounded them as they made their way through the gates, her skin crawling as she sensed a powerful ward protecting the mansion. Antony waved them away, promising to speak to them later.

"Thank you," Alba whispered. Antony had promised her a night of dancing, not a night of secret negotiations. Besides, how secret could anything *be* at this party? "Shall we dance?"

"Of course," Antony whispered back. "They'll be waiting for me after I see you home."

He led her into the mansion and onto the dance floor. Alba shook her head in disbelief at the sheer luxury, ranging from colossal tables groaning under the weight of food to golden statues and expensive paintings that dominated the room. A couple were explicit enough to make her blush. She had no idea how the artist had managed to convince *anyone* to do *that* long enough for him to make the preliminary sketches. Antony paid no attention to them, much to her relief. Hopefully, they wouldn't give him any ideas. She liked him more than she cared to admit, but she wasn't ready to do more than kissing yet.

Besides, there were other complications.

"We're just here to dance," Antony said, when a pair of middle-aged men tried to call him over. Alba was relieved. They'd been on the dance floor for nearly an hour, but neither of them wanted to leave just yet. "I'll be back in the office tomorrow."

Alba smiled at him. "What do they want to talk about?"

"Business." Antony beamed. "We're hot at the moment, you know."

"I know," Alba said.

She leaned in and kissed him, then jerked her head towards the door. Many of the younger boys and girls were heading home, clearly hoping to get back before curfew. She wasn't the only one who'd sneaked out, she was sure. Being caught at the dance, particularly as the night wore on, would ruin a young person's social life. Everyone knew what happened in the wee hours of the morning, even if no one could put it into words.

Antony grinned back at her as he led her through the doors and out onto the streets. The air felt colder now, a faint...*edge*...flickering at the periphery of her awareness, but she barely noticed. Antony led her back into the maze of alleyways, picking his way through the darkened streets with easy assurance. And yet...Alba found herself glancing from side to side as she realized what was missing. The alley was completely empty. It shouldn't have been, even at such a late hour. Beneficence was the city that never slept.

"We're nearly home," Antony said. He turned to face her. "Did you have a good time?"

"I did." Alba's heart was suddenly pounding in her chest. "I..."

She leaned forward, lifting her head so he could kiss her. His lips felt soft and warm against hers, just for a second. And then he tensed...

"I don't want to end up like Ridley," he said. "Is it safe...?"

Alba felt another flicker of irritation. Jaya, Alba's elder sister, had dated Ridley until he'd put his hand under her shirt and discovered, the hard way, that their mother had layered protective spells on her daughters. Alba had been too young to be interested in men at the time, but she still recalled the shouting match. Ridley hadn't even *known* she'd been protected until it was too late. Jaya had left the city afterwards and never been seen again.

"It should be," she said. She lifted her lips for another kiss. "As long as we don't go too far."

He kissed her again. The world seemed to darken, just enough for Alba to notice. An electric shock ran through the air. For a horrified moment, she thought she was wrong, that Antony's kisses had triggered a protective hex. And then her boyfriend looked up, his eyes looking past her. His mouth dropped open.

They were no longer alone.

Alba turned, one hand snatching her wand from her belt. She might not be a powerful magician, but she could make any unwary footpads regret they ever saw her. And then she froze as she saw the...entity...standing behind them. For a long moment, her eyes seemed to blur as her mind struggled to make sense of what she was seeing. The entity was no taller than Antony, yet he seemed infinitely tall; he was human, but somehow far more *real* than any mere human. His face and beard seemed carved from granite. His dark eyes were deep pools of shadow. She couldn't even *look* at him.

"Justice," Antony breathed.

Alba started. It was a trick. It *had* to be a trick. Some sorcerer's idea of a joke, perhaps. Or maybe her mother had decided to scare them both…she lifted her wand, casting a cancellation charm.

The entity didn't vanish. Instead, its presence seemed to grow stronger and stronger until it overpowered her. It was so *big*.

She heard her wand clatter to the ground. A moment later, she fell to her knees. She couldn't help herself. Her body felt utterly drained.

The entity strode forward, its footsteps shaking the cobbles below her knees. It was all Alba could do to keep watching as it came to a halt in front of Antony. Her boyfriend had fallen to his knees too. She saw him trembling as the entity stared down at him. Her mouth was dry, with fear and…and something she didn't care to identify. It couldn't be a *real* god, could it?

"Antony, Son of Emil," the entity said. It spoke in a quiet voice that boomed in Alba's ears, each word precisely enunciated. "You and yours have led this city to ruin."

Impossible, Alba thought. She could barely think clearly. *He's so young*!

"Mercy," Antony gasped.

"There is no mercy," the entity said. There was a *power* in its voice, a sheer conviction that every word it spoke was the unquestionable truth. "There is only Justice."

Antony's body blazed with light. Alba screamed, feeling as if daggers were being driven into her very soul. She squeezed her eyes closed, desperately trying to block out the pain. And then the light faded. She fell backwards, bumping her shoulder on the cobblestones. The pain made her jerk her eyes open…

…She was alone.

Her fingers touched her wand. The tingle, the sensation she felt whenever she touched a charged wand, was gone. She couldn't muster the energy to prepare a spell, let alone power it. The darkness seemed stronger, somehow, as if the moon and stars had been blotted from the skies. And yet…

She stumbled to her feet. Antony still knelt on the ground, utterly unmoving. She reached for his arm and touched cold stone. He'd been turned to stone…no, if he'd been petrified, she would have felt a tingle…wouldn't she?

The moon came out again, shining into the alleyway. And she screamed, again, as she caught a glimpse of his face…

It was twisted in horrific agony.

Chapter One

T HE AIR...*STANK.*

Emily was dimly aware, at the back of her mind, that someone was knocking on a wooden door. And yet, it didn't seem important. She wasn't even entirely sure where she was. The ground was shifting beneath her, sending up alarm bells she couldn't quite hear. And yet...

"Emily," a voice called. A *male* voice. "Wake up!"

Emily jerked awake. She was on a ship, she recalled; a merchant ship that did double duty as a warship, when the seafaring states went to war. And she was heading to Beneficence. And Casper was dead...

"I'm awake," she managed. She opened her eyes. Her stomach muttered rebelliously. "I'll be along in a moment."

"Good," General Pollack said. His voice was so close that she looked around in alarm before realizing he was on the far side of a wooden door. "Come meet me on the quarterdeck when you're ready."

Emily nodded as she heard the sound of his footsteps striding away. She was, as far as she knew, the only woman on the ship, although General Pollack *had* told her stories of young girls who'd run away to sea and somehow managed to conceal their gender for decades. Emily wasn't sure how that was possible – she'd seen the crew quarters and their complete lack of privacy – but she was prepared to take his word for it. She might have tried to run away too, if she'd thought it possible. And, perhaps, if she'd had any stomach for seafaring. She'd been on the boat for five days and she *still* felt seasick.

We should have teleported, she thought. They *had* teleported to the nearest port, then called a ship to pick them up. *But the general said it was tradition...*

She sat upright, glancing around the cabin. It belonged to the captain, who'd flatly refused to let anyone else give up their sleeping space to the young sorceress, noblewoman and war heroine. Emily would have been more impressed if she hadn't known that the captain had moved into his first mate's cabin, who in turn had displaced the officer directly below him...she shook her head, telling herself that she should be grateful. The cabin was cramped and smelly, despite the gilded wooden bulkheads, but it *was* private. She'd seen the way some of the sailors – and officers – gawked at her when they thought she wasn't looking.

Swinging her legs over the side, she stood, careful not to bang her head on the low ceiling as she slipped on her shoes. Sleeping in her clothes made her feel icky, but there was no way she'd wear a nightgown, let alone sleep naked, on the ship. She took some water from her canteen and splashed it on her face, then examined her reflection in the mirror. Her hair was a mess – she hadn't had a chance to take a hairgrowth potion back in Farrakhan – and her face was pale, dark circles clearly visible around her eyes. She looked distressingly like a raccoon – or, perhaps, someone who'd come off worst in a fight. Her shirt and trousers looked unclean, as if they hadn't been washed for a few days. Magic wasn't good enough to clean them. The only real consolation was that most of the crew looked worse.

We should definitely have teleported, she thought, as she felt the deck shifting beneath her feet. Her legs wobbled, just for a second. *I could have teleported us both back to Cockatrice and we could have crossed the bridge there.*

She took a sip of seasickness potion – it wasn't strong enough to provide more than minimal relief, but anything stronger would have impaired her mind – and headed for the door. General Pollack had insisted on taking his son's remains home via ship, despite her objections. In hindsight, Emily told herself, she should have asked to remain at Farrakhan with Sergeant Miles or even asked the sergeant to prolong her apprenticeship for an additional couple of weeks. But she hadn't.

The smell – too many humans in too close proximity, mingled with salt water – grew stronger as she pushed her way into the corridor. She could hear chatter coming from nearby, but she couldn't see anyone. A metal grate, set within the wooden deck, led down to the lower decks. The sailors would be down there, she knew; the night crew would be trying to rest, even as the day crew went to work. She wondered, absently, why some of the crew were talking. They'd be keeping their comrades awake.

Or maybe not, she thought, as she walked into the next compartment. *They'll be so tired they can sleep through anything.*

She drew in her breath as she saw the coffin, mounted neatly on a wooden block. It was a simple design, with a name and a handful of runes carved into the wood. And yet, it was empty. Casper's body had been blasted into dust, the remains drifting down towards the nexus point and vanishing. No spell she knew could salvage anything that was indisputably *Casper*. But General Pollack had insisted on taking a coffin home anyway. Emily didn't think that was healthy, yet she knew everyone grieved in their own way.

You'd think differently if you lost a child, she told herself. *You'd want to believe that some of him had been laid to rest too.*

A small book lay atop the coffin, protected by a simple wardspell. Emily felt a twinge of pain, remembering how many magicians and officers had written a brief farewell into its pages. Casper had deserved better than an early death, even if he *had* died a hero. Far too many others had already been forgotten, after dying in defense of the Allied Lands. No one, as far as she knew, had any idea how many soldiers and civilians had died. Most would only be mourned by their families.

She shook her head, then turned and headed for the outer door. A gust of cold air struck her as she pushed it open and stepped out onto the deck. *Willow* was rolling, gently, as she made her way along the green coastline, her deck shivering as she plowed her way through the uneven waves. Emily felt her stomach twist and swallowed hard, silently promising herself not to throw up in front of the sailors. Her legs felt unsteady as she forced herself to walk towards the quarterdeck. Every movement felt, to her, as though the ship was on the verge of capsizing. She told herself, firmly, that her mind was playing tricks on her, but it didn't feel convincing. She'd never managed to get her sea legs.

Willow felt *small* to her, even though she'd been in more confined spaces. Emily couldn't help thinking that she was *tiny*, compared to a ship on Earth. Ninety crew and ten guests, all crammed into her hull…she turned as she heard a shout, just in time to see a young boy scrambling up the mainmast and into the crow's nest. The boy couldn't be anything like old enough to shave, let alone go to Whitehall. It still surprised her, even now, to see children performing adult tasks. The four sailors who scrambled up to the forward sails dwarfed the cabin boy.

"My Lady," Captain Rackham said, once she reached the table on the quarterdeck. "Thank you for sharing my table."

Emily – reluctantly – held out her hand for him to kiss, then withdrew it as soon as she decently could. Captain Rackham looked like a pirate, right down to the black waistcoat and the cutlass on his belt. He probably *was* a pirate from time to time, she knew; *Willow* was fast enough to catch and overwhelm anything smaller than a full-fledged warship, if there were no witnesses. No one would ask too many questions, either. The Empire had worked hard to keep the seas clear of pirates, but it had been a long time since anyone had been in a position to patrol the waves.

"Please, be seated," Captain Rackham added. "My table is your table."

"Thank you," Emily said.

She sat next to General Pollack, silently welcoming the older man's presence as she nibbled a piece of bread and salt beef. A steward – probably under contract to the captain – passed Emily a glass of lime juice, his eyes flickering over her face as if he were trying to memorize every detail. Emily braced herself before emptying the glass at one swallow. It was so sour that she hadn't been surprised when the captain told her that some of the sailors refused to drink it, even though it was the only thing protecting them from scurvy. He'd made it clear that he expected *everyone* on his ship to drink their juice, even if they weren't part of his crew. It kept them safe.

And they didn't have time to restock when they picked us up, she thought, as she chewed her beef. *They're running short of supplies.*

The other passengers made small talk, making no effort to include her. Emily was silently grateful, even though she knew they probably considered it standoffishness. Her stomach left her in no state for idle chatter. She listened, saying nothing, as the passengers chatted about the war, bouncing question after question off General Pollack. Thankfully, none of them knew who she was. They'd be much more insistent on trying to open lines of communication if they'd known the truth. She might be in exile – technically – but she was still Baroness Cockatrice. Her word was gold.

King Randor probably feels otherwise, she thought, ruefully.

General Pollack elbowed her, gently. "Eat more," he warned. "We'll be heading into land soon."

Emily made a face as the midshipman placed a small bowl of stew in front of her, but tried to eat it anyway. It tasted faintly unpleasant, as if the meat had been cooked in vinegar. And yet, she knew she was eating better than any of the sailors. *They* were lucky if they got hardtack and salted fish. She'd seen a number of crewmen fishing during the voyage, trying to catch something to supplement their rations. Apparently, anyone who caught a fish was allowed to keep half of it for himself.

She glanced from face to face, reminding herself – again – that the Nameless World was strikingly diverse. Four merchants, one of them accompanied by his eldest son; three noblemen, who could presumably have used a portal; and a lone man who said nothing, his eyes flickering everywhere. The merchants were chatting loudly about steam engines and what they'd do to shipping, once the first steamboats set out on the open sea. Emily couldn't help noticing that the captain seemed vaguely affronted by the suggestion. *Willow* wouldn't be able to compete if – when – the steamboats lived up to their promise.

As long as they have wood or coal to burn, she reminded herself. *All this ship needs is a strong wind.*

"Come," General Pollack said. Emily looked down at her bowl and discovered, to her surprise, that she'd finished it. "We're just rounding the headland now."

Emily followed him, all too aware of eyes watching her as they climbed down the ladder and headed to the prow. The sailors might enjoy looking at a young woman, but the passengers were more interested in marriage alliances. General Pollack had had to explain that his charge was already engaged, much to Captain Rackham's amusement. He was the only one who knew the truth. Emily would have found it amusing if it hadn't been so annoying. Had they really expected that General Pollack would *give* them her hand in marriage?

They think you're his niece, she reminded herself. *And your uncle would have considerable power over your marriage.*

She pushed the thought aside as she joined General Pollack at the prow. A young lad sat at the front of the ship, mounted on the bowsprit above the wooden mermaid figurehead. Emily couldn't help thinking that he looked awfully unbalanced as he carried out his duties, but the cabin boy seemed to take it in his stride. He practically had the sea in his blood. Chances were, Emily recalled, he was a sailor's son, born and raised by the docks. Going to sea would have seemed natural.

"The captain is altering course," General Pollack commented. He pointed a finger towards the shoreline. "What do you make of that?"

Emily frowned, holding up her hand to block the sunlight as she peered into the haze. She saw a faint smudge of utter *darkness*…a black cloud, hanging in the air over a distant bay. It was raining…wasn't it? Underneath, there were jagged rocks and the remains of a building. A castle, perhaps, or a lighthouse. It stood on its own, completely isolated. There were no other signs of habitation. And yet, the cloud seemed to pulse, as if it had a malignant mind of its own…

A hand fell on her shoulder. She jumped.

"Careful," General Pollack said. "People have been known to be…to be *touched*, even at *this* distance."

Emily gave him a sharp look. "What *is* it?"

"It used to be called Roderick's Bay," General Pollack said. "Now, everyone calls it Bad Luck Bay."

He lifted his hand, making an odd gesture towards the cloud. "Roderick was a sorcerer, perhaps one of the most powerful sorcerers in the world," he added. "He was the lord and master of a small community on the edge of the Barony of Swanhaven. Thirty or so years ago, he vanished into his tower and started work on a new spell. A year after that, the tower collapsed into rubble and that thing" – he nodded at the cloud – "appeared over the remains. Since then, anyone foolish enough to go too close has suffered terrible bad luck. The community he ruled broke up shortly afterwards, most of its inhabitants heading south into Swanhaven. It was quite a scandal at the time."

Emily frowned. "What was he doing?"

"No one knows," General Pollack said. "But no one will risk going into the bay. Ships have been known to run aground on rocks that weren't there before the...well, whatever he did."

"And no one saw anything of him," Emily guessed.

"No one," General Pollack agreed.

The mist hanging over the coastline grew thicker as *Willow* advanced steadily westwards, the captain and first mate barking incomprehensible orders that rang in Emily's ears. Seagulls appeared out of nowhere, cawing to one another as they landed on the sails. The sailors cheered as the first bird touched down, then returned to their work. It was proof, Emily supposed, they were nearly home, even though they'd been close to land for most of the voyage. No one in their right mind would want to set sail on the Great Sea, let alone the Roaring Depths. Few ships that headed away from the mainland were ever seen again.

But there is a third continent, Emily recalled. She'd seen the map, carved into the stone deep below Whitehall. *What's waiting for us there?*

She smiled, despite herself, as she saw a pod of dolphins jumping through the waves, showing themselves briefly before disappearing back under the water. They didn't show any fear of the boat, even though fishermen sometimes hunted dolphins. Perhaps they were trained...or, perhaps, they realized the large ship wasn't a fishing boat, let alone a giant whaler. The sailors had told dozens of stories about men who'd set off to hunt the whales, only to discover that the whales could fight back. Without harpoon guns, hunting whales was a dangerous endeavor.

And that might change, she thought. *What happens when someone invents a harpoon gun?*

"Watch," General Pollack said. The mist was growing stronger, gusts of wind blowing water into her face. "You'll never forget this."

Emily took hold of the rail and held on, tightly, as *Willow* started to roll alarmingly. She saw – she thought she saw – glimpses of rocks, just below the surface, visible for bare seconds before vanishing under the waves. They weren't about to run aground, were they? She hoped – prayed – that the captain knew what he was doing. If worse came to worst, she told herself firmly, she could teleport off a sinking ship...

...If, of course, she had time to cast the spell.

The mist parted, suddenly. Emily sucked in her breath, honestly awed, as Beneficence came into view. She'd seen the city before, from the shore, but this was different. Beneficence was perched on a towering rock, a strange mixture of buildings mounted on buildings that reached towards the sky. Hundreds of people were clearly visible, climbing up and down ladders that went all the way down to the waterline, where they met tiny boats tied up by the cliff face. The sight took her breath away.

Willow rounded the edge of the rock, then spun in place before lunging into a giant bay. The Caldron was immense, crammed with ships of all shapes and sizes; behind them, Emily could see ladders and steps that led up to the city above. It felt almost claustrophobic to her, as if it were both large and terrifyingly small; the water heaved and boiled, threatening to push the ship in all directions. The tiny beach on one edge of the Caldron seemed almost an afterthought. There were so many children playing in the sand that there didn't seem to be enough room. Their older siblings scrambled over the rocks, scooping up crabs and dropping them into buckets. They'd make good eating, if cooked properly.

"We'll be the first off the ship, once we're tied up," General Pollack said. "Your bag will be delivered directly to the house."

Emily nodded. She hadn't brought much, beyond a change of clothes. Her staff and some of her other tools had been left with Sergeant Miles, who'd promised to take them back to Whitehall for her. There was nothing dangerous in her rucksack, certainly nothing of use to anyone else.

"Ah," General Pollack said. He pointed towards the docks. "The welcoming committee."

Emily smiled, despite herself. Caleb stood there, wearing a long, dark cloak. Beside him...

"Frieda?"

"Lady Barb suggested that your friend be invited too." General Pollack looked oddly amused. "I trust she will be a suitable chaperone?"

"I think so," Emily said. It was a shame to *need* one. "She can handle it."

"Very good," General Pollack said. *Willow* bumped against the dock, a trio of sailors scrambling down to secure the lines. "Welcome to Beneficence!"

Chapter Two

"EMILY," CALEB CALLED.

Emily's legs still felt wobbly, but she managed to make it down the gangplank and into his arms before she collapsed. She was glad, so glad, just to hear his voice again. Caleb wrapped his arms around her and held her tightly, just long enough for his father to clear his throat. Emily blushed as Caleb kissed her gently on the forehead, then let her go. Frieda coughed a moment later, warningly. She was clearly taking her chaperonage duties seriously.

"It's good to see you again," Emily said. She held Caleb's hand, reluctant to let it go. "And you, Frieda."

"And you." Frieda smiled as Emily glanced at her. "What did you do to your *hair?*"

"I had a little accident," Emily said. She didn't think she was allowed to talk about Wildfire, at least not in public. Master Grey had made it clear that the mere *existence* of the potion was a state secret. "I'll have it regrown in the city."

She stepped back and looked at Caleb. He wore a long, dark robe – a mourning habit, she realized suddenly. He was as tall and lanky as ever, but his eyes were shadowed and he held himself in a manner that suggested he was worried. His brown hair even seemed to have greyed, marginally. She might be imagining it, but he looked older. Beside him, Frieda was wearing a brown dress that made her look like a merchant's daughter. She'd tied her dark hair into two long pigtails that hung down to touch the top of her breasts. She looked paler too.

"You could always have it cut short," Frieda suggested. "Or just let it regrow naturally."

"It looks better long," Caleb objected. Emily had no trouble realizing, for once, that he wanted to talk to her privately. Frieda might not be an ultra-strict chaperone, but there were things neither of them wanted Frieda to hear. "Father…"

"Take Emily back to the house," General Pollack ordered. "I'll be along once I've made arrangements for the coffin."

A pained expression crossed Caleb's face. Emily had always had the impression Caleb didn't *like* Casper very much, but they'd still been brothers. Losing Casper had to hurt, even if they'd all known the dangers. Emily had no blood siblings. She had no real conception of what it was like to have brothers or sisters. Frieda was the closest thing she had to a sister, and they'd only *known* each other three years.

"Yes, Father," Caleb said.

He bowed his head, then turned and led Emily along the docks. Emily resisted the urge to walk closer to him, even though it had been a long time since they'd been together. It had only been a month, the rational part of her mind insisted, yet it felt as though it had been years, as though they'd both changed. She told herself, firmly, not to worry about it. They would have plenty of time together, once they got back to Whitehall.

Assuming I don't have to spend evenings and weekends trying to catch up with my work, she thought, wryly. *Grandmaster Gordian won't go easy on me just because I killed a third necromancer.*

The cawing of seagulls grew louder as they walked along the dockside. Emily glanced from side to side, drinking in the scene. Dozens – perhaps hundreds – of fishing boats were heading out through the gap in the cliff walls and onto the open sea, followed by a pair of midsized ships practically identical to *Willow*. Merchants and hawkers prowled the docks, making deals and selling their wares. A passing salesman held out a tray of salt fish, inviting them to buy a snack. Caleb shook his head, dismissing the man. Emily understood precisely how he felt. The food on the docks wasn't always safe to eat.

"This is a very odd place," Frieda muttered. Her eyes flickered from side to side as if she expected to be attacked at any moment. "I don't like it."

"It's home," Caleb said, bluntly. "And it's where the four corners of the world meet."

Emily nodded in agreement as a line of sailors hurried past them, heading to one of the larger ships. They were a diverse crowd, men as pale as herself mingling with the darkest men she'd ever seen…and others who were clearly the product of mixed marriages. A handful of women followed them at a more sedate pace, their dresses clearly marking them as whores. The guild sashes they wore made Emily smile, even though she knew it wasn't really funny. Whores might have their own guild in Beneficence, but they were still practically at the bottom of the social scale. Only slaves were lower.

"A couple of my friends had parents who were born on the other side of the world," Caleb added. "And others went to *live* there."

Frieda didn't look impressed. Emily didn't blame her. She'd gone from a mountain village to Mountaintop, then to Whitehall and Zangaria. Beneficence had to look chaotic to her, a melange of people jammed together on a small island. The city was roughly the same size as Manhattan Island, Emily thought, with far too many people crammed into its towering buildings. Indeed, some buildings along the edge of the cliff face had clearly been built on top of other, *older* buildings. The line of runes carved into the stone probably helped keep them upright. Emily hoped, for the sake of the inhabitants, that the magic never failed. The entire structure might collapse under its own weight.

You can build a house out of clouds, with enough magic, she thought. Beneficence didn't seem to have made *that* mistake, thankfully. The spells were common knowledge – and almost never used. *And if the magic fails, you'll plummet to your death.*

She listened, absently, as Caleb talked about the virtues of a cosmopolitan city. Beneficence drew on ideas from all over the world, ranging from complex spells to new building techniques…even their *cooking* drew on ideas from far and wide. In addition, Beneficence had become a center of the New Learning, spreading ideas across the world. Emily wondered, as they passed a pair of sailors who eyed Frieda and her with interest, what they'd say if they knew *she'd* founded the New Learning. Would they believe it was *her*?

"You'll like this," Caleb said, as they reached the edge of the docks. "You probably designed its grandfather."

Emily's eyes went wide as she saw the funicular. A small car – practically a tiny railway carriage – sat at the bottom of the track, its twin perched at the top. A steam engine puffed to life as the carriages began to move, one heading up the track while the other slid down. She couldn't help smiling as she realized what a particularly ingenious engineer had built. A funicular might normally be powered by humans – there were plenty of slaves in the city – but *this* one drew on steam. It was probably nowhere near as efficient as an electric motor, yet it advertised the potentials of steam technology to the entire world.

Caleb led them to the ticket booth and handed over a couple of coins. Emily followed him into the car, looking around with interest. Someone had pulled out all the stops, furnishing the interior with luxury seats and even a small bar…she shook her head with wry amusement at the sight. The trip would only take five minutes. They wouldn't be in the car long enough to have a drink. She turned her head to peer up the track and saw a stylized golden 'V' carved into the metal framework. Another was clearly displayed on the upper station. Anyone coming into the Caldron could probably see it, if they bothered to look.

"That's Vesperian's symbol," Caleb said. He stepped up beside her, wrapping his arm around her waist. "He's one of the richest men in the city, Emily, and he owes it all to you."

"Watch your hand," Frieda called. "And behave."

Emily felt her cheeks heat as Caleb pulled back. "You don't need to be *that* careful," she said, embarrassed. "We'll behave."

Frieda smirked. "Lady Barb made me promise to protect you," she said, sticking out her tongue. "And I don't want to disappoint her."

"No one wants to disappoint her," Emily said.

She felt a pang of sadness. She'd hoped that Lady Barb would accompany her to Beneficence, but Lady Barb had stayed with Sergeant Miles instead. Now that the necromancer was dead, the vast army that had assembled to defend Tarsier was breaking up and making its way home. Emily wasn't sure why Sergeant Miles had needed to stay in Farrakhan to assist Lord Alcott in disbanding the host, but he apparently hadn't had a choice. Half the other combat sorcerers had already returned to the White City, where Master Bone was facing an inquest. He might not have *known* that Gaius was a spy and a traitor, but he still had some pretty sharp questions to answer.

A low rattle echoed through the car, followed by a series of jerks. She and Caleb sat down hastily as the car started to move, inching its way up the track. Frieda giggled as she looked up, watching the other car heading down towards them. Emily knew – she *hoped* she knew – that it was perfectly safe, but it still looked ominous as the other car flashed past and headed to the bottom. Their car rattled into the upper station a moment later, the conductor unlatching the doors. Outside, the giant 'V' was everywhere.

"Welcome back." Caleb's voice turned regretful. "I wish you'd come under happier circumstances."

"So do I," Emily said. She'd found Beneficence to be a fascinating city, the last time she'd visited. "Caleb…"

Caleb squeezed her hand. "We'll talk about it later," he said, softly. "I…"

The streets were crowded, Emily realized, as they came out of the station. Thousands of people were hurrying from place to place as though their lives depended on them being on time. A long line of sailors headed down the ladders to the docks, choosing not to ride the funicular. It was probably too expensive for them, she reasoned. Indeed, she couldn't help wondering if it made enough to offset the original investment and running costs. There didn't seem to be any shortage of coolies carrying goods up the ladders and taking them into the city.

She took a breath and regretted it, instantly. The omnipresent stench of fish mingled with the scent of a primitive city: shit and piss, sweat and horse dung. Beneficence had slaves who were employed merely to clear the streets – as well as a reasonably modern plumbing system – but it still stank. She hated to think of how many diseases might be breeding in the streets. London had had a nasty outbreak of cholera that had been traced back to a single water pump.

Caleb pushed his way onwards, into the crowd. Emily gritted her teeth as she followed him, clutching to his hand as through it were a life preserver. She'd never liked crowds. Frieda stayed next to Emily, one hand raised in a casting pose. She probably didn't like crowds either. It was a relief when the crowds started to thin out…

"You came in with the morning tide," Caleb said, once they had some room to themselves. "I think everyone in the city is either going to the docks or leaving them."

Emily nodded, feeling sweat trickle down her back. Two-thirds of the city's economy depended on fishing or trade. No *wonder* so many people wanted to get down the ladders and onto the docks. And yet…she hoped General Pollack didn't have any trouble getting the coffin up to the house. She didn't pretend to understand *why* the general wanted to take an empty coffin home, but she respected his choice. It meant something to him.

The streets still thrummed with life. A handful of broadsheet singers shouted at the top of their lungs, inviting potential customers to buy a broadsheet and read the latest set of exclusives. Emily smiled as she saw the broadsheets, spotting a couple of titles she recognized from Cockatrice. The original broadsheet boom had slowed as the market grew saturated – too many printers had tried to go into the newspaper business – but the survivors were turning into reputable establishments. Their reputation for telling the truth was far stronger than any herald's.

That will change, she thought, cynically. *But people here worship the written word.*

"I picked up a copy," Frieda said, nodding towards one of the sellers. "There were only a couple of lines about the war."

"Too far away for most people to be interested," Emily pointed out. Beneficence *was* one of the most cosmopolitan cities on the Nameless World, but Tarsier and Farrakhan were still thousands of miles away. Farrakhan wasn't even on any of the major trade routes. "They wouldn't notice the war unless it impinged on them."

She frowned as they turned into a street lined with temples. Incense hung in the air, a cloyingly sweet smell that made her head swim. Large crowds were gathered outside the larger buildings, either waiting to join the service or chatting as they hurried down the street; street preachers stood on the pavement, calling to passersby. People glanced nervously at a set of statues, positioned outside one of the largest temples. Emily shuddered as she followed their gaze. The statues were...grotesque. They looked as though they were screaming in agony. The Nameless World worshipped some pretty odd things – there were cults everywhere – but the statues' aura chilled her to the bone.

"Caleb," she said. "What *are* they?"

Caleb frowned. "It depends on who you believe," he said, as he tugged her on. "I've been told they were Judged."

"Judged?"

"By Justice," Caleb said. "The witnesses claim that they *saw* the god petrify them."

Frieda looked up at him, disturbed. "Those are *people*?"

"A number of sorcerers claim they're just statues." Caleb's face darkened. "But if they *are* statues...what happened to the missing people?"

Emily shuddered. The Gorgon had petrified her, once. It had been an accident, but Emily knew she'd come far too close to losing herself. If her mind had faded away completely, she would have died. And the only thing left would have been a perfect stone statue. If the victims had been petrified, their souls destroyed...

"Surely the sorcerers could have done something," she said.

"If they were transfigured, the sorcerers should have been able to transfigure them back," Caleb said. "But they insist that the statues are just...statues."

Frieda had a more practical question. "How many?"

"There are five known statues," Caleb said. "Rumor says that there are more, *many* more."

Emily glanced around. She wasn't the most sensitive of people, but even *she* could sense an...*edge* in the air. The crowd was nervous. Fear clung to them warning her to be careful. The people on the street knew something was badly wrong. Even the chanting from some of the temples seemed curiously muted.

A trio of red-robed men appeared from one of the temples and headed down the street. The crowd parted to allow them to pass, their expressions fearful. Emily's eyes narrowed, remembering the last time she'd seen the men. The Hands of Justice, if she recalled correctly. They were the closest thing she'd seen to religious policemen.

Caleb hurried her through a maze of streets, coming out near a row of banks. Lines of people waited outside, their faces torn between enthusiasm and a kind of nameless dread they didn't seem to want to acknowledge. A mid-sized line of people outside the Bank of Silence quietly waited for...*something*. She promised herself, silently, that she would see Markus as soon as possible. The line of armed guards – and enhanced protective spells – surrounding the banks didn't reassure her.

"We'll have to go to the temple tomorrow," Caleb said. "And then..."

He glanced at Emily, then Frieda. "What would you want to do?"

"I don't know yet," Emily said, as they rounded the corner and walked into the magical district. "It depends."

She braced herself as she sensed the magic in the air, tingling against her wards. A pair of street magicians were playing with fire, young children clapping and cheering as they swallowed hot coals and breathed out gouts of flame. No one above the age of seven looked interested, she noted. Anyone raised among magicians would *know* that such tricks were simplicity itself, the spells so basic that anyone with a gram of talent could cast them. Behind them, a suspiciously intelligent horse was showing off its math skills. She studied the creature for a long moment, then rolled her eyes as she realized that the horse was actually a transfigured human. The watching crowd didn't seem to care.

"By tradition, there will be five days until the funeral," Caleb said. His words jerked her awareness back to him. "We'll have time to explore the city."

"I need to visit the bank," Emily said. "After that..."

"I'd better come with you," Frieda said. "Who knows *what* you'd get up to in the bank?"

Caleb looked annoyed. Emily didn't blame him.

"Mother wants to have a word with you, after dinner," Caleb said, making a deliberate effort to change the subject. "I suspect it has something to do with the courtship."

Emily resisted the urge to groan. "I look forward to it," she lied. She didn't think Caleb was fooled. "Caleb..."

"I understand," Caleb said. "But it has to be done."

True, Emily thought. *But that doesn't mean I have to like it.*

Chapter Three

CALEB'S HOUSE LOOKED SMALL, ON THE OUTSIDE. IT WAS A GRANITE BUILDING, ITS DARK stone exterior lined with protective runes. It did not appear large enough for a big family. And yet, merely owning the house proved that Caleb and his family were wealthy. Land was hideously expensive in Beneficence. There was a good chance that Caleb and his siblings would never be able to purchase their own homes. They'd have to go elsewhere if they wanted to own their own land.

She felt her heart start to pound as Caleb let go of her hand and tapped on the door, pressing his palm against a concealed anchorstone. The wards grew stronger, reaching out to brush against Emily's magic and confirm her identity. She hadn't expected to be keyed into the wards, but it was still a surprise when they took nearly five minutes to scrutinize her before the door clicked open. Caleb's mother stood in the opening, her dark eyes peering narrowly at Emily.

Emily nerved herself to look back as evenly as she could. Mediator Sienna of House Waterfall was a tall woman, a head taller than Emily, her hair a shade or two darker than Emily's own. She looked, in many ways, like an older version of Caleb... older, perhaps, than she'd been a year ago. It felt longer, far longer, since Emily had last seen her. Emily could barely believe that it had been only nine months since she'd visited Beneficence.

"Emily," Sienna said. Her voice was flat, emotionless. "I bid you welcome to my house."

"I thank you," Emily managed. She forced herself to fumble through the ritual. "I pledge to hold my hand in your house."

Sienna studied her for a long moment, then turned and led the way into the hall. Emily followed, looking around with interest. Someone had hung a surprisingly accurate portrait of Casper on the near wall, surrounded by black ribbon. Casper looked grimly resolute as he faced down a shadowy form. There was no sign of Emily or anyone else. Even the necromancer was just a dark shape. But she had to admit that the portrait conveyed the right message: Casper had laid down his life in defense of the Allied Lands.

"Remove your cloaks and make your devotions, then join us in the parlor," Sienna ordered, curtly. "My husband will meet you there."

Emily undid her cloak and hung it on the stand, then glanced at the household god. It was a tiny statue, carved to resemble a stern-faced man...probably one of the founders of House Waterfall. A single candle burned in front of the statuette, flickering randomly in all directions. It looked as though the wind was trying to blow it out, but there was *no* wind. A chill ran down her spine as she bowed to the statue, feeling faintly ridiculous. It was probably just magic. She'd seen no real evidence that the gods truly existed.

But you have met beings of immense power, she reminded herself, as Frieda knelt in front of the statue. *Does that not imply the gods might be real too?*

Caleb reached out and took her hand. "Mother hasn't taken Casper's death well," he whispered.

Emily nodded. She'd lost Grandmaster Hasdrubal, but he'd been over a hundred years old when he'd died. Sienna was mourning a son who should have outlived her by decades...who *would* have outlived her, if he hadn't gone to war. And with all the rumors swirling around, Sienna had to wonder just what had *really* happened at Heart's Eye. Emily, Lady Barb and Void were the only ones who knew the *full* story.

She looked up at Caleb. She'd planned to tell him about Heart's Eye, when they had some privacy. Frieda might as well hear about the former school at the same time. The idea of using the building – *her* building – to create a university was appealing. They'd planned to do it even *before* the war. Now...now they could make their dream real.

Caleb bowed to the god, then turned to lead them through the door. Emily followed him into a comfortable sitting room. Another painting hung over the far wall, showing a young child sitting on a stool. It took her a moment to realize that it was a seven-year-old Casper. The artist had been good, good enough to capture the essence of Casper's personality. She couldn't help wondering just how Casper had been bribed to remain still long enough for the artist to complete the preliminary sketches. Emily had been forced to sit for two portraits and she'd hated every second of it.

The sooner we invent cameras, the better, she thought.

"Karan, Marian," Caleb said. "Bid welcome to our guest."

Emily forced herself to smile as Karan and Marian rose to their feet. Karan looked very much like her mother, with a face full of character rather than conventionally pretty. Marian was blonde, but the bubbly young girl Emily remembered was gone, replaced by a somber teenager who eyed her through bright blue eyes. Magic flickered and flared around her...she'd be fourteen now, Emily thought. She'd clearly come into her magic earlier than usual. It was rare for anyone to enter Whitehall below fifteen, but Emily suspected an exception would be made for Sienna's daughter.

Someone's clearly been teaching her, Emily thought, as the younger girls embraced her. *She might never need to go to school.*

"You are welcome in this house." Sienna sat in a comfortable armchair, her back ramrod straight. "Please, be seated. Karan will fetch the drinks."

Emily sat on the sofa, feeling out of place. Caleb moved to sit next to her, but a sharp look from his mother sent him hurrying to a small armchair. Emily felt her cheeks heat – again – as Frieda sat down, her face expressionless. Emily knew her well enough to realize she was nervous. She was even more out of place in the house than Emily herself.

She took a glass from Karan – a fruit juice, she thought – and waited. No one seemed inclined to start the conversation, not even Marian. She'd definitely changed. Had Casper's death affected her *that* badly? Perhaps it had...Casper had been a bit of a bully to Caleb, but he might have treated his younger sisters better.

"I hear the railway line is being extended again," Caleb said, into the silence. "Is it now going all the way to Thornwood?"

"That's the plan," Karan said. "My friends and I rode the railway all the way to Cockatrice." She looked at Emily. "They named a locomotive after you."

"Emily the Tank Engine." Emily smiled, even though she knew no one else would get the joke. "I haven't seen the station for nearly a year."

"They've expanded it," Karan said. She gave Emily a guileless smile. "We had a few hours in Cockatrice before we rode back to the city. Your castle is very impressive."

"I believe we will be discussing your formal position later." Sienna's voice was cool. "Until then…"

Marian leaned forward. "Jan was saying that he got a five for ten deal on notes," she said, quickly. "I was thinking…"

Her mother skewered her with a glance. "No."

"Mother, it will pay off," Marian insisted. "Everyone says…"

"And if everyone were to jump off a cliff," Sienna asked sharply, "would you jump too?"

Emily glanced at Caleb, silently asking him what was going on. Caleb shrugged. Whatever it was, it was clear that Sienna objected to it. *And* that she would not be moved. Marian's pleas and protests fell on deaf ears. Emily was mildly surprised that Marian hadn't been sent to her room for cheek. Her pleas grew more and more frantic.

She looked up as the door opened, breathing a sigh of relief as General Pollack entered. He was followed by a young man who looked very much like Casper, save for his obvious youth and unscarred face. Croce, Emily guessed. Caleb's younger brother. Caleb, Karan and Marian rose to greet their father; Emily rose a second later, remembering the etiquette lessons that had been drilled into her at school. General Pollack was, at least in theory, the master of his household. Emily rather doubted that his wife paid much attention to conventional wisdom. She was a power in her own right.

"Welcome home," Sienna said. Her voice was very formal. She hadn't moved from the armchair. "I greet you, husband."

"I greet you, wife," General Pollack returned. His voice was equally formal, but there was a warmth in it that made Emily smile. They loved each other. "We have much to discuss."

"Indeed we do." Sienna rose. "Shall we eat?"

Emily felt her stomach rumble as Sienna led the way into the dining room. It was larger than she'd expected, large enough to make her wonder if someone had been experimenting with expansion charms. There were *ways* to make one's house bigger on the inside, but without the vast power of a nexus point they tended not to last long. Emily wouldn't have cared to trust her safety to a pocket dimension that *didn't* have an inexhaustible source of power.

"Take a seat." Sienna's lips crinkled into a humorless smile. "I think we can forget about the formalities, can't we?"

"Of course, my dear," General Pollack said. "Emily, please take a seat."

Emily sat and watched as the two girls hurried into the kitchen to fetch dinner. Had they cooked it? A wealthy family like Caleb's would probably be expected to hire servants, but the house was small and sorcerers liked their privacy. And yet... she found the idea of Sienna – or her young daughters – doing all the cooking and cleaning to be a little unbelievable. Perhaps the servants were merely expected to remain out of sight at all times.

A tasty smell wafted up from the tureen as Marian put it down in front of her father and removed the lid. It was a fish stew, the fish heads clearly visible within the white sauce. Emily was surprised to see the bowl of cooked rice that accompanied it, although rice was fairly common at Whitehall. It might not grow anywhere near the city, but the combination of shipping lanes and preservation spells would allow merchants to bring it from the other side of the continent. The meal might look simple, yet it was – in many ways – an understated display of wealth. Only the richest citizens would be able to afford rice.

General Pollack served Emily and Frieda first, then his wife and children. Emily reached for her spoon, then stopped herself, remembering that etiquette forbade her from eating until everyone was served. Caleb, sitting opposite her, gave her a reassuring smile. Emily smiled back, wishing they were alone. They'd taken picnics into the mountains at Whitehall, back before the war, back before everything had changed...

"Please, tuck in," General Pollack said. He picked up the tureen and moved it to the center of the table. "Take more if you wish."

"Thank you, Father," Caleb said.

Emily picked up her spoon and took a sip of stew. It tasted strong, stronger than she'd expected. And yet, the more she ate, the more she grew to like it. The blandness of the rice and boiled vegetables complimented the fish nicely. It was definitely better than most of the food she'd eaten during the war.

"So," Sienna said, holding up her spoon as though it was a knife. "What happened?"

Emily glanced at General Pollack, who shrugged. "My wife can hear everything," he said, dryly. "You can speak freely."

In front of two impressionable kids, Emily thought.

Sienna snorted. "Emily," she said. "What happened to my son?"

Emily forced herself to look back at her. "The necromancer killed him," she said. "He...he was blown to dust."

"I see," Sienna said. "Details?"

"We were out on patrol," Emily said. She had no wish to recite the entire story, but...Sienna had a right to know. Besides, she'd probably get the rest of the tale from her husband. "We didn't know Gaius was a traitor. He sent Casper away, then attacked me. I beat him, only to discover we were cut off from the city. Armies were already on the march. There was no way we could get back before it was too late."

Sienna nodded, inviting Emily to continue.

"We decided we could strike directly at the necromancer himself," Emily said. "He was at Heart's Eye, so we went there. We battered our way into the school and challenged the necromancer. And then we fought."

She sucked in her breath. There was so much she wanted to forget. Dua Kepala's incredible success – and the secret of his sanity. The moment when she'd watched in horror, helpless, as Casper died. And the sheer power of the revitalized nexus point, reaching out through her to tear the necromancer apart. She didn't dare tell Sienna everything.

"We had a plan," Emily said. "Casper died making it work."

It wasn't the complete truth, she knew. But it was true enough. Casper *had* died a hero, and that was all that mattered.

Sienna studied her for a long, cold moment. Emily looked back at her, hoping – praying – that Sienna didn't ask too many questions. There were secrets that *couldn't* be shared. And yet, didn't Sienna have a right to know? Her son had died in the war.

"You could have saved him," Marian said. "Couldn't you?"

"No," Emily said. She'd been drained after the first battle. Even if she'd known what was about to happen, she doubted she could have done anything about it. "He was dead before I could do anything."

"Emily would have saved him if she could," Frieda said, sharply. She shot Marian a challenging look. "She's *good* at saving people."

"So I have heard." Sienna's eyes had never left Emily's face. "And he was a dueling champion, was he not?"

"He took the title from me," Emily confirmed. It wasn't entirely true, but Casper *had* been impressive. She'd given him a tiny window of opportunity and he'd used it perfectly, winning the duel in a single moment. "He was the champion when he died."

"It wouldn't have brought him happiness." Sienna sounded tired, tired and sad. "It would only have gotten him killed."

Emily bit down, hard, on the comment that came to mind. Casper had worked hard to live up to his famous parents, the great military commander and the power-ful sorceress. And he'd never felt as though he *had* managed to move out of their shadow. He'd been on the verge of trying to commit drunken suicide when she'd accepted his challenge. She knew he'd been a prideful ass – he'd been one of the luckiest people in the world – but she also understood precisely how he felt. He'd still been an apprentice when his friends were completing their own masteries.

"He died a champion," Caleb said. "It was what he wanted."

"He was young," Sienna snapped. For a moment, her mask slipped. Emily saw grief and sorrow before it became hidden again beneath her expressionless face. "He didn't *know* what he wanted."

"He died a hero," General Pollack said. "And I will always be proud of him."

There was a long silence. Emily felt awkward, as if she were intruding on a fam-ily's private grief. They'd invited her to stay with them, to attend the funeral, but... part of her was tempted to leave. She could take Frieda and find lodgings somewhere nearby, easily enough. It wasn't as though she was short of money. Coming to think of it, she could ask Markus if they could stay with him.

"There was another sighting of Justice," Marian said. Emily could have hugged the younger girl for trying to change the subject. "Four workers claimed they saw him standing near the docks, watching the boats."

General Pollack made a rude noise. "And how much had they had to drink at the time?"

"Antony, Son of Emil, was replaced by a stone statue," Sienna said. "And while Alba was in shock, I don't think she was lying."

"Antony was turned to stone," Karan said.

Emily blinked. "Antony and Alba?"

"Alba is a friend of mine," Karan said. "Antony was her very brave boyfriend who was turned to stone."

"That's what it says in the books," Marian said. "Those who transgress against the god will be turned to stone!"

"*Magic* can turn someone into stone," Sienna said, curtly. "*You* know how to stop someone in their tracks, if necessary. There's no reason to believe the rumors. It would hardly be the first time someone claimed to have seen a god."

Emily leaned forward, interested. "What do the stories say?"

"That Justice will return to pass Judgement on us all," Marian said. "And those who defy his law will be turned to stone."

"Except there's still no reason to *believe* the stories," Sienna said. "The victims – *all* of them – might easily have been targeted by their enemies. All someone would need to commit the murders would be a warped petrifaction spell."

She shrugged. "And Speaker Janus, no doubt, has taken advantage of the rumors," she added. "Attendance at his services is up."

Emily glanced at Caleb. "Janus?"

"The High Priest of Justice," Marian said, before Caleb could answer. "He's a very powerful man."

"And this is not a suitable conversation for the dinner table," Sienna said. She gave her daughter a sharp look. "We'll discuss other matters later."

"Yes, Mother," Marian said in a sweet voice. "And what *should* we talk about?"

"Your schooling, perhaps," Sienna said. "You'll be off to school in a year." She looked at Emily. "You can give her some advice, perhaps," she added. "You've seen *two* of the magic schools."

Emily nodded, shortly.

"Later, perhaps," Caleb said. "We have much to do tomorrow."

"Indeed you do," Sienna said. "And we shall discuss it tonight."

Chapter Four

E MILY COULDN'T HELP MULLING OVER THE GODLY AFFAIR AS KARAN FETCHED THE DESSERT, a syrupy sponge so sweet she had to drench it in custard before she could eat it. Croce insisted on chatting with his father about life in the military, making it clear he intended to seek an apprenticeship as soon as he completed his time at Stronghold. General Pollack attempted to convince Emily to talk about life in the sorcerer's tent, but Emily had to admit she hadn't seen *that* much of military life. She'd certainly never taken a full apprenticeship with a combat sorcerer.

"Karan, I would appreciate it if you were to take Frieda to her room and sit with her for a while," Sienna said, once the dessert was finished. "Emily, would you please accompany me?"

Emily felt a cold weight settle in her chest as she rose, following Sienna through a pair of solid wooden doors. Someone had embedded spells within the wood, ranging from a simple protection and warding spell to a number of nastier tricks that would freeze, blind and – at worst – kill anyone who tried to enter without permission. The study behind the protections was simpler than she'd expected – a desk, a set of over-flowing bookshelves and a pair of wooden chairs – but it clearly belonged to a skilled magician. She could feel the hairs on the back of her neck prickling as the interior wards peered at her, assessing her power. If Sienna hadn't been there, Emily doubted she could have made it out before the wards tore her to shreds.

"Take a seat," Sienna said. Her voice was surprisingly calm. "We have a great deal to discuss."

Emily sat on one of the wooden chairs, feeling like a mouse being eyed by a cat. Sienna was powerful – and skilled, which made her dangerous. Emily didn't have any reason to *believe* that Sienna might want her dead, but she knew – all too well – that a grieving mother might not be in any state to think logically. Her eldest son had died because she'd convinced him to accompany her to Heart's Eye.

And would Lady Barb be any kinder, Emily asked herself, *if she'd had a son who died on your watch?*

Emily forced herself to remain calm as Sienna took her seat. Sienna was a combat sorceress, no small achievement for a woman. No allowances would have been made for her when she started working towards her mastery; indeed, her tutor would probably have pushed her harder, just to make sure she could keep up with the men. Even now, after giving birth to five children, Sienna was formidable. Emily couldn't help a pang of envy. Casper and Caleb – and their siblings – probably didn't realize just how lucky they were.

"I'm afraid the decision to send Frieda as your chaperone is quite awkward," Sienna said, curtly. It was, Emily realized, her version of small talk. "Her presence causes other complications."

Emily nodded, shortly. Caleb was taken, but Croce was only a year or so younger than Frieda...not enough to avoid a scandal, if he were caught spending unsupervised time with her. Emily doubted Frieda would be interested – she'd turned down a dozen offers at Whitehall – but it would still be embarrassing. People would talk. And while she doubted it would be *that* irritating, in the long run, she could see Sienna's point.

"I apologize on behalf of my advisor," Emily said. She wasn't sure if Lady Barb was *still* her advisor, given that she'd left Whitehall after the grandmaster's death, but Emily had no intention of choosing another. "I'm sure she would have come herself, if the war hadn't placed demands on her time."

Sienna smiled. It didn't touch her eyes.

"The war comes first," she said. "Even with the necromancer dead, there will be other…considerations."

"Yes," Emily said.

"There are points we have to discuss," Sienna said, shifting course. "And I expect you to *listen.*"

Emily tensed. *This* was the meat of the matter. "I will."

Sienna's face twisted. It took Emily a moment to realize that she was embarrassed.

"First, I am aware that you and Caleb have been sleeping together," Sienna said. "I trust…"

Emily's mouth dropped open. "He *told* you?"

Sienna snorted. "Can you imagine a young boy who'd *want* to discuss his love life with his parents?"

She pressed on before Emily could formulate a response. "Of *course* he didn't tell me, but it's obvious from the way you two react to each other."

"Oh," Emily said. She had to fight to resist the urge to cover her face. She *knew* she was blushing brightly. Caleb's mother *knew*…What on Earth was she supposed to say? "I…"

Sienna held up a hand. "I trust that you have been using precautions," she added. "What sort of protections?"

Emily groaned. "Do we have to…?"

"Yes, we do," Sienna said. "What sort of protections have you been using?"

"Contraceptive potion," Emily said. She forced herself to be clinical. "Both of us have been taking it."

"Good," Sienna said, stiffly. "I assume you know how to cast a protection charm?"

"Lady Barb talked me through it," Emily said. God! She'd thought *that* conversation was embarrassing. Barrier charms were perfect, *if* they were cast properly. But they didn't last long, so they had to be cast shortly before penetration. Did *anyone* have the mental discipline to cast such a charm under such circumstances? "But we normally rely on potions."

Sienna nodded. "There are two important points I want to make to you," she said. She pointed a long finger at Emily. "First, you are *not* to sleep together under my roof, not until you're married. There's a charm on your room that will alert me if Caleb enters without my permission. Or any other man, for that matter. I understand the urges you'll have, as a healthy young woman, but I won't allow you to slake them under my roof. Do you understand?"

Emily felt her cheeks grow even hotter. "I understand."

"Caleb will hate me for this," Sienna added. She looked at the bookshelves, her face oddly pensive. "But it's for his own good."

"I don't think he'll hate you," Emily said.

"He certainly won't be pleased." Sienna smiled, rather thinly. "But I have made it clear to him that he *will* regret it if he defies me."

Ouch, Emily thought.

Sienna cocked her head. "And that leads us neatly to the *second* point."

Emily braced herself. She didn't think anything could be worse than having the talk with her boyfriend's mother, but she knew she could be wrong. Not that she blamed Sienna, not really. An unplanned pregnancy – or a scandal – would have all sorts of unfortunate repercussions. She had no idea what Sienna could do to her, beyond kicking her out of the house, but Caleb could be disowned – or worse.

"Just under two years ago, Caleb came to us – his parents – to request our blessing for a Courtship," Sienna said. "We discussed the matter at great length before agreeing, provisionally, to grant him our blessing. You were a child of many worlds, the daughter of a great sorcerer as well as a great noblewoman in your own right. Caleb's decision to court you carried risks."

"Not that many," Emily said.

"You might have rejected him, which would have been a blow to his pride," Sienna said. Her face flickered with droll amusement. "And if you'd done it publicly, it would have embarrassed the family and turned us into laughing stocks. But even if you didn't, Emily, it ran the risk of entangling us with the affairs of your father and Zangaria. We seriously considered denying Caleb our blessing because of the risk of being dragged into politics. My *dear* grandfather would certainly have been concerned about the danger."

Emily swallowed, hard. "Your grandfather?"

"The Patriarch of House Waterfall," Sienna said.

She shook her head, holding up a hand to stave off any further questions. "We consented to the courtship, Emily, because we believed the risks could be managed. Caleb is – was – a second son. His marriage is understandably of personal importance, but not particularly important to anyone outside the immediate family. We could have disowned him if things had threatened to get out of hand."

Emily stared at her. "You would have disowned your son for marrying me?"

"*Not* for marrying you," Sienna said. "For dragging us into a political morass. I believe your friend Markus was disowned for similar reasons."

"Yeah," Emily said.

She kept her thoughts to herself. She'd never thought about it like that before - she wished she didn't have to think about it now. It wasn't something that made her feel comfortable.

"Things have changed," Sienna said. It was an understatement. "Caleb is now my heir. A year ago, I would have said there was no hope of him succeeding my grandfather, but…things have changed. If he marries you, Emily, he'll be in a very strong position indeed. And yet, there is your current...disagreement with King Randor. Where, exactly, do you stand?"

"I chose to leave," Emily said, stiffly. She needed time to think – and, perhaps, discuss the matter with Caleb. "I am no longer the Baroness."

"You are, even if you're in exile," Sienna corrected.

She sighed, heavily. "You entered into the courtship on the understanding that you were going to be marrying a second son. Caleb was not expected to inherit anything beyond a small legacy. You may, if you wish, back out now. No one would blame you for taking a moment to reassess your position."

Emily met her eyes. "Do you *want* me to marry Caleb?"

"I want you to be aware of the problems facing you," Sienna said. It wasn't an answer. "And there is a further problem. There are *already* rumors that you deliberately killed Casper to clear the way for your boyfriend."

Emily felt a flash of hot temper. "I did not!"

"If I thought otherwise, young lady, we would be having a very different discussion," Sienna said, dryly. "But people *will* talk. If you were to marry Caleb – and he were to become Patriarch of Waterfall – you'd be combining magical and aristocratic power to make a formidable power base. Even if he didn't become the formal Patriarch, he'd be in a strong position to steer family affairs from behind the scenes. And you, behind him, would be pulling the strings."

"You didn't answer my question," Emily said. She felt her magic rising with her temper and ruthlessly forced it down. Sienna could probably sense it already. "Do you *want* me to marry Caleb?"

"What I want doesn't matter," Sienna said. She looked down at the wooden floor. When she spoke, there was a hint of pain in her voice. "Emily...for people like me... like *us*...marriage is rarely a matter of personal choice. We make the matches that suit our families and hope that love blossoms. I've known girls and boys who were broken-hearted because they couldn't marry the people they loved, or were disowned after they eloped. I was the youngest daughter of the youngest son, and yet I had to argue for *weeks* to convince the Patriarch to bless my marriage."

Emily frowned. Alassa had said much the same, when she'd been preparing to meet her first set of potential suitors. She'd even admitted that her father might pick one of the young noblemen who'd traveled to Zangaria, dismissing whatever concerns Alassa might have about the match. Emily hadn't been able to understand it, not really. Alassa was the Crown Princess – and she would be Queen, in time – but she didn't have much choice about who she married. It had been sheer luck that she'd remained unmarried long enough to start a proper relationship with Jade.

And yet, it wasn't something Emily wanted for herself. She liked Caleb...she even loved him. She simply didn't know enough about love to be *sure* of what she was feeling. The idea of outsiders discussing her marriage, even trying to manipulate it, was horrific. She had no intention of trying to use the match as part of a stealth takeover of House Waterfall...

But they have reason to worry, she thought, grimly. *Fulvia might well have gotten started that way too.*

She looked down at her hands, studying the ring Void had given her. It sparkled under the light, magic glittering against her pale skin. Was it fair to ask Caleb to give up his family for her? *She* wouldn't give up Lady Barb and Void for anyone, even Caleb! And she didn't want to give Caleb up either. And...

"You married a mundane," she said. She touched the snake-bracelet with her fingers, tracing out the scaly pattern. "Doesn't that..."

Sienna's face darkened. The magic level jumped, sharply. An insult ... she'd given Sienna an insult. For a moment, Emily was sure Sienna would throw a curse...or simply slap her ... before Emily could even formulate an apology.

"I would not have married him if I hadn't felt he was a good person," Sienna said. Her voice was icy cold. "And my grandfather would not have approved the match if he hadn't felt that Pollack would bring something to the family."

She met Emily's eyes. "And someone less forgiving than I would have taken *that* as a challenge to a duel," she added. "Dueling champion or not, I suggest you learn to watch your tongue."

"I'm sorry," Emily said, quickly.

"So you should be," Sienna said. "I would have been thrashed to within an inch of my life if I'd said that at your age."

She gave Emily a sharp glance. "Your father neglected a very important part of your education, young lady. Etiquette is what keeps us magicians from tearing ourselves apart."

"My father was always more interested in magic," Emily said. Sienna didn't know – couldn't know – the truth. Explaining that she'd come from an alternate world would have stirred up questions that she couldn't begin to answer. "Much of my education came from the servants."

Sienna sniffed in disapproval. "Servants are not good tutors for young magicians," she said, shortly. "They are rarely versed in the background required to teach properly."

She shrugged. "You're here for a couple of weeks, before the three of you go back to Whitehall," she said. "I *suggest* that you spend some time considering what I told you. If you and Caleb wish to proceed with the courtship, you may do so with your eyes wide open."

"Thank you," Emily said.

She sat back, feeling oddly drained. It wasn't the worst conversation she'd ever had, but it was definitely the most embarrassing. And it was almost *surreal.* What sort of choice was she supposed to make? The idea of tying herself down, at twenty-one, was terrifying. And yet, she was part of this culture now, for better or worse. She promised herself, silently, that she would write to Lady Barb – and Void – asking for advice. Maybe she could ask Sergeant Miles too. He'd have a different perspective on everything.

And Sergeant Harkin too, if he'd survived, she thought. She felt a pang of guilt. The sergeant would have been very disappointed in her, if he'd realized her mistake. *I wish I'd had a chance to thank him for everything.*

Sienna rose. "I'll take you to your room. Caleb and I will be having a long talk this afternoon, then I'll be taking him to the temple. I suggest you catch up on your sleep. Karan will be downstairs if you need anything. Everyone else will be going out."

Emily glanced at her watch. It was early afternoon.

"I don't know how long I'll sleep," she said. She felt tired, but going to sleep now would only make it harder for her to sleep in the evening. "Do we have the run of the house?"

"Stay out of the bedrooms and any room that's warded closed," Sienna said. She motioned for Emily to follow her. "There's a small collection of books in the living room, including a couple that were passed down from my great-grandfather. You might like them. Or you can ask Karan for anything she might have."

"I understand," Emily said.

Sienna gave her an unreadable look. "I am aware this isn't easy for you. Just bear in mind that it isn't easy for anyone else either."

"I know," Emily said. "I am truly sorry Casper was killed."

"So am I," Sienna said. She looked older, just for a second. "I always knew there was a possibility that he'd die, but I didn't want to believe it. None of us did. And now...his death has opened up a whole new can of worms. And we have to deal with them now."

She shook her head. "Come with me."

Emily rose and followed her through the doors and up a narrow flight of stairs. It was so narrow that Emily doubted a large man could get up the stairs without getting stuck. She thought of the servant corridors in King Randor's castle, the tiny passage-ways intended to keep the servants hidden from their lords and masters. She'd used similar corridors to sneak around at Whitehall.

She glanced up at Sienna. "Do you have any servants?"

"I have a cook and a maid," Sienna said, briskly. "They work regular hours and live outside the house. The maid is *not* there to help you with your hair. I've had to make that point clear to both the girls, regularly. It never seems to sink in."

They reached the top of the stairs and walked down a short corridor. "This is your room," Sienna said, as they reached an unmarked wooden door. She knocked smartly and waited. "You're sharing with Frieda. Remember what I said – do *not* invite Caleb into the room."

"I won't," Emily said.

"And don't go into his room either," Sienna added, sharply. The door swung open, revealing Frieda. "It'll just get you both in hot water."

"I understand," Emily said. She couldn't help feeling annoyed. She'd missed sharing a bed with Caleb. It was hard to believe, now, that she'd ever been reluctant to let him do more than kiss her. "Did my bag get sent up?"

"It's here," Frieda said.

"Have a good nap," Sienna said. "I'll see you at dinnertime."

Chapter Five

"So," Frieda said, as she closed the door. "I've been told I have to set some ground rules."

Emily scowled at her. "And who told you that?"

"Lady Barb," Frieda said. She winked. "You don't want to argue with her, do you?"

"I also happen to know she's not here," Emily said, wryly. "Do *you* get to set the ground rules?"

Frieda looked embarrassed, a hint of a blush on her face. "This is serious," she said. "Emily…"

Emily resisted the urge to roll her eyes. Frieda was no more a part of the city's culture than *she* was. Her upbringing in the mountains hadn't taught her how to comport herself in the big city. She would have been married off by now, if she'd lived long enough to grow into womanhood. Only the discovery of her magic had saved her from a life of total obscurity.

She looked up, inspecting the room. It was small, smaller than her bedroom at Whitehall, but larger than the one she'd shared with Lady Barb nine months ago. A pair of beds, no larger than the bed on the ship, reclined against the wall; a small dressing table, complete with a mirror spell on a reflective surface, was positioned neatly under the window. Someone – probably Sienna – had carved out a set of runes around the window frame, each one configured to uphold the household wards and keep intruders from breaking in. They wouldn't be enough to keep her from forcing the window wide open, she thought as she walked to the window and peered out, but they'd probably make it impossible to sneak in and out of the house without triggering the wards. The street below was so busy, she doubted anyone could climb up without being noticed.

Frieda cleared her throat. "Emily, Lady Barb was serious."

"I know," Emily said. She felt a flicker of amusement, mingled with annoyance. It was nice to have someone looking out for her, but did Frieda have to be so overbearing? "I won't do anything with him under this roof."

"People will talk," Frieda pointed out. "You have to be careful."

Emily smiled. Frieda had grown up in a village where everyone knew what everyone else was doing. There was no real privacy, even for married couples. A pair of teenagers couldn't find time to themselves without being caught and punished. She couldn't help wondering, as she had the first time she'd visited the Cairngorms, if a particularly devious suitor sometimes set out to entrap a girl into marrying him. It didn't have to be a boy, either. A girl could easily try the same trick.

"I'll be careful," she promised. She turned and picked up her bag. She'd only brought a couple of outfits, neither of which were really suitable for city life. "Did Lady Barb send some clothes, too?"

"There's a trunk under the bed," Frieda said. "I have orders to take you to a dressmaker if they don't fit."

"Thank you," Emily said. Lady Barb wouldn't have opened *her* trunk at Whitehall, even if it hadn't been heavily warded. No one, not even Grandmaster Gordian, would have broken *that* taboo unless he saw no alternative. "What else did Lady Barb say?"

She opened the trunk and dug through the small collection of clothes as Frieda spoke. "Just that you have to respect the family's mourning period," she said. "And that you should take part in their ceremonies, even if things don't work out. And that I have to behave myself."

Emily looked up and smiled. "My, what *have* you been doing?"

Frieda smiled back. "I...um...I managed to catch Master Tor in one of my spells, back when I was playing Freeze Tag," she admitted. "He was *not* amused."

"Oh dear," Emily said. She tried hard, very hard, not to giggle. "I imagine he was furious."

"He was," Frieda said. "I would still be in detention if I hadn't been summoned here."

"Ouch," Emily said.

She pulled a dress and a set of undergarments from the trunk and placed them on the dressing table, then poked her way through the rest of the trunk. A small bottle of contraceptive potion she doubted she'd have a chance to use, a notebook and set of pencils...and, buried right at the bottom, a collection of books and a short note. She picked up the note and read it, then glanced at the book titles. Lady Barb expected her to have them read from cover to cover before she returned to Whitehall.

"They're for your studies," Frieda said. She looked doubtful. "You'll have to work hard to catch up."

"There goes my summer," Emily said. Sergeant Miles had promised to help her study over the summer, if she needed to retake her end-of-year exams. She'd hoped to be able to explore more of the Nameless World, but exams came first. "Do you know what *you're* doing for summer?"

"I've put my name down for work experience," Frieda said. For a moment, she looked agonizingly young. "I don't know if I've been accepted yet."

"I'm sure you will be," Emily said, reassuringly.

She put the books on the dressing table, then closed the trunk and shoved it back under the bed. Technically, she knew she should have locked it with magic, but there was nothing particularly valuable inside. Besides, she knew from Lady Barb that some household wards reacted badly to locking spells. It would be better to check with Sienna before doing anything that might provoke a reaction.

"I need a nap." She also needed a wash, but she was too tired. "Will you be all right here?"

"Of course." Frieda tapped her own trunk. "I've got schoolwork too."

Emily nodded as she checked the door. The wardspell was simple enough, keyed to bar men – and only men – from touching the handle and opening the door. The maid would have no trouble entering the room, if she dared. *Emily* wouldn't have cared to work in a magician's house, particularly when the magician's older children would be using their magic to keep intruders out of their domain. Touching the wrong thing, even in perfect innocence, could get the maid turned into a frog. She grimaced at the thought. The games students played at Whitehall were less amusing when played outside school.

She undressed rapidly, then climbed into bed and closed her eyes. It felt odd to lie in an unmoving bed, after five days on a sailing ship. She told herself she would get over it and concentrated on her mental discipline. She didn't expect sleep would come easily – she'd never found it easy to sleep in a new place, at least for the first few days – but it would come. She heard Frieda opening her trunk just as the darkness rose up and overwhelmed her...

A hand touched her shoulder. She jerked up, one hand raised to cast a spell. Frieda jumped back, raising both of her hands in surrender. Emily caught herself, and sat upright in bed, shaking her head in annoyance. The light pouring in through the window was dimmer, somehow. It had to be dusk.

"It's dinnertime," Frieda said. "Did you sleep well?"

Emily shook her head. She hadn't dreamed, and she felt as if she hadn't slept at all. Her body felt tired and grimy. She swung her legs over the side and stood, her legs wobbling as if they expected the floor to shift under her weight. It took her a long moment to remember that she was no longer on the boat, that the floor wasn't going to be rolling back and forth...she rubbed her eyes, tiredly. The sooner she got over the last few days, the better.

Frieda bit off a curse. "What *happened* to you?"

Emily looked down at herself. "I fought a traitor and a necromancer," she said, as she studied the bumps and bruises. Most of them had healed, but enough remained to remind her that she'd been in a fight. She rubbed at a particularly nasty bruise on her upper arm, silently grateful that it was no longer sore. The fight had been so vicious that she honestly didn't know when she'd been struck. "I'll heal soon."

"You should go find a Healer," Frieda said. She glanced towards the window. "We could go now..."

"There's no pain," Emily assured her. She touched one of the scars, remembering the moment when white flames had lashed out at her. The pain had been so excruciating that her memories were jumbled. "I'll recover in time."

"Make sure Caleb knows you're not quite recovered," Frieda said. "And I'll hex him if he tries to make you do anything *too* energetic."

Emily sighed, torn between embarrassment and irritation. She knew Frieda didn't like Caleb.

"I'm sure he'll respect his mother's wishes," she said, reluctantly. A low chanting sound echoed through the window. She turned to peer through the glass, watching as a number of worshippers hurried out of their homes and headed to the temples. There were a dozen religions, she recalled, that prayed at sunrise and sunset. "Is there a toilet here?"

After Frieda pointed them out, Emily used the surprisingly modern facilities, then changed into a long blue dress and inspected herself in the mirror. Her hair was still a mess, but the rest of her looked reasonably presentable. She should be grateful, she supposed, that Lady Barb had packed her trunk instead of Queen Marlena. Alassa's mother would have sent along enough dresses to outfit every girl in Whitehall, along with gifts and other largess intended to forge a bond between them. She glanced at her bag, wondering if she had time to write a brief message to Alassa and her other friends. She really should have done it as soon as she arrived, but she'd been too wrapped up in other matters.

Later, she told herself firmly.

"Come on," Frieda said. "Being late for dinner would be insulting."

Emily nodded as they walked down the stairs. There was no sign of General Pollack or his youngest son when they reached the dining room. Caleb sat at the table, reading a book, while his mother quizzed him relentlessly on his studies. Emily winked at him as the two girls entered, carrying more bowls of stew. She had the feeling they were going to be eating fish for the foreseeable future.

"I trust you slept comfortably," Sienna said, once the food was served. "I'm afraid we don't have any better rooms."

"It's better than sleeping in a tent," Emily said. It helped that she wasn't sharing close quarters with five other magicians – all men. "Or on a boat, for that matter."

Sienna gave her an understanding glance. "Your legs still wobbly?"

"Just a little." Emily rested her palm on the table. "I keep feeling as though the room is going to heel over."

"You get over it," Sienna said. She smiled, rather dryly. "I used to love boating when I was a child."

"Perhaps we could take a fishing boat out through the gap," Caleb said. "Fish tastes better if you catch it yourself."

"But not if you cook it." Marian stuck out her tongue. "Don't marry my brother for his cooking, Lady Emily. He can't boil water without ruining it."

"My cooking is worse," Emily said. It was true. On Earth, she'd had no time to learn any more than the basics. Her mother had never been particularly interested in cooking anything more complicated than scrambled eggs. "I throw perfectly good ingredients together and wind up with a mess."

"I dare say that qualifies you to become an army cook." Sienna's lips twitched. "I've yet to meet a military cook who *couldn't* turn a silk purse into a sow's ear."

Emily had to smile. "Is that why so many aristocrats brought along their own cooks?"

"Naturally," Sienna said. "And I imagine they brought their own food too."

She cocked her head. "The official excuse is that poor food puts the men in a fighting mood," she added. "But the truth is that hardly anyone can be bothered to organize proper food for anyone who doesn't have a title."

Emily nodded in grim agreement. She'd seen enough during the campaign to know that Sienna was right. The aristocrats – and the combat magicians – had eaten well, while the common soldiers were lucky if they got enough to sustain themselves.

Farrakhan had been on the verge of collapsing into a bloody revolution because *its* nobility had collected all the food, leaving the poor to starve.

She tasted the stew. It was similar to the stew they'd had for lunch, but with a spiciness she found disconcerting. Marian passed her a piece of freshly-baked bread, which she dipped into the liquid. It countered the spice, making it easier to eat.

"You'll enjoy sailing on a little boat," Caleb said. "Would you like to try?"

"If we can get through the gap," Emily said. She hadn't liked the look of those waves. The currents might have pushed the ship into the harbor, but they could easily dash the vessel against the rocks if the crew lost control. "Is that safe?"

"We'd probably hire a boat from the outer docks," Caleb said. "Anyone who tries to pass through the Dragon's Teeth in a small boat is taking their life in their hands."

"It's been done," Karan said. "Jolly did it on a bet…"

"Jolly nearly drowned when he tried to get back in," Sienna said. "Idiot should have had the sense to realize the currents were against him. If he'd let himself be pushed back out to sea, he could have found his way to the outer docks or tried again at high tide."

"He was brave," Karan said.

"There's a difference between bravery and stupidity," Sienna said. She shot her oldest daughter a sharp look. "I hope you weren't *too* impressed."

Karan colored. Marian snickered at her discomfort.

"We'd have to scramble down the ladders, but it should be safe enough," Caleb said. "Magic will break our fall, if we lose our grip."

Emily made a face. She wasn't sure she *liked* the idea of scrambling down wet ladders, even if she *did* have magic. Walking into a necromancer's lair had been incredibly dangerous, but she'd known – all too well – that she didn't have a choice. Taking on the necromancer directly was the only way to stop him from devastating an entire country. But taking a fragile boat out onto the open sea…she knew she could teleport away, if things went to hell, yet she still didn't like it.

"We'll see." She suspected Sienna was judging her, although she had no idea what would appeal to the older woman. "It sounds like fun."

"Caleb will take you to the temple tomorrow," Sienna said, briskly. "You can say a prayer before the god of the ocean, if you wish."

"You do have to pay your respects to Beneficence," Caleb added. "I don't think you've been there before, have you?"

Emily shook her head. She hadn't stayed long, the last time she'd visited the city. Lady Barb hadn't seemed inclined to take her to the temple, either. She wasn't sure she wanted to go, but she knew it was important to Caleb and his family. Besides, she was curious. She'd only been to one other temple in her life, back in Zangaria. Her mother had certainly never bothered to take her to church.

"Make sure you take some fruit," Sienna ordered. "And afterwards…?"

"I need to visit the bank," Emily said. Markus had said he was in his office every day. If he wasn't, for whatever reason, she could leave him a message. He might take a day off every so often to visit Melissa. "And then…I'm not sure."

"I'd like to visit the bank," Karan said. "I…"

"Perhaps later," Sienna said. She glanced at Frieda. "Caleb and Karan will be happy to show you the city."

"Thank you," Frieda said, politely.

Emily concealed her amusement. Frieda would probably be happier exploring on her own, if Emily couldn't accompany her. She really didn't *like* Caleb that much. Maybe she'd get on better with Karan. She was only a year or so older than Frieda, after all.

"I have a bottle of sleeping potion, if you wish to take it," Sienna said, when the dinner came to an end. "Or you can read until you feel tired."

"I have letters to write," Emily said. She owed Alassa and her friends an update. "I'll get some rest afterwards."

Sienna nodded, and led her daughters out of the room. Caleb sent Emily an embarrassed look — it was clear he didn't know quite how to act when his mother and his girlfriend were in the same room — and nodded to the door. Frieda gave him a mock-suspicious look as they walked up the stairs. Emily shot her a warning look in return. She understood Sienna's concerns — and Lady Barb's — but she wasn't going to allow either of them to control her life.

"We'll be outside tomorrow," Caleb whispered. Frieda slipped past them and hurried into the room, carefully leaving the door ajar. "I wish…"

He leaned forward to kiss her. Emily kissed him back, tensing as she sensed the spells crawling through the house. Caleb wasn't in her room…surely, mere kissing wouldn't set off the spells. He wrapped his arms around her, holding her tightly. She hugged him back, feeling a sudden hot flush. Her body was reminding her, sharply, of just how much she'd missed him.

"I look forward to it," she whispered back. "Are you going to be sneaking through the house at night?"

Caleb looked embarrassed. "Mother would *not* be pleased," he said. "And she *would* notice."

Emily nodded. She'd seen monitoring charms at Whitehall, but Sienna's spells were an order of magnitude more complex. Sienna would know, if she cared to ask, precisely what her children were doing at all times. Emily couldn't help thinking there was a fine line between being protective and smothering…and that Sienna, for all her obvious concern for her children, was on the wrong side.

"I understand." She kissed him again, just as she heard Frieda clearing her throat inside the room. "I'll see you tomorrow."

She kissed him one final time, then stepped into the room and closed the door.

Chapter Six

EMILY WAS MILDLY DISAPPOINTED, WHEN SHE WOKE THE FOLLOWING MORNING, TO DISCOVER that Caleb *hadn't* tried to sneak into her room. He'd said as much, but still…she shook her head, telling herself not to be silly. She wasn't the only person in the room. The prospect of Caleb accidentally sneaking into the wrong bed was the stuff of bad romantic comedies, not real life. Frieda would be understandably horrified if Caleb climbed into *her* bed.

She washed, changed into a new dress and then checked the chat parchments. Alassa, Jade and Imaiqah had written brief replies, but they were clearly distracted by greater matters. The Gorgon had added a reply of her own, talking about a new piece of magic that linked into some of her older spellwork. Emily couldn't help feeling a flicker of wistfulness as she read her words, then added a comment. She hadn't had the *time* to explore new spells over the past few weeks.

And Caleb and I have to continue our project, she thought. It would be harder, she thought, now they were sleeping together. *How are we supposed to remain focused?*

Frieda came out of the bathroom, wearing a long, dark dress that fell to her ankles. She'd clearly put some effort into her appearance, something that surprised Emily. Frieda was pretty enough, in her own way, but she rarely bothered trying to enhance her looks with charms or beauty products. She couldn't help wondering if Frieda was trying to impress someone.

"You look good," she said. "Are you meeting someone?"

"No." Frieda colored. "I just thought I should try to look better if I was walking next to you."

Emily looked down at herself. The blue dress was one of ten that had been chosen by Queen Marlena, after her first attempts to clothe Emily had ended poorly. It suited her, Emily felt; it drew attention to her face and hair without being *too* tight around her bust or hips. And yet, it was hardly *fancy*. The only thing that made it stand out from something Karan or Marian would wear was the expensive cloth, which wasn't noticeable unless someone happened to touch her sleeve. She could walk through the city without attracting attention, just another unmarried girl of marriageable age. She'd just have to keep her hair hidden behind a small glamour.

"I think you look fine," she said. She held out a hand. "Shall we go downstairs to breakfast?"

She wasn't surprised, when she reached the bottom of the stairs, to discover that Sienna and Caleb were chatting quietly. Emily couldn't help wondering precisely *what* they'd been talking about. Caleb's mother *might* have decided to caution her son against *kissing* her, as well as everything else. Or she might have sat him down for a long talk about the courtship and precisely where he saw it going. The thought caused her a bitter pang. Casper's death had changed so much. As a younger son, Caleb's marriage wasn't important; as the oldest surviving son, his marriage would shape the future of the entire family.

Which isn't just the general and his wife, she reminded herself. *There's an entire clan of magicians who might be affected.*

"Please, eat." Sienna waved a hand towards a plate of bread and honey. "I believe the honey comes from Cockatrice."

Emily nodded, meeting Caleb's eyes. He looked embarrassed, suggesting that she was right to worry about what his mother had told him. She forced herself to look away as Sienna hurried out of the room, leaving the three of them alone. A moment later, Karan entered, yawning loudly as she took a seat.

"We'll buy some fruit on the way," Caleb said. He took a piece of bread and slathered it in honey. "And we might as well take some bread too."

"The god will appreciate it." Frieda chewed her bread with every evidence of enjoyment. "It's very good."

"We have a good cook." Karan glanced at Emily. "Try not to let my brother eat *too* much outside the house. There's a big meal this evening."

"She means she wants you to take me for lunch so there's more food for her," Caleb said. He sounded more natural, now his mother was out of the room. "But we could go visit one of the new burger bars if you wish."

Frieda snickered. Emily rubbed her forehead, embarrassed. *She'd* founded the burger bars – or at least she'd introduced the concept, when King Randor had given her Cockatrice. It still amused her, in so many ways, that burgers and pizzas had become luxury foodstuffs all around the continent. Fast food still wasn't particularly *fast* – it would be years before the Nameless World had anything to match McDonalds or Pizza Hut – but it was clear evidence of the changes she'd wrought.

"I might enjoy it," Emily said.

"They've become places for youths to hang out," Karan informed her. "I go to the nearest one whenever I come home."

Caleb grinned.

Emily washed her hands and checked her appearance as soon as they finished breakfast, then followed Caleb and Frieda onto the street. It was nearly ten o'clock, local time, but the streets were already crowded. The street magicians were doing their best to attract attention, casting brilliant spells into the air; street sellers were calling out to passing tourists, inviting them to sample their wares. The racket was deafening. Emily checked the charms on her money pouch carefully – Lady Barb had warned her that the streets were often teeming with pickpockets – and then placed another charm on herself. Anyone who tried to touch her without permission would be in for a nasty surprise.

She forced herself to remain calm as the crowd shifted around her, making way for a black carriage and two horses. The driver was cracking a whip loudly, waving it around as if he intended to start flogging the crowd. Emily half-expected to hear people screaming in agony, then be forced to watch helplessly as the rest of the crowd attacked the carriage, but it seemed the driver had *just* enough sense not to actually hurt anyone. She couldn't help wondering why the passenger didn't simply get out and walk. The streets were so crowded that getting from one side of the city to the other would be easier on foot.

"That's one of the guildmasters," Caleb said, when she asked. "They're the only ones allowed to use carriages at all times."

Frieda bumped against Emily. "Perhaps we should have waited for another hour," she said, as they elbowed their way through the crowd. "The streets would be calmer then."

I hope so, Emily thought.

They left the carriage – and its cursing driver – behind as they slowly made their way to the temples. Emily hadn't realized, when they'd walked through yesterday, that there were actually two streets, with a single massive temple at the crossroads. A long line of people waited outside, some clearly visitors from outside the city. Caleb waved to a street salesman as they joined the line, purchasing a small bag of apples. Emily couldn't help wondering if those, too, had come from Cockatrice. Her barony was the closest place where apples grew.

Caleb muttered instructions in her ear. "When you walk into the temple, proceed through the left door – that's the women's section. Kneel in front of the statue to make your devotions, then place the fruit with all the other donations. And then walk out the back and wait for us there."

Emily glanced at him. "What happens to the fruit?"

"Officially, the god eats it." Caleb's face twisted in droll amusement. "Unofficially, the priests distribute it to the poor and the needy."

"Oh," Emily said.

She glanced up as she heard a bell ring, just once. The line inched forward, then stopped again. Two men were arguing in front of her, chatting about…*something*. Three more walked past her, heading towards the other temples. They wore the red robes she'd seen before. And they weren't the only ones. There were so many people on the streets that it was hard to be sure, but there were at least thirty Hands of Justice within eyeshot. They patrolled, moving up and down the street. Their eyes missed nothing.

There's more of them now, Emily thought. She couldn't help finding that ominous. A number of Hands were carrying whips. *And what are they doing?*

It felt like hours before the line finally reached the door. Caleb gave her hand a squeeze as they stepped into the temple – it was strikingly cool inside – and motioned to the left-hand door. The women ahead of her waited, as patiently as they could. Every time the bell rang, one of them walked through the door and vanished. Emily felt a shiver run down her spine as she reached out with her senses. Magic, powerful magic, was woven into the temple. No matter how hard she looked, she couldn't see anything beyond the door. She wasn't even sure what summoned the *men* to enter the temple.

Emily stepped through the door as the bell rang, feeling vaguely silly. She'd never believed in the Christian God, let alone Loci Gods that belonged to a lone city. She *had* met powerful creatures, yet they weren't *gods*. And yet…she felt a stab of pain between her breasts, a warning that there was subtle magic in the air. She touched the rune she'd carved on her chest, and glanced behind her. It wasn't exactly a surprise to see that the door she'd come through had vanished. There was no way back.

Bracing herself, she walked down the corridor and into a shrine. The subtle magic grew stronger, forcing her to grit her teeth in pain. A non-magician would have been swept away without realizing something was wrong...hell, a trained magician without specific protections would still have had problems. The air seemed *still*, somehow, as she looked around the shrine. It felt as though something was just biding its time before happening...

Her eyes swept the room, warily. A single statue stood on a plinth, looking down at her. It was human, she thought, yet *idealized*, practically perfect in every way. The outfit it wore was smart without being pretentious. She couldn't help thinking that the Beneficence Loci looked more like a trader than the kings or aristocrats she'd seen depicted in Zangaria. And yet, didn't that fit the city? Beneficence had been a hive of innovation even *before* she'd introduced the New Learning. It had certainly been a center of commerce.

She looked past the god, seeing the pile of food and drink at the far end of the room. The walls were bare, save for a handful of powerful runes. Preservation runes, she realized, established so long ago that their magic was firmly in place. It was an impressive piece of work, all the more so for − presumably − not having been designed by trained magicians. A piece of food, left in the room, would not decay. Time would only resume, for the food, when it was removed. The priests wouldn't accidentally poison anyone.

Did she *have* to kneel? She wasn't sure. She didn't *believe* in the god. It meant less to her than Christmas or Easter, two religious celebrations that had become secular holidays more noted for shameless materialism than religious contemplation. She'd certainly never *met* a god. Alassa was the only one of her friends who'd become a devotee and Emily had never been sure if her friend genuinely believed or if Alassa had merely found a way to annoy her father. Emily couldn't help wondering what Jade thought of it. The Crone was hardly a comfortable goddess to follow.

Caleb would be hurt if I didn't pay my respects, she thought.

But he'll never know, the nasty part of her mind pointed out. *No one will know what happened inside the temple.*

She stared at the statue for a long moment, then knelt − briefly. Nothing happened. There was no sense of heightened presence, no awareness of something greater than her. She'd felt greater things while encountering demons, or falling helplessly through time...here, there was nothing but carefully-shaped magic. Feeling oddly disappointed, she rose and walked over to the food. Countless worshippers had passed through the room, leaving everything from pieces of meat to bottles of drink. She put the apples down, silently hoping the priests didn't eat them themselves, then walked out the rear entrance. Caleb already waited there.

"You were in there a while," he said. His tone was light, but his eyes were worried. "Are you all right?"

"Yeah," Emily said. "It was just my first time inside a major temple."

Caleb gave her an odd look as they waited for Frieda. He knew the truth of her origins now, but she suspected he had a hard time believing it. It was *easier* to believe she was Void's daughter, raised in isolation, than that she might have come from a whole other world. She wondered, absently, what he'd make of the Christian God. A single all-powerful being made more sense, she felt, than hundreds of limited entities. A god wasn't anything more than another powerful creature.

Frieda joined them, a moment later. "I've never seen such a large temple," she said. "How many people does it *feed*?"

"I have no idea," Caleb said. "But anyone can come for a meal, if they wish."

Emily kept her thoughts to herself as they walked down the steps and onto the street. It was less crowded now, although there were still too many people around for her peace of mind; priests, citizens, tourists...a dozen more Hands of Justice, walking around as though they owned the place. The handful of city guardsmen gave them a wide berth. Emily couldn't help wondering precisely what was going on, behind the scenes.

"Another statue," Frieda said. She jabbed a finger towards the center of the road. "That wasn't there yesterday."

Caleb nodded and led them to the statue, pushing his way through the crowds. Few people seemed to want to get too close, as if something about the statue spooked them. Emily studied it with some interest, reaching out with her senses in the hopes of touching whatever magic had been used to make it. But there was nothing, no wisp of magic at all. The only clue that the statue had once been human was its sheer perfection. No sculptor ever born could carve so much detail into stone.

She reached out to touch it. But all she felt was cold stone. Marble? She wasn't sure.

Screams split the air. Emily jumped back, expecting...she wasn't sure *what* she expected. She readied a spell, turning around to see the crowds moving back from the Temple of Justice. The screams grew louder...she glanced around, looking for a proper vantage point. Perhaps if she climbed up...

The crowd parted. Seven people – five men, two women – knelt in front of the temple. Their shirts had been removed, leaving them topless. A Hand of Justice stood behind each of them, holding a nasty-looking whip. Emily watched in growing horror as they brought the whips down again and again, drawing blood as they lashed bare flesh. The victims screamed, then pleaded for mercy. She wasn't sure who – or what – they expected to answer.

Emily reached for her magic, then stopped. She didn't know what to do. Could she help them? Should she help them? They were making no attempt to escape. Even the women – both bare-breasted, both barely older than Emily herself – weren't trying to hide themselves, let alone trying to run. Had they *chosen* to be whipped?

She looked away, feeling sick. The sound echoed in her ears, the screams mingling with the crowd roaring after every stroke. Men and women cheered, mocking the victims as they suffered. Insults and catcalls echoed, followed by whistles and lewd suggestions. She recoiled, then forced herself to move. Caleb and Frieda followed, pushing their way through the growing crowd. She couldn't help realizing that both of them seemed to take the punishment in stride. It was just part of their world.

The screams faded, slowly, as they made their way down the street. But her ears still rang.

"They would have offered themselves for punishment to balance the scales," Caleb said, quietly. A dozen youngsters pushed past them, no doubt eager to see the whipping before it was over. "Justice is *about* balancing the scales."

Emily shook her head. She'd heard that argument before. An eye for an eye, a tooth for a tooth, a life for a life...such punishment didn't really change *anything*. The scene she'd unwillingly witnessed was more about retribution than anything else, a grim reminder that anyone could face such horrific punishment. She'd seen men and women in the stocks, or forced into slavery as payment for their crimes, but public whippings were worse...

"It's sick," she said.

"They chose it," Caleb said. "They thought it would provide balance."

"My father said the same thing," Frieda said. She shivered. "He was always drunk at the time."

Emily reached out and squeezed Frieda's shoulder. Her friend rarely talked about her childhood, but Emily had seen the scars. Frieda had been beaten savagely, time and time again, from an early age. She'd been lucky, very lucky, to be sold to a passing magician and taken away to Mountaintop. She'd certainly never shown any interest in going home.

But if they chose to be whipped, she asked herself, *is it wrong?*

Despite herself, she had no answer.

Chapter Seven

THE BANK OF SILENCE WAS AN IMMENSE BUILDING, EASILY LARGER THAN MOST OF THE temples she'd seen as they made their way to Bankers Row. It was larger than every other bank on the street, with a longer line of customers waiting outside. And yet, Markus had hired more guards to patrol the walls and placed more complex wards around the building. He clearly expected trouble. The other bankers had hired guards of their own.

"We'll be taking a look at the shops," Caleb told her. "Do you know how to find your way to Railway Street?"

Emily shook her head. "I'll ask someone." She wished, suddenly, that she'd thought to bring the chat parchment with her. It was astonishing how much she'd grown to miss cell phones over the last few years. How had people *coped* in bygone days without their friends and family at the touch of a button? "If I meet you in a couple of hours…?"

"If you can't find us, just go back to the house," Caleb said. "We'll come back eventually."

"Try not to get into trouble," Emily said. She glanced at Frieda. "And don't get him into any trouble either."

Caleb rolled his eyes, but said nothing. Frieda smirked.

Emily watched them go, then turned and walked to the front door. A pair of armored guards eyed her with professional interest, their eyes lingering on her face rather than her chest. Emily couldn't help thinking they looked more like soldiers than most of the men she'd met during the war. And yet, there was a *falseness* around them that bothered her, an attitude that made her think they hadn't seen real combat. Sergeant Harkin had been crude, rude and willing to do whatever it took to turn his students into combat sorcerers, but he'd been a *man*. He'd seen the elephant and survived. These men…she thought they'd never seen war.

A clerk, standing behind them, studied her for a long moment. "Yes?"

"Inform the manager that Lady Emily wishes to speak to him," Emily said, firmly. The clerk's eyes opened wide. "And then escort me to the waiting room."

The clerk stared at her. "I…I need to see some proof…"

Emily reached out with her magic and brushed it against the wards. Markus had keyed her into the outer defenses back when he started the bank, pointing out that she *was* one of his best customers. The clerk jumped, then turned and scurried into the bank. Emily followed him, pretending not to notice the guards hiding smiles. There must be no love lost between them and their social superior.

Markus must have been alerted by the wards, because he entered the waiting room while the clerk was still trying to offer her food, drink or the latest broadsheets. Emily smiled as he dismissed the panicked man, then opened a hidden door and invited Emily to walk upstairs to his office. He was only three years older than Emily, but he held himself like an older man. She told herself that it probably wasn't surprising. He was, after all, the *de facto* head of the Bankers Guild.

His office was large, easily five times the size of a bedroom at Whitehall. A marble desk sat in the middle, under a pair of giant glass windows; a small set of comfortable chairs and sofas sat in the corner. Emily had to smile when she saw the portrait of Melissa hanging over the fireplace. It was so accurate that Melissa had clearly sat for it, not so long ago. A pair of maps – one showing Beneficence and the surrounding lands, the other showing the known world – dominated the other wall.

"Emily," he said, motioning for her to take a seat. "It's good to see you again."

"Thank you," Emily said, sincerely. She'd always liked Markus, more than she'd liked Melissa. "I would have written ahead, but..."

"I heard." Markus rang a little bell on his desk. "You've been to war."

A young, dark-haired woman materialized out of a side door and bowed. Like so many others, she looked to be mixed-race, a combination of Chinese and Indian features. Her dress was professional, but surprisingly tight around her breasts. And yet, there was an innocence about her that Emily found a little amusing. She suspected, from the glint in the woman's eye, that she dressed that way so she was always underestimated.

"Kava, please," Markus said. He looked at Emily. "Would you like something to eat?"

"No, thank you," Emily said.

She leaned back in her chair as the secretary returned, carrying a tray of mugs, a pot of Kava and a small collection of pastries. Her stomach rumbled as she saw them, reminding her that she hadn't eaten *that* much for breakfast. Perhaps she could take one or two, just to be sociable. Markus wouldn't mind.

"Help yourself." Markus sat down facing her, taking a mug and a single pastry. "I believe we all owe you a debt."

"It came at a high cost," Emily said. Had Markus *known* Casper? He might well have known *of* him. Most magical children were taught the names and family lines of their peers. "But we won the war."

"Yes, you did," Markus said. He leaned back in his chair. "Did you read the last stockholders report?"

Emily shook her head. It would have been sent out three weeks ago, but naturally *her* copy would have gone to Whitehall. Markus wouldn't have known where else to send it. She'd find it when she returned to school.

"There were a lot of people coming in and out of the banks," she said, instead. "And the city feels...*odd*."

"There's been an investment boom." Markus tapped his nose, meaningfully. "The microloans we've been offering, along with the other banks, have galvanized a massive boost in industry. Investment in steam engines and railways has skyrocketed. *Everyone* is buying stock."

"If they can afford it," Emily said.

"If they can afford it," Markus agreed. He frowned, nodding towards a pile of letters on his desk. "The requests for loans – more significant loans – are coming in, day by day. My staff are more than a little overwhelmed."

Emily frowned. "How secure *are* these loans?"

"Some are good, some are bad." His face darkened. "I've earned a reputation for being stingy, I'm afraid. I won't loan money unless I think there's a better-than-even chance I'll recoup my investment."

"That's common sense," Emily pointed out.

"Not according to some of the newer broadsheets," Markus said. "They're insisting that I'm putting the brakes on the industrial boom by not providing money to fuel it."

He sighed. "It isn't that easy to judge prospects," he admitted. "I can seize the property of someone who takes a loan, if they are unable to pay it back, yet...what do I do if they just don't have enough to compensate me for the loss? A client took the loan I gave him and bought a ship, then vanished when it became clear he'd never be able to *keep* the ship. She's probably been renamed and repainted by now, somewhere on the other side of the world."

Emily nodded in grim agreement. There was no international system for tracking down criminals, let alone debtors. A man who reached the next country, perhaps even the next city, with enough untraceable goods could probably vanish, taking a new name and finding a new place. There wouldn't even be *many* problems in hiding an entire ship. It wasn't as if there was a giant list of every ship sailing the seas.

"And I don't want to snatch their children," Markus added. "Melissa would kill me."

"Good for her," Emily said. The concept of taking someone's *children* to pay their debts was horrifying, even though it was technically legal. Melissa, who'd been used as a pawn herself in her family's affairs, had good reason to hate the practice. "How *are* you coping?"

"I've hired extra staff to research business opportunities," Markus said. "We do have a slush fund, and money coming in from most of the microloans, so we should be safe enough as long as we don't start cutting into our seed monies. It means we get some bad press, but most of our larger investments have managed to pay off."

"So the bank itself is fairly stable," Emily said.

"I think so," Markus said. He took a sip of his Kava. "We can't control what people do when they remove their money. There have been times, over the past few weeks, when I've been worried about the sheer number of people trying to invest. I've even noted a number of customers who've taken the financial hit, just to get their money out of the bank. They gave up a sure thing just to play the investment game."

"And if they lose, they lose," Emily said.

"Yeah." Markus glanced at the window. "And I'm really not sure what's happening with the other banks. The Bankers Guild isn't big on sharing information."

"I thought you were the guildmaster," Emily said.

"Only by courtesy," Markus said. He grinned. "I was the first bank manager in the city, unless you count the handful of sorcerers who used to run protective vaults. Some of *them* think *they* should have the title, to be fair. With or without them, Emily, we bankers don't have an established guild structure. I imagine one will sort itself out, sooner or later, but it may not be in place when we need it."

His expression darkened. "And without some limited information sharing," he added, "it's hard to know *just* how well the other banks are coping."

Emily nodded. "I thought that a number of banks *did* fail."

"Seven did," Markus said. "Five of them folded very quickly. I believe the original investors didn't realize they had to offer incentives, beyond basic security. They had few customers and collapsed when they couldn't repay the original investment. The sixth had a major break-in, a couple of months after it opened. Their customers lost a great deal of gold, which led them to simply abandon the bank completely."

"Unsurprising," Emily commented. "And the seventh?"

"I don't know what happened to it," Markus admitted. His face twisted in annoyance. He'd always liked to know things. "One day, everything seemed to be fine; the next, the doors were shuttered and the bank manager had done a runner. Thankfully, there weren't *that* many customers who lost out. I think the manager realized he couldn't repay his original investors and vanished, taking everything he could carry with him."

"It sounds likely," Emily agreed.

"We may never know for sure," Markus said. "The investors stripped the building, then sold it to Vesperian for a song."

"I keep hearing that name," Emily said. "Who *is* he?"

"The Railway King," Markus said. "Vesperian Industries built the Beneficence-Cockatrice Railway, as well as a number of prototype steamboats and improved steam engines. They're currently plowing their profits into the planned Beneficence-Zangaria Railway. Or Vesperian's Track, as they call it. There's been a *lot* of investment in the line."

Emily lifted her eyebrows. She'd approved the original plans for the railway, two years ago, but she hadn't realized it had expanded so far. And yet, it wouldn't be the only thing that had grown rapidly, when imaginative minds took what she'd taught them and ran with it. Right now, there were printing presses far superior to the primitive designs she'd introduced. Why *not* steam engines? How long had it taken Earth to move from the Puffing Devil to the Flying Scotsman?

"We were involved in some of the early investment," Markus added. "I took the liberty of adding some extra investment after the first track started to pay off."

Emily smiled. "Did it repay its investors?"

"I believe so," Markus said. "Moving goods from Beneficence to Cockatrice is quicker now, thanks to the steam engines. But merely encouraging closer relations between the artisans in Cockatrice and the workers here has produced all sorts of interesting spin-offs. I believe that a number of new factories are being opened in Cockatrice, if only because we don't have the room for them. Some of the guildmasters were actually thinking of trying to buy land from you."

"They'd have to talk to the king," Emily said. Cockatrice was entailed. She couldn't divide her lands amongst her children, let alone sell a small patch of ground to the highest bidder…not without the king's permission, at least. "It would be vulnerable, would it not?"

"I doubt that has escaped their minds," Markus said, dryly. He pointed to the map. "If we surrender the protection of the river, who knows *what* King Randor will do?"

Emily nodded in agreement. Beneficence was cut off from Zangaria by the Tribune River, a fast-flowing body of water that would be hell to cross without modern technology – or powerful magic. The four bridges linking Beneficence to the mainland could be blocked easily by the City Guard, if necessary. She had a feeling, from what she'd seen when she'd crossed the bridges with Lady Barb, that the bridges could be cut completely if there was a realistic chance they'd fall. There was definitely enough gunpowder in the powder mills to smash them beyond easy repair.

But having territory on the wrong side would make it easier for Randor to strangle them, she thought. *And the Kings of Zangaria have conceded the city's permanent independence.*

"You could always colonize one of the smaller islands to the north," Emily mused. "Zangaria doesn't have *that* much of a navy. You'd have no trouble smashing a blockade."

"Perhaps," Markus said. "But getting the trade goods to their destination might prove rather more difficult."

"Trade-offs everywhere," Emily mused.

Markus nodded. "The real problem is that we don't have *much* of an international contract enforcement system," he said. "Most merchant families are *families*, Emily, linked by ties of blood. They trust each other. That's always been a problem because it limits expansion – either a family reaches its natural point and stops, or it starts making so many marriage alliances that they start to contradict each other."

He smiled. "You'll have discovered that yourself, I suppose."

Emily felt her cheeks heat. "Does *everyone* take an interest in my life?"

"You're an interesting *person*," Markus said, with a wry smile.

Emily blushed, harder. If she hadn't known Markus was happily married, she would have taken his banter for flirting.

Markus smirked. "And, given who you are, the person you marry is likely to be of considerable interest too. Poor Caleb."

Emily sighed. "People will talk," she muttered. "They do nothing else."

"If they're talking," Markus countered, "they're not plotting."

His secretary returned, carrying a sheet of paper in one hand. Markus took it, scanned it with a practiced eye, and passed it back to her.

"No," he said.

"Yes, sir," his secretary said. "Shall I have security escort him out?"

"Please," Markus said.

He watched his secretary sashay out, then looked back at Emily. "I do think we will remain fairly stable," he said, "but I don't like some of the rumors I'm hearing. Gods prowling the street, people being turned to stone…it's worrying."

Emily looked down at her hands. "Do you believe in the gods?"

Markus shrugged. "I've always believed in power," he said. "Turning someone into stone permanently isn't *difficult*, with enough magic. Cloaking yourself in a godly seeming isn't difficult either. I could put together a spell to do it in a few hours, if I had the time. And there is a suspicious uniformity to the confirmed cases that bothers me. I think we have a magic-using assassin, not a god. The rumors are just muddying the waters."

"And growing in the telling," Emily said. She suspected Markus had a point. There were so many stories about her, she knew all too well, that some of the people who *met* her were disappointed. She *hadn't* crushed Shadye with her bare hands, let alone seduced him into lowering his guard. There were probably more stories about Dua Kepala circulating now. "Are you watching your back?"

"I've taken a few precautions," Markus said. "There's an emergency tunnel I can use to get in or out of the bank, connected to a nearby house. I'll key you to the wards."

He waved his hand. Emily felt the wards shifting around her, then resettling into the background. She couldn't help being impressed. It was a neat piece of spellwork.

"Officially, the house belongs to a sorceress called Robyn," he said. Emily couldn't help flinching. A sorcerer – and DemonMaster – called Robin had tried to rape and enslave her, nearly a thousand years in the past. "Unofficially, I own it. Just ask for the Robyn House and people will direct you."

"Thank you," Emily said.

Markus rose. "I hope to see you again, before you leave," he said. "Perhaps you and Caleb can join Melissa and me for dinner."

"Melissa would probably prefer to spend time with you," Emily said. She rose. "But I'll see you soon."

She walked back down the stairs and into the lobby. A pair of burly guards were escorting a pale-faced man out of the bank. His mouth opened and closed frantically, but no sound came out. Someone had clearly slapped a silencing spell on him, muting any protests. The customers looked amused, rather than angry. Some of them even laughed.

A man stepped in front of her. "Lady Emily?"

Emily blinked. *That* hadn't stayed a secret long, had it?

She studied the man for a long moment. He was dark-skinned, probably around the same age as Sergeant Miles. His gold-rimmed spectacles helped him to project an air of reassuring competence. The grey robes he wore reminded her of school robes, but she couldn't sense any magic on him beyond a handful of protective charms. He looked more like a lawyer – or another clerk – than a magician.

"Yes," she said, finally. She carefully cast a privacy charm, trying to hold it in place without making it obvious. "I am."

The man bowed. "I am Callam, Son of Patrick." His voice was artfully flat. "Assistant to Tryon Vesperian. He requests the pleasure of your company."

Emily hesitated, glancing at her watch. She still had nearly an hour before she was due to meet Caleb and Frieda, assuming she could *find* them. And she was curious. If nothing else, she wanted to know how her cover had been blown.

"Of course," she said. "It will be my pleasure."

Chapter Eight

EMILY WAS NOT SURPRISED TO DISCOVER THAT VESPERIAN'S MANSION WAS LOCATED IN Starry Light, the richest part of the city. It was one of a dozen mansions, each surrounded by small gardens and protected by private guards. Their owners had gone to some trouble to try to make the buildings unique, placing statues of their ancestors or the gods outside their homes. Vesperian had placed a giant, stylized 'V' outside his mansion, just like the one she'd seen in the funicular. It glittered gold in the noonday sun.

She tensed as she passed through the gates, silently readying a handful of protective spells. It hadn't occurred to her until she'd already agreed to go that it might well be a trap, although she knew no one in Beneficence who might want to do her harm. She certainly couldn't recall meeting Vesperian – even *hearing* of him – before she'd headed off to war. It was possible that he'd been one of the industrialists who'd flocked to Cockatrice as the New Learning became more prevalent, but Byron and Paren had been in charge of handling such matters. She'd chosen to keep her distance.

Which might have been a mistake, she told herself sternly.

She reached out with her senses as they reached the door, which swung open as they approached. There were a handful of protective wards – one tuned to keep out supernatural vermin, the remainder aimed at anyone entering with bad intentions – but they didn't *feel* directly linked to a sorcerer. Given time, she knew she – or any reasonably competent magician – could probably break into the house. The butler, wearing a long dark robe, bowed politely as Callam led her into the hallway. She couldn't help thinking that he lacked the loyalty and devotion she'd seen in some of King Randor's liegemen.

Vesperian hadn't lived in the mansion long, she realized, as she looked around the hall. It looked as though he and his family had only moved in a year or so ago. The walls were lined with paintings and portraits, the former showing a combination of real steam locomotives and remarkable designs that wouldn't have been out of place in a steampunk universe. Some of the latter would take years to build, even assuming steam technology continued to advance; the remainder were probably doomed never to materialize, unless technology went in unprecedented directions. She couldn't help smiling as she followed Callam down the hallway. Vesperian, whatever else could be said about him, didn't lack imagination.

But he *did* lack taste, she noted. Everything he'd placed on display showcased his wealth: golden statues clashing uncomfortably with old paintings and artifacts that dated all the way back to the pre-imperial days. There was no overall theme, none of the quiet elegance she'd seen in Whitehall or Queen Marlena's private chambers. The servants wore striking clothes, the men showing off their muscles while the women displayed their breasts and legs. She couldn't help thinking Vesperian had designed everything to call attention to himself and his wealth. He was definitely *nouveau riche*.

King Randor has to show off his power, she thought. She understood the logic, the need for the king to show off his power even when funds were running low, but she'd never cared for the style of King Randor's court. *And Vesperian has to show off his wealth.*

She felt a twinge of pity, mingled with amusement. Vesperian had no title, no long family history he could call upon to back up his claims. The older families in the city had probably sneered at him, once upon a time. She wondered, as they stopped outside a large wooden door, if they were laughing at the *parvenu* now. A man who had purchased – or rented – a mansion in Starry Light could not be dismissed.

The doors swung open. "Lady Emily," Callam said. "Please allow me to introduce Tryon Vesperian."

Emily braced herself as she strode into the office. It was huge, easily larger than a small classroom at Whitehall. The walls were lined with bookcases, save for one wall dominated by a giant painting of Vesperian and his family. She sensed three more protective wards, one of which was definitely a supercharged privacy ward. The other two didn't seem to have any purpose, as far as she could tell. They were clearly designed to resist outside probing. She pulled back her awareness before she provoked a reaction. God alone knew what the wards were designed to do.

Tryon Vesperian rose to his feet and bowed, politely. He was tall, probably in his early forties, but running to fat. His face was pale, but his almond eyes suggested that he, too, had some mixed blood in him; his hair was orange, a neatly-trimmed goatee dominating his chin. It was a statement, Emily suspected. An unkempt beard would have suggested a nobleman, one dominated by his lower impulses. She'd seen too many of them at King Randor's court.

Vesperian wore fine clothes, cut from the most expensive silk; a pair of black trousers, a white shirt and a black waistcoat. That too was a statement, she suspected. Vesperian had come far in the world, far enough to afford such materials, yet he hadn't forgotten his humble beginnings. The shirt wasn't *too* different from what a common laborer would wear, but the silk would cost more than a thousand laborers could earn in a year.

"Lady Emily," Vesperian said. His voice was polite, tinged with a hint of aristocracy. "I've wanted to meet you for a long time."

His handshake was firm, Emily discovered, as he shook her hand. It made her smile as he invited her to sit, summoning maids to bring food and drink. His manner suggested that he considered her an equal, perhaps *more* than an equal. She found it oddly refreshing. He wasn't bowing or scraping to her...or dismissing her, as some noblemen in Zangaria had tried to do. They'd never wanted to take women seriously...

And yet, there was something about his manner that set alarm bells ringing at the back of her mind.

"I've been following events in Cockatrice with great interest," Vesperian said, as a maid arrived with a tray of drinks and small cakes. "I'm glad to hear that most of your...innovations remain in effect."

"They haven't been changed," Emily agreed. She couldn't help noticing that the maid's dress was terrifyingly short. "I find they bring in considerably more tax revenue."

"Of course," Vesperian said. The maid withdrew, as silently as she'd come. "And they are spreading, are they not?"

"Swanhaven has adopted some of my innovations," Emily said. She covertly tested the drink and cakes for poison, finding nothing. "I don't know how far they'll spread beyond there."

"The new Baron has considerable influence," Vesperian said. If he'd noticed her test, he didn't bother to comment on it. "And you know him, do you not?"

"Yes," Emily said, flatly. King Randor had given Swanhaven to Jade, after both of the baron's legal heirs had died. She couldn't decide if Randor had done his son-in-law a favor or given him a poisoned chalice to drain. Swanhaven had been on the verge of outright rebellion only seven months ago. "He has many other duties to attend to."

She nibbled one of the cakes, tasting sugar on her lips. It was sweet enough to make her teeth hurt – yet another display of wealth. Sugar was expensive, even in a trading city. The cake probably cost more than an entire month's supply of food, for a poor family. She wasn't particularly impressed. There was a fine line between showing off one's wealth and naked conspicuous consumption.

Vesperian chatted about everything from politics to magic. Emily listened, feeling an odd sense of respect mingling with irritation. On one hand, he asked for her opinion and actually *listened*; on the other hand, he hadn't said anything of particular consequence, certainly nothing that explained why he'd asked her to visit. She could have had the same conversation with almost anyone. And yet, somehow, she doubted he just wanted a chat.

"The railway is coming along well," Vesperian said. "Have you ridden the line to Cockatrice?"

"Not yet," Emily said. Technically, she wasn't allowed to return to Zangaria without King Randor's permission. Practically speaking, Randor had no way to keep her out as long as she was careful, but it would put Alassa and Imaiqah in an awkward position if he found out. And Jade, who might be ordered to arrest her. "I hear it's spectacular, though."

"It is," Vesperian said. He grinned. Oddly, she thought it was the first *genuine* emotion he'd shown. "We started with a single track, which might have been a mistake; we had to add a *second* track within a month, just to run engines in both directions at once. Right now, we can move goods from Beneficence to Cockatrice City in just under two hours. We're currently working on extending the line further into Zangaria."

His smile grew wider. "My investors have been very happy," he added. "Each individual payment is quite small, of course, but they've been mounting up rapidly. I've made them very wealthy men."

Emily nodded. "I'm sure they're pleased."

"They are," Vesperian said. His smile lit up his face. "And extending the line into Zangaria will bring them more money."

"One would hope so," Emily said. "Do you have permission to take the line further south?"

Vesperian shrugged, dismissively. "There are some diplomatic headaches to be sorted out," he said. "And minor technical bugs."

Emily frowned. "Diplomatic headaches?"

"A number of aristocrats are reluctant to allow us to take the railway through their territory unless we come to terms with them first." He sounded irked. "Each of them holds out for the best deal he can get, but whenever one of their fellows gets a better deal...they want the same deal for themselves. They just don't stay bribed."

He shrugged. "But we have enough agreements in place to extend the line into Swanhaven and up towards the Iron Hills," he added. "The profits will be considerable for those who cooperate."

Emily wasn't so sure. "Do either of them have anything to offer your investors?"

"The railway line will open up promising new investment opportunities," Vesperian said. He rose and walked over to his desk, returning with a large paper map. "Shipping iron ore, for example, has always been a problem. A working railway line will make it cheaper to ship ore around the country, as well as creating new markets for coal. The mines down south have never been fully developed."

He placed the map on the table, inviting Emily to inspect it. The map was practically a work of art, an order of magnitude more detailed than any of the rough maps she'd seen on campaign. She silently applauded the mapmaker, noting how he'd carefully sketched out the distances instead of guessing wildly. It wouldn't be perfect, of course, but it was good enough to showcase Vesperian's plans. He'd even added the local boundary lines between the different noble estates.

Her finger traced the railway lines on the map. The line between Beneficence and Cockatrice was relatively straight. It curved to avoid a couple of hills, but nothing else. The planned line beyond Cockatrice, however, looked as though someone had drawn a jagged line on the map. It swung around widely, adding hundreds of miles to its final length. Some of the alterations made sense – there were places where building a bridge would be difficult – but others seemed to come out of nowhere. The planned track meandered at random.

"This will add considerably to the final cost," she mused. "Why does it...?"

She tapped the line. It was strikingly inefficient.

"We've had problems getting permission to take the line through some of the estates," Vesperian reminded her. "In the long run, however, it will work in our favor. Clear proof of profit will convince the holdouts to join us, allowing us to expand the network through their territory. We'll be in a better position to dictate terms when we no longer *need* them."

Emily wasn't so sure. She'd met enough aristocrats to know they reacted badly to anything that threatened their power. The railway, in and of itself, wasn't much of a threat. It might even be profitable. But it would introduce a whole new world to the peasants laboring on the farms. Who knew what would happen when peasants could purchase a railway ticket to Beneficence...

...And never come back.

It's hard enough catching runaways who flee to the nearest city, she thought, grimly. She'd had to deal with hundreds of complaints from her neighbors, the last time she'd been in Cockatrice. Too many of their peasants were fleeing into her territory. *How much harder will it be if the runaways can cross the entire country?*

It wasn't the only problem, either. Building a line over relatively flat countryside was simple enough, but cutting through hills and mountains would be considerably harder. Vesperian would have to build bridges and stations, install crossings...everything necessary to run a railway line up to the Iron Hills. And there would be an ongoing demand for maintenance that would eat up the early profits...

"It's an impressive scheme," she said. It wasn't a lie. It *was* impressive. But she doubted that profits would materialize as quickly as he suggested. "Why did you want to show it to me?"

Vesperian leaned forward. "I wanted to give you the opportunity to invest," he said, confidently. "I can give you notes at a rate of ten-to-fifteen."

Emily blinked. Marian had mentioned *notes*, hadn't she? But she hadn't gone into detail.

"You want me to invest," she said, slowly.

"Yes," Vesperian said. "Unfortunately, such a large project requires a sizable investment."

"It would," Emily agreed.

She listened as he outlined what he had in mind. Thankfully, listening to some of her tutors had taught her how to follow speakers who weaved backwards and forwards, sometimes changing the subject at random. It was simple enough, at least on first glance. She would invest ten thousand gold crowns, publicly, into Vesperian's Track. In exchange, she would receive *fifteen* thousand crowns when the profits started rolling in. Vesperian himself wouldn't take any profit until his investors had been serviced.

It sounded good. It sounded too good to be true.

They might not be able to get the line built, she thought, looking down at the map. The line between Beneficence and Cockatrice served as a proof of concept, but it was also relatively simple. Scaling it up, even pushing the line to Swanhaven, would be expensive. *And if they can't get permission to build the line, everything will be wasted.*

And yet, she *knew* the railway line was necessary...

"I will consider it," she said. "However, before I offer *any* money, I will require a good look at your accounting books."

Vesperian's face froze, just for a second. "My books?"

"I need to know just how profitable the first part of the railway has been," Emily said. It seemed the obvious thing to check. "You do keep figures, don't you?"

"Of course I do," Vesperian said. "The line has been profitable, *strikingly* profitable."

Then you should be willing to prove it, Emily thought.

She looked back at him. "I am unwilling to invest any money until I know that the line is profitable," she said, flatly. She wasn't Bryon – or Imaiqah – but she knew a few things. "I will require a look at the accounting books, a comprehensive cost-benefit analysis for the future expansion and a full list of your investment collateral."

Vesperian's face darkened. "There are details I cannot share," he said. "My investors..."

"Should have no objection to anything I demanded," Emily said. Had Vesperian's original investors bothered to do any due diligence? "I believe they would be interested in seeing the books too."

Vesperian rose, firmly. "Thank you for coming, Lady Emily," he said. It was clearly a dismissal. "I may not be able to offer so good a deal in future."

"I will not change my mind," Emily said. "I cannot even *consider* a loan before seeing your books."

"As you wish," Vesperian said. He snapped his fingers. The door opened a moment later, revealing Callam. "My assistant will escort you back to your bank."

My bank, Emily thought.

She looked at him. "How did you know I was here? At the bank, I mean?"

Vesperian smiled. "That would be telling."

Emily sighed. She'd announced herself to the clerk, in front of two guards. Any of them could have tipped off Vesperian. They might not even be breaking their contracts with Markus! Or...perhaps someone had put two and two together and realized that she was staying with Caleb's family. It wouldn't be *that* hard to deduce her identity. Caleb and she hadn't made any sort of formal announcement, but the magical community probably knew they were dating. The thought made her more uncomfortable than she cared to admit. Her private life was none of their business.

She nodded to Vesperian, catching a hint of...*something*...crossing his face. He hid it well, but he clearly hadn't been brought up in an aristocratic household. He was... fearful? Or worried?

Perhaps he has reason to worry, she thought.

She followed Callam out of the house and through the streets. They seemed tenser somehow, although it was hard to put her finger on it. The crowds milled around, small groups forming only to break up moments later. She was missing something, she was sure. But what?

"Lady Emily," Callam said, breaking into her thoughts. "Where do you want to go?"

"Railway Street," Emily said. She was due to meet Caleb and Frieda there. "I hear it's quite impressive."

"It is," Callam assured her. "I'll be happy to take you there. It's Mr. Vesperian's pride and joy."

Chapter Nine

Railway Street was dominated, unsurprisingly, by a steam engine that was only three years old, but already outdated. The *first* steam engine was in Alexis, on display near Paren's former workshop; this one, according to the placard underneath it, was the first steam locomotive to be designed in Beneficence. It looked like a giant wooden kettle, mounted on a wooden carriage. Emily suspected it had been outdated long before it had first been driven up the track, but building it had probably taught the local artisans a great deal about how to complete the job.

She took a moment to admire the sight, then allowed her gaze to wander down the street. A dozen other steam engines stood there, all clearly wooden mock-ups rather than real locomotives. Dozens of children clambered over them, waving to their friends and families as they posed on the tops or jumped down to the street. One of the engines – a little tank engine – had a large smiley face drawn on the front. The children seemed to find it delightful.

"Emily," a voice called. She turned to see Caleb, hurrying over to her. "Did you have a good time?"

"I had an odd invitation." Emily gave him a quick hug, then drew back. If Vesperian and Callam had identified her, who *else* might be watching? She'd have to use a glamour if she wanted to go out in public. "Where's Frieda?"

"Just visiting the bookstalls," Caleb said. "I said I'd wait for you here."

Emily had to smile. Frieda hadn't made a bad guess. Emily probably *would* have visited the bookstalls, if Caleb hadn't found her first. Frieda had certainly followed Emily through a dozen bookshops and stalls back in Dragon's Den. She took Caleb's hand and allowed him to lead her into a side street lined with small stalls. A dozen of them sold newly-printed books. Beyond them, a broadsheet singer offered the latest broadsheets from three different printers.

"There she is." Caleb nodded towards one of the larger stalls. "Do you think you should be concerned about her reading matter?"

"Not as long as she doesn't take it back to Whitehall," Emily muttered, as she saw a particularly lurid cover. "She'll be in trouble if someone catches her with it."

She shook her head in annoyance as they walked over to join Frieda. She'd introduced the printing press, knowing it would make books cheaper...yet she hadn't considered all of the ramifications. Textbooks had become cheaper and more widely distributed, true, but the publishing industry had also boomed. Cheap novels had started to spring up all over the continent, including hundreds – perhaps thousands – of blue books. She supposed she shouldn't have been surprised by the growing mass of erotic fiction, almost all of it tame compared to some of the fan fiction she'd read, but it was still disconcerting. Blue books were banned at Whitehall, Mountaintop and probably every other magical and mundane school in the world. Somehow, that hadn't put a dent in their popularity.

"Emily." Frieda turned, holding a pair of books tucked under her arms. Emily decided it would be better to pretend she hadn't seen the cover. She doubted anyone's body could bend that way. "What happened at the bank?"

"I'll tell you over lunch," Emily said. "Coming?"

Frieda paid, then jerked a hand towards the furthest store. "You probably should take a look at that one," she said. "There's stuff about Zangaria there."

Emily frowned. "Stuff?"

"About King Randor, about Alassa…about everyone," Frieda said. "I glanced at a couple of pamphlets, Emily. They make Alassa out to be like one of the girls from *Sapphic Sorceress Sisters*. She's having an affair with her handmaid as well as her husband…"

She led Emily down the street and up to the stall before Emily could formulate a coherent response. The stall was covered in pamphlets and broadsheets, including a handful of hand-drawn cartoons. She glanced through a couple, then shook her head in disgust. Alassa wasn't the only one being slandered, depending on the writer. King Randor, Baroness Harkness and Baron Gaunt were accused of all sorts of perversions, while Sir Roger of the Greenwood had apparently been partying in Farrakhan during the war. That, at least, she knew to be a lie. He and his men had played a major role in saving the city from the first enemy attack.

"They've been fighting the battle of the broadsheets for a long time," Caleb said, quietly. "I don't think anyone's managed to ban them from the city."

Emily nodded, reluctantly. Journalism in Zangaria – and the rest of the world – was still in its infancy. Truth and justice took a backseat to sensation and titillation. King Randor had probably banned most of these broadsheets – she could pick out a couple of familiar names – but he'd find it impossible to keep them out of his kingdom completely. The printers could pay a couple of kids to distribute them, then pull up stakes and vanish. They'd never be caught.

"I'll have to discuss it with Alassa," she said. She suspected it would be pointless – Alassa couldn't do anything about it either – but it probably needed to be mentioned. The tensions in Zangaria continued to rise, from what she'd heard. Slanderous suggestions about the Crown Princess's personal life would only undermine her position when she took the throne. "Do you want to pick a place for lunch?"

Frieda nodded and led the way back to Railway Street. Emily followed, holding Caleb's hand and thinking hard. Were there stories about *her* on the stall? It was hard to imagine anything worse than the songs she'd heard, shortly after defeating Shadye, but she knew her imagination in such matters was limited. The bards had come up with all sorts of explanations for her victory, ranging from the possible to the outrageous. And there was nothing she could do about that, either.

"Burgers," Caleb said, as Frieda pointed to the eatery. "Coming?"

Emily sighed, dismissing her concerns. "Yeah," she said. "Can you get us a private booth?"

She followed them into the burger bar, looking around with interest. It could have passed for a fast food restaurant on Earth, if the chairs and tables hadn't been wooden and the burgers larger and generally more attractive. She reminded herself to be careful what she put on her burger as a waitress led them to a private booth. The local mustard was far stronger than the yellow crap she'd eaten back home.

"So," Caleb said, once they were seated and orders had been placed. "What happened?"

Emily ran her hand through her hair. "I've been noticed," she said. She cast a privacy ward before continuing. "Vesperian himself asked me to visit."

Caleb blinked. "And you went *alone*? Without telling us where you were going?"

"I beat a necromancer," Emily reminded him. She knew he had a point, but that didn't stop his concern being irritating. "And I didn't know where to find you."

"Ouch," Frieda said. She shrugged. "What did he want?"

"A loan." Emily went through the full story as they waited for the burgers. "He wanted ten thousand crowns."

Caleb muttered a rude word under his breath. Emily didn't blame him. The value of money on the Nameless World was a little variable, largely because coinage hadn't been standardized for long, but ten thousand crowns was an immense sum. She had a feeling it was well over ten *million* dollars, perhaps much more. Even a well-paid alchemist would be lucky if he made over a hundred crowns in a year.

Frieda shook her head. "Do you *have* that sort of money?"

Emily winced, inwardly. She'd never liked discussing money.

"He thinks I do," she said, finally. Vesperian might well be right. Even if she didn't have ten thousand crowns at hand, she *could* – presumably – use her position as Baroness Cockatrice to take out a loan. Hell, Imaiqah would probably send the money if Emily asked for it. "But I asked him for a look at his books, and he refused."

Caleb's eyes narrowed. "That's probably not a good thing."

Frieda glanced at him. "*Probably?*"

"On one hand, opening his books would help to convince someone to offer him a loan," Caleb pointed out. "But on the other, it would also reveal the names of his investors…who could then be targeted, if someone wanted to ruin his business. The Accountants Guild was noted for using their inside information to cause trouble, back before the New Learning."

Emily nodded, slowly. "If he wants so much money…"

"That's probably not a good thing either." Caleb leaned forward. "Do you remember what Marian said, yesterday?"

"She was talking about notes," Emily recalled. A thought struck her. "Vesperian offered me fifteen for ten."

Caleb met her eyes. "You wouldn't be the first person to be offered such a good deal," he said. "The price of notes has been going up and up…"

"And it will come down," Emily finished.

Frieda held up a hand. "Notes?"

Emily and Caleb exchanged glances. "Vesperian has been selling promissory notes to everyone with the money to buy them," he said. "He started out by offering eleven for ten, from what I heard, but the rate has been going up over the last few months. People have even been exchanging the notes or selling them on."

"Shares," Emily muttered.

She shook her head in disbelief. It sounded like a recipe for trouble.

"I don't understand," Frieda said. "What does it *mean?*"

"Suppose I loan you ten crowns," Emily said. "We set the repayment rate at fifteen-to-ten, with a due date of…well, next month. You have to pay me fifteen crowns and, if you don't, I have the right to claim something of yours."

"I don't think I have *anything* that's worth fifteen crowns," Frieda mused.

"You're a poor investment risk," Caleb gibed.

Emily ignored him. "We write the terms of the loan down in a promissory note," she added, carefully. "I could then sell that note onwards to Caleb…for eleven crowns, perhaps. Caleb then makes a profit of *four* crowns when you pay him the full fifteen."

"Except you would have given up a profit of four crowns," Frieda said, slowly. "Why would you do *that?*"

"I might need the money before the note came due," Emily said. "You wouldn't be paying out the full amount before then."

"Assuming you *can* pay," Caleb pointed out. He sounded disturbed. "What happens if you *can't* pay? What happens if you don't have anything to cover the cost?"

The burgers arrived before Emily could think of an answer. They were huge, cooked to perfection and slathered with melting hunks of cheese. The server brought them a small collection of condiments and a basket of oversized chips, then hurried away again. Emily reminded herself, again, to be careful with the sauces. They were *nothing* like the ones she'd used at home.

Healthier, though, she thought. *But we might have to skip dinner.*

"I don't know what would happen if someone couldn't repay the loan," she said, slowly. She tested the burger, just to make sure it was safe to eat. "If they didn't have anything that could be seized…"

"They'd be in some trouble." Caleb picked up his burger and took a careful bite, then a larger one. "Ten thousand crowns…how many of his bills are coming due?"

Emily winced. If she was right – and she had no reason to think otherwise – Vesperian was borrowing money to repay the first set of loans, rather than investing it in his railway. Ten thousand crowns could repay a lot of debts, as well as convincing some of his creditors that there was no need to panic and demand repayment. He might even be able to use the sudden influx of money to get *more* loans.

But the wheels will fall off, sooner or later, she thought. Vesperian and his investors were playing musical chairs for high stakes. *When the music stops, and it will, who's left out in the cold?*

She'd seen it happen, back on Earth. Someone took out a loan, then another loan, then struggled to repay the interest…sinking further and further all the time. She'd known people who had been so deeply in debt that they hadn't had a hope in hell of escaping. And *they'd* dealt with relatively small sums of money, hardly noticeable to the banks and credit card companies. What would happen if a giant corporation went the same way? It would be a nightmare.

"I don't know," she said. "And without further information, I'm not going to invest."

"Mother banned Karan and Marian from investing," Caleb said. "She told them they weren't allowed to use any of their allowance to invest."

"I don't blame her," Emily said. Karan and Marian would be annoyed, she was sure, but she suspected their mother was right to be wary. There was no way either of the girls would be counted amongst the major creditors once the hammer fell. "How did they take it?"

"Poorly," Caleb said. His face twisted. "Their friends are bragging about scoring good deals, and they're out in the cold."

"They might have the last laugh." Frieda dunked a chip into something that smelled like Tabasco, then nibbled it thoughtfully. "What happens if their friends don't get their money back?"

Emily shrugged. A schoolchild's allowance was nothing, in the grand scheme of things. A handful of cents wouldn't amount to much. The teenagers would be embarrassed and humiliated, but there wouldn't be any major consequences beyond annoyed parents...would there? She found it hard to believe that *anyone* in Beneficence would give their children *that* much pocket money.

"They'll be laughing," Caleb predicted. "And their friends will be hurt."

"We should investigate." Frieda looked up, interested. "How far can this possibly go?"

Emily considered it, carefully. She'd read about financial bubbles, but most of the details had slipped her mind. Even a relatively low-tech society could have a sudden upswing in share prices, followed by an equally rapid crash when the shareholders realized their mistake and tried to withdraw their money before it was too late. What would happen if investors realized Vesperian couldn't repay them?

It would be bad, she thought, numbly.

"I don't know," she said, finally. "It would depend on too many factors."

She forced herself to think.

How much did Vesperian actually own? His mansion...did he own it? If he was renting the building, there was no way he could sell it to recoup his losses and repay his investors. The railway and its rolling stock? Or...what else did he have?

She didn't know. But she did know was that the only people who came out ahead in a pyramid scheme were the ones right at the very top.

"Don't invest," she said.

Frieda laughed.

"Good advice," Caleb said. "I just hope my sisters listened."

He paused. "I hope *Casper* listened," he added, after a moment. "He was certainly old enough to make his own decisions."

"I don't think he would have had enough money to make a difference." Emily took another bite of her burger, enjoying the taste. "Did Master Grave give him an allowance?"

"I don't know," Caleb said. He grinned. "Did Sergeant Miles give *you* an allowance?"

Emily shook her head. It had never occurred to her to ask for one. She'd taken enough cash with her to meet all her *personal* needs, given that the army supplied the sorcerers and their apprentices with food, bedding and everything else they needed. And she'd never been one to gamble. It wasn't as if the other apprentices had invited her to any high-stakes games.

"He *could* have asked our parents for an advance on his inheritance," Caleb mused. "But I don't think they would have agreed."

"Probably not," Emily said. "How would *that* have worked?"

"Poorly," Caleb said. "He was the Heir, after all."

Emily met his eyes. "What did your mother say to you?"

"Nothing I can talk about here." He shot Frieda a glance. "But we do have to talk."

"I'm sure I can trust you to behave," Frieda said. She glanced from Emily to Caleb, then looked at her watch. "There's a train due in thirty minutes. I could wander off afterwards, leaving you two alone."

"Thank you," Emily said. She knew Frieda meant well, but her constant supervision was annoying. "We won't do anything stupid."

"Vesperian must be getting desperate," Caleb mused, as he finished his burger. "I would have expected him to send you a formal invitation to dinner, not have one of his flunkies accost you outside a bank. It smacks of something put together on the spur of the moment, rather than a carefully thought out plan."

Emily nodded. She hadn't thought about it like that, but Caleb was right. By any reasonable standard, Vesperian should have wined and dined her before requesting a loan…and, perhaps, put together a better case. It sounded more like he'd taken advantage of an unexpected opportunity rather than planning everything down to the last detail.

Frieda had a different thought. "Did he really expect you to write him a bank draft at once?"

"Maybe." Emily had met enough aristocrats to know they didn't bother to pay much attention to money. A baron might run short of ready cash, but his lands and properties would eventually refill his wallet. And if he needed the money quickly, he could just squeeze the tenants until they pleaded for mercy. "Or perhaps he thought the mere promise of the money would be enough to save his bacon."

She finished her burger and rose, carefully concealing a tip under the plate. The waitress would scoop it up before anyone else arrived. "Let's go," she said. "I want to see the railway."

Chapter Ten

"I T'S GROWN," CALEB SAID, AS THEY ENTERED THE STATION. "IT WAS MUCH SMALLER, THE last time I visited."

Emily nodded. Beneficence Station was larger than she'd expected, a combination of platforms, sheds for rolling stock, and roving salesmen trying to sell everything from shares in the railway to food and drink. Uniformed conductors walked everywhere, supervised by a fat man in a top hat and black waistcoat. Emily was disappointed to realize that people couldn't get onto the platforms themselves without a proper ticket, although she understood the problem. There were too many spectators for it to be safe.

She looked from side to side, shaking her head in amusement. Vesperian had covered almost everything with his giant 'V,' save for a handful of advertisements and a giant portrait of himself. Almost all of the advertisements were for guildmasters, urging guildsmen to vote for free trade candidates. Emily wondered, absently, if Vesperian had banned any other candidates from advertising in his station. She rather suspected he had. Someone more inclined to raise trade barriers would not find favor with him.

Frieda nudged her. "Here it comes!"

Emily smiled at the note of excitement in Frieda's voice – and the crowd's intake of breath – as the steam engine slowly came into view. Steam billowed up from the south, growing closer and closer until the locomotive itself appeared, half-hidden in a cloud of smoke. The whistle blew as the train roared past and headed into the station, pulling four large carriages to the platform. Emily had to admit that steam technology had improved over the last couple of years. Earth had taken decades to make the same leap.

But they didn't have my half-remembered diagrams to point them in the right direction, she thought, as the train came to a halt. *They had to progress by trial and error.*

The whistle blew, again. She tilted her head, watching as the doors were opened from the inside and the crowd poured out. Most of them looked like merchants, but a number were clearly peasants from Cockatrice. The idea of going on a holiday, even a mere two hundred miles from home, would have been alien to them, once upon a time. Now…she wondered, absently, just how many of them would never go home. There was always work for willing hands in the big city.

"It's impressive," Caleb said. "And there's no magic in it at all."

Emily shrugged. Some of Paren's early designs had included a spell to keep the boiler from bursting, if the steam ran right out of control. She had no idea what Vesperian – or his designers – had included. A handful of simple runes might make the difference between success and failure. She heard a grinding sound and turned to watch, just in time to see the engine moving away from the coaches. Unless she missed her guess, there would be a set of points – further into the station – that would allow the driver to turn the engine around and move it around the coaches. The engine practically vanished in another whoosh of steam as the driver moved it away, quickly. Seconds later, another engine appeared on the far side and was quickly hooked up to the coaches. It looked as though there were quite a few engines in the sheds.

"It is impressive," she agreed. There was so much *energy* in the station that it was easy to believe Vesperian's Track could reach all the way to the Iron Hills. Young men lined up in front of a recruitment office, clearly hoping they'd win one of the coveted driver positions. There were even a couple of young women! "But can it make money?"

They walked through the station, allowing her a chance to look around. Prices were relatively low, something that puzzled her until she realized that most of the first investment had already been sunk into the infrastructure. Besides, low costs would encourage more travelers. Large placards talked about how the track's expansion would bring a new era of economic development to Beneficence, a boom that would never stop. Emily knew that was a lie, even if all the political and financial barriers suddenly vanished. There were limits to how far the boom could go.

Here and there, she spotted people who looked...concerned. They hid it well, but their faces were pale and they spoke in low voices. Others muttered angrily, seemingly unconcerned about listening ears. She picked up enough to know that matters weren't as settled as Vesperian had suggested, although she wasn't sure of the details. There were costs and cost overruns and unanticipated side effects...

She heard the engine puffing out of the station behind her. She didn't look back.

"You could probably get a tour," Frieda said. She jabbed a finger towards another line of youngsters. "They're getting a tour."

Emily shook her head. "I don't think we'd be told anything useful." Her name could probably get them a private tour, if Vesperian still thought she might loan him money. "I'd be astonished if they talked about any problems."

A young woman materialized in front of her, carrying a large manuscript book. "I'm selling notes," she said, giving Caleb a sweet smile. Emily felt her hackles rise in irritation. "We're offering sixteen for twelve, repayment due in two years."

"Two years," Frieda said. She smirked. "And what happens then?"

The woman's mask dropped, just for a second. She looked younger, probably no older than Frieda herself. Emily felt a stab of pity, despite her earlier annoyance. Unless she missed her guess, the woman was only paid in commissions. Vesperian – intentionally or otherwise – had created a pyramid scheme.

"Don't listen to her," someone snarled. Emily turned to see an older man, carrying a bottle of beer in one hand. "I can't get a decent price on iron because of that... that..."

He waved a hand at Vesperian's portrait, beaming benevolently down on the assembled crowds. Emily gritted her teeth, unsure what to do. More and more people were turning towards them, some heckling and catcalling the older man while others seemed inclined to support him. And then two burly private guardsmen pushed their way through the crowd, grabbed the older man and marched him off to the entrance. Emily allowed herself a moment of relief as the crowd started to disperse, then followed the guards.

"Come on," she hissed. "I want to talk to him."

The guards pushed the older man out of the entrance, then stood there until he started to head down the street. Emily made her way past them, followed by Caleb and Frieda. The older man turned to look at her, his gaze flickering over her face without a hint of recognition, then started to look away.

"I need to ask you some questions," she said. "Can we talk?"

"Maybe." The man grunted and looked down at the bottle in his hand. "You're too pretty to be a whore and too forward to be a wife. You must be a magician."

His eyes landed on Caleb. "And you're the general's son. What do you want?"

"To talk," Emily said. She glanced at Caleb. He didn't look pleased, either at being recognized or the man's comment to Emily. "Please."

"Polite, too." He walked over to a bench and sat down. "Anything for the general's son."

"Thank you," Caleb said, tartly. "And you are?"

"Jack," the man said. "I was a soldier, once upon a time. Your father was my commander. He actually knew what he was doing, unlike the weak-chinned blue blood they landed us with afterwards."

Emily cleared her throat. "When you said you couldn't get any iron," she asked, "what did you mean?"

"I meant I couldn't get any iron," Jack said. "Or wood. You can't get the wood, you know."

He snorted, rudely. "The army performed a remarkable spell and turned me into a blacksmith. I've been a blacksmith ever since. I used to make swords and horseshoes and everything else the troops needed. And then I came here and started my own business. Not that I ever got much money out of horseshoes!"

"No horses here," Frieda said.

"Not many." Jack agreed. He glared towards the station. "I found a wife, had a couple of little ones, things looked good. And then that man--" he spat "--started building his *railway* and soaking up all the iron. And just about everything else! Every blacksmith in the city is running out of iron because that man is driving prices up and up and up and up…"

He looked down at his bottle. "It's happening everywhere," he added, softly. "Fishermen can't get the supplies they need because the railway is consuming everything. My customers are going away because I can't give them what they want. And when I complained, they had the nerve to suggest that I should go *work* on the railway. That man destroyed my life, and they want me to *work* for him!"

"I'm sorry," Emily said, quietly.

"It wasn't your fault, missy." Jack jabbed a finger towards the station. "It's that *man's* fault!"

He laughed, bitterly. "They keep promising that the railway will take us to a land of milk and honey," he added. "Where iron will be so cheap that *everyone* can have a suit of armor…hah! They've got *one* line. How are they going to finish it when they can't get the iron to complete the next set? Or make those moving kettles? Or…"

Emily nodded. Jack had a point. If Vesperian was driving prices up – and he was, because all the sellers knew he *needed* their wares – what was it doing to everyone else? What *other* effects would it have?

Her blood ran cold as she considered the problem. What if most of the fishing boats were unable to fish? The city might run out of food.

They could go back to wooden boats, she mused. *But if the price of wood is also being driven up…*

"I can't meet my obligations," Jack said, breaking into her reverie. He shook his head. "I'll be taking my family out of the city in a week or so, I think. Better to go to Cockatrice or Swanhaven than see my little girls turned into slaves. I'll strip the forge bare, sell what I can and go."

"My father would help," Caleb said, awkwardly. "He…"

"Might feel obliged to report me instead," Jack said. He laughed, humorlessly. "My wife came here to get *away* from some nobleman who was sniffing around her. Brute thought he was being all noble and such when he didn't just force her into his bed. But now we're going back in that direction. There's a baroness in the castle now. At least *she* won't be chasing my daughters."

"No," Emily agreed. Baron Holyoake had been beheaded, after taking part in the coup against King Randor. His lands had even been renamed when Emily had been ennobled, just to make sure that no trace of their former master remained. "She won't."

Jack looked at Caleb. "Tell your father to do something about that man, if he can. He's going to drag a lot of others down with him."

"I will," Caleb promised. "And I won't mention your name."

"Very good," Jack said. He laughed, again. "Maybe your father can do something. But I doubt it. That man is unstoppable."

He jerked as another engine whistled loudly. "I have grown to hate that sound," he growled, lifting his bottle to his lips and taking a swig. "I'm not the only one."

"No," Caleb agreed.

Jack rose. "They say that Justice is walking the streets. But he hasn't punished the worst sinner of all." He turned and strode off, rather unsteadily.

Emily watched him go, feeling cold. She'd assumed that the investors would be the only ones who lost out, if – when – the scheme collapsed, but it might be much worse. She made a mental note to visit Markus again and discuss it with him, although she wasn't sure if he could do anything. They didn't even know, not for sure, just how bad things really were.

Her thoughts mocked her. *And how much of this is your fault?*

It wasn't a pleasant thought. She'd been the one to introduce railways, and banking, and even microloans. She'd seen them as nothing more than a way to galvanize small businesses and encourage innovation, but Vesperian had taken the concept and run with it. And he'd had just enough success to make further expansion seem desirable. And yet...

I also destroyed the Accounting Guild, she reminded herself. She hadn't regretted it at the time – everyone she'd met had distrusted and disliked the Accountants – but it had had an unexpected side effect. *No one was watching as the bubble started to grow.*

She forced herself to think, yet nothing came to mind. Vesperian wouldn't give her a look at his books – if what she suspected was true, he wouldn't let *anyone* see them. Only a complete lunatic would loan someone money after discovering that costs were skyrocketing and profits were nowhere in sight. No wonder he had abandoned his attempts to convince her after she'd insisted on seeing the books.

"Poor man," Frieda said. Her words broke into Emily's thoughts. "A blacksmith can normally find work anywhere."

"I know." Caleb sat next to Emily, just close enough to be comfortable. She leaned against him, ignoring Frieda's disapproving look. "But if he can't get the raw materials, what can he do?"

"Nothing," Emily said.

She shook her head. It would be easy to write Jack a letter of recommendation for Imaiqah. Her word would be more than enough to get Jack a place at Cockatrice. But he was one person, with a small family. How could she help *everyone* who would be affected, directly or indirectly, by Vesperian? She couldn't find them all jobs. Even *trying* might set off the crash.

If I loaned him money, she thought, *the best that will happen is the crash will be put off for a few months.*

"He's bit off far more than he can chew," she said. No matter how she looked at it, she couldn't see the line being profitable for years, perhaps decades. "And it's going to blow up in his face."

She looked back at the station. More crowds gathered as *another* steam engine crossed the bridges and made its slow way towards the platform. A third locomotive? How many locomotives did Vesperian have? And how much were they worth? She couldn't imagine them being *that* useful outside the railway, although she supposed one of them could be turned into a steamboat engine.

Or someone could melt them down, she mused. The thought was horrific, but she could imagine someone deciding to do just that. *That would solve the iron shortage, wouldn't it?*

Caleb rose. "Frieda, we'll see you at sunset," he said. His tone was firm. "If we meet you by the horse statue I showed you two days ago...?"

"Far enough from your mother's wards to be safe." Frieda smiled. "Be careful, all right? Lady Barb will kill me if you get Emily into trouble."

"I don't think she'll *kill* you," Caleb said. He put on a pedantic tone. "I think she'd merely thrash you to within an inch of your life."

"That isn't an improvement," Frieda said, tartly.

"You'd still be alive," Caleb pointed out. "Sore for weeks, perhaps, but alive."

"I hope you two weren't bickering all the way to the city," Emily said, rising. Caleb and Frieda would have taken the portals, she thought, but they would still have had to cross the bridges to reach his home. It would have seemed a very long trip. "We won't get into trouble."

"You *attract* trouble." Frieda pointed a finger at Caleb. "See?"

Emily snorted, then spoke before Caleb could fire back with a devastating insult of his own. "Remind me which one of you two started an in-school rebellion that nearly got the instigator sentenced to death?"

"Well...that wouldn't have happened without you," Frieda countered. She looked down at paving stones. "Emily...I'll...I'll try and get a tour at the station, then have a wander around the city, see what I can pick up."

"You're good at that," Emily agreed. Frieda was much better at reading people than Emily was, let alone coaxing them to talk. "See what everyone is saying."

"And try not to get into trouble," Caleb added. He sounded amused. "Emily would kill *me*."

Frieda gave him a rude gesture, then hurried off towards the station. Emily watched her go as another whistle blew, echoing through the air. Another locomotive was moving into view, larger than the others she'd seen. Cylinders flexed as the engine picked up speed, heading towards the bridges. It pulled a long line of muddy-looking trucks. She couldn't help thinking that they looked ominous.

Caleb touched her hand. "We have a few hours," he said, glancing at the sun to note its position. He suddenly looked hopeful. "Do you want to find a hotel room?"

Emily hesitated, briefly. Sienna hadn't told them not to make love, merely not to do it in her house. And it had been a long time...she cast a glamour around her, then gave him a tight hug. As long as they weren't recognized, everything would be fine.

She leaned forward and kissed him. "Why not?"

Chapter Eleven

"PRICES ARE GOING UP HERE TOO," CALEB SAID, AFTERWARDS. HE LAY NEXT TO HER, HIS body moist with sweat. "I had to pay twice as much as normal for three hours in a room."

Emily shot him a sidelong glance. "Have you done this before?"

Caleb flushed. "No, but I had to organize hotel rooms for some of our guests last year. They got a much better deal for an entire *week* in a room."

"We're not going to be here for a week," Emily pointed out. "And while *we're* in the room, they can't rent it to anyone else."

She leaned back and looked around the tiny room. It was cramped, barely large enough for two grown adults. The bed was hard and uncomfortable, the window nothing more than a tiny lattice, and the bathroom thoroughly unpleasant. Technically the bathroom had a shower, but she had a feeling that they'd get cleaner if they stood on the roof during a rainstorm. She'd cast a number of privacy wards before she'd felt comfortable enough to start undressing. She had slept in worse places, to be fair, but she hadn't had to *pay* for them.

But it didn't matter. It was the first time they'd been alone for months, and she intended to make the most of it.

She snuggled closer to Caleb. "We haven't had a chance to talk properly," she said, allowing him to wrap an arm around her. "Are *you* all right? I mean, after Casper…"

"He was my brother," Caleb said, reflectively. "Casper…could be a terrible prat, at times. He didn't think much of me – I think he thought I was an embarrassment. But he was still my older brother. I never thought he'd die."

His face softened, slightly. "But it was how he wanted to go," he added. "He died a hero, and that's how he will be remembered."

"I would have died without him," Emily pointed out, mildly.

Caleb grimaced. "I know."

His voice was curiously flat. But then, she knew his culture didn't regard manly tears as appropriate. She couldn't recall seeing *any* men cry on the Nameless World, not even when Grandmaster Hasdrubal had been laid to rest. General Pollack hadn't cried when he'd heard the news, certainly not in public. His military subordinates would have thought less of him if he had. He'd chosen to celebrate his son's heroism instead.

I would have owed Casper my life, if he'd survived, Emily thought. *Would it have balanced out, or would I have owed him a permanent debt?*

"He did well," she said. There were truths she'd already decided not to mention. Casper's drinking, the possibility of suicide…it would only hurt Caleb and his family if *that* ever came out. "That's something to remember, isn't it?"

Caleb lifted himself up so he could look at her. "You don't have any siblings, do you?"

"No," Emily said, flatly. It was possible, she supposed, that her long-gone father had sired other children. But she hadn't seen him since she was a baby. If he *had*, she didn't know about them. She certainly hadn't *met* them. "Why?"

"You can pick and choose your friends," Caleb said. "Family...you don't get to choose *them*."

He sighed. "Casper was my brother." There was a hint of pain in his voice, combined with something Emily didn't care to identify. "And I will miss him."

"I'm sorry," Emily said, quietly.

"He got what he wanted," Caleb said. His voice hardened, although she wasn't sure it was directed at her. "We need to remember that too."

Emily nodded and changed the subject. "What did your mother say to you?"

"She promised dire retribution if she caught us doing anything under her roof," Caleb said. "I wouldn't *dare* sneak into your room."

"Probably for the best," Emily pointed out. "This isn't Whitehall."

Caleb laughed. "Mother would make a good teacher," he said. He sounded more like his usual self. "No one would misbehave in *her* class."

"I suppose not," Emily said. Being taught by one's mother, particularly in a packed classroom...it would be embarrassing. "Is she *planning* to teach?"

"I hope not," Caleb said. "But Marian is going to school soon. Mother wouldn't have to stay in the city, after that. She could take up a job somewhere else if she wanted."

Emily lifted her eyebrows. "What does your mother *do*? Now, I mean."

"She does some consulting work for the City Guard, I believe," Caleb said. He didn't sound particularly interested. "Mother *is* a trained Mediator with an unblemished record. But she chose to spend the last twenty years raising us."

Emily nodded, slowly. Sienna had become a mother relatively young. She'd have time to go back to work for decades, or forge a whole new career, before she began her second retirement. It was fairly common among sorceresses, Emily had been told. Lady Barb was one of the very few exceptions.

Except she's dating Sergeant Miles, she mused. *And they could have children.*

The thought cost her a pang. Lady Barb was the closest thing to a mother – a *real* mother – she had. And yet, it was selfish to expect her mentor to always be there. She couldn't rely on the older woman indefinitely. Sooner or later, she'd have to sink or swim on her own.

"You're a long way away," Caleb said, reaching out to touch her chin. He sounded as though he was only half-joking. "Come back to me?"

Emily had to smile, then sobered. "Your mother told me that you were now the Heir. What did she tell you?"

Caleb looked...pained, as if he was reluctant to talk. Emily waited, patiently. Lady Barb had told her that trying to drag answers out of men, particularly young men, only caused bad feelings. It might work, she'd warned, but it tended to weaken relationships. It was better to wait until the man was ready to talk.

"That I'd inherit the house and much of the family fortune," Caleb said. "But we don't have much of a fortune, so it may not matter *that* much."

"The house would be worth a few hundred crowns," Emily pointed out. "It's in a good location, isn't it?"

"If you happen to be a sorcerer," Caleb said. "But you're right – I wouldn't have any trouble finding a buyer. The house isn't really attuned to a specific bloodline."

He leaned forward to kiss her on the forehead. "There's a bit more to it than that." He sounded as though he didn't want to think about it. "If my parents die – if my mother dies, for anything magical – I'll be in charge. I'll have to supervise my siblings, make sure they marry well…"

Emily tensed. "You'd choose their husbands?"

"I wouldn't dare," Caleb said. His lips twitched. "Have you ever seen Karan try to hex someone?"

"No," Emily said.

"She's good." He smiled. "I once saw her put a hex right through Casper's wards. He was sprouting boils for days afterwards."

He sobered. "I wouldn't choose her husband, but I would have to make sure she chose well. And if she picked badly…I'd have to give her the choice between giving him up, or being disowned."

"That's horrible," Emily said, quietly.

"It's for the family," Caleb said. "That's what Mother said. It's for the family."

Emily shook her head in disbelief. "Would a poor choice really affect the whole family?"

"It could," Caleb said. "And then, there's House Waterfall. I'd have to steer a course between their demands, which will intensify when Mother dies, and my siblings."

"Ouch," Emily said.

She shuddered. Fulvia had treated her granddaughter as a pawn in her schemes. If Caleb's uncle was anything like her, Karan and Marian would be seen as assets on the marriage market. Coming to think of it, Caleb and Croce would be in the same place. Caleb wouldn't find it easy to assert his family's independence against an older, wiser and probably more powerful magician. They might be threatened with complete disownment if they didn't fall in line.

Which might not be so bad, she mused.

"And there's another problem," Caleb said. He looked…he looked as though he didn't want to say anything. And yet, it was clear he knew he had no choice. "I'll be expected to marry as soon as I gain my mastery."

Emily froze. Caleb had been a second son when they'd begun their courtship. Sienna had made that very clear, but she hadn't bothered to spell out the implications. Perhaps she'd assumed that Emily had *known* them. Casper's marriage would probably have been arranged as soon as he completed his training…for all she knew, it had already been arranged and both sets of parents were only waiting for him to graduate before formalizing the arrangement. It wasn't as if Casper would have felt any inclination to discuss it with her…

A thought struck her. If there *was* an arranged marriage, one that had been planned before Casper's death, would *Caleb* be expected to stand in Casper's place?

She swallowed. She didn't want to know. But she had to ask. "Did…did Casper have a planned match?"

Caleb looked relieved. "I don't think so. There would have been interest, of course, but Mother wouldn't have finalized anything until Casper gained his mastery."

He looked down at the rough bedding, seemingly unwilling to meet her eyes. "Would you marry me after I gain my mastery?"

Emily hesitated. She didn't know.

"You wouldn't have to stay here," Caleb said. He sounded as though he was trying to convince himself, not Emily. "You could complete your own mastery before we have children. You'd…"

His voice trailed off. "I don't know…"

Emily forced herself not to look away. She *still* didn't know. She liked Caleb a lot. He was nothing like her stepfather, nothing like the boys at school she'd feared… nothing like Hodge or Robin. He lacked the sheer energy of Jade or Cat – or Casper, for that matter – but he was intelligent, stable and *decent*. She'd chosen to sleep with him, to give him her virginity…she didn't regret it, not really.

And yet…marriage?

It would change her life. She would be tied down by laws and customs that weren't hers, that probably never *would* be hers. And, given her position, there would be hundreds of minor conflicts. Caleb was no longer a free agent, no longer someone who could walk away from his family to marry a baroness. There would be consequences if he stayed with his family and other, different, consequences if he left. Or if they disowned him.

"I don't know," she said, again.

She felt a pang of bitter regret, mixed with frustration. They'd talked of hopes and dreams, of plans for the future…plans they'd implement, once they left school. Those plans were gone now…perhaps. Caleb might be called back at any moment to succeed his mother. And she, as his wife, would have to go with him…or people would talk. She understood, now, precisely why Sienna had chosen General Pollack for a husband. He brought no new obligations to the match.

"You'll have to choose soon," Caleb said. He sounded haunted. He'd had dreams too. "I will respect your choice, but…"

Emily gritted her teeth in anger. Yes, he *would* respect her choice. She *knew* he'd respect her choice. And yet, what *was* the choice? To marry him as soon as he gained his mastery, or leave him, knowing they were both poor choices? Or to watch as he was introduced to a succession of eligible beauties by his mother, who would pressure him to get married and start working on the *next* generation as soon as possible?

And if I say no now, she asked herself, *what then?*

"I'll choose soon," she said. She knew she was only putting off the moment when she *would* have to make a choice, but it was the only thing she could do. She needed to talk to Lady Barb or someone else who could give her proper advice, not make a decision on the spur of the moment. "And I wish…"

"I know," Caleb said.

Emily sat up and looked down at him. Caleb wasn't the handsomest man in the world – she admitted that freely, if only to herself – but she would have been suspicious of a handsome man. And yet...

She shook her head. "I captured a nexus point," she said. "It's *mine*."

"I heard," Caleb said. "Everyone – and I mean *everyone* – was talking about it before we left school. You locked *everyone* out."

Emily smiled. She'd been there – literally – when Whitehall's nexus point had been tamed, nearly a thousand years in the past. She was the only living person who knew how it had been done, let alone how to repeat the process. Other nexus points had been tapped for power, of course, but no one had managed to duplicate Whitehall's spells. Heart's Eye would remain sealed off until she was ready to return.

"I own it." She met his eyes. "And I thought it could become our university."

Caleb's eyes flashed with pain. The university had been *his* brainchild, not Emily's. He'd been the one to dream of a day when the various masteries were studied together, once students had completed their regular schooling. They'd talked it over, planned how to raise money and recruit teachers, but without a nexus point...

They had a nexus point, now. But they also had other obligations.

"Perhaps I can convince Mother to let us work there," he said. "There's no reason to *think* she's going to die, is there?"

Emily shook her head. Sienna was a formidable sorceress. She was powerful enough to cope with almost anything, short of a necromancer or a handful of other sorcerers. And she knew how to extend her life. The chances were good, very good, that Sienna would remain alive for decades to come. There was no reason to *think* she'd be dead within the next ten years.

"No," she said. "But it will complicate matters."

"In more ways than one," Caleb said. "We always knew it was going to be tricky."

Emily felt a sudden urge to giggle. *Tricky*. Yes, they'd known it was going to be *very* tricky. She'd been a baroness – a baroness with real power – while he'd been the second son of a military hero and a powerful sorcerer. He would have made a decent consort for her, just as Jade had made a decent consort for Alassa, because he couldn't threaten her power. But he was now – potentially, at least – a major player in the magical community. Their marriage would have all sorts of political implications...

And I can't even get away from them, she thought, sourly. King Randor might have exiled her, but he hadn't stripped her of her title. It would have been politically impossible. *Maybe we should just change our names and run.*

It was a silly thought. She had no family to leave behind, but Caleb did. He wouldn't want to abandon them. His parents might be a little overbearing, and his siblings annoying, but he loved his family. And she wouldn't ask him to give them up for anything, even for her.

"We'll get through it somehow," she promised. "I just don't know how."

She glanced at her watch, then sat up and peered out the window. The sun was steadily setting. Frieda might turn a blind eye if they were late, but Sienna would not be quite as forgiving. She hurried into the shower, cursing under her breath as she realized it was even worse than she'd thought. The water was cold. She washed any-way, then dried her body with a spell. There was no time to share a shower, not now.

Back at Whitehall, she told herself, firmly. *We can shower together there.*

"Make sure your glamour is in place," Caleb reminded her, as they dressed. "We don't want to be seen leaving this place."

Emily nodded, casting the spell. She wasn't used to being *recognized.* Normally, no one connected her with the Necromancer's Bane. Everyone knew the Necromancer's Bane was a towering woman of stunning beauty and terrible power. But *Emily* was an uncommon name, even after she'd made it famous. Anyone who heard *Emily* would think of the Necromancer's Bane.

Caleb dressed, then cast his own glamour. Emily stared at it for a long moment. She knew the spell was in place, but it was still hard to see his *real* features under the illusion. No one would notice unless they had a reason to look *very* closely. Her own glamour would attract even *less* attention. She wouldn't be the first young woman to hide some imperfection behind a spell.

"Very masculine," she said, dryly. "I think you've overdone the muscles."

"It should make it harder for people to get in the way," Caleb said, flexing illusion-ary muscles. "And even if someone does realize that they're illusions, they might not look any further."

He held out a hand. "Shall we go?"

Emily took one final look around the room, making sure they hadn't left anything behind, then followed him down the cramped staircase. The owner hadn't asked any questions, much to her relief. He'd just told them the rates, and pointed to the stairs. The lobby was deserted as they walked through; they left the key on the desk. Outside, the temple singers chanted loudly, calling the faithful to prayer...

And yet, she could *feel* the tension in the air. Something was going to blow. And soon.

"We'd better hurry," she said, as more and more people spilled onto the streets. "Frieda will be waiting for us."

Chapter Twelve

"**Y**OU HAVE MAIL," SIENNA SAID TARTLY, AS EMILY FOLLOWED CALEB INTO THE LIVING room. "And two people who came to find you, both of whom left visiting cards."

"The secret's out," Caleb teased. "They know who you are."

Emily winced. So much for remaining un recognized.

Sienna snorted. "I ordered a third man to leave after he wanted to stay here and wait for you," she said, passing Emily a small collection of envelopes. "He wouldn't take *no* for an answer until after I turned him into a frog and kicked him out the front door. He'll turn back. Eventually."

Emily swallowed as she checked the letters for unpleasant surprises, then glanced at the visiting cards. They were from two men, both completely unknown to her. They'd both invited her to dinner, offering to let her choose the time and place. She passed them to Frieda and then opened the first envelope. Three pages of greetings and salutations – and a great deal of flattery – boiled down to a *third* dinner invitation. She rolled her eyes at the way the writer sang her praises to the skies, then opened the next envelope. This writer, at least, was more concise. He talked about an investment opportunity she might be interested in, if she cared to visit his office. The name at the bottom belonged to yet another stranger.

"I'm surprised they weren't lurking outside the house," Frieda said, reading the visiting cards. "They clearly *want* to talk to you."

"The sorcerers on the street would have used them for target practice, if they'd stuck around," Sienna said, briskly. She looked up as her two daughters entered the room. "If you don't want to keep those letters, drop them into the fire."

Emily glanced through the remaining letters, one by one. Three of them were just as flattering as the first, while the others talked about opportunities without going into detail. They reminded her of the proposals she'd read at Cockatrice, although she'd made a point of clearly expecting a reasoned argument when the writers finally got to see her or her representative. She wasn't going to hand out loans as if money grew on trees.

"They're investment opportunities," she said. She wondered if Vesperian had considered sending a paper letter too. "And none of them are very detailed."

"Vesperian merely got his oar in first, then," Caleb said.

Karan looked up. "Vesperian?"

"He tried to talk Emily into giving him a loan," Caleb said. "It didn't work."

"And a good thing too," Sienna said, glowering at her daughter. "Vesperian was a schemer before the New Learning, and he's still a schemer after the New Learning. Nothing has really changed."

"It's a great opportunity," Karan said, wistfully. "I could earn money…"

"No, you couldn't," Emily said, sharply. "He's heading for a fall."

Sienna gave her a cold look. "And you know this how…?"

"He wouldn't show me the books," Emily said. "And that means he has something to hide."

"Something so big it couldn't be concealed in the paperwork," Sienna agreed. She looked approving, just for a second. "Do you have any actual *proof*?"

Emily shook her head. "I think he's overextended himself. He's buying up material, driving prices up…but he has very little to show for it. Taking the railway to Swanhaven alone might be a step too far."

"And the second set of notes are coming due soon." Sienna shook her head. "I *knew* he was trouble."

Caleb blinked. "You *know* him?"

"We've met," Sienna said. Her lips thinned. "His father was a fisherman, a very conservative fellow. Vesperian went into business on his own, building newer and better boats. Some worked, some didn't; he had an eye for opportunity, but no real sense of just how far he could go. He married well, coming into money; his wife's dower allowed him to purchase more boats, then design a few newer ones. He was one of the first people to see the potential of the New Learning…I'll give him that much."

She shrugged. "I remember him arguing that the railway line would bring in a colossal profit. The guilds were reluctant, but they couldn't stop him once he'd secured the first set of investors. The guildmasters were getting a lot of pressure from their lower ranks, too. So he built the first railway, and then started offering to allow anyone to invest in it."

"My friends are investors," Karan said. "They're *proud* to invest!"

"They'll lose their money," Emily predicted. "You'll have the last laugh."

She looked at Sienna. "What should I do with these letters?"

Sienna shrugged, again. "Are you asking a future mother-in-law, or an impartial Mediator?"

Emily had to smile, despite the pang Sienna's words caused. "Whichever one is more useful."

"They'd both be useful," Sienna said. "As your mother-in-law, I would advise you to chuck the whole lot on the fire and go wash your hands afterwards. But as an impartial Mediator, I'd tell you to write each of them a polite refusal, whistle for a lad to deliver them, and *then* chuck them on the fire."

"And then go wash your hands," Marian said.

"But this could get you a lot of money," Karan protested. "Should you not hear them out, at least?"

Emily looked back at the letters. They didn't improve on second reading. None were specific, none went into details. She assumed they planned to make their pitches in person, when she would find it harder to refuse. But she had to assume they were talking about the railway. If they *were* investors, they might be interested in selling her their notes before time ran out.

They must be scenting trouble now, she thought. *If the man on the street is aware that something is about to go wrong…*

"You'll have time to go, if you wish, over the next two days," Sienna said. She shot Caleb a glance. "Did Caleb tell you what is going to happen?"

Emily shook her head. "No."

Sienna looked irked. "Casper's coffin has been placed in the Temple of War. It is where all the brave heroes are buried, after their funerals. The funeral itself will be held in two days, during the Fire Festival. There will be a wake and two days of formal mourning after we consign his body to the flames, then we will bid him farewell for the final time."

"I understand," Emily said.

She tried, hard, to keep her face completely expressionless. Did Sienna *know* there was no body? Surely she must know that her son had been disintegrated. General Pollack would have told her. And yet...Sienna was treating the coffin as if it held an intact corpse. Emily didn't want to ask. She wasn't sure she wanted to know.

"Caleb will be formally confirmed as Heir after the mourning period is over," Sienna continued. She sounded as if she was chewing on a lemon. "Once the ceremony is over, the three of you--" she glanced at Frieda "--can return to Whitehall and resume your lessons. I'm sure your teachers expect you to do well."

"I'll be spending most of the summer catching up," Emily predicted, gloomily.

"It won't be the end of the world," Sienna said. "Having to repeat the entire year would be worse."

Emily had to smile, although she was sure that killing a necromancer – a *third* necromancer – would count as a suitable excuse. It wasn't as if she'd spent half the year partying in her bedroom, or anything else that might convince the tutors there was no point in allowing her to retake the year. But then, Gordian *was* the Grandmaster. Perhaps she should be worried after all.

"I suppose," she said.

"Caleb will spend the next two days with me, learning what he needs to know before his formal confirmation." Sienna's gaze was suddenly so sharp that Emily *knew* she knew what Emily and Caleb had been doing. "I trust that Frieda and yourself will have no difficulty staying out of trouble?"

"I should probably go back to the bank," Emily said. "And then we can explore the city."

She was torn between an odd mixture of relief and regret. She would have loved to spend more time with Caleb, but she also needed time to digest what he'd told her and decide what it meant for their future.

All of a sudden, she understood Imaiqah very well. She'd never let herself get attached to any of her boyfriends. It had made it easier for her to let go.

"Very good," Sienna said.

General Pollack entered, followed by Croce. "There was a fight down at the docks," he said, as he undid his cloak and passed it to Karan. "I'm not sure what caused the original explosion, but it was turning into a riot when I left."

Sienna sniffed. "Too many drunkards in one place."

"No doubt." General Pollack sat, heavily. "Going to the council was a complete waste of time. They were too busy discussing Justice to talk about a dead necromancer."

"Justice has been seen again," Marian said. "No one died this time, but they saw him…"

"Drunk," Sienna snapped. "Or maybe they saw an illusion."

"It was no illusion," Marian insisted. Her eyes were wide with passion. "Mother, they weren't *lying*."

Sienna looked unimpressed. "Any halfway competent sorcerer could cast a glamour and mingle it with a few hexes to create a godly image," she said. "And as long as they didn't get caught, they'd get away with it."

"People *died*," Marian said. "They were turned to stone!"

"Which is a common spell," Sienna said. "You'll be turning your classmates into stone next year."

"I wouldn't *kill* them," Marian protested.

Sienna gave her youngest daughter a sharp look. "Let's consider it for a moment," she said, slowly. "Justice – the god – is prowling the streets, looking for sinners. There's no shortage of sinners in this city. I don't let you go down to Fishing Plaice after dark because it is not a safe place for a young girl, magic or no magic. A half-drunk sailor would probably have his way with you whether you wanted it or not."

Her gaze hardened. "A city filled with sinners. And yet, only five people are petrified and killed. Five people, three of whom were industrialists; two of whom were connected to industrialists. Why isn't Justice going after the *real* bastards?"

"He is," Marian insisted.

"There's a man in a cell who's going to be taken to the castle and tossed off the Watchful Rock tomorrow afternoon," Sienna said. "He kidnapped, raped and murdered seven young girls, the oldest of whom was nine years old. And he was only caught because he made a mistake and drew the guards to him. There were grown men vomiting in horror because of the stories he told, when they poured truth potions down his throat."

Her voice grew stronger. "Why didn't Justice kill *him*?"

"We caught him," Marian stammered. Her face was pale. "Didn't we?"

"He claimed his first victim two years ago," Sienna snapped. "And he was only caught last week! If this…*god*…is a *real* god, why didn't he kill him, instead of leaving him alive to kill six more girls? Children! The bastard killed *children*! Tossing him from the rock is more mercy than the bastard deserves!"

She turned and stalked into the dining room. "Come. We have dinner to eat before bedtime."

Emily glanced at Caleb, then followed the others into the dining room. Marian looked subdued, taking her seat and staring at the empty plate as if she didn't want to meet her mother's eyes. Emily didn't blame her, even though she suspected that Sienna was right. If a *real* god was stalking the streets, why would he leave a *real* sinner alone? Or, perhaps, go after *more* sinners. What counted as a sin? Or…

She looked up at Sienna. "The victims…were they all connected to Vesperian?"

Sienna frowned. "They could be," she said. "A couple of them would definitely have been tapped for supplies. But the younger two victims had barely reached their majorities. They wouldn't have any *direct* connection to him."

"They might have been investors," Karan suggested, as she started ladling out the food. "If my friends can buy notes, why not *them*?"

"They wouldn't have been major investors." Sienna sounded confident. "No parent ever born would allow their child enough ready money to be a *major* investor."

"Maybe Vesperian has hired an assassin," Caleb speculated. "Perhaps the targets were all investors who wanted their money back."

Emily nodded. "If they were owed money, what would happen to it?"

Sienna frowned. "It would go to their heirs, I assume," she said. "The notes would be treated as just another piece of property. There *might* be a clause in the original contracts specifying that repayment only had to be made to the original investor, but I can't see any competent lawyer allowing that to pass."

She shook her head. "And if the estate wants the money back immediately, they could take Vesperian to court."

"Which would cause him a great deal of trouble," Emily noted. "Even if he had to just pay back the original loan, without interest, he'd still have to find the money."

"Unless he had *just* enough to pay back the original loan," Caleb offered. "The estate managers might be glad just to get *that* back."

"It would still be risky," Emily countered. "The managers might be prepared to wait long enough for the notes to mature."

She sighed. "The whole thing is a disaster waiting to happen. I think you should be glad we don't have any money invested in the scheme."

"I am," Sienna said. Her lips thinned. "And we will not be investing any money either."

"You're assuming that Vesperian is killing his own investors," General Pollack rumbled. He looked oddly amused. "And you're *also* assuming that no one else has noticed the pattern."

"It *is* obvious," Sienna pointed out.

Her husband smiled. "I'll give you an alternate explanation. Someone *else* wants Vesperian to fail. They're killing his investors to cause problems for him."

"They'd just have to wait for the scheme to collapse under its own weight," Emily said, after a moment. "Why risk exposure when all they have to do is sit tight and wait?"

"If it fails," Karan pointed out, crossly. "What happens if it succeeds?"

"It will be a long time before it makes any profits," Emily said. "There will be no return on the investment."

"You don't *know* that," Karan snapped.

"*Karan*," her mother said.

Emily took a moment to gather her thoughts. "Vesperian is trying to build two extensions to the railway," she said. "One runs to Swanhaven, the other to the Iron Hills. Getting the track as far as Swanhaven City will probably not pose any political problems, as the current baron is supporting the project, but the engineers will still have to bridge a number of rivers, dig tunnels and install everything from signals to stations. It took nearly a year to build the original track, which runs through smoother terrain. *This* one will take longer, even if there are no other problems.

"The second track *will* have political problems," she added. She had no doubt of it. She'd dealt with too many noblemen who had nothing, but a name. "There are upwards of a thousand noblemen who will have to be consulted, then flattered and bribed into staying out of the way. And the terrain south of Cockatrice is even worse for railway lines. I'd be astonished if the original line could be completed in less than five years, assuming that all the political problems just...*go away*. Vesperian has bitten off more than he can chew."

Karan cleared her throat. "But..."

"It will take time, also, to develop a market for the railway," Emily added. "Merely expanding the mines would be difficult, too. I would be very surprised if the railway becomes profitable in less than a decade."

There was a long silence. Karan looked shocked, as if she didn't want to believe what Emily was saying; Sienna's face was expressionless, while Caleb looked as if he was trying to hide his amusement. General Pollack and Croce didn't seem inclined to argue. And Marian...Marian was looking contemplative.

"There are elderly couples who have invested," Sienna said, quietly. "They won't have a hope of starting again."

Emily nodded. Sienna was right.

And when the music stops, Emily thought, *chaos will follow.*

She ate her food quickly, silently hoping she was wrong. But she doubted it. She'd seen the plans when Paren and his artisans had designed the first steam engine. It would be a long time, they'd said, before the country was criss-crossed in railway lines...and that was with King Randor backing the project. Here...Vesperian might put a good face on his jagged railway line, but Emily knew it was an admission that politics weren't proving as simple as he'd hoped. It was possible, she supposed, that there would be a major breakthrough...

"I'll speak to some of my friends," General Pollack said. "Sienna, you could speak to the sorcerers..."

"I don't know what they'd be able to do." Sienna's lips twitched. "We can't magic Vesperian out of existence."

"And if we did," General Pollack said, "we'd only make matters worse."

Caleb glanced at Emily. "Is there no hope?"

"I don't know," Emily admitted. There had been boom and bust cycles on Earth, but she couldn't recall any of them being stopped in their tracks. Bailing out the banks might have staunched the bleeding, if one took an optimistic view, yet it hadn't fixed the underlying problems. "I don't even know where to begin."

Chapter Thirteen

"IT'S GOOD TO SEE YOU AGAIN, EMILY," MARKUS SAID, AS EMILY AND FRIEDA WERE SHOWN into his office. "I'm glad to see you've regrown your hair."

Emily shrugged. "It was a mess." The potion had made her scalp itch uncomfortably for hours, but it had worked. Her hair was now as long as it had been before she'd gone to war. "You remember Frieda, of course."

"Of course." Markus took Frieda's hand and kissed it. Frieda's eyes widened in shock. Emily wasn't so sure he actually *remembered* Frieda – she'd been a common-born magician at Mountaintop, well below his notice – but Emily gave him points for trying. "You are more than welcome in this place."

"Thank you," Frieda said. "This is a fascinating place."

"I'm impressed you managed to say that with a *straight* face," Markus said. "I keep losing junior employees to the railway."

He called for food and drink, then motioned for them to take the sofa. "I'm glad you decided to visit," he said, as he sat down. "I need to ask you a question."

Emily's eyes narrowed. "Not you, too?"

Markus looked perplexed, just for a second. "I've heard a rumor that says you invested thirty thousand crowns in Vesperian's Track," he said. "Is that true?"

"*No*," Emily said, sharply. Thirty thousand crowns was enough money to outfit an army, perhaps even to run a small kingdom. "He asked me to invest, and I declined."

"I thought as much," Markus said. Emily hid her irritation. Markus was well placed to know the rumor had no basis in fact. He was her banker. And yet, he'd been worried. "How much did he ask for?"

"Ten thousand crowns." Emily took a breath. "He invited me to visit him just after last we met."

She ran her hand through her hair. "Markus...all hell is about to break loose."

"The railway," Markus said, flatly.

Emily nodded. "He wouldn't let me see the books. But I can't see how he can repay his investors. The notes are due in a couple of days, unless he manages to roll them over somehow. But there's too much money involved for that to be easy. He needs a fresh set of investors, and I don't think he's going to get them."

"That was my thought too." Markus looked grim. "Do you know how many of my customers have invested money in the railway?"

"No," Emily said.

"A lot," Markus said. "I think some of my *board* have invested money, despite my objections. They're not going to give it up without a fight."

Emily nodded in agreement. Frieda and she had wandered the streets for the last couple of days, eating in small cafes and chatting with strangers. She hadn't truly realized how many people had bought notes until they'd talked to a string of investors in a row, each extolling the blessings the railway would bring to the city. They'd all sounded like cultists, from the young girls who'd invested their pocket money to the cooks who thanked Vesperian for their new customers. A couple had even tried to convince her to invest.

Others, they'd discovered, hadn't been so happy. Vesperian seemed to be buying up resources, from every scrap of iron he could find to bronze, copper, timber and dozens of chemicals. It was a boom time for suppliers, but everyone else was being frozen out of the market. Fishermen couldn't get items they desperately needed for their boats; bridge repairmen couldn't keep up with wear and tear on the giant structures...she was sure that, sooner or later, something would go badly wrong. There were even people muttering about damned foreigners entering their city in search of work.

"You need a contingency plan for when the notes come due," Emily said. "Do you have any ideas at all?"

Markus sighed. "I don't think the bank itself is going to be directly affected," he said. "We didn't invest in the railway ourselves. But if there is a sudden demand for ready cash, we're going to be in some trouble."

Emily made a face. In some ways, the concept of the bank being crammed with gold and silver coins was a polite fiction. Much of the money placed into the bank existed only as notes in a ledger, a promise to repay based on the theory that the bank would *never* have to repay all the loans at once. Markus might be able to meet *some* demand, even though it would mean cutting into his seed money. He wouldn't be able to repay all of his customers at the same time.

She gritted her teeth. The Bank of Silence wasn't the flashiest innovation she'd introduced, but it might well do more good than anything else in the long term. Merely giving people a safe place to store their money made life better, while micro-loans ensured that innovators had the backing they needed to turn their ideas into reality. The thought of it crashing down in ruins, through someone else's financial mismanagement, was appalling. And yet, if hundreds of customers demanded their money back, how could anyone say no?

"This could break the bank," she breathed.

"It's a possibility." Markus looked down at the wooden floor. "I'm very glad that Melissa is safely in Whitehall."

Emily swallowed. "She might be safe." She was on better terms with Melissa these days, but she still didn't like her very much. "But what about you?"

"I don't know," Markus said. "Emily, this could destroy your fortune as well."

"I know," Emily said. "And I have no way to move the money out before it's too late."

She cursed under her breath. In hindsight, she might just have outsmarted herself. She'd put half of her fortune into the Bank of Silence, both to give Markus some seed money and to keep it safe from King Randor's grasping hands. But now...she couldn't even move it back to Cockatrice! The mere *hint* that someone was moving their money out of the bank might start everything rolling downhill to disaster...

...And she had no way to guess at just how big the disaster was likely to be!

"You could buy up the notes," Markus said. "That might limit the scale of the crash."

Emily shook her head. There were just too *many* notes. Even if she bought them at their original value, she'd still run out of money fairly quickly. And the bank would have the same problem. Perhaps, if *all* Vesperian needed was ten thousand crowns, something could be done. But if he needed more...

He wouldn't have asked for so much if he wasn't desperate, she thought, grimly. *And perhaps he has good reason to be desperate.*

"The investors would want full price," she said. "They wouldn't take less than that until it was too late."

"And the notes become worthless paper," Markus said.

He rubbed his eyes. "I'm going to call an emergency meeting of the Bankers Guild. If we discuss the matter in a body, we can approach Vesperian and demand he shows us the books. I've got accountants who can go through every last scrap of paper and pull together a complete picture of his affairs."

Frieda leaned forward. "And what if he refuses to cooperate?"

"We can advise people not to buy any further notes," Markus said. "Beyond that... there isn't much we *can* do."

There's no financial authority to regulate transactions, Emily thought, numbly. *And no international police force to track Vesperian down if he grabs everything he can carry and runs.*

"You could always put in a demand for repayment," Emily pointed out. "Couldn't you threaten to seize the railway?"

"The Guild Council would have to approve it," Markus said. "And Vesperian has a *lot* of allies amongst the guildsmen."

"They bought his notes," Frieda said.

"And he's been creating jobs," Markus added. "The Ironworkers Guild loves him. So do most of the Woodworkers. The guildmasters would hesitate to take firm steps against him until the disaster was obvious."

"And then it would be too late," Emily said.

She frowned, thinking hard. Vesperian had definitely overreached himself. That much was certain. But...had someone else backed him? Had someone offered to pick up the tab, then defaulted. Who would benefit? King Randor was the most likely suspect, but the economic shockwaves would wash over Zangaria too. Alassa's father had grown increasingly paranoid over the last couple of years, but he wasn't stupid. He'd know better...wouldn't he?

Or was she over-thinking it? It wasn't as if any outside player was necessary. Vesperian might have created the disaster without any outside help at all. And then...

She met Markus's eyes. "Who's the richest person in the city?"

Markus smiled. "The richest person that I know about is *you*."

Frieda giggled.

"If one believes rumors," Markus continued, "Vesperian and Grand Guildmaster

Jalil are worth thousands of crowns apiece. Below them, there's a boatload of other wealthy men...why?"

Emily looked down at her hands. "If I was feeling cunning," she said, "I'd wait until the crash came, then buy up everything Vesperian has for a song. The railway and its rolling stock would be mine. I'd cut back on the planned expansion and concentrate on milking everything I could out of the existing infrastructure."

"And possibly do more expansion later," Markus said. "Once you had everything on solid ground again."

He made a face. "Do you think someone is waiting to do just that?"

Emily shrugged. "We can't be the only ones who see impending trouble," she mused. "And who knows *what* Vesperian will do, if he is truly desperate."

"It could take years to unravel the mess," Markus said. "Emily...do you want to attend the meeting? You *are* a major shareholder in the bank."

"I think the bankers would prefer to deal with you," Emily said. She didn't enjoy big meetings. Working with people one on one was much less stressful. "And I have to discuss the matter with others."

"You might need to mention it to King Randor," Markus said. "You *are* one of his aristocrats, even if you're technically in exile. He probably needs to be warned."

"And Imaiqah," Emily said. She could send a letter to Randor. It would give him time to think before he wrote a reply. "Cockatrice is right next door."

"Close enough for trouble to spill over." Markus stood and paced over to the window. "I wonder if any of us will have a pot to piss in when all of this is over."

"I wish I knew." Emily finished her drink, then rose. Frieda followed her. "Be careful, all right?"

"You too." Markus turned to face her. "And if anyone asks about those rumors, what should I say?"

Emily made a face. On one hand, the thought of allowing Vesperian to keep spreading lies was unappealing. If, of course, it *was* Vesperian spreading lies. But on the other hand, an outright denial might make matters worse. Anyone who thought the railway was about to collapse, dragging half the city down with it, would do everything in their power to get their money out before it was too late. And, in doing so, they'd start the collapse.

"Tell the general public that you're not allowed to comment," she said, slowly. It was true enough. The Bank of Silence prided itself on not sharing information with anyone. "And tell the bankers that I *won't* be putting any money into the railway."

"As you wish," Markus said. He glanced back out the window. "Do you want to use the tunnel to leave?"

"I think we'd better," Emily said. "I don't want to be noticed."

"That might be too late," Markus said. "But try and stay out of sight as much as possible."

Emily cast a glamour over herself as she followed the secretary down a long staircase and into a servant's corridor. The air hummed with powerful wards, blurring together into a sensation that made her head spin. It was a relief when they stepped into the tunnel, cast a set of light globes and walked under the road. The wards faded as they hurried away from the bank.

"It feels...*surreal*," Frieda said.

Emily glanced back at her. "Pardon?"

Frieda looked...as if she didn't quite believe herself. "I thought I knew threats," she said, softly. "My father approaching me with a belt was a personal threat; a blight on the crops or a harder frost was a threat to the whole village. I've had people threaten me with beatings or hexes or...the walls trying to crush us. That's a threat too."

She glanced up at the low ceiling. "But this threat is...is so strange, so hard to see. There's no foreign army at the gates, no fires threatening to burn down the entire city, just...pieces of paper. It's insubstantial. There's no sense of threat. And yet you're saying it could bring down everything."

"The fires will come," Emily predicted. "Once the truth gets out..."

"It feels like nothing," Frieda said.

Emily understood exactly how she felt. Caleb and his family had grown up with money, even if it had been the rough gold and silver coins of the Nameless World rather than a standardized currency. Frieda had probably never touched money until she'd been sold to Mountaintop, perhaps not even until Emily had given her money in Cockatrice. She'd grown up in a world of barter, where a blacksmith or a cobbler might trade their work for food and families pooled their resources just to stay alive. To her, the growing crisis was so nebulous that it might not even *exist*.

"Look at it this way," she said. "Pretend you have ten crowns in your money pouch."

"I wish," Frieda said.

Emily snorted. "You loan me those ten crowns, after I promise to repay you fifteen," she said. Vesperian had offered her such terms, after all. "But I can't repay you. What do you do?"

Frieda shrugged. "Take it out of your hide?"

"You could," Emily agreed. It was *precisely* what Frieda's family would have done. "But in the meantime, your bills come due. You have to pay ten crowns yourself to *your* creditors. And you can't pay them, because you gave me the money. There's a limit to what you can get out of my hide. Perhaps I don't own my house, or tools... perhaps I don't own anything. Or maybe I abandon ship and run before you can start tearing me to pieces. What do you do then?"

"My creditors try to take it out of *my* hide," Frieda said.

"Precisely," Emily said. "Do you own a house? They'll take the house. Or...or whatever you have. *That's* the threat. It isn't just about large sums of money evaporating into thin air...it's about what happens when that money is never repaid."

They reached the end of the tunnel and made their way through a set of complex wards and into the house. Emily had expected someone to meet them at the far end, but the house looked deserted. They walked to the door and opened it, recoiling in shock at the sudden noise. A small procession was making its way through the streets, chanting a single word over and over again.

"Justice! Justice! Justice!"

Emily fought the urge to cover her ears as the procession marched past the door. It was led by the Hands of Justice, but hundreds of others from all walks of life had joined the chanting parade. A set of grim-faced stewards ran from place to place, pushing and shoving marchers in and out of line; a handful of young girls in flowing white dresses handed out pamphlets to interested onlookers. Emily took one absently and scanned it, noting that the claim that 'Justice' had killed hundreds of sinners. It was long on gruesome detail and short on accurate facts.

This can't be true, she thought. *We'd be seeing statues everywhere if hundreds of people had been killed.*

She folded up the pamphlet and pocketed it, then hurried down the street. It was barely mid-afternoon, but crowds were already forming everywhere. There was an ugly note in the air, something she remembered from Farrakhan. The city was on edge, again. She hoped they could get back to Caleb's house before something happened. It felt as though they were standing on a powder keg.

We are, she thought.

There was another batch of letters waiting for her when they reached Caleb's house. Sienna passed them to her without comment, muttering something about impudent correspondents when she turned away. Emily looked past her, hoping to see Caleb, but there was no sign of him. Karan was the only one in sight, sitting on a sofa darning her socks.

Emily sat on the chair and glanced through the letters. They were all the same, inviting her to dinner with vague promises that it would be made worth her while. Sighing, she started to write out another set of polite, but firm, rejections while Frieda read her book and made notes for her fourth year project. Emily envied her. *She* didn't have to worry about banking problems and financial disasters...

"Dinner time," Sienna called. "Come now if you're coming."

There was no sign of General Pollack, Caleb, or Marian at the table. Conversation was stilted: Sienna seemed occupied with some greater thought, while Karan and Croce kept throwing odd glances at Emily. Emily felt uncomfortable, wishing she could speed up time in order to escape. She'd never known what to say at the dinner table.

A messenger arrived midway through the meal, carrying a note from Markus.

Vesperian refuses to talk, it read. *Now what?*

Chapter Fourteen

"WAKE UP," FRIEDA SAID. "EMILY?"

Emily opened her eyes. "What ... what *time* is it?"

"Time to get up," Frieda prompted, quietly. "You have to get dressed."

Emily nodded as she sat upright and stood. Sienna had taken one look at her when she'd come down for breakfast, deduced that Emily hadn't slept well at all and ordered her back to bed after a light snack. Emily had been too tired and restless to argue, but when she'd returned to her bed she hadn't been able to sleep. She'd been too busy trying to figure out a way to defuse a ticking time bomb. And yet, she must have slept. Her watch insisted that it was after midday.

She stumbled into the bathroom, removed her nightgown and splashed water on her face. It didn't help. The face she saw in the mirror looked pale enough to pass for a vampire, with dark circles around her eyes. She rubbed her eyes in annoyance, then stepped under the shower. She'd been told, in no uncertain terms, that she wasn't to use a glamour or anything else to alter her appearance during the funeral. It was, apparently, tradition.

"Hurry," Frieda called. "We'll be leaving in thirty minutes!"

"I know." Emily stepped out of the shower and looked at herself, critically. The cuts and bruises were fading, thankfully, but she still felt tired. "I'm coming."

Frieda pushed past her into the shower as Emily entered the bedroom. The mourning clothes were already waiting for them, hanging behind the door. Emily pulled on an undershirt, then took the larger of the two black robes from the hook and pulled it over her head. It was shapeless, as shapeless as the robes she wore at Whitehall. Karan and Marian had spent the last two days sewing them for the funeral. It looked simple, yet there were a handful of complex designs stitched into the cloth. They weren't magic, as far as she could tell. She had no idea what they meant.

She tied her hair back, then inspected herself in the mirror. There was no sign that she was wearing *anything* underneath her robe, thankfully. Imaiqah had joked about wearing her robes and nothing else at school, but Emily knew she couldn't do the same. Someone might *just* try to levitate her and flip her over. They'd get in awful trouble, she knew, yet it might not be enough to deter some of the boys. Or even some of the girls.

"You look like a ghost," Frieda said, coming back into the bedroom. "It isn't going to be *that* bad."

"I *feel* like a ghost," Emily muttered. "I'll get better."

Frieda dressed quickly, then tied her hair into a pair of pigtails. "How do I look?"

Emily examined her, critically. "Ready to go," she said, grabbing her shoes. "Shall we?"

She could hear the bell tolling as she walked down the stairs and into the living room. Sienna, Karan and Marian waited for her, all wearing the same black robes. Sienna's face was hidden behind a black veil that made her look sinister, while both of Casper's sisters were bareheaded. They'd left their hair completely untied.

"Very good," Sienna said, after a quick inspection. "Come."

The bell tolled louder as they made their way to the door. It hung above the porch, sounding again and again...Emily resisted the urge to cover her ears as she walked underneath the bell. No one was touching it, she saw. Sienna must have charmed the bell to sound constantly.

Outside, a small crowd had already gathered. They were a diverse collection: guildmasters, priests, sorcerers and even commoners. Most of them wore black, although only a handful wore formal robes. The coffin itself stood at the center of the road, with General Pollack, Caleb and Croce standing behind it. Emily tried to catch Caleb's eye, but he was staring at the coffin. Perhaps he hadn't really grasped that his brother was dead until the funeral had begun.

Sienna stepped forward. Silence fell.

"My son fell in battle," she said. Her voice echoed on the air. "Today, we lay him to rest."

She lifted a hand, pointing at the coffin. Emily felt the spell a moment before the coffin rose into the air, then started to glide down the street. Frieda pulled her into position beside the coffin as they walked beside, Sienna and her husband taking the lead. The streets were lined with people, all present to bid Casper farewell. Emily couldn't help wondering how many of them were there because they'd known Casper, and how many of them had come just to be seen. Whatever he'd been in life, in death Casper had become the city's favorite son.

The crowd was silent as the coffin went past them. Emily couldn't hear anything, even a cough. She reached out with her senses, picking up the edges of a powerful silencing spell. It was an impressive piece of work, blanketing the coffin and surrounding crowds. She wasn't sure she could have cast anything like it herself. Sienna was a *very* skilled magician.

No wonder Casper was so determined to prove himself, she thought. *He wanted to impress both of his parents.*

She glanced at Caleb. His head was bowed. What little she could see of his face was somber. Casper had been his brother, for better or worse. She knew the two boys hadn't been close, but still...they were family. No, they'd *been* family. They wouldn't see each other again. Unless, of course, there really *was* life after death...

The Temple of War rose up in front of them, standing amidst the other temples. It was a massive building, made from white stone and covered in hundreds of statues. There were men – all men – holding weapons, ranging from clubs and swords to crossbows and even muskets. The latter statues looked new, she thought. They would have to be. There hadn't been any guns on the Nameless World until she'd introduced them.

She followed the coffin into the temple, careful to keep an eye on Karan. When the younger girl stepped to the side, Emily walked after her. Frieda moved up beside her, touching Emily's hand lightly, as Caleb walked to the other side. General Pollack and Sienna followed the coffin into the exact center of the building, moving to each side as the coffin drifted down onto a stone altar. Emily glanced around, taking in the decorations. The interior of the temple was covered in carvings, each one showing a single man standing against overwhelming odds. Most showed humans or orcs as the enemy, but one showed a single amorphous creature and another showed no enemy at all. And yet, the Old Script written around the carving suggested there should be *something* there...

Silence fell. A single man, wearing a golden suit of armor, clanked his way to the coffin and turned to face the crowd. He was the priest, she realized. Every square inch of him was covered in armor, save for his dark face. His voice, when he spoke, was so full of gravitas that Emily found herself paying close attention. There was no magic in his words. Merely...*presence.*

"A man who goes to war goes to prove himself," he rumbled. "He may stand firm against the enemies of all...or he may break and run. He may prove himself a man or he may run like a woman. War...proves him."

Emily concealed her amusement. She didn't know anyone who would dare suggest Lady Barb or Sienna hadn't proven themselves in war. Hell, *she'd* been in the war too. But she understood what the priest meant. Sergeant Harkin had said much the same, when she'd been pushed into his class. War was the ultimate expression of masculinity, he'd said. A woman who wanted to succeed had to *act* like a man.

And there are very few female non-magicians who fight in wars, she recalled. Lady Barb had made no bones about that, either. *Even a trained woman can be dangerously outmatched if she meets a skilled opponent.*

"Casper of House Waterfall went to war," the priest continued. "And while he fell, he fell in battle. He fell in honorable combat. He did not run. He did not hide. He stood up to the enemy and died in glorious battle."

Emily shivered, fighting down a flicker of anger. It hadn't been glorious. She'd had half a plan, a plan that had threatened to go off the rails even *before* they'd discovered the necromancer's secret. She knew she'd been scared, when she walked into Heart's Eye. Casper, she was sure, had felt scared too.

Feeling fear isn't the problem, she recalled. *The problem lies in allowing your fear to dominate you.*

"For those who fall in battle, death is not the end," the priest said. "They rise to the heights of war, to serve the gods in their battles with evil. They will feast in the halls of war, then go out to fight and then return, brothers in arms with the gods themselves. We honor their memory just as we look forward to joining them."

Emily kept her face expressionless. The prospect of spending eternity feasting and fighting didn't appeal to her, although she could see why some people might like it. A godly realm might turn war into a game, rather than a life-or-death challenge. The slain might rise again to feast and fight, after they fell in heavenly war. But it didn't strike her as restful. It wasn't what *she* wanted.

And it might be a lie told to encourage the troops, the cynical side of her mind noted, sarcastically. *Why fear death if it is merely the gateway to eternal reward?*

"Casper died, and died well." The priest held up one hand in a rough salute. "And we deem him worthy to pass through the Iron Gates and take his place among the elect."

There was a long pause. Emily risked another look at Caleb. He was watching the coffin with grim eyes. General Pollack was completely expressionless, even as he stepped forward and drew his sword. The blade shone so brightly that she was *sure* it had been charmed.

"From birth, life is a risk," General Pollack said. His face was as immobile as granite. "Parents swiftly come to learn that they cannot shield their child from danger, that they cannot protect them against the world…that even *trying* can do terrifying damage. It is never easy to strike the balance between supporting one's children and letting them make their own mistakes, between being there to help them and allowing them to deal with the consequences of their ignorance. Parenting…is not easy.

"My son chose to follow his father into the military. I was proud of him even as I feared for his life. Casper was my firstborn son, the fruit of my loins. I did not want to lose him. I wanted him to remain safe and well. And yet, I could not stand in his way. A youngster has to make his own mistakes before his parents die, before he stands alone against a hostile world.

"He thought I knew nothing, of course. Such is the folly of youth."

He paused. Emily kept her thoughts to herself. If Casper's father had told him that before he died …

"It is tragic when a father outlives his son," General Pollack said. "I believed there would come a time when Casper carried the torch to my coffin and lit the fire. Instead, I must watch as my son's coffin burns. I mourn for his loss…

"And yet I am proud of my son.

"Like me, when I was young, he wanted to prove himself. Like me, he chose war as his *way* to prove himself. He sought out a challenge, then another challenge… when the time came, he did not flinch. He was no coward. His death did not shame him or any of us."

There was a second pause. This time, it seemed to last forever.

"It is never easy to know how one will react, when one faces the challenge." General Pollack held up his sword and considered it reflectively, then returned the blade to his belt. "It is not something you learn until you actually do it. And then, you find out what you actually are…

"My son could have hurried back to the army. It would have been easy for him to justify a tactical retreat on the grounds that *someone* had to take a warning to the city before it was too late. But he didn't. When the time came, when he was tested, my son proved himself worthy of his heritage. And so I am proud, even as I mourn his loss."

He stepped back, smartly. Emily found herself blinking away tears as Sienna moved forward, her gaze sweeping the hall. General Pollack hadn't been *that* good a father to his oldest son, she knew. Casper had been trapped between his father's expectations and his father's legacy…he'd even been on the verge of suicide before he'd finally had a chance to prove himself. And yet, the general truly mourned his son. Casper had grown up, but there had been no time to mend their relationship.

"We bring our children into the world." Sienna's voice was so composed that Emily *knew* she was in distress. "We birth them, we bathe them, we teach them their lessons and show them how to behave. And we watch, helplessly, as infants grow into children and children grow into adults, pushing gently against us all the time. There always comes a time when the cord must snap, when the newborn adult must stand on his own, when...

"I have seen war. I have seen skirmishes and clashes; I have campaigned against the necromancers and hunted rogue sorcerers until only one of us emerged victorious. When Casper came to me to ask for my blessing, I knew I would sooner go back to war myself than let him go. In my mind, he was still the little boy I'd raised from birth. I did not want him to die.

"But I looked him in the eye," she added. "I told him to make me proud. I told him to live up to the legacy of *both* sides of the family. And I hated myself for saying it, because I *knew* that war kills. I have lost friends and family in battles, some killed outright while others were never the same afterwards. I knew my son could die.

"I let him go.

"I could not have stopped him. How *could* I? He was a grown man, as little as I might care to admit it. He would have resented me if I'd stopped him from going, even – perhaps – hated me. I've seen lives ruined because they couldn't go to war, because they were mocked and belittled until harsh words became a cancer gnawing at their souls. Casper wanted to go, and I could not stop him. I had to let him go.

"I will never see my little boy again," she finished. "But I am proud of the man he became."

Emily had to wipe away her tears as Sienna stepped back. The priest turned to face the coffin, chanting in a language she didn't recognize. General Pollack waited until the priest finished, then drew his sword again and placed it on the coffin. A moment later, he bowed and strode out of the temple. Caleb and Croce followed him, bowing to the coffin before heading for the rear door. The remainder of the men followed them. Sienna waited until the last of the men had bowed before leading the women past the coffin and out into the rear garden.

I'm sorry, Emily thought, as she looked at the coffin. The *empty* coffin. *I wish I could have brought your body home.*

Frieda slipped her hand into Emily's as they walked out into the garden. It was strange; a handful of plants had grown up around dozens of statues. A handful of men in silver uniforms milled around, carrying trays of drinks. Emily took one, and sniffed it carefully. She was no expert, but she thought there was enough alcohol in the earthen bowl to make a strong man drunk. Hopefully, no one would notice – or care – if she didn't drink.

The wake was a strange affair. Some of the mourners were clearly grieving, others were drinking beer as though there were no tomorrow, laughing and dancing as the sun started to fall towards the horizon. She was torn between revulsion and a kind of rueful understanding that the celebration *did* make sense. Casper might be dead, but he'd died well. And he'd gone on to Valhalla.

Or something along the same lines, she thought. *Fighting and feasting for all eternity.*

She watched Caleb as yet another stranger walked up to him to express his condolences – and, perhaps, to open up discussions. Caleb was the heir now, even if he hadn't been formally confirmed. Emily couldn't help thinking that her boyfriend looked stressed, perhaps even on the verge of collapse. His hands shook as they held a glass. She had no idea how much he'd drunk, but it could easily be far too much. Some of the younger men were having a drinking contest...

And then she sensed the presence of...*something.*

She looked up as the crowd scattered, the magically-sensitive reaching for spells or ducking for cover. A man stood on top of the nearest building, a tower that was easily one of the tallest buildings on Temple Row. He was right on the edge, staring down at the crowd. And there was...*something*...billowing around him, a haze that touched her senses and scrambled them. Something was very wrong...

"Vesperian," someone breathed.

And then the man jumped.

Chapter Fifteen

S OMEONE SCREAMED.

Emily barely heard it as she tried, desperately, to muster a levitation spell. It should be simplicity itself to catch Vesperian before he hit the ground and smashed himself into a pancake. She wasn't the only sorcerer trying, either; magic boiled around the crowd, reaching towards the falling man...

...And breaking up, fading into nothingness.

She blinked in astonishment. It felt almost as though someone had wrapped a basic protective ward around Vesperian. But it was wrong ... She tried again, tightening her spell. There were so many spells trying to catch Vesperian that one of them, at least, should have worked. No protective ward should have been able to break up so many spells.

And yet, Vesperian kept falling. He hit the ground with a terrible thud.

"Justice," someone breathed.

Emily looked up. But the rooftop was empty.

She heard the sounds of panic behind her and turned, yanking Frieda towards Caleb and his family as the crowd started to go wild. The priest shouted for order, but his words fell on deaf ears. Emily heard someone screaming that Vesperian owed him money, before the words were lost behind an incoherent sound. Outside, she heard chanting. The Hands of Justice were on the way.

Sienna cast an amplification spell. "REMAIN CALM," she ordered. Her words had little effect. Several of the younger men were already fighting each other, although Emily had no idea why. Others tried to climb over the walls or flee back into the temple, as if they thought it would be safe. "REMAIN CALM!"

General Pollack shot Emily a relieved look as she reached them. "This isn't good," he said, stiffly. "We have to get back home."

Emily nodded. A team of city guardsmen had already arrived, pushing their way into the garden, but they looked edgy. There were sorcerers in the panicking crowd, sorcerers who might blast the guardsmen at any moment. Their commander hurried his men to the body of Vesperian and surrounded it, although Emily didn't have the slightest idea what he thought he was doing. Somehow, keeping the crime scene free of containments seemed pointless.

"It's him," the commander called. "Vesperian is dead!"

"Idiot," Sienna swore.

The sound of chanting grew louder, seemingly coming from all directions. Emily glanced around, trying to determine the safest way out of the temple. She reached for her magic, preparing to teleport them home, but stopped herself abruptly. If... *something*...had kept a crowd of magic-users from saving a falling man, what would it do if she tried to teleport?

"Justice." Marian sounded dazed. "I saw Justice!"

"Be quiet," Sienna snapped.

"We have to move," General Pollack said. His voice boomed over the crowd. "I'll take the lead; Caleb, you and Croce bring up the rear. Don't hesitate to use magic to clear the way if necessary."

Emily swallowed, hard, as they hurried towards the gate. Men and women swarmed the streets, fleeing in all directions. Groups of worshippers fought, pouring out of their temples and into the fray. The Hands of Justice seemed to be stalled, but they fought with a discipline that surprised her. She hadn't seen so much discipline from the footsoldiers she'd watched during the war. The remainder of the City Guard was nowhere to be seen.

"They'll be setting up wards along Sorcerers Row," Sienna called back. "Let me go first when we reach the entrance."

"Of course, dear." General Pollack sounded pained. "But we have to get out of here first!"

Emily felt her body shake as they made their way down the street. The sheer emotion unleashed by the riot was staggering, a wave of rage and hatred that threatened to suck her into the mob. She readied a spell in one hand and clutched Frieda with the other, trying to escape a very primal terror. Cold logic told her she had enough magic to protect herself, but it wasn't enough to make her feel safe. The crowd would rip her to pieces if it could lay hands on her.

"Stand aside," Sienna snapped.

Emily looked up. A dozen men charged towards their small group, faces twisted with fury. They all wore dark green tunics and caps, marking them out as devotees of the Horned God. Now...she braced herself, just as Sienna threw an overpowered force punch at the leader. A blast of magic picked him and his comrades up, tossing them through the air and slamming their helpless bodies into a nearby temple. They fell to the ground and lay still. It was easy, even at a distance, to tell that some of them were badly wounded, perhaps even dead.

"Keep moving." Sienna glanced back at Emily. "We have to get home fast!"

Emily swallowed, but did as she was told. Sienna was right. Emily just didn't like it. She braced herself as another group of Hands of Justice came around the corner, readying a spell, but the fanatics ignored them. They were more intent on slamming into the rioting worshippers and teaching them a lesson. The clubs they carried were less dangerous, she supposed, than swords, yet she knew hundreds of people were going to be hurt – or killed.

She shivered as the chant grew louder. "Justice...Justice...Justice..."

The streets grew quieter as they hurried away from the temple. Dozens of guardsmen had materialized at one street corner, setting up barricades and turning away anyone who wanted to head to the temples. They looked terrified, a couple even sidling away as soon as they had the chance. Emily didn't blame them. There were enough rioters in the area to smash through their lines, if they decided to rampage through the rest of the city. She wasn't sure there were *enough* trained guardsmen to put an end to the riot.

They'll have to use magic, she thought. A pair of black-clad sorcerers, wearing blue armbands, hurried up to join the guard. *And who knows what that will do?*

"General," a guardsman called. "Is it true?"

General Pollack slowed. "Is *what* true?"

"Is he dead?" the guard asked. Others looked up, hoping to hear the answer. "Is Vesperian dead?"

Say no, Emily urged, silently. Rumors were already spreading...but, if they were lucky, perhaps they could keep them from spreading too far. People wouldn't *want* to believe that Vesperian was dead. *Don't pour fuel on the fire.*

"Yes," General Pollack said. "I saw him die."

Emily cursed, inwardly, as they picked up speed again. Telling the guardsmen the truth had been a mistake. Even with the best will in the world – and that was lacking – Vesperian's death would cause economic shockwaves. Now...who knew how many people would run out of money while the council tried to figure out what to do? Or how many others would seek redress through violence?

A cold shiver ran down her spine. Beneficence was battening down the hatches, shopkeepers slamming their doors and sealing the windows while stallkeepers hurried away in all directions. A number of young men massed outside some of the shops, carrying all sorts of makeshift weapons. Emily couldn't tell if they intended to do some looting or prevent it. Perhaps they didn't know either. Their gazes flickered over the small group, then looked away. No doubt they'd recognized General Pollack or his wife.

The noise dimmed, slightly, as they turned into Sorcerers Row. A handful of sorcerers were hastily raising wards, casting charms over anyone who stepped through them. Sienna spoke briefly to the leader, who nodded shortly and motioned for the group to enter the street. Emily was surprised to note that the various magic-users seemed to be working together surprisingly well. Normally, getting powerful sorcerers to cooperate was a little like herding cats.

The prospect of a mass riot might just have concentrated a few minds, she thought. There were so many wards and defensive charms flickering through the air that she suspected some of them were interfering with the others. It was not going to be a peaceful night. *And they might have decided to put old grudges aside to defend their homes.*

She turned, peering back towards Temple Row. A cloud of smoke rose into the air. Beneficence had a working fire service, but she doubted the firemen could get to the fire while the mob raged. The flames might not be a major problem on Temple Row – the temples were all built of stone – yet if the fire spread further, it would turn into a disaster. Most of the homes in Fishing Plaice were built of wood. The poorest and most helpless citizens would find themselves without a roof over their heads.

"Get inside," Sienna snapped. Emily could feel the wards, cracking through the air. "Now!"

She hurried into the house. Sienna slammed the door. A moment later, the wards crashed down too. Emily tested them, briefly. They were simple but tough, linked directly to Sienna's mind. Breaking them would be a complex task, one almost certainly beyond her. No one could enter or leave the house without Sienna's permission.

"The coffin," Karan said. "We left it behind!"

"They won't touch it," Sienna said, shortly. "I saw to that."

You charmed an empty coffin. She wondered just what Sienna thought was *inside* the coffin. And yet, it wasn't a question she dared ask. *You went to a lot of effort...why?*

A pale-faced girl appeared in the doorway. Emily started, then caught herself. The newcomer must be the maid. She looked to be around the same age as Karan, but she was so thin and pale that Emily couldn't help wondering what she ate. Her dark hair framed a pale face that was vaguely Oriental in shape.

"Mistress," she said. "What happened?"

"A riot," Sienna said, shortly. "Fetch drinks for us, now."

The maid curtseyed, then retreated. Emily shivered, helplessly, as she followed the others into the living room. She would never grow used to servants, never. There was something creepy about having someone to serve her, someone who *had* to do as they were told. Void had urged her to hire a maid, to have someone tend to her house during her absences, but she would be damned if she was enslaving anyone.

Sure, her own thoughts mocked her. *And how would you know your secrets were safe if you didn't?*

"I was going to meet a couple of friends," Croce said. "I..."

"You will be staying here," General Pollack said, firmly. "Riots are dangerous, even for young sorcerers."

Croce looked as if he were about to argue, but said nothing. Emily studied him for a long moment, then turned her head. Caleb sat on the sofa, looking tired. His hands shook slightly, a legacy of a nasty alchemical accident. Emily didn't blame him. He had drunk too much even before all hell had broken loose.

The maid returned, carrying a tray of mugs. Emily took the offered drink, then tried to shoot the young girl a smile. The maid looked shocked, just for a moment; she handed out the rest of the mugs and departed as fast as possible. Emily felt a stab of sympathy as she sipped her Kava. Working for Sienna had to be a difficult task.

"I saw Justice." Marian looked up, defiantly. "He was on top of the tower."

"I very much doubt it," Sienna said, sharply. "Be silent."

"I *saw* him," Marian insisted. "Mother, Vesperian jumped to avoid being petrified!"

Sienna gave her youngest daughter a quelling look. "You will be quiet!"

Emily thought, fast. *Something* had been up there, but what? She'd definitely sensed *something.* And every spell she'd cast to stop Vesperian's fall had failed, the magic breaking up and fading out of existence. She'd seen protective wards that worked like that – they were among the first she'd learned to cast – but she'd never seen one that had deflected so many spells. Whoever had cast the ward, if it *was* a ward, had been a powerful magician.

Or they could have configured the spell to feed off the unleashed magic, she mused. *It wouldn't last indefinitely, but it might hold out longer...*

She tossed the equations 'round and 'round in her head. The *real* downside was that the ward wouldn't discriminate. It would happily absorb both incoming and outgoing spells. But if someone didn't *have* magic – and she hadn't seen proof that *Vesperian* had magic – it wouldn't matter. They wouldn't be doing anything the ward might block.

Marian came to her feet. "I *saw* him!"

"No, you didn't," Sienna said. "You don't know *what* was up there. Nor do I!"

"Justice," Marian insisted. "Mother, I..."

Sienna rose. "Go to your room," she ordered, in a tone that suggested further arguing was pointless. "I will be up shortly."

Marian glared at her, then rose and stamped through the door. Emily could hear her crashing her way up the stairs and slamming her bedroom door. She felt a moment of pity for the younger girl, mingled with contempt. Sienna was right. There was no real *proof* that a god was walking the streets. Whoever had killed the original set of victims might finally have caught up with Vesperian himself.

"Emily," Karan said, into the chilly silence. "What will happen now he's dead?"

Emily shook her head. She'd had a quick look through the law books, but Beneficence didn't have *anything* resembling a modern regulatory framework. A person could go bankrupt, a *family* could go bankrupt...there hadn't been any large corporations until the New Learning, certainly nothing as large as Vesperian's business. The largest institutions she knew had been trading firms, and few of them had operated more than a handful of ships.

"I don't know," she said. "This has never happened before."

"Not here," Caleb said.

Emily nodded, shortly. "I suppose it depends on what happens to the estate." The notes had been due tomorrow, if she recalled correctly. Vesperian's estate probably wouldn't be paying out on them, not immediately. There would be hundreds, perhaps thousands, of people watching their life savings evaporate. "It will take weeks to figure out just how much he owes."

Sienna peered at her, narrowly. "You've seen it happen before?"

"Only in theory," Emily said. It wasn't entirely true – she'd been on Earth when the dot-com bubble burst – yet she hadn't really taken notice. The crash hadn't made her life any better or worse. "We discussed the possibility in Zangaria."

Sienna didn't look convinced. Emily winced, inwardly. She didn't want to tell Sienna the truth, not yet. Perhaps not ever. Who knew *what* Sienna would do if she learned alternate worlds and dimensions existed? And yet, Caleb's mother had probably figured out there was *something* odd about her prospective daughter-in-law. She would certainly want answers, sooner or later.

Karan coughed. "And what did you conclude?"

"That we should be careful," Emily said. "I don't know *what* we can do."

"The council may push for a moratorium on payouts," General Pollack said. "If Vesperian had no reason to expect his death, he might not have updated his will."

"He certainly *should* have," Sienna said. "Death can come at any time."

She rose. "Emily, Frieda, I suggest you have a rest," she said, as she headed for the door. "I don't think anyone will be foolish enough to try to break through the wards, but you never know. Don't try to leave the house."

"We won't," Emily said.

"I'll be in my office," General Pollack said. "Don't hesitate to call if you need anything."

Caleb followed Emily and Frieda up the stairs, then jabbed a meaningful finger at their bedroom door. Frieda hesitated, glancing towards Marian's door before opening her door and hurrying though. Caleb reached out and hugged Emily the moment the door was half-closed, holding her tightly. His hands were still shaking.

"I'm sorry I wasn't with you during the ceremony," he said. "I…"

He shook his head. Emily wondered, again, just how much he'd had to drink. She'd seen Caleb angry, but not maudlin. And yet…Casper had been maudlin when *he'd* been drinking alone. She hadn't liked seeing that either.

"It wasn't your fault," she said. Caleb hadn't designed the ceremony. The rules had been laid down hundreds of years ago. Men and women were separated as soon as they entered the temple. Hell, she'd had the impression that women were rarely allowed to visit. "I'm sorry the service was ruined."

"Casper is probably looking down on us now and laughing," Caleb said. "His funeral turned into a riot…he'd find that amusing."

He shook his head. "I hope he's happy, wherever he is."

"Me too," Emily said.

"And everyone asked me when I was going to get married," Caleb added. "They all seemed to want to know."

"That's because you are now the Heir," Sienna said. Emily jumped. Sienna stood in Marian's doorway, holding a wooden hairbrush in one hand. "I believe I explained that earlier."

Caleb took a step backwards. "Why do they care?"

"Because they have to know what's going to happen in the next few years." She cocked her head, thoughtfully. "If there's a city left, that is."

"There will be," Caleb said.

"Perhaps," Sienna agreed. "We shall see."

Her voice hardened. "Go to bed," she ordered. "And make sure you take a sober-up potion before you close your eyes."

"Yes, Mother," Caleb said.

"And remember what *else* I told you," Sienna added. "*Not* under my roof."

Emily flushed. They hadn't been doing anything, apart from hugging. But she knew Sienna was in a dark mood. The funeral had been ruined. Casper might be laughing, as Caleb had suggested, but his parents had to be furious. They might need to hold the ceremony again.

"Sleep," Sienna ordered. "And behave."

Emily stepped into her room and closed the door.

Chapter Sixteen

"THAT WAS CARELESS," FRIEDA SAID, AS EMILY SHUT THE DOOR. HER TONE WAS LIGHT, BUT her eyes were serious. "You could have been in *real* trouble."

Emily shrugged, locking the door and pulling off her robe. She'd faced necromancers and a whole host of other monsters. Sienna was intimidating, but not that scary. Her nightgown was where she'd left it; she pulled it over her undershirt, then lay down on the bed. The wards were a reassuring presence at the back of her mind, but she knew sleep wouldn't come easy. It felt like hours before she fell into darkness...

"It's breakfast," Frieda said. "Did you sleep well?"

"You're joking," Emily said, in shock.

She glanced at her watch. Frieda *wasn't* joking. She'd slept for over ten hours. Odd, when she'd barely drawn on her magic. Maybe she'd accidentally charmed herself to sleep. She hoped not. There were stories about young magicians who'd done just that and wound up trapped in their own minds. None of them ended well. She pulled herself out of bed, splashed some water on her face and pulled on another blue dress. Trousers would be better if she had to run, but she had none. Maybe she could borrow a pair from Karan.

"I hope you slept," she said, as they opened the door. "Did you?"

"For a while," Frieda said. "And then I studied instead."

They walked down the stairs. It was dark outside, the sun barely glimmering below the horizon. There was no sign of Caleb, Croce, or Marian at the breakfast table; General Pollack, Sienna, and Karan sat there, eating lumpy bowls of porridge. It dawned on Emily, as Sienna pointed to a chair, that starvation was a real possibility. If they couldn't get out of the house...

"The riots seem to have simmered down," General Pollack said, by way of greeting. Emily would have been more impressed if he wasn't still wearing his sword. "There was no trouble up here."

"They went looking for easier targets," Sienna said, as Karan served Emily and Frieda. "I don't think many rioters would be stupid enough to challenge the wards."

Emily hoped Sienna was right, but she doubted it. Rioters weren't even as clever as the stupidest person in the mob. It was easy to imagine crowds pushing against the wards, forced into contact by their fellows. Pain wouldn't stop them when the pushers weren't the ones being hurt. But then, the sorcerers should be able to make their wards strong enough to keep the crowds out without seriously hurting anyone.

She chewed her porridge carefully. It was strikingly bland, without sugar, milk or anything else that might make it more edible. She told herself, firmly, that she should be glad to have it. There were people on the streets who might be starving by now. God alone knew what had happened outside the wards.

Karan took the bowl as soon as Emily had finished and carried it back into the kitchen. Emily suspected Karan was looking for something to do, to keep herself occupied.

Sienna cocked her head. "We've got visitors," she said. "Come into the living room."

Emily tensed as she rose. *Hostile* visitors? But Sienna didn't look alarmed...

She watched as Sienna parted the wards and opened the front door. Two men stood there: one wearing a long red robe, the other a blue uniform with a silver star on the collar. A guardsman, she guessed. The robed man looked to have had too much comfortable living – he was strikingly pudgy, with a long white beard that fell to his chest – but his companion reminded her of General Pollack. His scars told her that the guardsman had been through too much to let himself run to fat.

"Guildmaster Jalil," Sienna said. "And Captain Haverford."

"It is always a pleasure, Mediator," Jalil said. His voice was so perfectly aristocratic that he would have fit in at King Randor's court. "And Lady Emily, I believe. It is a pleasure to meet you at last."

"Guildmaster Jalil is the current Grand Guildmaster," Sienna said, as she led the two men into the living room. Emily frowned. She was fairly sure that Jalil had been one of the people who'd sent her letters. "Captain Haverford is the current head of the City Guard."

"That I am." Haverford had a curt way of speaking that reminded her of Sergeant Harkin. Emily was fairly sure that Haverford was not a man to play politics. "And time is not on our side."

Sienna nodded. "Your bodyguards will get impatient," she agreed. "You have a small army waiting outside."

"The streets are not safe," Haverford said. "The Guard is overwhelmed."

Jalil cleared his throat, looking directly at Sienna. "As the Grand Guildmaster. I am formally requesting your assistance with the investigation."

Sienna lifted her eyebrows. "Mine?"

"Your word is good, Mediator," Jalil said. "We need to know what happened to Vesperian, now. Did he commit suicide? Did he fall off the building by accident? Or was he pushed?"

There was something up there, Emily thought. *But what?*

"An understandable request," Sienna said. "I will require the usual compensatory package, as well as a warrant from the Council to question witnesses and go wherever I deem necessary."

Jalil reached into his robes and produced a piece of old-style parchment. "I took the liberty of convincing the Council to sign," he said, holding it out to Sienna. "They are desperate for answers."

"Then I will be off presently," Sienna said. She glanced at Emily. "I will be taking Lady Emily with me, of course."

Emily stared at her. "Me?"

Jalil...showed no visible reaction at all. "If you are willing to assume responsibility for her, then I dare say we can offer no objection. But please be careful."

"Of course," Sienna said.

"And we would also like the services of your husband," Haverford added. "The City Guard is being reinforced."

"It will be my pleasure to serve," General Pollack said.

"Then we will take our leave." Jalil rose, ponderously, and bowed. "I look forward to your report."

Emily stared after them until they'd left the house. "You're taking *me* along?"

"Everyone knows you have an odd sense for magic," Sienna said. "And besides, I don't want to leave you and Caleb alone."

She ignored Emily's flush. "Get your cloak. We'll be leaving in ten minutes."

Emily swallowed the angry response that came to mind. She wasn't Sienna's daughter-in-law, not yet. Sienna couldn't order her around as if she were a servant. And yet...she *was* curious. Jalil was right. They did need to know what had happened to Vesperian as soon as possible. She hurried back to the kitchen, told Frieda what had happened, and went to grab her coat. It would be chilly outside.

The streets were surprisingly clear, even after they passed through the wards, but there were signs of damage all around. She saw watching eyes peering from upper windows as they walked down the street, past damaged storefronts and a handful of dead bodies lying in the gutter. Small squads of city guardsmen marched from place to place, carrying their clubs as if they expected an attack at any moment. Perhaps they were right, Emily thought. She was sure one of the bodies had been wearing a guardsman's uniform.

Temple Row was a mess, she saw, as they turned the corner. Hundreds of statues had been damaged or destroyed, while several temples had been desecrated. Priests and their devotees tried to clean up the mess, watched by patrolling guardsmen. A small pile of bodies, some hacked to pieces, had been dumped at the edge of the street. She hoped someone removed the bodies before they started to decay. Beneficence had enough problems without a disease outbreak.

The Temple of War was a shadow of its former self. The stone walls still stood, but the interior had been thoroughly devastated. Sienna let out a grunt of pain as they approached the coffin, then a sigh of relief as she checked the wards. The coffin remained intact, thankfully. Emily wanted to say something – anything – as Sienna paused, but nothing came to mind. Eventually, Caleb's mother led her out into the back garden. Vesperian's body still lay on the ground.

"It's definitely him." Sienna paced around the body, muttering to herself. "His fall must have been slowed, a little. The face is remarkably intact for someone who fell ten stories and landed hard."

Emily glanced at Sienna with respect. *She* hadn't thought of that.

Sienna looked up. "He fell from the Temple of Stone," she added, thoughtfully. "How did he even get to the roof?"

The temple was deserted, they discovered. Sienna pulled a wand from her belt and waved it around, then stepped back in puzzlement. The wards that should have been in place, keeping out supernatural vermin and unbelievers, were gone. Instead, there was a faint sense of...*absence* that chilled Emily to the bone.

She looked at Sienna. "Was Vesperian a...I mean...did he go to this temple?"

"If he had any religious beliefs, I don't know about them." Sienna sounded as though she was worried by some other thought. "There should be someone here at all times, Emily. I don't like the look of this."

Emily frowned. "They could be hiding at home?"

"A priest would normally be here, whatever happened," Sienna said. "And there are no wards to bar our way."

She led the way further into the temple. Emily glanced around, taking in the rough stone statues and the layers of rock embedded within the walls. She knew nothing about the temple's precepts, but she had to admit its priests had crafted a remarkable building. Water flowed down the side of the stairs as they walked up, pooling in a silver pond at the exact center of the temple. Sienna didn't seem to find it out of the ordinary. Emily decided it must be part of the design.

A cold breeze blew across the roof when they reached the top and stepped into the open air. Emily shivered, looking north. A dozen ships were making their way through the Gap and heading out onto the open sea, so desperate to leave that their skippers ran the risk of a collision. She had no idea what would happen if two sailing boats collided, given the currents flowing around the jagged rocks, but she doubted it would be pleasant. And yet, staying in the city might not be pleasant either…

Sienna held up a hand to keep Emily from walking further onto the roof. "No footprints. That dust has been here for years."

Emily wasn't so sure. The breeze wasn't *that* strong, but it should have kept a layer of dust from forming. And the rain would have washed the dust away…a thought struck her and she looked around, already knowing what she would find. A handful of runes had been carved into the stone, directing the wind and rain away from the temple. The breeze…

"There shouldn't be a breeze," she said. "But there is…"

Sienna followed her gaze. "Well spotted," she said. She shot Emily a brilliant smile. "The magic has failed."

She knelt beside the nearest rune. "It's dead," she said, running her fingers over the carving. "Not weakened…it's dead. No charge of magic at all."

Emily shook her head in disbelief. Subtle magic runes drew *mana* from the environment, slowly building up their power. It was what made them so dangerous. The magic was so hard to detect – it might as well be part of the background noise – that the effects were rarely questioned until it was far too late. And yet, Sienna was right. The runes had no magic charge at all.

"They're intact," she said. "Right?"

"Right," Sienna agreed, grimly. "What does *that* mean?"

Someone hit the reset button, Emily thought. *Could a magician have drained the charge…?*

She reached out with her senses, carefully. She'd always been more sensitive to background magic than many of her friends, if only because it wasn't as natural as breathing to her. If there was any magic on Earth, it was well hidden. She'd certainly never believed magic existed until she'd first set foot on the Nameless World. And yet...

"I can't feel magic," she said. "It wasn't just the runes. The entire area has been drained."

"Impossible." Sienna held out a hand, palm upwards. A spark of light danced over her fingertips, then faded. "I've never seen anything like this."

Emily frowned, taking a step forward. It felt as if something was subtly wrong, as if...she tried to put it into words, but failed. It wasn't the presence of something... more like a shift in the world itself. And yet...

The forest near Whitehall – *past* Whitehall – had been glowing with magic. It had affected her, she recalled, the surges of raw magic toying with her emotions. She couldn't help a pang of guilt as she remembered kissing Robin...she ruthlessly pushed the thought out of her mind. She hadn't been in her right mind. *Present* Whitehall's forest wasn't anything like as infused with magic. Tapping the nexus point had clearly allowed the background *mana* to fall to a more normal level.

But here...here, something had drained the magic completely.

She looked up at Sienna. "Can someone drain a rune of power?"

"I don't think so," Sienna said. "They certainly wouldn't get very *much* power."

Emily nodded. It wasn't power that made undiscovered runes dangerous. She had no idea how long the runes had protected the temple, but they couldn't have gathered enough *mana* to make absorbing the energy worth someone's while...

"No footprints," Sienna said. "Vesperian could have levitated himself to the edge and fallen..."

"Maybe whatever kept our spells from saving him also drained his magic," Emily said. "If he *had* magic."

"He didn't," Sienna said. "But he could have easily afforded something that would have let him fly."

"Unless it failed," Emily said. "There was *something* up here, wasn't there?"

She scowled. She'd been disappointed, at first, when she'd discovered that witches and wizards didn't fly on broomsticks. It wasn't as if making flying brooms was difficult. And then she'd found out how easy it would be to knock someone off a broomstick. Even basic levitation could be dangerous if someone wanted the flyer dead.

"I sensed something," Sienna agreed. "But it was probably someone concealing their presence."

Emily shrugged. "Was Marian the only person who thought she saw Justice?"

Sienna rounded on her. "Gods do not walk the streets, Emily. And people who say otherwise are lying."

She jabbed a finger towards a building at the bottom of Temple Row. "That temple was founded by a fisherman who claimed to have seen a god at the bottom of the ocean. Right now, countless fishermen go there to pray and leave tributes every day before setting sail. And you know what? Some of those fishermen have never come home!"

Emily held herself steady. "You think it's a con?"

"I don't know what he saw," Sienna said. "Or even if he saw anything. But you'd think that a god of the oceans could protect his worshippers, wouldn't you?"

She sighed as she headed for the steps. "I've handled cases where rogue sorcerers have summoned creatures out of the Darkness. Maybe those creatures could be mistaken for gods, if they weren't so malevolent! Those cultists who worship them rarely live to regret it. And the higher gods, the greater gods…

"People are wasting their lives worshipping creatures who can't or won't intervene in human affairs," she added. "The time spent praying could be better used elsewhere. The food donated to the temple could be given directly to the poor. If the gods were good, they'd help anyway; if not, they wouldn't. And all the stories make the gods out to be spoilt brats in need of a good thrashing. They may be more powerful than us, but that doesn't make them *good*."

Emily said nothing. She'd read enough about the Greek and Roman gods to know that Sienna had a point. The gods had been assholes, demanding worship on one hand and cursing random people on the other. And yet, if religion caused no harm, why bother to worry about it?

Her thoughts answered her. *Because no religion is as good as its god. It is only as good as its followers. And some of those followers are worse than their gods.*

They reached the bottom of the stairs. "Something clearly happened up there," Sienna said, "but what?"

"I don't know," Emily said. A Manavore *might* be able to drain the local magic field, but she hadn't seen one of them in the present day, not even in the history books. They'd been forgotten hundreds of years ago. "What do we tell the guildmaster?"

"Nothing, yet," Sienna said. "I think we'd better go visit an old friend of mine – and her daughter. She might be able to tell us what she saw, the night her boyfriend died."

Emily nodded. "And then what?"

Sienna looked, just for a second, much older. "I wish I knew," she said. "Right now, we can't even swear to it being murder…or suicide."

"And *if* he committed suicide," Emily finished. It didn't seem likely – there *had* been something on top of the temple – but it was possible. "Everyone is going to want to know *why* he committed suicide."

And they'll demand their money back, her thoughts added. *What happens then?*

Chapter Seventeen

THERE WERE MORE GUARDS — AND HANDS OF JUSTICE — ON THE STREETS AS THEY LEFT Temple Row and headed towards the docks. The homes were darker here, bolted and locked...sometimes even guarded by hired toughs. Men gathered outside bars, chatting to one another in hushed voices, their eyes flickering from side to side as if afraid of being overheard. There were few women on the streets at all. Emily resisted the urge to walk closer to Sienna as she felt sharp-edged protective spells drifting through the air. None felt friendly.

"Be on your best behavior," Sienna warned, as they stopped outside a small house. "Sarnia is not one to tolerate incivility."

Emily glanced at her, then nodded. The house — Sarnia's house — was surrounded by hundreds of protective spells, meshed together into a network that would be difficult to break without setting off all kinds of alarms. Emily could feel them probing at her, warning her to keep back. There were so many redundancies built into the spellwork that she had no doubt Sarnia was a powerful and experienced sorceress. And then the wards fell back, allowing them to enter.

"This way," Sienna said.

She led the way to the door, which opened smoothly. A tall woman stood just inside the porch, her eyes studying Emily with undisguised interest. Emily looked back, evenly. The woman — Sarnia, she assumed — could have passed for an aristocrat. Her stern face, cold eyes and greying hair suggested it wouldn't be easy to change her mind about anything. Her black robes made it clear she was a sorceress.

"Sienna," she said. Her voice was cool and composed. "I welcome you to my house."

"Thank you," Sienna said. "Sarnia, may I present Lady Emily?"

Sarnia looked unimpressed. "You are welcome, Lady Emily."

"Thank you," Emily said. "I pledge to hold my hand in your house."

"Very good." Sarnia's voice was still composed. "You may enter."

Emily followed the two older women, looking around with interest. There was no household god, no sign of any religion...merely hundreds of runes, carved into the walls. Sarnia had linked them into the wards, she noted. It would make it harder to starve the wards of power instead of breaking them down one by one. Sarnia led them into a small living room, so picture-perfect that Emily couldn't help wondering how long Sarnia — or her servants — spent cleaning and dusting it every day. *Everything* had its place.

"I assume this is not a social call," Sarnia said, as she motioned for them to sit down. "Shall we get right to the point?"

"We're investigating Vesperian's death," Sienna said, briskly. She sounded pleased. Emily wondered if she'd been dreading a few minutes of pointless chatter before getting to the point. "We need to talk to Alba."

"Alba is not in a good state at the moment." Sarnia's face didn't change, but Emily thought she saw pain in the older woman's eyes. "Do you *have* to talk to her?"

"I'm afraid so," Sienna said. "She *was* a witness to one of the petrifications."

Sarnia looked displeased. "I shall summon her," she said. She cocked her head, interacting with the house's wards. "Do you want my insights while you wait?"

"Of course," Sienna said.

"Alba snuck out of the house, two weeks ago." She smiled an odd little smile. "My daughter believes I didn't know she was sneaking out."

"Just like you did at her age," Sienna said.

"Indeed," Sarnia agreed. "She had the usual collection of protective spells – and her wand, of course – so I believed she could go in reasonable safety. And the next thing I know, a guardsman is knocking desperately on my door, babbling something about my daughter being frightened out of her wits. I checked the tracking spell, and it was gone."

Emily leaned forward, shocked. "You had a tracking spell on your daughter?"

"Yes," Sarnia said, flatly.

There was a long pause. "The spell was configured to alert me if anyone tried to remove it," she added, slowly. "Even *I* couldn't have unravelled it without setting off the alarms. But it was gone, completely. There was no way to find her."

Sienna nodded. "And then?"

"I checked the other spells, as soon as I reached the scene," Sarnia said. "They were all gone, all of them. Worse, her wand had been purged of spellwork and her reserves were completely drained. She hasn't been able to cast even the simplest spells for the last two weeks."

"Gods," Sienna breathed. "She lost her magic?"

"It is regenerating, but very slowly," Sarnia said. "I haven't seen anyone so drained since the Trellis Ritual."

"Which killed a number of older sorcerers," Sienna finished.

Emily winced. She'd been in rituals herself. Even the simplest rituals were draining. "What *were* the other spells?"

"One to summon her home, if necessary," Sarnia said. "One to alert her if something happened to either of her parents. And one to make sure that no one could take her maidenhead. The results would be unpleasant for anyone who tried."

Emily blinked. "You put spells on your daughter?"

Sarnia studied her for a long, cold moment. "When you have children, Lady Emily, you'll understand. Until then, I have a duty to protect *my* children."

The door rattled open before Emily could think of a response. A young girl stepped into the room, her face pale and wan. Her hands were clasped together to keep them from shaking, while her eyes flickered from side to side as if she expected a brutal attack at any moment. Emily would have wondered if Sarnia had been abusing her daughter, if Alba hadn't gone immediately to her mother and sat down next to her. She looked like a toddler cuddling up to its mother.

"Alba," Sarnia said. "Auntie Sienna and Lady Emily need to talk to you."

Alba still shook. Her mother wrapped an arm around her, holding her gently. Alba wasn't much smaller than her mother, but her fear made her smaller, almost elfin. Emily felt a stab of pity, mingled with concern. Magical families seemed to believe, firmly, in tough love. And yet, Sarnia was obviously willing to indulge her shaken daughter. It boded ill. Alba was in a very bad state.

"He d-died," Alba stuttered. "He died in f-front of me."

Sienna leaned forward. "Tell us what happened," she said. "Please."

Alba swallowed, hard. "I snuck out of the house. I...I was due to meet Antony. We were going to go to Vesperian's ball, at his mansion..."

Her voice trailed away for a long moment. Emily felt another stab of pity. She'd seen shocked people before, but Alba looked to have been pushed well past her breaking point. Sarnia was right. Her daughter had been scared out of her wits.

"We had a good time, dancing." Alba didn't look at her mother. "We danced. That was all we did. We danced. Everyone was there...we left, a few hours later, and started to walk home. And then *he* was there."

"Describe him," Sienna ordered.

Alba's shaking grew worse. "I can't. He was...he was *there*."

She stared down at her lap. "I...I...I...I...couldn't do anything. I...he just over-whelmed me. His *presence*...I couldn't help myself. I dropped the wand...I could only watch."

"It's all right," Sarnia breathed. "You're safe now."

"No one is safe," Alba burst out. "A *god* is walking the streets!"

She thrashed around, as if she were being held tightly and trying to break free. But she wasn't. She seemed torn between clinging to her mother and running for her life. Her entire body shook helplessly...

"There was pain," she whispered. "There was light, powerful light. And then...he was stone. Antony was stone. He'd been turned to stone and..."

"Her screams brought the Guard." Sarnia held her daughter tightly, sweeping her into a hug. "They called for both sets of parents."

"I can still *see* him," Alba said. "He's behind my eyes every time I try to sleep. I can't forget him. Antony is dead and...and...he's dead..."

"It's going to be all right," Sarnia promised.

No, it won't, Emily thought. *There's no one here who can help her.*

Sienna looked pained. "Did you run any tests on the statue?"

"All my spells insisted that it was stone, had always been stone, would always be stone," Sarnia said. "There was no magic there at all. And yet, it was very definitely Antony. He always looked very much like his father."

She didn't look up. "I didn't approve of Antony," she added, "but he didn't deserve to die like that. His face...he died in agony."

"I see," Sienna said.

Emily frowned, inwardly. Sarnia was willing to put spells on her daughter to pro-tect her, yet unwilling to forbid Alba from seeing Antony? *That* didn't quite add up. Unless, of course, Sarnia was prepared to allow her daughter to make some mistakes under controlled conditions. And yet...Emily couldn't help shivering at the thought of someone laying spells on her without her consent. The spells might be designed to do far more than protect their subject.

Sienna shook her head. "Did you check the surrounding area?"

"No," Sarnia said. "The Guard summoned two of their sorcerers to do the work. They found nothing, from what I heard."

"No traces of magic," Sienna mused.

"Nothing," Sarnia agreed. In her arms, Alba began to cry. "If you have other questions, please let me know. Otherwise…"

"We'll show ourselves out," Sienna said. "And thank you."

She didn't say anything else until they were outside, walking back through the darkened streets. "Alba was always a fun-loving girl," she said, softly. "I considered attempting to arrange a match between her and Croce. To see her broken like that…"

Emily shivered. "A Nightmare Hex?"

"It's possible," Sienna agreed. "And yet, Sarnia would have sensed it. It would have left traces."

"And it *wouldn't* have killed a man," Emily added. Nightmare Hexes weren't dangerous, in and of themselves. She knew that for a fact. It was what someone did, under the influence, that was truly dangerous. A magician who lost control of his powers and lashed out in fear could easily get himself killed. "What can do *that*?"

"I wish I knew." Sienna turned the corner, walking down a narrow alleyway. "It just doesn't add up. Alba was drained of power, yet she didn't cast a single spell; Antony was killed, yet…whatever turned him into stone left no traces."

"Unless you have something that vacuumed up all traces of magic," Emily pointed out. "A magic-absorbing ward would do that, wouldn't it?"

"Only active magic," Sienna said. "I've never heard of anything that drained a person's reserves…"

She stopped, dead. Emily sensed it too, a moment later. An…*absence*…an absence of…*something*. She looked around, noting that they were standing in a place where four alleys met. And yet, something was missing. The background *mana* was almost completely gone.

"It happened here," Sienna said. "And the magic field has been disrupted."

She walked from side to side, casting a handful of spells. Emily closed her eyes, trying to sense the ebb and flow of magic. It felt as though something had drained the *mana*, leaving a region that was completely devoid of magic. The remainder of the field was slowly filling the hole, she noted, but it was moving so slowly she couldn't help thinking it would be years before the region returned to normal. Her reserves didn't seem affected, but runes and anything else that depended on the background magic field would fail as long as the area remained dead. She wondered, grimly, just what would happen if she tried to cast a spell within the dead zone.

The spells would have to be modified, she thought. *And I would have to put out more power.*

"*Something* was definitely here," Sienna said. "But what?"

Emily shook her head. A necromancer could drain power, true, but Alba wouldn't have survived the experience. *And* every sorcerer within the city would have sensed the power surge. Unless someone had invented something new…it was possible. Dua

Kepala had been revoltingly ingenious, and the Allied Lands had paid the price.

"It seems impossible to believe it was a god," Sienna added. "The killings *do* follow a pattern. People linked to Vesperian, directly or indirectly..."

"And now Vesperian himself," Emily agreed. Sienna was right. If Justice was *real*, why wasn't he going after the *real* monsters? Why target Antony when it was his *father* who was working with Vesperian? "Did you *know* Antony?"

"Vaguely," Sienna said. "A young man, one of many. Nothing too remarkable...no magic, as far as I know; the promise of inherited wealth, yet no wealth of his own. I believe his parents were looking for a match for him, but they never expressed interest in *my* daughters."

Emily glanced at her. "Would you push Karan or Marian into marriage?"

"They're powerful magicians," Sienna said. There was a hint of pride in her voice. "It would be unwise."

"Fulvia tried to push Melissa into a marriage," Emily pointed out.

"And look how well *that* worked out," Sienna countered. "I would prefer that my daughters choose their own partners."

Emily nodded, slowly. She wasn't sure she wanted to ask the next question, but it had been nagging at her mind. "Do you...do you put protective spells on your daughters?"

"There are some on Marian," Sienna said. "Karan is too advanced a magician to allow me to give her protections."

She gave Emily a searching glance. "Does that bother you?"

Emily hesitated. Part of her – the part that had grown up feeling vulnerable – would have welcomed such protections, if they kept her safe. She might even have *asked* for such protections. But she also felt as though it would be unwarranted interference in her life, carried out by a parent who didn't understand her. She had a right to make her own mistakes, didn't she?

"I don't know," she admitted, finally.

Sienna looked amused. "My mother was a strict disciplinarian. She ruled the household with a rod of iron. I chafed under her rules and promised myself that, when I had children, I would treat them differently. And then I had children, and discovered my mother had actually had good reason for her actions. You'll feel differently too, when you have children. It isn't a safe world."

Her smile widened. "There aren't any spells on Caleb, if *that's* what you're asking. Or didn't you notice that you *didn't* get struck blind when you kissed him?"

Emily stared at her in shock. "Is that...is that what Sarnia's spell did?"

"It might have," Sienna said. "There was a minor scandal involving Alba's elder sister and *her* boyfriend."

"I don't think I want to know," Emily said. "Does she...does she have the *right* to put spells on her children?"

Sienna shrugged. "When you have children, you'll feel differently," she commented. "Trust me on that, Emily."

"Alba had a wand," Emily said. "Was she...was she a strong magician?"

"She didn't have enough talent to justify sending her to school," Sienna said. "Her mother made the decision to teach her at home. She had promise, but...not enough."

Emily swallowed. "Was it the right choice?"

"Good question," Sienna said. "Sarnia is a good teacher, but no one can cover *all* the basics."

She looked down at Emily. "I know what you're thinking. You're thinking that Sarnia is too strict with her children. You're probably thinking that I'm too strict with *my* children. And you might be right. It's never easy to balance between protecting your children and preparing them for adulthood. Some mistakes have to be made to allow your children to learn from them. Others...others shouldn't be made at all.

"There are worse parents out there," she added. "Parents who ignore their children, parents who spoil their children, parents who *abuse* their children. Focus your ire on them."

Emily felt herself flush. *Her* mother had been a drunkard, her father had vanished long ago and her stepfather...she shuddered. A protective spell would have been helpful, back when she'd been trapped in a dingy apartment. She might have felt safer. It might even have given her the courage to stand up to the older man.

"I'm sorry," she said.

"Ah, youth," Sienna said. "The age when you know everything."

She turned in a circle, casting a set of spells into the air. "And if you *do* know everything, tell me what did this?"

"I don't know," Emily said, irked.

She glanced up, readying a spell, as she heard the clatter of footsteps. A young man wearing a green tunic hurried up to them and fell on one knee.

"Lady Emily," he gasped. A herald, Emily realized. King Randor's wore finer clothes, but the principle was the same. "The guildmasters request the pleasure of your company at the guildhall."

Emily glanced at Sienna, who shrugged.

"It will be my pleasure," she said, formally. She frowned. How had the herald known where to find her? They certainly hadn't told anyone where they were going after the Temple of Stone. "I'll be on my way in a moment."

"I will accompany you." Sienna smiled, as if something was humorous. "We wouldn't want you to get lost along the way."

"Thank you," Emily said. The herald turned and hurried off. "How...how did he know where to find us?"

"There's a tracking spell on my papers," Sienna said, with an odd little smile. "And they knew you were accompanying me."

"Oh," Emily said.

Chapter Eighteen

E MILY COULDN'T HELP THINKING, WHEN SHE FIRST SET EYES ON THE GUILDHALL, THAT IT looked rather like a smaller version of the Capitol building. It sat in the center of the city, overshadowed by the giant castle and surrounded by hundreds of statues, each one representing one of the guilds. The City Guard were out in force, patrolling the streets around the guildhall as if they expected trouble. Emily suspected they were right. Sienna led the way to the doors, spoke briefly to one of the guards, and walked into the building.

"They'll be meeting in one of the smaller chambers," Sienna said. Emily had no idea how she knew *that*. "This way."

Emily followed her, looking around with interest. Someone had spent a great deal of money on the giant building, paving the floors with marble and lining the walls with paintings, each one showing a former guildmaster. She couldn't help noticing that most of them were men, although a handful were definitely female. They all wore fancy robes, so fancy that Emily suspected they were copied from Zangaria's aristocracy. And yet, anyone who became a guildmaster had to be competent. Family connections could only go so far.

There was another pair of guards outside a door, one of them clearly a sorcerer. Emily tensed as she sensed a pair of spells probing at her, but relaxed as the door opened. The smaller chamber didn't look friendly. Grand Guildmaster Jalil sat in a chair that looked like a throne, flanked by eight other men wearing guildmaster robes. General Pollack stood in front of them, next to two men Emily didn't recognize. She couldn't help thinking that the room looked like a courtroom, with the guildmasters acting as judges. It made her feel almost as if she'd done something wrong.

The door closed, loudly.

"Lady Emily." Jalil sounded friendly, but there was an edge to his voice that made Emily look up and pay attention. "We have...*invited*...you here to answer some questions."

Emily resisted the urge to look at Sienna for support. She'd spent far too long answering questions after the war had ended, after Gaius had turned traitor and both Casper and the necromancer had been killed. This time, at least, she was fairly sure she didn't have anything to hide. There were no secrets that could get her killed.

"I understand," she said.

"I must also warn you that lying to the council, either directly or through omission, will be counted against you," Jalil said. "If there are questions you do not wish to answer, you must say so."

Emily nodded, slowly. "Ask your questions."

Jalil paused, taking a moment to compose his first question. "We have been informed that you invested a considerable sum of money in Vesperian's Track," he said. "The figure mentioned was fifty thousand crowns. Is this true?"

"No," Emily said.

One of the other guildmasters started to splutter. Jalil silenced him with a look and then turned back to Emily. "Did you invest *any* money in Vesperian's Track?"

"No," Emily said.

A guildmaster leaned forward. "We have been reliably informed that you *did* invest a substantial sum into the project. These reports..."

"I was unaware that *rumor* was considered a reliable source these days," Sienna said, before Emily could formulate a response. "Grand Guildmaster, point of order. Is that a legitimate question?"

Jalil's face darkened. "No," he said. "Guildmaster Merriam, you will apologize."

Merriam looked down at Emily. "I apologize for my tone," he said, bluntly. "On behalf of the ironworkers, however, I require a straight answer. Did you invest in Vesperian's Track?"

Emily forced herself to contain her irritation. "I have already answered that question," she said coldly. "I did not invest any money in the project."

She paused, weighing her options. "It is true that Vesperian wanted me to invest. The figure mentioned was *ten* thousand crowns, not *fifty*. His offer seemed good, but I declined."

Another guildmaster met her eyes. "Can I ask why?"

"I wanted to see the books before making my final decision," Emily told him. "He refused to allow me to inspect them. Accordingly, I told him that I wouldn't invest any money in his project. The rumors have no basis in fact."

And yet, someone might have started the rumors to stave off disaster for a few more weeks, she thought, grimly. *Vesperian could certainly have lied to his other investors...*

Jalil looked grim. "What did you make of the project?"

Emily hesitated. "I didn't see the books." She wasn't sure she *should* answer the question. "All I have to go on is...is my gut feeling. And my gut feeling is that Vesperian tried to move forward far too fast. I didn't think he had any reasonable hope of paying off his investors before it was too late."

Shock ran through the room. "I've invested thousands," a guildmaster breathed. "I..."

"You weren't the only one," Jalil said.

"My guildsmen have invested too," Guildmaster Merriam said. He was pale. "What will happen to them? Who owns the track now?"

Good question, Emily thought.

Jalil slammed the table. "We have to remain calm. We don't even know the scale of the disaster..."

"Vesperian owed my guild thousands of crowns," Guildmaster Merriam said. "If that isn't paid within the next few weeks, we won't be able to make our own payments! We might not even be able to resell the iron rails, wooden ties and other railway truck items we produced for him, if we repossess them..."

"Which we can't, until we have a formal determination of who is owed what," another guildmaster said. "This would never have happened on *my* watch!"

"This isn't the time for gloating, Harman," Jalil snarled.

"No," Guildmaster Harman agreed. "But if Vesperian had hired a proper set of accountants, we might not be in this mess."

"You lost most of your business because you were taking advantage of your customers," Merriam pointed out. "And now you expect us to *trust* you?"

"I expect you to face the facts," Harman said. "And the facts are that two-thirds of our entire population invested in the track. Some people invested a few crowns, others gave Vesperian their life savings. When it sinks in that all the money has vanished...what then?"

Sienna nudged Emily. "Harman lost the post of Grand Guildmaster when the Accountants Guild took a hit," she muttered, as the guildmasters began to squabble. "It was sheer luck he managed to keep his seat on the council. Being right isn't always a good thing."

Emily nodded in agreement. The Accountants Guild *had* been corrupt – something that had only become evident when the New Learning had arrived, introducing the world to the joys of Arabic numbers and double-entry bookkeeping. And yes, it *had* been a brake on progress, ensuring that the money supply remained limited. But it had also made it impossible for Ponzi schemes to work. Vesperian would never have been able to attract so many investors before the Accountants Guild had collapsed.

She looked back at Sienna. "What are they going to do?"

"I don't know," Sienna whispered. "I don't think they know either."

General Pollack cleared his throat. "You need to decide how to proceed." He stood in the center of the room, his hands clasped behind his back. "You have asked me to take command of the City Guard, but I don't have the manpower to control the streets if all hell breaks loose. Even with the Hands of Justice backing us, Guildmasters, I cannot even guarantee to protect this building."

Emily frowned. The Hands of Justice were backing the City Guard...?

"Declare martial law," Merriam snapped. "Tell the population to stay in their homes, or else."

General Pollack snorted. "Or else *what*? We don't have the manpower to enforce that, *sir.*"

"The investors want their money back," a tired-looking man said. He was so colorless, his grey face matching his grey robes, that Emily wondered if he was ill. "But it will take years to calculate how much is actually owed, let alone to whom."

"Nonsense," Merriam said. "Give the bastards their money."

The grey man shook his head. "Over the last twenty hours, my office has received over two *hundred* demands for immediate repayment and statements of claims on Vesperian's estate. We lack even the *basic* data we need to calculate who is owed what. I don't know if he kept an accurate register of who invested – and what notes they were given – but the notes have been swapped around so much that it will probably be worthless. This is not a simple assessment, Guildmaster."

"And we're running out of time," General Pollack said. "How many people believe their notes will come due in--" he made a show of checking his watch "--seventeen hours?"

"There are already lines forming outside his offices, demanding repayment," Harman said, wryly. He sounded amused. "And what will happen when the notes are *not* repaid?"

"Chaos," Emily blurted.

"Which we will be unable to control," General Pollack said. He glanced at Emily, then back at Harman. "Right now, the sole thing standing between us and rioting is the belief that those notes will be repaid."

"And they can't be repaid," the grey man said. "Even if the paperwork is in order, it will take months to sort everything out..."

"We don't *have* months." Harman nodded to General Pollack. "We have seventeen hours."

Merriam looked as if he wanted to panic. "Then tell them...tell them..."

Jalil snorted. "Tell them *what?*"

"Tell them that we are assessing the situation," Harman said. "I can put together a team of accountants and take them to Vesperian's offices. We can study his paperwork and put together a list of investors and debtors, then calculate the precise value of Vesperian's assets."

"Confiscate his mansion," a guildmaster suggested.

"It doesn't belong to him," Merriam snapped. "He *rented* it."

"It isn't uncommon for a freeze in payments to take place after someone's death," Harman continued. "Tell the investors that we will begin paying out once we know what is actually owed."

"They might not have the time," General Pollack said, quietly. "How many people do *you* know who are *depending* on their notes being repaid tomorrow?"

"Then tell them to wait," Harman said.

General Pollack looked back at him, evenly. "And what if they *can't* wait?"

Jalil slapped the table, hard. Everyone jumped.

"We have a problem," he said, sharply. "Right now, our sole priority is finding a way to *solve* the problem before we run out of time. We can assign blame and rewrite the laws later, once we have some breathing space. Vesperian's death cannot be allowed to tear the city apart."

Emily winced, inwardly. She had a feeling it was already too late. Buying back the notes for face value was the simplest solution, but who had *that* sort of money? The only person she could think of who *could* afford such an investment was King Randor, yet she knew better than to expect him to solve the independent city's problems without payment. He'd probably want to put a garrison in the city, for starters. Perhaps the guildmasters could put together a fund to buy the notes...

Except those who didn't invest will resent having to pay for those who did, she thought, grimly. *And then they won't be happy either.*

"Lady Emily," Jalil said. "Would *you* be prepared to join the investigation team?"

Emily took a moment to consider it. She was no accountant. Indeed, she had the feeling her appointment would rub far too many people the wrong way. And yet, figuring out just how much money Vesperian owed – and to whom – was the first step in defusing the time bomb before it exploded. If General Pollack wasn't confident of controlling the streets, when the investors realized that *none* of the money would be repaid on schedule, she knew the riots were going to be bad. The rioters might even blame the guildmasters for the disaster.

"I would," she said. A thought struck her. "And I would like to propose that Markus be invited too."

"A banker," Harman muttered.

"He understands modern banking." Emily had her doubts about Harman. The accountant had every reason to want to see the newfangled paper banking system collapse into rubble. "And I have faith in him."

"Very well." Jalil looked at the grey man. "Harriman?"

"I will serve," Harriman said. "However, I do not expect quick results. This is an unprecedented situation. We do not even know – yet – who Vesperian named as his heirs."

"He had a son," Merriam pointed out. "And a wife."

"And we don't even know if the project is viable," Harriman added. "If we seek to complete the project, sir, we have one set of decisions to make. But if we decide to wind it up and sell the remains to the highest bidder…"

Emily groaned, inwardly. The railway line between Beneficence and Cockatrice was a wonder, even though the planned extension was almost certainly a financial disaster waiting to happen. She didn't *want* to watch, helplessly, as it was broken down for scrap, the engines melted down and the railway lines torn up. Hell, merely selling the rails would send the price of iron plummeting. The accountants might not reclaim even a fraction of their paper worth.

"We will assess the situation first," Jalil said. "We will work out what actually *happened* to the money. And then we will decide what we want to do."

He looked at Emily. "Guildmaster Harman and Harriman will escort you to Vesperian's offices."

"I can't come with you," Sienna muttered. "Be careful when you come home."

"I will," Emily promised. "And thank you."

General Pollack moved to stand next to her and spoke quietly, pitching his voice so only she could hear. "Be *very* careful. The Guard has managed to keep a dampener on any major riots, but small fights are constantly breaking out all over the city. Too many people in bars, drinking themselves silly; too many rumors, each one worse than the last. Quite a few involve you."

Emily grimaced. "Do I want to know?"

"Probably not," General Pollack said. He motioned for her to accompany him - and Sienna - out of the room. Sienna cast a privacy ward as soon as they were outside. "But you *should* know."

He sighed. "The most common rumor is that you either loaned or agreed to loan Vesperian a great deal of money. Each retelling credits you with ever more fantastical sums of money – right now, there are rumors that insist you loaned him *millions* of crowns."

"There *isn't* that much," Emily protested. "I am nowhere near that rich."

General Pollack shrugged. "Those are the decent rumors," he said. "We have various rumors suggesting that you promised investment, only to pull it out at the last minute so the project would fail. Or that you charmed him into overextending himself so you could sneak in and claim the railway for yourself. And then we have suggestions that King Randor used you to destabilize the city so his armies could march in and take over. And then..."

Emily scowled. She didn't want to believe someone could think *that* of her, but she knew – all too well – that rumors grew in the telling. There was no internet on the Nameless World...not that the internet would have made things better. If anything, the internet would probably have made matters worse. By now, people were probably implying that she'd made a deal with the Necromancers and was working to undermine the Allied Lands from within.

"I'll send Caleb to join you too," Sienna said. "You may need his help."

"Thanks." Emily wasn't sure if Caleb *could* help, but she knew she'd welcome his presence. And then another thought struck her. "General...is it wise to ask the Hands of Justice for help patrolling the streets?"

"We're short of manpower," General Pollack said, grimly. "A third of the City Guard has decided it's a good time to desert. Others bought notes of their own. We just don't have many choices if we are to keep the streets relatively calm."

"It won't last," Sienna said. "Prices are already going up."

And then most of the population will be unable to buy food, Emily thought, numbly. *There'll be food riots.*

"You should ask the council to send out more fishing boats," she said, instead. "That would keep the city going, wouldn't it?"

"Yes," General Pollack agreed. "But who will pay for the catch?"

He scowled, his moustache quivering unpleasantly. "A number of boats have not returned. Either they're still fishing...or they've gone to other ports. There are plenty of places along the coastline where a fishing boat can sell its catch without anyone official paying much notice. Fishermen have to eat too."

Emily shuddered. "They can eat," she said, grimly. Were the fishermen being selfish – or practical? How long would the fishermen work if the council confiscated half their catch to feed the starving masses? "There must be something we can do."

"Yes," General Pollack said. "We can solve this problem as quickly as possible."

He looked past her. "Good luck, Emily."

Emily turned. Harman was walking towards her, followed by Harriman. The accountant bowed politely to her, then nodded to the door. Emily readied her magic, testing a series of protective spells before saying goodbye to General Pollack and his wife. She hoped, despite herself, that Markus and Caleb joined her soon. She had the feeling that neither of the older men were going to be useful.

"I'll have my staff join us at the office," Harman said.

"I'm sure they will be helpful," Harriman said. "Perhaps we can organize the paperwork quickly enough to start making payments soon."

Emily sighed, inwardly. She hoped Harriman was right.

But she had a feeling he was being optimistic.

Chapter Nineteen

EMILY HEARD THE CROWD LONG BEFORE IT CAME INTO VIEW, A BAYING MASS OF HUMANITY jeering outside the offices. Vesperian had purchased – or rented – a large building near the railway station, one that would have given anyone an aura of respectability in better times. Now, she hoped that anyone in the nearby buildings would have vacated the premises when things got ugly. The angry mob might not stop with Vesperian's offices when – if – it gave in to the urge to destroy.

"This way," Harriman said.

He led the way towards the mob, holding his head high. Emily stared at his back, then hastily prepared a dozen more spells as she followed him. A line of guardsmen spotted them a moment later and advanced, driving back the mob to allow them to reach the gates and open the doors. A man stood in the lobby, unable to move. A guard sorcerer caught her eye and winked. He'd clearly frozen the man when he'd tried to enter.

"I thought it would be better to hold him until you arrived," the sorcerer said. He was a young man, probably only two or three years older than Emily. "I didn't want him trying to burn anything."

"Good thinking," Harriman said. "Ah, Callam. Lady Emily, if you would…?"

Emily blinked in surprise – the frozen man *was* Callam, Vesperian's assistant – and then undid the spell with a wave of her hand. Callam fell to the floor, groaning loudly. Harman strode past him, further into the building, while Harriman helped Callam back to his feet. Emily took a moment to check him for spells and found nothing. He didn't even have a protective amulet.

"I thought I should be here," Callam said. "Mr. Harriman, I…"

"Good," Harriman said. "Where are the books?"

"Upstairs," Callam said. "Do you want to see them?"

"Yes." Harriman nodded towards the stairwell. "Shall we go?"

Emily followed them up the stairs, reaching out with her senses as she walked. There were no wards at all, as far as she could determine…not even a basic anti-theft ward. Had they all died with Vesperian? Or had someone – or *something* – beaten them to the offices? She glanced into a pair of smaller rooms as they reached the top of the stairs, half-expecting to see another statue waiting for them. But there was nothing. The rooms seemed completely empty.

She reached out and tapped Callam's shoulder. "What have you been doing since Vesperian's death?"

"Waiting to see who I work for," Callam said. "I believe Vesperian left most of his property to his son, but there were some…unusual bequests in the will."

Emily frowned. "Unusual bequests?"

"Later," Harriman said, as they entered an office. "I…"

His voice trailed away as they took in the scene before them. The office was a mess, pieces of paper and parchment lying everywhere. Emily glanced into the next room and saw a collection of filing cabinets, each one a jumbled mess. A dozen account books sat on a table, filled with entries in spiky handwriting. She wasn't sure if someone had searched the building, looking for the money, or if Vesperian had simply left behind a tremendous mess. If there was a filing system, she couldn't see it.

Her heart sank as she opened one of the account books. Vesperian had ignored all of the basics, making the books incredibly difficult to follow. He'd left notes or initials to represent his investors, but he hadn't said if they owed him money or he owed *them* money. Emily picked her way through the pages, trying to determine if there were even any *dates*. She had no idea how each entry could be matched to a specific note, let alone used to figure out how much the note-holder was entitled to collect. She didn't even know where to begin.

"Gods," Harman breathed.

Emily turned. Harman had entered the room, his expression falling as he saw the chaos. She hadn't expected much from him, but…she shook her head, fully understanding his dismay. How many account books *were* there? And how did they relate to one another? It might take years to sort them out, assuming it was even *possible*. Vesperian had clearly figured that his memory would be enough to put the pieces together, perhaps with a few prompts from his notes. She'd read books by sorcerers who'd seemed to follow the same principle.

"He was supposed to have hired accountants," Harman said. "Where *are* they?"

"They didn't show up for work," Callam said. "Besides, Vesperian handled these accounts himself."

Emily felt despair gnawing at her soul. "Where do we even start?"

Harman looked at Callam. "Which one of these ledgers is the oldest?"

"I think it's stored in the vaults," Callam said, as Markus and Caleb entered the room. "I'll go find it, shall I?"

"A very good idea." Harriman glanced at Caleb. "Perhaps you could escort him, young man. We don't want him getting lost along the way."

Caleb nodded and followed Callam out of the room.

"I'll have my staff here within the hour," Harman said. "Markus, you and your staff can focus on the notes – who bought them, when and where, for how much. I'll concentrate on the big investments and whatever assets remain to the company."

Emily heard a whistle. She turned and walked over to the window, just in time to see a train puffing out of the station and heading for the bridge. She wondered, grimly, who was running the station. Were they certain Vesperian's son would take over the family business or were they trying to put a brave face on matters?

Callam returned, carrying a bunch of dusty books under his arm. "These date back to the start of the original track," he said. "Anything older would be in Cockatrice."

Harriman looked at Emily. "Could you find the records for us?"

"I can try," Emily said. She had no idea who'd started the original railway, let alone sold it to Vesperian. Imaiqah would have to find out. "I'll send a message tonight."

Harman opened the first ledger. Dust drifted up from the pages. "We'll start as soon as my staff arrives," he said. "Hopefully, we'll have some answers by the end of the day."

Emily enjoyed reading old spellbooks and figuring out the missing steps the ancient sorcerers had used to conceal their secrets, but she had to admit – as the minutes turned into hours – that accountancy was mind-numbingly boring. There was no prospect of danger if she transposed a rune or added the wrong ingredient to an alchemical brew, merely the certainty that a tiny mistake would eventually turn into an accounting disaster. She felt her head starting to pound, even as Harriman, Harman and Markus delved further and further into the files. Vesperian's filing system made so little sense that Emily thought he'd just shoved paperwork into the files at random. It was a nightmare.

"He has an ongoing contract with the ironworkers to purchase thousands of tons of iron rails," Harriman said. "He owes them upwards of five thousand crowns."

"And another with the artificers," Harman added. "They're paid per engine, I think."

"And he's paid some of them in notes." Markus's voice was grim. "I think they won't be repaid in a hurry."

Emily rubbed her forehead. It was starting to look as though, if anything, that they'd underestimated the situation. Vesperian's Ponzi scheme had grown and grown until it had started to consume everything else. Nearly every industry within the city limits had been selling...*something*...to the railway, from simple iron rails and steam engines to rope and luxury furnishings. And most of the debts had never been paid. It looked as though she'd been right, when Vesperian had asked her for a loan. He'd been taking out new loans and using them to pay off the older loans.

And sooner or later he would have run out of money, she thought. *He* did *run out of money.*

She looked up from the account book, caught Caleb's eye, and nodded to the door. Harman took the book without comment and added it to the set to be studied as Emily and Caleb walked out. The upper floors were crammed with accountants and bankers, each one trying to put together a giant jigsaw puzzle, but the lower floors were deserted. Even the angry mob outside was quieter, somehow...

"It's a nightmare," she said. "It'll take years to get through it all."

She sat down on a chair, resting her head in her hands. Tomorrow, the bill would come due; tomorrow, the city would realize that the bills would not be paid, that the notes weren't even worth the paper they were printed on. And then...she swallowed, hard. Thousands of people would wake up to the news that they would never get their money back, no matter what they did. It would set off a chain reaction that could bring the city to its knees.

Caleb moved up behind her and gently started massaging her shoulders. She looked up at him, feeling a sudden rush of genuine affection. He had to have been bored, watching and waiting while the accountants worked their way through the books...she silently blessed him for staying with her. She wouldn't have blamed him if he'd wanted to leave. His fingers reached further down, working out the kinks...

"I love you," she said, quietly.

His fingers seemed to freeze, just for a second. She hadn't said that to him often, had she? She wasn't sure she'd said it at all. And yet, she *did* feel something for him. Their relationship was...stable. Maybe she would never have Imaiqah's series of romances mixed with break-ups and new romances – or Alassa's passionate relationship with Jade – but she didn't want it. She wanted someone who would be there for her, someone she could trust with her life...

The thought caused her a stab of guilt. She hadn't trusted him completely, had she?

"I love you too," he whispered.

His lips pressed against the back of her neck. She shivered as he kissed her, then lifted her head so he could kiss her lips. A thrill of excitement ran through her body, mingled with a fear of discovery. This wasn't Whitehall. There would be consequences if they were caught making out when there was work to be done. She dreaded to think what Caleb's mother would say if they embarrassed the family. And yet...part of her wanted to throw caution to the winds.

She stood, turning so she could hug him. "We can't," she whispered. "Not here."

Caleb nodded in grim understanding. His arms wrapped around her, running down her back...her body thrilled to his touch, even though she knew it was dangerous. She met his eyes, seeing regret clearly written there, then let go of him and stepped back firmly. They couldn't be caught, not now. Even finding an inn would be problematic. She rubbed her face clean, hoping her lips didn't look *too* puffy. They had work to do.

She jumped as she heard someone shouting at the bottom of the stairs. The racket was so loud that she thought, just for a second, that they *had* been caught. And then she turned and hurried down the stairs. Someone else – Markus, probably – was already coming down from the top floor. Caleb followed her, his footsteps echoing. The noise grew louder as she reached the bottom of the stairs.

"And I'm telling you that I have every right to view his papers," a young man was shouting, despite an older man trying to restrain him. "He was my *father*!"

"And I'm telling you that this building has been sealed," a guardsman was saying. "Sir, please leave..."

The younger man looked past him. "Lady Emily," he called. "Can we talk?"

Markus clattered down behind Caleb. "Tryon, I'm afraid this building *has* been sealed."

The younger man shot him a nasty glance, then looked at Emily. "Can we talk?"

"I suppose." Emily didn't want Tryon – Tryon Junior, she assumed – interrupting the accountants. "We'll find a room."

"Thank you." Tryon bowed low, then rose. "This is Vespers, my family's advocate."

Lawyer, Emily translated.

"There's a room on the second floor," Caleb said, turning to lead the way up the stairs. "I'm sure it will be suitable."

"Of course," Tryon said.

Emily studied Vesperian's son as they walked up to the meeting room. He was tall, but otherwise he looked like a younger version of his father. And yet, there was a nervous energy about him that would have worried her, if she'd met him five years ago. He looked as though he would lash out at any moment. She reminded herself, firmly, that she had more than enough magic to stop him in his tracks if he tried anything stupid.

"The will has been read," Vespers said, once they were seated. He had a plummy voice that put Emily's teeth on edge. "The controlling interest in Vesperian Industries has been passed to my client. I must therefore ask that you refrain from any further disruption until my client takes possession of his heritage."

Emily cursed, mentally. She should have asked Harriman to join them. *He* was the one with *real* authority.

Markus leaned forward. "I have a question," he said. "Are you filing a legal demand that we stop inspecting the account books?"

"They're mine," Tryon said. "I'm the one who decides what happens to them."

"The information contained within the accounts may also be confidential," Vespers added, smoothly. "My client and his investors would be most displeased if certain details were revealed."

Emily exchanged glances with Caleb, then spoke. "Has your client been following the details of his father's investments?"

Tryon colored. "My father handled all such matters himself!"

He stood and started to pace the room, as if a chair couldn't contain his nervous energy any longer. "I was groomed to succeed him." He turned to look at Emily. "And I will not allow anyone to get in my way."

Markus snorted. "Do you understand the codes your father used in his account books?"

"There are accountants to handle the details," Tyron insisted. "That's what they're *paid* to do!"

"Yes, I suppose there are." Markus looked at Vespers. "The Guild Council granted the investigation commission wide latitude to open the account books and carry out a complete audit of Vesperian's finances. As you are no doubt aware, such a commission can only be overruled by the Guild Council itself."

"Such a commission is only legal if the city itself is at risk," Vespers pointed out.

"The city *is* at risk," Emily said, quietly.

"Nonsense," Tryon thundered. He glowered at her. "My father loved this city!"

"The figures are clear," Markus said. "Tomorrow, your father's corporation will be expected to pay out upwards of twenty *thousand* crowns in repayment of investments, not to mention his debts to various industries. So far, we have been unable to uncover anything like enough funds to cover the debts. Your father's total free cash, as far as we have been able to determine, is somewhere around two thousand crowns – a respectable amount, to be sure, but not enough to cover his debts."

"Impossible," Tryon thundered. "My father was a great man, his dreams destroyed by small-minded fools..."

"The preliminary report will be presented tomorrow." Markus's voice was even. "We may uncover more cash reserves, but I have my doubts. Vesperian could have settled most of his debts if he had the cash."

"You're lying," Tryon said. His gaze switched to Emily. "This is all your fault, you..."

Vespers elbowed him. "What my client means to say," he said smoothly, "is that it was reported that you made considerable investments in the track."

"Such reports are lies," Emily said. "I invested no money."

"My father wouldn't lie," Tryon said. "I demand..."

"You can make your demands to the Guild Council," Markus said. "I'm sure they will make the best possible decision, once you've stated your case. Until then, the investigation will continue."

"I'll own your bank by the end of the week," Tryon snapped. "You're not an accountant, you're not even an *advocate*! The lawsuit will..."

"I *would* advise you to grab what you can and flee the city." Markus's expression twisted into something that could charitably be called a smile. "But seeing you probably wouldn't take my advice, I won't bother."

Tryon stamped up to the table and glared at him. "This is an outrage!"

Markus lifted a hand. Emily felt a spell forming, a moment before it drained back into nothingness. "No," he said. His voice was so calm that Emily *knew* he was faking it. "What *is* an outrage is your father building a financial scheme that will wipe out the savings of countless people who trusted him. Now, you can leave here peacefully or I'll turn you both into frogs and dump you in the nearest pond."

Vespers rose and stalked out of the room. Tryon gave Markus a nasty look, shot a nastier one at Emily, then followed his lawyer. Emily resisted the urge to hex him in the back as he left – barely. Beside her, Caleb was bristling. She took his hand and squeezed it lightly.

"He'll go straight to the council," Markus predicted. He sounded oddly amused. "But they'll probably do their best to ignore him."

"Good." Caleb looked at Emily. "How long do we have?"

Emily glanced at her watch. "Fifteen hours," she said. "That's when the notes fall due."

Chapter Twenty

D ESPITE CALEB'S TENDER TOUCH – AND A PAINKILLING POTION SHE'D KEPT IN HER POUCH – Emily's headache had only grown worse by the end of the day. Vesperian's account-keeping had been so poor that it was impossible to say with any certainty just what he owned, let alone what it was worth and who needed to be paid. Even Harman's snide remarks had drained away as he and his staff struggled to figure out the truth. There was no hope of a quick resolution.

"We could sell everything we *know* he owns," she said to Caleb, "but it wouldn't raise enough money to buy back the notes."

"And the richest and most powerful investors would want their money back first," Caleb pointed out. "Everyone else would be screwed."

Emily winced. Caleb was right. The ordinary investors would be lucky if they got *anything* back. She doubted selling the steam engines and railway lines would bring in much money, not when it would take years for them to repay the investment. The guildmasters might reclaim their money, but everyone else…? She closed her eyes in pain. Everyone who had trusted Vesperian with their life savings was about to lose everything.

She peered out of the window over the city, wondering what would happen when the notes finally came due. There were already rumors…what would happen when those rumors were confirmed? The crowd outside the office had grown, despite the best efforts of the guardsmen. They hadn't been able to convince the crowd to disperse, even as night began to fall. Emily didn't blame them for not pushing harder. The guardsmen were outnumbered fifty to one. And besides, some of them probably had relatives in the crowd.

"Lady Emily," Harriman said. Emily turned as the clerk entered the small office. The grey man didn't look very tired, even though he'd put in more work than any of the accountants and bankers. "We are not going to find a quick answer."

Emily nodded. Vesperian seemed to have almost no money. There were no secret bank accounts, no caches of pre-banking coins…everything he'd collected, it seemed, had been invested into the railway or used to pay his older debts. It certainly didn't *look* as though Vesperian had intended to flee the city, taking everything he could carry with him. But there hadn't been much he *could* carry.

"It looks that way," she agreed.

"So far, his total debts appear to be upwards of seventy *thousand* crowns," Harriman continued. "His total assets, assuming they were sold at purchase price, come to ten thousand crowns at most."

"And they won't be sold at purchase price," Emily finished. Vesperian had driven prices up, simply by buying everything he could get his hands on. The price of iron had quintupled over the last two months alone. "We'll be lucky if we get back a tenth of what he paid for them."

"I'm afraid so." Harriman looked downhearted, just for a moment. "I will have to present this to the council, tomorrow. It will not go down well."

"No," Emily agreed. She shook her head, tiredly. "I have no solution."

"Nor do I." Harriman nodded towards the window. "Everyone who can leave the city is going now."

"I know," Emily said.

She yawned, wishing – more than anything – that she could lie down in Caleb's arms and sleep. The headache, never far from her mind, kept pounding away inside her skull. Her entire body felt drained...

"I'm going to have the building sealed for the night," Harriman said. "The most important documents will be transferred to a bank vault for safekeeping. There are already suggestions on the street that Vesperian kept his money here..."

He sighed. "I suggest you get some rest. You may be called upon to testify tomorrow."

Emily was too tired to argue. "I'll see you tomorrow." She glanced at Caleb. "Shall we go?"

"Please," Caleb said. "We both need to rest."

The roar of the mob grew louder as they – and the rest of the staff – emerged from the building. Emily felt the primal waves of rage and helplessness washing through the crowd, driving them into a frenzy. Someone had passed out bottles of beer and wine, perhaps in the hope that the crowd would drink itself into a stupor. Or perhaps, the cynical side of her mind added, they *wanted* a riot. The guardsmen kept their hands near their weapons, exchanging nervous glances as the mob roared its anger. Emily couldn't help noticing that there seemed to be fewer guardsmen on the streets. She wondered, as she readied her magic, how many of the guardsmen had gone home to protect their families.

They didn't sign up for this, she thought, numbly.

She held Caleb's hand, gritting her teeth as the roar grew louder. The railway station was also under siege, hundreds of men and women gathered outside despite the curfew. Emily suspected the council had made a mistake by ordering everyone to be inside by nightfall, even though she knew they'd had little choice. They lacked the manpower to enforce it, let alone any more draconian measures they might have in mind. Even with the Hands of Justice backing them up – and there were no Hands in sight – the Guard was still badly outnumbered.

The roar faded as they made their way through the crowd and down the street. She didn't envy the clerks, many of whom were carrying documents to Bankers Row. Markus accompanied them, along with a handful of other magicians, but she had a nasty feeling that there were magic-users who had also lost their investments. Sienna might have banned her children from investing in the railway, yet others might not have been so prudent. In hindsight, she should have asked if Alba and *her* family had invested...

A dull red glow appeared in the distance, casting an eerie light over the city. Emily tensed, glancing from side to side. The handful of people on the street – hurrying home, she assumed – didn't look threatening. And then she realized the glow was coming from the richer part of the city...

She looked at Caleb. "What's that?"

Caleb's voice was grim. "Fire."

Emily swallowed, hard. Beneficence had a fire service, she'd been assured, but would the firemen get to the blaze in time to save whatever was burning? Or would the flames spread out of control? The city was built of stone, but that might not make a difference if the wind fanned the flames. If the poorer parts of the city caught fire, hundreds of thousands of people would die or be rendered homeless. The fire service would just have to wait for the blaze to burn itself out.

"I can't see what's burning," Caleb added. "But Vesperian's mansion is over there."

"Yeah," Emily agreed.

Caleb was probably right. She had a feeling he *was* right. Vesperian's mansion was the most logical target for the mob, after all. The City Guard might not have had the manpower to protect the mansion. Or, perhaps, they would not have tried. Letting the mob run riot for a few hours might just burn off its energy before it started rampaging through the city at random. Who knew? Perhaps the guardsmen had studiously looked the other way. They'd lost money too.

She wondered, as they turned down a street, if Tyron and his mother had escaped. They'd been advised to flee, but *had* they? She wondered if *she* would have fled, if she'd found herself in such a trap. It *was* a trap, too. Tyron owed more money than he could possibly repay. The smart move would be to grab whatever he could and run for his life before the mob caught him.

Caleb muttered a curse under his breath as they turned a corner. A nasty-looking crowd had gathered outside a closed bar, yelling loudly for the bartender to come out and start pouring the booze. Emily didn't blame the bartender for not showing, not when the crowd looked disinclined to pay for the drinks. A number were already drunk, singing tunelessly as they poured more and more beer down their throats. Others picked up makeshift weapons and hacked at the door, trying to break it down. Emily hoped – prayed – that the bartender and his family didn't live above the bar. But, judging from the other bars she'd seen, she suspected it was a forlorn hope. The bartender wouldn't be able to afford lodging away from his bar.

The crowd rippled. "A whore," someone shouted. "A whore!"

Emily felt a flicker of panic as the crowd surged towards her. They didn't know who she was, part of her mind noted; they certainly didn't care. They'd just seen a young woman with only one protector. They thought they could just brush Caleb aside and do whatever they liked to her...

She stepped forward, casting a spell. The magic billowed around her, then lashed out, picking up the crowd and throwing them down the street. She felt a pang of guilt as some of them landed badly, breaking bones; she forced the guilt away, reminding herself that the crowd wouldn't have hesitated to gang-rape her, then beat her to death. And they would have killed Caleb too...

The magic grew stronger, slamming into the stunned crowd. How *dare* they? How *dare* they? A mundane woman wouldn't have stood a chance if they'd caught her, no matter who or what she was. Emily felt her anger grow stronger, felt the ground shaking under her feet…

Caleb caught her arm. "You'll bring down the whole street. You have to stop!"

Emily rounded on him, then caught herself as she controlled her rage. She'd nearly lost control. The magic faded, slowly. A roof tile fell to the ground with a clatter. Further down the street, she thought she heard something shatter into a million pieces. The remainder of the crowd – those who could still walk – ran for their lives. Emily couldn't help feeling, with a flicker of grim satisfaction, that they weren't drunk *now*.

She walked onwards, looking down at the moaning bodies. No one had died, as far as she could tell, but a number definitely had broken bones. Their blood looked black in the darkness…she wondered, numbly, if she should try to help them. But they'd intended to rape her, then rip her to shreds. And if they'd managed to catch a defenseless victim, they would have done just that. She told herself, firmly, that she shouldn't feel sorry for them.

Caleb said nothing as they reached the end of the street and hurried on, leaving the bodies behind. Sorcerers Row came into view a moment later, guarded by strong wards and a team of patrolling magicians…although it didn't look as though the community was in any danger. Emily wasn't particularly surprised. If she'd been able to flatten a crowd of rioters with a single spell, more experienced magicians would be able to do a great deal more damage to anyone stupid enough to attack them. Caleb spoke briefly to the sorcerer on duty at the corner, then waved Emily down the street. There were so many wards drifting through the air that Emily suspected some of them were actually weakening the others.

"No one trusts his closest neighbors to ward his house," Caleb muttered, when she mentioned it. "Too much espionage amongst magic users."

He tapped on the door, which opened. Karan stood just inside, holding a silver knife in one hand and a spell in the other. Frieda stood behind her, looking bored. She hurried forward as Emily entered and gave her a tight hug, then released her a moment later. Emily undid her cloak, placed it on the hanger and followed Frieda into the living room. Croce sat at the table, writing in a journal. There was no sign of anyone else.

"Marian hasn't come home," Karan said to Caleb. "Mum and Dad haven't returned, either."

"Dad's got a new job." Caleb looked up, sharply. "Where did Marian go?"

"I don't know," Karan said. "She said she was going to visit Lepta."

"She couldn't stay there after sunset," Caleb said. He sounded alarmed. "Take care of Emily, please. I'll go look for her."

Emily glanced up at him. Her head was still throbbing. "Do you want me to come with you?"

"You need your rest," Caleb said, shortly. He pulled his cloak over his head. "She's just down the road. I'll be quicker on my own."

"Okay," Emily said, torn between annoyance and understanding. She knew Caleb meant well, but she didn't want him to go out alone. Sorcerers Row would be safe enough, she was sure, yet…"I'll be here."

"Don't go up to Starry Light," Karan said. "Vesperian's mansion is on fire."

Emily looked at her. "How do you know?"

"I saw the flames from my window," Karan said. "The entire building is on fire."

"Someone probably used a burning spell," Croce commented. His voice was rough, as if he was as tired as Emily herself. "The flames looked impossible to quench without powerful magic, but they don't seem to have spread beyond the mansion or its grounds."

"Be careful, Caleb," Karan said. "There are riots on the streets."

"We know," Caleb said. He snorted, rudely. "I don't *think* she'll have gone outside Sorcerers Row"

He shook his head. "Why did you even let her go?"

"It's just down the street," Karan whined. "You know what she's like when she really wants something."

"You should have stuck her feet to the floor or sealed the wards," Caleb said, rubbing his forehead. "This isn't the time for a temper tantrum."

"She's not had a good time of it," Karan said. "You've been away…"

"So have you," Caleb snapped back.

He caught himself with an effort. "I'll be back soon, hopefully with her," he said. "If Mum comes back, let her know where I've gone."

If, Emily thought. *The council might have found something else for her to do.*

She saw the worry on Caleb's face and silently forgave him. His family was important to him, even though she knew he sometimes wondered how he and his siblings could come from the same parents. They were different in so many ways. But Caleb would fight for them, if necessary, and they would do the same for him. She couldn't help feeling a flicker of envy as Caleb turned and hurried to the door. The thought of having siblings who loved her…

Karan passed her a mug of hot chocolate, then left the room. Croce looked at Emily and Frieda for a long moment, before following his sister. Emily's tired mind wondered if it was appropriate for Croce to share a room with two unmarried girls, even though one of them was courting his older brother. Who knew how his parents would react?

Poorly, she thought, as she sipped the drink. *Croce and Frieda are both of marriageable age.*

"It's been a long day," Frieda said. She sounded tired – and sullen. "What happened to you?"

"You can come help with the accounts if you like," Emily said, feeling another stab of tired guilt. Frieda had been trapped in the house all day, unless she'd decided to sneak out despite the chaos on the street. She did have homework to do, but that wouldn't keep her occupied indefinitely. "Right now, my head feels like there's a troll living in it."

"Ouch." Frieda reached out and touched Emily's hand. "Is it going to be bad?"

"Very bad." Emily rubbed her eyes. "The streets are on edge…noon tomorrow, when the bills come due, there isn't going to be any money to pay. And then all hell will break loose."

Frieda gave her a searching look. "Should we leave?"

Emily frowned, honestly unsure. She'd promised General Pollack she would stay until the mourning period was completed, but she had no idea what had happened to the coffin, let alone the farewell ceremony. Sooner or later, she'd either have to go back to Whitehall or resign herself to repeating Fifth Year. And she didn't think there was anything she could do to help Beneficence. There were no necromancers to kill, no dark wizards to catch…all she could do was watch helplessly as vast sums of money evaporated.

She rubbed her forehead. She didn't have the money to buy back the notes at face value. She didn't know anyone, save for King Randor, who *did*. And his assistance would come with strings attached. Beneficence might prefer being broke to bending their knee to a king.

Which won't help anyone who's starving, she thought, coldly. *They'll be too hungry to care who's in charge.*

Frieda nudged her. "Emily?"

Emily jumped. She'd nearly drifted off.

"Emily." Frieda touched Emily's hand, again. "Should we leave?"

"Not yet," Emily said. She didn't want to leave Caleb – and she knew he wouldn't leave, not until his family was safe. And she knew neither Sienna nor General Pollack would turn their backs on their city. "I promised I'd stay until Casper was buried."

"And I promised I'd stay with you." Frieda squeezed Emily's hand. "And I think you'd better go to bed."

"Thanks." Emily yawned, covering her mouth hastily. First Harriman, now Caleb and Frieda. "Why does everyone want me to get some rest?"

"Because you need it," Frieda said. She helped Emily to her feet. "And because tomorrow might be a better day."

Emily shook her head. She knew that wasn't going to be true.

Chapter Twenty-One

Emily could hear Sienna's voice echoing up the stairs as she dressed and then led Frieda down to breakfast. Marian was in trouble, judging by the racket. It sounded as though Caleb *hadn't* managed to find her last night…Emily searched her memory, but she couldn't recall hearing Caleb coming back to the house. Had he spent all night looking for his sister? She hoped he'd managed to get some rest too.

"You're nowhere near old enough to be wandering the streets in the dark." Sienna was glaring at her daughter as Emily entered, her anger matched by her obvious fear for Marian's safety. "And the streets are *very* unsafe…"

"I didn't go out of Sorcerers Row," Marian snapped back. She looked, just for a moment, like a younger version of her mother. "Mother, I was perfectly safe!"

"Fifty people were killed last night — and that's just the ones we know about," Sienna said. "I can't even guess at how many were injured or raped or…"

She slammed her hand down on the table. "I gave you specific instructions to stay in the house. Why didn't you listen to me?"

"I was safe," Marian insisted. "I'm not a child!"

"You *are* a child," Sienna said. "You are too young to learn magic, too young to get married, too young to be on the streets on your own! And you are too young to decide for yourself what orders can be safely ignored, and…"

Marian glared at her mother, then switched her glare to Emily. "I…"

Her face flushed, brightly. She'd been so angry that she hadn't even noticed Emily and Frieda entering the room. Abruptly, she pushed past them and stormed out, her footsteps echoing as she stomped up the stairs. Sienna moved to follow her, then stopped herself. Emily did her best to avoid the older woman's eyes, wishing she'd thought to stay in her bedroom. She'd never enjoyed being told off in front of the entire class, and it had to be a good deal worse in one's home.

"I apologize for my daughter, Emily," Sienna said, finally. She sounded as though she was trying to keep her temper in check. "Rest assured, she will be suitably punished."

"She's under a lot of stress," Emily said, trying to be kind. Marian had lost a brother. "I…"

"Her conduct is inexcusable," Sienna said. "Caleb had to spend hours looking for her."

Her face darkened as she motioned for Emily and Frieda to sit. Karan entered a moment later, carrying two plates of scrambled eggs and bread. She looked weepy, suggesting Sienna had already told her off for letting her younger sister leave the house. Emily didn't blame Sienna for being angry, but…she shook her head, inwardly. At least Sienna gave a damn about her children. *Emily's* mother hadn't cared about anything but the next bottle of cheap wine.

"The Guild Council has decided that there will be a meeting at noon," Sienna said, as Emily tucked into the food. "Apparently, Clerk Harriman will be presenting his findings. I've taken the liberty of arranging places for us."

"Thank you," Emily said.

"Karan, Croce and Marian will remain here," Sienna added. She looked older, just for a second. "The mob burnt down Vesperian's mansion last night."

"I heard," Emily said. "Was anyone hurt?"

"No." Sienna sat down, resting her fingers on the table. "The servants managed to get out before the blaze consumed them."

There was a pause. "He didn't even *own* it," she added. "The poor bastard who *did* own it will now have to rebuild the mansion or surrender the land back to the council. I don't know if he can *afford* to rebuild it."

Caleb entered the room before Emily could think of a reply. She looked up and frowned in concern. Caleb looked…tired, dark rings clearly visible around his eyes. He held himself as if the only thing keeping him upright was sheer force of will; his clothes looked as if he'd slept in them. Emily opened her mouth to tell him to go back to bed, then reminded herself – sharply – that she wasn't his mother. Sienna would tell him to get some rest if necessary.

"Get a drink, then a shower," Sienna ordered, curtly. She glanced at the clock. "We'll be leaving in an hour."

Emily met Caleb's eyes. "Are you all right?"

"I only had a couple of hours to sleep," Caleb said. "I'll be fine. The little brat led me quite a dance."

"I'll show you how to use the tracking spell." Sienna rose, looking regretful. "And I also need to…*discuss*…matters with her."

Caleb nodded. "Did father come home?"

"He's still with the City Guard." Sienna sounded as though she couldn't care less, but Emily caught a hint of worry in her eyes. General Pollack was a brave man, yet he had no magic to protect himself. A dozen rioters could beat him to death if they wished. "I dare say we won't be seeing much of him until the crisis is over."

Her eyes moved to Karan. "See to it that neither of your siblings leave the house until we return. And if they won't stay still, use magic."

Karan looked down at the table. "Yes, mother."

Emily watched Sienna go, feeling a stab of sympathy for Marian. Sienna didn't seem the type of person to bother trying to find out *why* her daughter was so upset. And yet, she didn't blame Sienna for being concerned – and angry -- that her youngest daughter had deliberately put herself in danger. The rioters who'd attacked her on the streets would have no trouble tearing Marian to pieces, if they'd caught her instead.

"Change into trousers," Caleb advised, when they'd finished their breakfast. "You might have to run."

"Good thinking," Frieda said. Emily shot her a sharp glance. "Or we could just teleport home."

Caleb looked back at her, evenly. "Can *you* teleport?"

"Emily can," Frieda said.

"Then you'd better be prepared to run." Caleb sounded as though he was trying – hard – to keep himself under control. "Because, you know, you might get separated in the crowd."

He cleared his throat. "Emily, you *can't* teleport into Sorcerers Row," he said. "If you have to teleport out, aim for somewhere on the far side of the river."

Emily nodded. There were enough wards surrounding the house to make teleporting extremely dangerous, if not fatal. She was fairly sure it *would* be fatal. Lady Barb and Void had warned her that teleport spells were easy to disrupt, even by low-power magicians. A lucky magician might *just* realize the danger in time to abort, but the timing would have to be terrifyingly precise. She doubted she could handle it.

"I'll be careful," she promised. "What happened last night?"

"She wasn't with her friend," Caleb said, flatly. "I don't know *where* she was."

"Ouch," Emily said. Alba had sneaked out too, she recalled. But Marian was too young for a boyfriend, wasn't she? "Is she going to be all right?"

"Probably." Caleb smiled, humorlessly. "At her age, getting grounded is a fate worse than death."

Emily nodded as they hurried back up the stairs to change. Marian didn't have a computer, let alone the internet; she didn't even have television or a radio. Being locked in the house would probably feel like going to prison. There were books, of course, but Emily suspected Sienna would confiscate any novels Marian owned. By the end of the day, Marian might be begging for something – anything – to do. Maybe her sister would put her to work cleaning the house. God alone knew what had happened to the maid.

She changed into her borrowed trousers and a shirt, then hurried downstairs. Sienna stood at the door, speaking to a young man Emily didn't recognize. He nodded politely to her, then hurried away as Caleb and Frieda joined them. Caleb had changed, but he still looked tired and wan. Frieda looked surprisingly neat in a black shirt and trousers. Sienna flickered her eyes over the shirt – a size or two too tight, Emily noted – and then looked away. Emily was silently glad *her* shirt wasn't so daring.

"The meeting will be held in the Square." Sienna waved a hand in the air, adjusting the wards before she opened the door. "We have to hurry."

Emily took a breath as they stepped into the morning air. A faint taste of ashes hung over the city; glancing north, she saw a plume of smoke rising into the air. Vesperian's mansion was still burning, then. She wondered, absently, what spells had been used to make the blaze impossible to subdue. There were several that needed specific countermeasures to stop, if she recalled correctly. Or maybe the firemen had lost money too and simply decided to let the building burn to the ground.

The streets were crowded with hundreds of people making their way towards the Guildhall, some carrying weapons and wearing armor. Emily couldn't help staring at a man who carried a sword almost as big as himself, wondering how he managed to swing the blade. Someone had probably charmed it, she decided. Sergeant Miles had taught her a great deal about charmed weapons, although he'd always been careful to point out that a charmed blade didn't make the bearer invincible. A blade could be charmed to cut through anything, or weigh as much as a feather, but a crafty magician could always undo the spell at the worst possible time.

"Too many people on the street," Frieda muttered, as they turned into the square. "Is the entire city here?"

"No." Caleb glanced from side to side, his eyes grim. "But it will certainly feel that way."

Emily nodded. The square – just in front of the Guildhall – was crammed with people, from wealthy merchants, industrialists, and priests in fine robes to commoners wearing clothes that had clearly been handed down from generation to generation. Many of the latter carried pieces of paper bearing the stylized 'V' – their notes, Emily realized. Others held weapons or muttered angrily to their neighbors as rumors sped through the crowd at terrifying speed. She couldn't recall seeing commoners carrying so many weapons before, but Beneficence wasn't Zangaria. Anyone who wasn't actually a slave could carry a sword, if he could afford it.

"That's Speaker Janus," Caleb said, as Sienna led them towards the small gathering of dignitaries outside the Guildhall. "He's talking to father."

Emily followed his gaze. A tall, thin man, with dark hair and a goatee that reminded her of Disney's Jafar, stood next to General Pollack, speaking to him. The red robe he wore was identical to the robes worn by his followers, save for the gold trim around the hood. Emily glanced around, noting that there were nearly thirty Hands of Justice within eyeshot and probably many more out of sight. She couldn't help thinking that they were waiting for something. But what?

"Lady Emily," a voice said. She turned to see Harriman, wearing a grey suit that matched his personality. "I trust you slept well?"

"Well enough," Emily lied.

"Good, good," Harriman said. She thought she heard...*fear*...in his voice as he held up a set of papers. "I have to speak to the crowd, once the Grand Guildmaster has made his speech."

Emily winced in sympathy. She disliked the idea of speaking in front of a crowd too, even when the crowd wasn't angry. Harriman might put the mob to sleep, if he recited facts and figures at them, but they'd wake up angry. She silently prepared a number of spells as a single trumpet blew, bringing silence in its wake. The meeting was about to begin. She reached for Caleb's hand and held it, tightly, as Grand Guildmaster Jalil took the stand.

"Citizens," he said, calmly. His voice was boosted by a spell, ensuring everyone could hear. "Our city stands tall against the waves, our city..."

"Get to the money," someone shouted. Others took up the cry. "Get to the money!"

"He owes me," someone else shouted. "Where's the money?"

"Hecklers," Sienna muttered. She sounded troubled. "*Paid* hecklers."

Jalil cleared his throat. "We have faced many crises in our time," he added, grimly continuing with his speech. Emily wasn't sure if he was being brave or stupid. "And yet, we have overcome them all..."

"Where's my money?" a heckler shouted. "He stole it all!"

The crowd roared with anger. Emily glanced from side to side, realizing there were too many people crammed into the square for the guards to restore order. The hecklers continued to shout, their taunts boosted by their own magic. Jalil, not used to such blatant disrespect, paled rapidly. Pieces of rotten fruit began to fly through the air...

"Give us back our money," a voice shouted. Or was it many voices? "Give us back our money!"

Jalil steadied himself. "Clerk Harriman has inspected the accounts," he said, holding onto the podium as though it were a life preserver. Surprisingly, the roar quietened. And yet...odd flickers of magic were running through the air. "He will now present his findings."

Caleb squeezed Emily's hand as Harriman walked forward and took the podium. He shook like a leaf. Emily silently prayed for him as she peered around the square. General Pollack muttered orders to a messenger; beside him, Janus watched Harriman, a faint smile flittering over his face. Their eyes met, just for a second. Emily thought she sensed...*something*...looking back at her through Janus's eyes.

"Ah...my team has gone through the first set of accounts." Harriman looked down at his set of notes. Emily wondered if he'd planned a long speech before seeing the angry crowd. "We have determined that the Vesperian Track – and Vesperian Industries – has debts of roughly seventy-five thousand crowns..."

The crowd seemed too stunned to respond. It was a figure so immense as to be beyond easy comprehension. On Earth, it would have been billions – perhaps trillions – of dollars, enough money to buy or run a country. And it existed – it *had* existed – as nothing more than pieces of paper. Vesperian hadn't had a hope of paying off his debts.

And the total keeps going up, Emily thought. *When will it stop?*

Harriman paused. "The estate's total assets are worth no more than *twelve* thousand crowns," he added, after a moment. Clearly, Emily noted, he'd gone back to the account books in the morning. She wasn't sure if she should salute his dedication or reprimand him for making matters worse. "This is, in many ways, a best-case estimate. The sellable value of his goods may be much lower..."

"I want my money back," someone shouted. Again, others took up the cry. Harriman stood at the podium and waited, holding himself upright through sheer bloody-minded determination. Emily felt a flicker of admiration as the noise grew louder. "I want my money!"

"We are currently assessing the precise debts owed by the estate to his creditors," Harriman continued. "Once we have a clear picture..."

"Theft," a heckler shouted. "I paid a hundred crowns to that bastard!"

"A thousand," someone else shouted. "I want my money!"

Emily glanced at Caleb. He looked pale. The crowd moved, a handful of members hurrying off while others started towards the podium. Harriman still stood there, one hand crumpling his papers. He knew, as well as she did, that there was no hope of recouping enough money to pay *all* the investors. The rich men – the industrialists – would be paid first. There wouldn't be enough left for the others...

...And, judging by the growing anger running through the crowd, the realization was finally sinking in.

"I want my money back," a woman yelled. "I have debts!"

"Give me my money," a man added. Emily ducked as pieces of rotting fruit started to shower down on the podium. She felt panic howling at the back of her mind. A man could fall in the crowd and be trampled to death before anyone realized he was in trouble. "Give me the money!"

Jalil hurried forward. "Be calm," he pleaded. "We'll give you the money."

The crowd roared. Emily winced as she pulled back, grabbing hold of Frieda's arm and pulling her back too. It had been *precisely* the wrong thing to say. The crowd was a wild animal now, scared of the future and whipped up by hecklers...someone had put the hecklers there, she thought. She looked around, desperately. Janus walked calmly towards the podium, a faint smirk clearly visible on his face. There was no sign of General Pollack...

...Or Harman.

"Vesperian's goods will be sold to buy back the notes," Jalil insisted. It had no effect. Of course it didn't – Harriman had told the crowd that Vesperian's total assets couldn't be sold for more than a fraction of the debt. "I..."

"You have led this city astray for far too long," a new voice said. Janus stood by the podium, looking as calm and composed as a man ordering dinner. There was a sense of *righteousness* around him that transcended the chaos. "You have led your people into sin and depravity. No more."

Silence fell like a hammer blow. The crowd milled uneasily, angry yet unwilling to challenge the priest. It was a long, chilling moment before Janus spoke again.

"This is the time of Justice."

And then Emily sensed the presence.

Chapter Twenty-Two

SHE TURNED, SLOWLY.

The presence was overwhelmingly powerful. It was like staring into a bright light, yet being unable to look away. The...*entity*...stood at the edge of the square, its sheer power so staggering that her knees threatened to buckle. It thrust itself into her awareness, existing on multiple levels at once...she thought, suddenly, of the nexus points. The entity wasn't even doing it deliberately, part of her mind noted. It was so powerful she couldn't help looking at it.

Its power thrummed on the air, deafening her. She wanted to kneel, to prostrate herself before its immensity. It was so *real* that she felt like an illusion, like something that didn't quite exist. No wonder Alba had been so badly shocked when she'd seen the entity; no *wonder* she'd termed it a god. And yet, something kept Emily from surrendering her will completely. It *could be* a trick.

She forced herself to take a mental step back, then another. The entity stood there, her senses swimming as she tried to study it. It was huge, infinitely large, so enormous its head touched the sky...she tried to comprehend how it could be both utterly immense and yet standing calmly in the square. Her head spun as she pulled back again, glancing from side to side. A good third of the crowd had fallen to the ground, prostrating themselves in front of the entity. Others cowered or ran in all directions...

It's a lie, she thought, as she touched her chest. The rune wasn't burning, which meant...what? No subtle magic? A compulsion on such a scale wasn't impossible, if one had enough power. But there was no nexus point in the city, was there? No one could have kept a nexus point hidden, not when anyone with a hint of magic could detect it. *It has to be a lie.*

Caleb coughed, tugging at her arm. Emily realized, dully, that her hand was throbbing in pain. Caleb had squeezed her tightly enough to hurt. And yet, she'd barely noticed – no, she *hadn't* noticed. She pulled her hand free, then glanced at Frieda. Her friend was wavering, looking as if she might fall to the ground at any moment. Emily caught her shoulder and yanked her back, hoping to break the connection. Frieda jumped, then looked away from the entity.

"I AM JUSTICE," the entity said. There was so much power in its voice – so much *compulsion* – that it was hard, very hard, to doubt it. It spoke as if it, and it alone, possessed the truth. "I HAVE BEEN SUMMONED TO TEND TO MY CAUSE."

The power surged, suddenly, as the entity raised its hand. A bolt of lightning flashed from its fingertips, reaching out to strike Jalil. The older man screamed in pain as his entire body blazed white, then turned to stone. Emily knew, on a level that could not be denied, that he'd died...and that he'd died in agony. The knowledge beat on the air like a giant heartbeat, impressing itself into her soul. She looked around as the lightning flashed again, seeking out Guildmaster Merriam. Merriam screamed and ran, but the lightning followed him. There was something cruel in the spell, Emily thought dully. It moved in slow motion, just slowly enough to give the impression that Merriam might manage to escape. But it was a lie...

She looked away, shielding her eyes, as Merriam died.

Too much power, she thought, numbly. It hurt to even *try* to probe it with her senses, but she had to try. Even a protected nexus point didn't have so much calculated malice woven into its very nature. The entity was designed to hurt anyone who tried to analyze it. She found her head starting to hurt – again – as she tried to study the power. *There's too much power being thrown around too freely.*

Her mind raced as Sienna pulled her back, shouting for her husband. A necromancer would have such power, but almost no control. Was she looking at a necromancer wrapped in an overpowered glamour? It didn't seem possible. A necromancer would have slaughtered the entire crowd by now, instead of merely making examples out of a couple of guilty parties. She glanced back at the entity, trying to focus on how it channeled and used power. But it was too powerful for her to track the ebb and flow of magic surrounding it...

"THIS CITY WILL COME TO KNOW THE WAY," the entity boomed. Its presence seemed to grow stronger, but this time Emily was ready for it. "THE SINNERS WILL BE PURGED. A DAY OF PEACE WILL RISE."

Emily sensed another surge of magic and turned her head. A set of sorcerers were screaming defiance, hurling dozens of spells at the entity. Justice made no attempt to move, let alone to defend itself. The spells struck its exterior and vanished, snapping out of existence as if they'd struck a brick wall. And yet...Emily reached out again, frowning as she watched the second set of spells strike home. The magic was unravelling, the *mana* breaking down and falling towards the entity...

They're feeding it, she realized.

"JUSTICE WILL BE DONE."

The three sorcerers suddenly blazed with white light. When it faded, three more statues stood in the center of the square. The crowd broke, half falling on their knees, the other half running in all directions. Fistfights broke out as they struggled to get out of the square before it was too late, sorcerers and magic-users panicking and lashing out with their powers as they ran. Hundreds of people were going to die, Emily realized dully, trampled to death when they fell to the ground. Justice – whatever it actually was – would be responsible for them all...

She felt the *presence* ebb, just a little, and turned to look. Justice seemed smaller somehow, yet still impressive. His face was indistinct, but rigid; she saw flashes of his features, rather than a complete picture. A black beard, flashing black eyes, a stern chin, a muscular body...she thought he was garbed, but his clothes refused to come into focus. She couldn't help thinking of Judge Dredd or – perhaps – an Old Testament prophet, coming home to lay down the law. There was a solidity about him that caught her attention, something that convinced her she wasn't looking at an illusion...

"This way," Sienna snapped.

Emily caught sight of Janus as Sienna led the way towards the Guildhall itself. The Speaker stood beside the podium, his hands clasped behind his back as he watched the carnage. He looked at Emily, just for a moment, and nodded politely to her. There was an oddly beneficent look on his face that was more terrifying, somehow, than any smirk or scream of rage.

He did this, Emily thought. The screams were growing louder. *He knew it would happen.*

She saw Harriman, lying on the ground near the doors. Blood poured from a nasty gash on his forehead. She hurried over to him, but it was too late. He made a gurgling sound, then died in her arms. She stared down at him for a long moment, knowing that she didn't have the time to try to get his body out of the square. He'd deserved better than to die in such a way…she took his papers, then stood. Janus had turned back to look at her.

Magic boiled around her fingertips, demanding release as he watched her through cold, dark eyes. She could kill him right now, she could end it…but she knew it wouldn't be enough to save the city. Justice's mere presence would change everything, even if Janus died. They had to find a way to stop something that might as well be a god…

"Emily!" Caleb shouted.

Emily turned to run. She felt tired, her legs starting to hurt…she felt almost as if she were swimming through molasses. It felt like a nightmare when she couldn't move, no matter how much she tried…she knew, all too well, that *something* was coming up behind her. She could feel the presence growing stronger, feel her knees threatening to bend…her body wanted to turn, to surrender…she raised her hand, somehow, and slapped her face. The pain gave her just enough focus to break free and run.

"We have to get out the rear," Sienna snapped. "Hurry!"

She tossed a spell at the doors as soon as they were inside the building, slamming them closed. A second spell locked them, although Emily suspected it wouldn't last more than a few seconds. Justice had more than enough power to reduce the entire building to dust, if it wanted. She heard the sound of falling masonry in the distance as the ground shook…she wondered, as she followed Sienna and the others through a maze of ornate corridors, if the island was tectonically stable. A major earthquake might do real damage…

Or a volcano, she thought. There were stories about magicians who'd triggered volcanoes, although most of them were cautionary tales. *What if the city was built on a dead volcano?*

The building shook, again. A large painting of a stern-looking guildmaster fell from the wall and crashed to the floor. Others followed, forcing them to jump. A lantern dropped from a great height and smashed against a tapestry, starting a fire. Sienna snapped a spell at it, quenching the flames in a heartbeat, but it was only a matter of time until something else caught fire. The shaking was growing worse.

"ALL WILL BE JUDGED," Justice said. The voice was so *near* that Emily glanced over her shoulder, half-expecting to see the entity right behind her. Given its power, she suspected the entire city could hear it. "YOU WILL ALL COME TO ME IN TIME."

Sienna threw the back door open. A small group of Hands of Justice stood behind the Guildhall, handing out weapons. Sienna didn't hesitate. She raised a hand and threw a spell at them, knocking them to the ground. Emily's hair stood on end as she sensed the residues. It was a killing spell, but not one she knew. Whatever it was, she thought as she watched Frieda scoop up a short sword, the Hands hadn't stood a chance.

"Stop," a voice shouted. A spell flashed over their heads. "Stop and be judged!"

Emily turned. A dozen more Hands ran towards them. One of them waved a wand in the air, threateningly. The others carried swords and staffs...the latter, perhaps, charged with magic. She noticed, as she readied a spell of her own, that they wore different insignia over their chests. It looked like a clenched fist...

"No," Sienna said.

She threw a spell at the leader, knocking him back. Emily and Caleb threw fireballs too, then force punches; Frieda cast a spell of her own, a lightning storm that lashed out at everyone within range. The Hands scattered, then regrouped. Sienna struck them with another force punch, chanting words under her breath. The small group was flung in all directions with terrifying force.

"ALL WILL BE JUDGED," Justice said.

"Run," Sienna ordered.

Emily turned and ran for her life, followed by Frieda and Caleb. She was vaguely aware of Sienna doing...*something* before she ran too, something that sent more shivers down her spine as the spell detonated. The screams behind her cut off abruptly as Sienna joined them, pounding down the street. Thankfully, the streets were largely empty. Emily didn't want to *think* about what that meant for the crowd left in the square.

"Janus knew." Emily reached out with her senses. Justice was easy to sense, just like a nexus point; a flickering awareness of *presence* that seemed to ebb and flow around the center of the city. And yet...there was something odd about it, something that nagged at the back of her mind. What was it? "He knew something was going to happen..."

"Less talking, more running." Sienna didn't even sound winded. "We have to get back home before anything else."

Emily nodded. Sienna was right. And yet...she couldn't keep herself from thinking. Janus had known, right from the start, that something would happen. No, perhaps it was worse. Vesperian's death hadn't started the whole nightmare, making it impossible for the city's population to delude themselves any longer. It had only made matters worse...

If Janus knew the whole scheme was about to collapse, she thought as she forced herself to run faster, *he might have tried to take advantage of it. And yet...*

"Stop," a voice bellowed.

Sienna swore out loud as they came face-to-face with another group of men. They carried staffs and wore silver armor, covered in runes…Emily gritted her teeth, remembering the first time she'd faced men in protective armor. They could be beaten, she knew, but it took time. Or she could use a larger spell…

"Emily," Frieda said. "Watch me."

Emily had only a second to realize what Frieda intended to do before it was too late. Her body seemed to blur as she threw herself at the Hands, her sword flashing like lightning in the bright sunlight. She moved too fast to be seen clearly, slashing out at the men before they could react. Emily gritted her teeth as she saw five men fall in less than thirty seconds, knowing that Frieda would pay a high price for her bravery. The Berserker spell was too dangerous to use for long. Emily had never dared use it since her first year at Whitehall.

A man broke free and hurled himself at Sienna. She darted to one side, yanking a virgin dagger out of nowhere and inserting it into his eye. He yelped and dropped to the ground, dead. Emily reached for her own magic as another man came at her, only to have Caleb slam a force punch into his chest. The sheer force of the impact picked the man up and blasted him into a building hard enough to leave a mark. He slumped to the ground, his legs twisted out of shape. He might never walk again.

"Now," Sienna said.

Emily looked up, then ran forward. Frieda had killed all of her enemies, but now she twitched helplessly as the spell ran its course. Emily readied a cancellation spell as she reached Frieda, casting the spell a moment before Frieda lunged at her, too far gone to tell the difference between a friend and an enemy. Emily felt a flash of pure horror, then grunted in pain as Frieda bowled her over, landing hard on the solid pavement. Frieda drew back a fist, then stopped a moment before she slammed it into Emily's throat…

"Emily," Frieda said. "I…"

She sagged, nearly falling on top of Emily. Sienna helped Frieda to her feet, then picked her up and slung her over her shoulder in a fireman's carry. Frieda looked as though she was struggling to stay awake, even though her body must be screaming for rest. Berserker drained the caster completely unless it was stopped.

"Take the armor," Sienna ordered. "Hurry."

Emily glanced in both directions, then hastily started to undo the first set of armor. Warding spells snapped at her fingertips, but they were already fading. It might be hard, she thought, to re-enchant the armor. But it might come in handy for something…she collected three sets of intact breastplates, then stood. Caleb had removed four sets himself. She looked down at the bodies for a moment, wondering what they'd been thinking when they'd joined the Hands, before following Sienna down the road. The noise behind them grew louder…

I can sense the entity, she thought. She didn't want to label it with a name, even in the privacy of her own mind. *And so can everyone else.*

She sagged in relief as they finally reached Sorcerers Row, passing through a tangled network of wards guarded by a dozen sorcerers. Sienna slowed to talk to one of them, explaining what had happened in a hushed voice. The sorcerers didn't look as though they believed her, which didn't come as a complete surprise. Emily had *seen* the entity firsthand and part of *her* mind refused to believe it.

You've seen demons, her own thoughts reminded her. *Why not a god?*

"Come inside," Sienna said.

Emily looked back towards the center of town. More smoke was rising, suggesting...what? That the Guildhall had caught fire? Or that other buildings were burning too? Or...she could still sense the presence, even at a distance. It pervaded her thoughts, an itch she couldn't scratch, taunting her with its sheer presence. The sensation grew stronger the more she looked, drawing her back...she shook her head, pinching herself. God alone knew what would happen when they slept.

We'll have to tune the wards to block it out, she thought. *If we can...*

"Emily," Caleb hissed.

General Pollack was still out there, somewhere. Emily hoped he was safe, but she knew he'd been in the midst of the crowd. What if he was dead? Or compelled to kneel before the entity and pledge himself to its service? What if...her heart twisted in pain at the thought of more misery being inflicted on Caleb and his family. They deserved a break, didn't they? They deserved a chance to heal from their earlier wounds...

She closed her eyes for a long moment, then turned and walked through the door. Behind her, Caleb slammed it shut.

Chapter Twenty-Three

IT WAS BLESSEDLY QUIET INSIDE THE HOUSE.

Emily allowed herself a sigh of naked relief as she felt the entity's presence fade from her mind. Whatever it was, the wards kept it out. Oddly, she found that reassuring. A *real* god would have no problems working through the wards. She sagged against the wall, trying to catch her breath. Her thoughts and impressions were hopelessly jumbled.

Karan appeared, popping out of a side door. "What happened?"

"Get some soup," Sienna ordered. She carried Frieda into the living room and placed her on the couch. "Now!"

Emily followed her into the room and sat on the chair, suddenly feeling exhausted. Her entire body felt drained. Alarmed, she tested her power reserves as Karan returned and discovered they were untouched. Resisting the entity's sheer presence had been enough to exhaust her. She rubbed her forehead, feeling yet another headache blooming to life. The entity hadn't been focused on her, and yet it had had an effect...

"Caleb, test the wards," Sienna snapped. "And then send Marian and Croce down here."

"Yes, mother," Caleb said.

Karan reappeared, carrying a bowl of thin soup. Sienna took it and started to feed Frieda, holding the spoon to her lips as if she were feeding a baby. Emily watched as Frieda sipped, wishing she could reach out and hold the younger girl. The Berserker spell had been stopped before it had drained Frieda completely, but it had still left her tired and worn. And yet, without it, they might not have reached home.

"Tired," Frieda said. "I..."

"Lie still," Sienna ordered. "You'll need to eat something more solid once you regain your strength."

Frieda looked at Emily, then relaxed. "What...what *was* it?"

"I wish I knew," Emily said. She could see a dozen ways to cast an illusion that would *look* like a god, particularly one designed to allow its target's perceptions to fill in the gaps, but the entity had clearly been far more substantial. And it had wielded magic. She had no doubt that Jalil and the others were dead. What could do *that?* "But it can't get to us in here."

"Yet." Sienna's voice was grim. "The wards are strong, but not unbreakable."

Marian came into the room, looking mutinous. "Mother, Karan..."

Her voice trailed off as she saw Frieda. "What happened?"

"Good question," Sienna said. "There was...*something*...at the square."

Caleb returned, followed by Croce. "The wards are fine, mother," Caleb said. "But there's an odd resonance that worries me. Someone might be probing the edge of our defenses."

"I'll take a look at it." Sienna helped Frieda sit upright, then passed her a piece of bread and butter. "Emily, make sure Frieda keeps eating. She's going to need to eat until she feels stuffed."

"I'm all right," Frieda said. "I…"

"Eat," Sienna said, firmly. "I've seen that spell kill people who didn't have someone looking after them already."

Marian cleared her throat. "Mother," she said, sounding scared. "What happened?"

"We saw an entity that claimed to be a god," Sienna said. She rose, allowing Emily to sit next to Frieda. "Caleb can fill you in. I have to check the wards."

Karan's voice rose. "Where's father?"

"I wish I knew," Sienna said.

"But you can find him," Marian said. "Can't you?"

"I don't have a tracking spell on him," Sienna said, sharply. "I don't know *what* happened to him."

She walked out of the room, closing the door firmly behind her.

Marian looked at Caleb. "What *happened?*"

Emily forced herself to concentrate on Frieda as Caleb told the story. Frieda was growing stronger, thankfully, but she still looked weak. She would have to get some rest soon, Emily knew, yet she had to eat first. The Berserker spell would have drained her reserves to the limit. If she went to sleep without eating something, she might never wake up.

"Justice," Marian breathed, when Caleb finished. "It's *him.*"

"And father is still out there somewhere," Caleb said. "Where *is* he?"

Emily swallowed. General Pollack was tough, but he didn't – he couldn't – have any active defenses against outside influences. Given time, Emily knew, *she* could have twisted his mind into a pretzel. She had no doubt that Justice – whatever the entity actually was – could do the same. Hell, merely being in its presence for a few hours would probably be enough to wear down the strongest defenses. And then…

The general has a blood tie to his family, she thought. *The entity could find us…*

"You're the man of the house," Karan said. "Go find him."

"Casper would have gone by now," Marian added.

Caleb looked hesitant, glancing between Emily and his sisters. Emily understood, all too well. Caleb loved his father, wanted to save his father…but the streets were in chaos and the wards might not remain secure. Who knew *what* had happened to General Pollack? Finding him might prove impossible…

Or all too easy, her thoughts mocked her. *But we might not like what we found.*

"Dad is strong," Caleb said. "He could have escaped another way."

Emily winced. General Pollack had been far too close to Janus for her peace of mind. She had no way to know if Janus had magic, but the priest could have used a wand or simply knocked General Pollack on the head, if he'd wanted a prisoner. Or stuck a knife in his back when the entity first appeared. God knew everyone had been so focused on Justice that Janus could have done anything without anyone taking a moment's notice.

"You have a blood tie," Karan said, again. "You could find him…"

"I'll go," Marian said. "I've got a blood tie too."

Karan glared at her. "Do I have to stick your butt to the chair again?"

"You're too young," Caleb said. "You have to stay here."

"I'm not a child," Marian snapped.

Emily felt a stab of sympathy for Marian, even though she was being a brat. The youngest member of the family *had* to feel as though she had a lot to live up to. And yet…Caleb was right. Marian was too young to go out on the streets alone, particularly now. She might be caught and killed by a mob before she managed to escape.

"Yes, you are," Caleb said. "Marian…"

"You need to decide what to do," Frieda said, weakly.

Emily glanced at her in surprise. Frieda sounded…scornful.

"I don't *know* what to do," Caleb snapped.

"*Casper* would have known what to do," Marian said.

Shit, Emily thought. Caleb would *not* take that calmly.

"Casper is *dead*." Caleb's face reddened. "I don't even know what we're dealing with!"

"And you don't have time to work it out," Frieda said. She shot Caleb a nasty look. "You *always* hesitate. You don't have the nerve to…"

"Enough," Emily said, quietly. She knew Frieda was tired and stressed – they were *all* tired and stressed. But that didn't excuse her picking on Caleb. "Frieda, behave…"

"He *does* hesitate," Frieda insisted. "Emily…"

"Shut up," Caleb thundered. "I…"

The door opened. "I think you should both be quiet," Sienna said, stepping back into the room. "Karan, fetch us all some Kava – and some more stew and bread for Frieda."

"I don't need it," Frieda protested.

"Yes, you do," Sienna said. She looked at Caleb. "I couldn't locate the source of the resonance. That *alone* is worrying."

Emily nodded, slowly. If someone had been attempting to break down the wards – or study them, in hopes of finding a weak spot – there should have been a clear link between them and the wards. Sienna should have been able to locate the would-be burglar and fry him. But if the resonance *couldn't* be found…? Were the wards reacting to the entity's aura or…or were they being probed from a distance?

Which should be impossible, she thought. *But so is a god walking the world.*

She glanced up as she heard the front door rattle, readying a spell. Sienna and Caleb did the same, while Croce and Karan took up positions behind them. If someone broke through, somehow bypassing all the defenses, it would be the last thing he did. And then the door opened, revealing General Pollack. Emily couldn't help a surge of relief. He looked to have aged twenty years in the last couple of hours, but he was alive.

"*Dad*," Caleb said.

"Stay there." Sienna's voice was so cold it froze Caleb in his tracks. "Watch and wait."

General Pollack stopped, holding his hands in the air to prove they were empty. Sienna stalked towards him, the wards gathering around her. Emily sensed them probing General Pollack, confirming he was alive, unharmed and definitely *not* under outside control. Sienna relaxed, then kissed her husband with a passion that made Emily look away. It was suddenly easy to believe their marriage had been a love match.

"I'm glad to see you alive." Sienna relaxed, slightly, as she led her husband back into the living room. "What happened?"

"That...that...*thing*...was killing people," General Pollack said. He sounded as tired as Emily felt. "Most of the council...a dozen guardsmen...it recited their crimes and then turned them to stone. I...I had to stab myself with my knife just to break free and run."

Sienna laughed. "I always knew you'd make it."

"Thank you," General Pollack said.

Emily felt a flicker of wistful envy as Karan hugged her father tightly. It would have been nice to have a father she knew, a father she actually *loved*. Someone who had been there for her from the moment of her birth...she shook her head, telling herself that there was no way to change history. If she'd had a loving family, she might never have left Earth at all.

But my life would have been better there, she told herself. *And then...who knows?*

"We have a major problem," General Pollack said. "That...*thing*...is dangerously powerful."

"He's a *god*," Marian insisted. Her eyes were fever-bright. "He *is*."

"It can't be," Emily said. "If it was a *real* god, none of us would have escaped."

She sighed, wishing she felt better. "It's a trick of some kind. We have to figure out how it's done."

"Justice only has power over those who deserve punishment," Marian said. "Father doesn't *deserve* punishment."

Emily looked back at her. "Did Antony?"

"You don't know what he might have done in the dark," Marian pointed out. "He could have committed all sorts of crimes that were never revealed."

"And if that were true," Sienna said, "how many others also deserve punishment – and didn't get it?"

Emily thought as fast as she could. If Justice was all-powerful, they were doomed. *That* was beyond dispute. Resistance would be utterly futile. She could remember a couple of books and comics where all-powerful characters had been beaten, but most of them had only worked because the omnipotent enemy hadn't had brains to match his power. The real world was rarely so helpful.

And yet...

She'd never studied any of the local religions, but she'd always had the impression they talked about immensely powerful entities rather than all-powerful beings.

They were very much like the Norse Gods, if she recalled correctly. Thor and Loki were powerful, she knew, yet they could be beaten by mere humans. But then, they were really nothing more than supercharged humans. The Norse – and the Greeks, Romans and Celts – hadn't conceived of a single being who lived on a whole different scale, whose existence comprised the universe. The concept of *God* had come later.

The Norse Gods weren't all-seeing, she thought. *And that meant that they could be beaten.*

She wished, suddenly, that she'd spent more time reading about the myths. How much of what she knew came from the original legends, instead of the comics and movies? The movie versions of Odin, Thor and Loki might bear little resemblance to the older versions...

"He's a god," Marian said. "His motives might be beyond us!"

"He's slaughtered the council," General Pollack said. "I don't know if any of them survived."

"You might be the last," Sienna said, quietly.

"I was never on the council," General Pollack reminded her. "My appointment didn't come with a council seat."

"They deserved it," Marian said. "How many lives were blighted because the guildmasters ran the city to suit themselves?"

"The guildmasters weren't perfect," General Pollack said. "But there were worse criminals in the city."

"This looks very much like a coup," Sienna added. "Use Justice to slaughter the former government and cow resistance, while the new government is imposed."

"He's a god." Marian's eyes shone with tears. "And all of the stories agree that one day he will return!"

"They say that about *all* the gods," Sienna said. "Have you ever *seen* a god?"

"*You* have," Marian insisted. "Mother..."

"It's a trick," Emily said, quietly.

Marian rounded on her. "It's no trick!" she thundered. "Everyone *knew* he was coming back to judge the sinners! Everyone heard the stories! They just didn't want to believe it!"

"It has to be a trick," Emily said. "A *real* god would have overwhelmed all of us. A *real* god would be...would be convincing. We would know him the moment we laid eyes on him."

She took a breath. "Our wards and protections kept us from being overwhelmed. We could feel his presence right until the moment we stepped into the house. What sort of god is kept out by simple wards?"

"Everything he's done, so far, could have been done by magic," Sienna added. "And his targets were more than *just* random sinners."

Marian glared at her mother. "You *want* to believe that." She swung around to face Emily. "*You* want to believe that too!"

"I *do* believe it," Emily said. "I've met powerful creatures, seen powerful spells... there's no reason to assume that *this* entity is any different."

"Emily's right," Caleb said. He looked contemplative, as if his mind was occupied by some greater thought. "Given time, I could cast a series of spells that would have the same effect."

But probably not on such a scale, Emily thought. *The power requirements would be astronomical.*

She mulled it over and over in her mind, wishing she had a moment to sit down and work out the spells. Compelling people to drop to their knees – and surrender their free will – would require a focused spell. Doing it for a single person would be relatively straightforward, but doing it for hundreds – perhaps thousands – of people at once would be difficult. The entity was extremely powerful, whatever else it was. And it had done a great deal more than *merely* overwhelm the weaker minds.

Or the minds more inclined to believe it is a god, her thoughts reminded her. *I'm the only person on this world who knows about monotheistic religion.*

"Of course she's right," Marian snapped. "Lady Emily is *always* right. That's all we ever hear!"

She glared at Emily. "He was telling us all about how wonderful you are." She sneered. "He made you out to be a goddess, someone who could do no wrong. So sweet, so kind, so clever, so beautiful, so wonderful, so adorable, so…"

"That will do," Sienna said.

"Not *this* time." Marian jabbed a finger at Emily. "Casper died because of you!"

"*Marian*," Sienna snapped. "Be quiet!"

"I will not be silenced." Marian's voice trembled with rage. "Casper died because of you! Caleb is the Heir because of *you*! You killed Casper to make sure Caleb would become Heir!"

Her voice grew louder. "And you deny Justice because he will come for you!"

Emily stared at her in shock. It was hard to think of a response. She hadn't killed Casper. He'd accompanied her to Heart's Eye, knowing the risks…and even then, he'd been blindsided by the necromancer's secret weapon. *None* of them had known what to expect. How *could* they have? If anyone else had ever stumbled across the secret, they'd kept it to themselves.

Frieda broke the silence. "You little *bitch*!"

She lifted a hand, readying a spell. "I'll…"

"*Enough*," Sienna said. The anger in her voice would have stopped any sane man in his tracks. "Marian…"

"Casper is dead!" Tears ran down Marian's cheeks, her entire body shaking with rage. "And she's the only one who benefited!"

"Emily, take Frieda to the bedroom and make sure she gets some rest," Sienna ordered. "No magic, not until she's recovered fully. I'll talk to you later."

Her voice was calm, but there was an edge to it that made Emily shiver. Everyone was on edge, yet…she looked at Marian and recoiled at the naked hatred in the younger girl's eyes. She believed, truly believed, that Emily had deliberately led Casper to his death, clearing the way for Caleb to inherit. And yet…

She forced herself to move, helping Frieda to her feet. Marian stepped aside, moving with deliberate slowness even after her mother snapped at her. Raw magic crackled around her, a grim reminder that she would be going to school next year. Emily hoped, privately, that she didn't go to Whitehall. Thankfully, if she did, she'd be someone else's problem.

"That was uncalled for," General Pollack said, as Emily helped Frieda up the stairs. His voice was grim. "You know better."

"It had to be said." Marian's voice echoed upwards. She sounded much like her mother in that moment. "Casper would have lived if he hadn't been with her."

And that, Emily knew, was all too true.

Chapter Twenty-Four

"LITTLE BITCH," FRIEDA SPLUTTERED, AS THEY STUMBLED INTO THE BEDROOM. HER VOICE was tired, so tired that Emily suspected Frieda didn't know what she was saying. "I should turn her into a frog. Teach her a lesson. Show her..."

"It's all right," Emily said. She helped Frieda to the bed, then undid and removed her shoes before she lay down. "You need to sleep."

It wasn't all right, she knew, as she sat next to Frieda. Marian's accusation had *hurt*, badly. Her entire body shook as it sank in. Marian had accused her of practically murdering Casper to clear the way for Caleb to inherit. She couldn't really think that Emily had deliberately gotten Casper killed, could she? And yet, Marian hadn't been there. She didn't know the full details; no one did.

Marian's words echoed in her head. *And you deny Justice because he will come for you...*

She looked down at the wooden floorboards, then rested her head in her hands. The seeds of doubt had been sown. Whatever happened, Caleb and the rest of his family would wonder if Emily had been instrumental in Casper's death, if she'd calculated that marrying Caleb would bring her even more wealth and power. Why not? Fulvia had married into a magical family and turned it into her personal power base. Why couldn't Emily do the same?

I didn't kill him, she thought, feeling tears forming in her eyes. *I didn't mean to get him killed.*

She blinked the tears away, angrily. It had been a long day and...she looked out the window, noting that the sun hadn't even begun to sink towards the horizon. God alone knew what was going on out there, beyond the wards. Sienna had called it a coup, and Emily suspected she was right. Janus had used Justice to clear the way for his takeover, and that meant...

It has to be a trick of some kind, she told herself. *But what?*

She looked down at Frieda, sleeping peacefully. Her friend had risked her life to save them, yet she'd also snapped and snarled at Caleb...Emily knew she'd have to tell Frieda to apologize, when she woke up. They were *all* on edge, Frieda and Marian included, but that didn't excuse any of them. Justice might not have managed to worm his way into their minds, as far as she could tell, yet he'd definitely left his mark.

There was a faint tap on the door. Emily hesitated – it could be Marian – and then rose, opening the door and peering out. Caleb stood there, holding a broom in one hand and a mug of Kava in the other. It took Emily a second to realize he'd actually used the broom handle to knock on the door, just in case Sienna had booby-trapped it. There were so many wards protecting the house that it would be hard for anyone to pick out a specific spell.

"Emily," Caleb said. He looked relieved. "Is she awake?"

"She's sleeping," Emily said. She could hear the faint sounds of an argument echoing up the stairs. "Caleb, I..."

"Mother wants me to sit on the roof," Caleb said. "Do you want to sit with me?"

Emily hesitated. She wanted to be with him, she wanted reassurance...and yet, she knew they'd both be in deep trouble if Sienna caught them. Caleb's mother had too many problems already. The sounds from downstairs were growing louder. Marian didn't seem to know when to stop.

"Yeah," she said. "Just let me get my cloak."

She couldn't help feeling cold as she followed Caleb up a wooden ladder and out onto the roof. The wards floated through the air, roughly a metre above their heads... she sensed smaller spells snapping and snarling at any trace of rogue magic, far too close for comfort. She kept her head down as Caleb turned, gazing around the city, then sat on the roof. After a moment, Emily sat next to him.

Beneficence was burning. Smoke and flames rose from a dozen separate places, all to the north. She could taste smoke on the air. It was hard to tell *what* was burning, yet all the fires were clearly concentrated in the same general area. And yet, it was terrifyingly quiet. She couldn't hear anything louder than her own breathing.

Caleb wrapped an arm around her shoulders. "I'm sorry about Marian. She..."

"Don't worry about it," Emily said. She'd never had an older brother. She had no idea what it was like to have someone like that in her life. And yet, if she'd blamed someone for killing Caleb or Jade, she wouldn't have hesitated to let them know either. "She's young."

"That's not an excuse," Caleb said. He sounded pained. "She should never have said that to you."

"Thanks," Emily said.

His arm tightened, just for a second. "I spent half my life trying to get out of Casper's shadow. And now I find myself reprimanded for not *being* him."

And Casper spent his life trying to get out of his father's shadow, Emily thought, remembering Casper's drunken confession. *And...*

"You don't have to be him," Emily said. "You're nothing like him."

"Six months ago, I would have said that was a good thing." Caleb looked down at the rooftop as a gust of cold wind brushed against them. "Now...I never realized just how much Casper had to learn, when everyone thought he would inherit. All the little things I have to remember, all the obligations that come with being part of House Waterfall..."

Emily hugged him, awkwardly. Caleb had never been particularly interested in power for its own sake. He was a born scientist, a researcher into magic...she smiled in sudden warmth as she remembered their ever-evolving joint project. Caleb would have been happy to build their university and then vanish into it. Now...he had responsibilities that came with his family. He couldn't walk away from them.

And yet, she was tempted to tell him to do just that. She had money and a house, enough to support both of them for the rest of their lives. They could move to Heart's Eye and build their university in peace, then open it for other seekers after truth. But she knew he wouldn't be comfortable, if she supported him. Lady Barb had warned her, more than once, that men *needed* to feel useful. They had to feel as though they were earning their keep.

But he wouldn't have any difficulty supporting himself once he graduates, she told herself, dryly. *He could pay me back then, if he wished.*

She shook her head, telling herself she was being selfish. She couldn't ask Caleb to abandon his family, to walk away from his parents and siblings…she couldn't ask that of him. How could she? She rarely looked back at her mother and stepfather, despite the long, dark shadow they had cast on her life – she would be happy if she never saw either of them again – but Caleb had been raised in a loving environment. He might fight with his family from time to time, yet he loved them…

"You'll be fine," she said, softly. "I have faith in you."

"Thank you," Caleb said.

She leaned into his embrace, forcing herself to *think*. Justice was…*what*? The entity wasn't a simple illusion, not when she'd felt the presence centered on it. Whatever it was, it could clearly use magic at will. And yet…it definitely wasn't human. A Manavore? She'd seen spells strike them and vanish, back in the past. Or a Mimic?

Perhaps someone should have tried to cast a dispelling spell on it, she thought. She kicked herself, mentally. She should have thought of that, back in the square. *And yet, a Mimic couldn't go after more than one target at once.*

She considered it for a long moment. Justice hadn't *behaved* like a Manavore, although she had to admit that she'd only ever seen *one* type of Manavore. There could be others, lost somewhere in the past. And yet, based on what she knew, Justice *wasn't* a Manavore. It had certainly shown no sign of being unable to target mundanes as well as magicians. A Mimic was a much more likely answer…

But Mimics kill and replace their targets, she mused. She was, as far as she knew, the only living person who could build a Mimic from scratch, at least in theory. She'd never dared try. *Justice killed.*

She forced her tired mind to work. A Mimic could replace someone perfectly, perfectly enough to fool even their closest friends and family. She shivered against Caleb as she remembered Travis, mocking her as she'd waited outside the Warden's office. She'd been talking to the Mimic, she knew, but there hadn't been anything to give it away. The Mimic had duplicated Travis perfectly.

Although I didn't know him that well, she mused. Travis had been an asshole, an older student who'd resented her – not without reason. She'd certainly done her best to have as little to do with him as possible. *Someone who was close to him might have sensed something wrong.*

But Justice had spoken in simple terms. He'd sounded as though he was speaking by rote.

"A supercharged spell," she said. "Compulsion, but on a terrifying scale."

Caleb looked at her. "A necromancer?"

"A necromancer couldn't use compulsion like that," Emily said. "Could he?"

She looked down at her hands. Shadye had used blood magic…but that depended on having a sample of the target's blood. Dua Kepala hadn't used any blood magic or compulsion spells, as far as she knew. Gaius had cast them for him, back when he'd been undermining Farrakhan's defenses. More complex compulsion spells would be beyond most necromancers, as they relied on fine-tuning to overwhelm resistance. Even Mother Holly, who'd understood a great deal about making use of limited resources, hadn't been able to use such spells after she'd become a full-fledged necromancer.

"The spell was blunt," Caleb said. "It didn't adjust itself to crack through wards and protections."

"True," Emily agreed. "Necromancers *do* use overpowered spells..."

And Mimics draw their energy from something similar, she added, silently. *But a Mimic would be able to cast spells, wouldn't it?*

"Maybe one of the priests became a necromancer," Caleb said. "But before he took the plunge, he swore a set of oaths that kept the madness in check."

"Risky," Emily said. Perversely, a selfish necromancer had a greater chance of surviving the necromantic rite than someone who wanted to do good. A fanatic *might* be dedicated enough to turn into a necromancer, but as the madness grew stronger he'd lose whatever sense of focus he'd managed to retain after the transition. "I wouldn't care to take the risk."

"They might," Caleb said.

Emily frowned. A compulsion spell...more than one, mingled with an illusion and probably some subtle prompts to keep people from thinking logically. How could something be *both* infinitively huge and yet small enough to fit into the square? And the petrification spell, strong enough to not only turn someone into stone, but lock them that way permanently. She remembered the statues, screaming in agony, and shuddered. Sienna had been sure the victims were killed outright, but what if she was wrong? What if their souls remained trapped in the statues?

But what would happen, she asked herself, *if a necromancer tried to use a transfiguration spell? Would it be so powerful that the victim would be trapped permanently – or killed?*

"They must have known about Vesperian," Caleb said. "The Hands of Justice must have guessed what was coming."

"Probably," Emily said. Vesperian's Ponzi scheme had been doomed for months, once the borrowing had gotten out of hand. The notes – and the massive financial losses – would have weakened the city's government, undermining the people's faith in their leaders. Combined with a real god, or at least something that looked like one, the Hands of Justice might be able to take over without much opposition. "And they targeted his investors deliberately, just to speed up the collapse."

"And then killed him themselves," Caleb said. His hand ran down her back as she leaned against him. "And that started the collapse."

"We need more information," Emily said.

"A very good idea," Sienna's voice said. "And you also need that hand removed."

Emily jumped. She hadn't heard Sienna coming up the ladder behind them. Caleb yanked his hand away from her behind and tried to look innocent, even though it was futile. They might not have been making out on the rooftop, but they'd definitely been closer than mere friendship would allow. Besides, their relationship was no secret. Someone who saw them would know the truth.

"Mother," Caleb said. "The wards would keep anyone from getting a good look at us."

"I believe I told you to behave when you were under my roof." Sienna gave Emily a sharp look. "Did your father not teach you that a sorcerer's home is his castle? That you should follow the rules?"

Emily hesitated, unsure what to say. Her mouth was very dry.

"Apparently not." Sienna sounded regretful, rather than angry. But she also sounded tired. "Caleb, go downstairs to your room and stay there unless the wards are threatened."

"Yes, Mother," Caleb said.

Emily watched him go, then looked at Sienna. Her face was so composed that Emily *knew* strong emotions churned behind the mask. She tried to keep her own face composed, even though she knew they were in trouble. Sienna would be within her rights to kick both Emily and Frieda out of the house for disobeying the rules – or worse.

"Your father may not have told you this," Sienna said, "but the reputation of a young woman can come back to haunt them. You do *not* want people discussing your choices behind your back."

"I already have people talking about me behind my back," Emily said.

"And you really *don't* want to give them more ammunition," Sienna snapped. She stepped forward, towering over Emily. Somehow, she looked more terrifying than a necromancer. "Your reputation overshadows you. You *have* to be careful."

"I know," Emily said.

Sienna didn't look convinced. "What you do in private isn't important." She knelt down, facing Emily. "But what you get *caught* doing in public *is* important."

"We're not in public," Emily said.

"That's the sort of excuse I expect from a five-year-old," Sienna said. "I *suggest* you be more careful."

She sat back and sighed, heavily. "I must also apologize for my daughter's harsh words. Please rest assured that she will be suitably punished."

Emily winced, inwardly. Marian was lucky there had been no outside witnesses. Caleb wasn't the only one whose actions reflected on his family. Sienna would have been judged by how well she'd handled the situation. Her community might have turned on her if she'd allowed her daughter to get away with such unpleasant accusations.

And the story of The Boy Who Cried Feud *is all about dealing with it*, she thought. Lady Barb had advised her to read the stories, explaining that they would help her to understand magical society. *It's better than* The Boy Who Cried Wolf.

"She is young," Sienna said. "She will grow into maturity."

Emily swallowed. "You don't have to punish her. I...I know what it's like to lose someone I loved. I don't blame her for being angry."

Sienna met her eyes. "Her behavior was appalling," she said. "And she tried to leave the house this morning."

"I don't blame her," Emily said.

"And I am glad of that," Sienna said. She sounded relieved. It dawned on Emily, slowly, that she could have demanded compensation for the accusations. "But I cannot allow Marian to grow up in the belief that lashing out at people is acceptable. The next person she mouths off to may demand a far more exacting price."

Emily shivered. A nobleman insulted by a little boy might draw his sword and behead the child. Or break bones or...she'd seen it happen in Zangaria. A magician might hex the child, or demand payment from the child's parents. Sienna was far more able to defend herself and her family than any peasant woman, but even *she* couldn't stand up to everything. Her community would have shunned her if she'd allowed her children to run wild.

"She's young," she said, finally.

"Yes," Sienna said. "And I want her to grow up."

"I didn't want Casper to die," Emily said. "I..."

Sienna smiled, humorlessly. "If I believed you had deliberately set him up to die, Lady Emily, I would have killed you the moment you entered the house," she said. "I might have had to let him go off to the war, but I could certainly have avenged his death."

Her smile faded. "But the necromancer who killed him *is* dead. And I thank you for it."

"You're welcome," Emily said, automatically.

Sienna turned to look over the city. "Go back to your room and get some rest," she said, gruffly. "I'll have some more food sent up for Frieda when she awakes."

Emily rose. "Thank you," she said. "And I'm sorry about her conduct too."

"You can put her to work scrubbing the floors, if you wish," Sienna said. It took Emily a moment to realize that the older woman was joking. "And I suggest you do tell her to apologize."

"I will," Emily said.

"And don't let me catch you and Caleb too close again," Sienna said, as Emily clambered down the ladder. "I'll have to take notice next time."

"We'll behave," Emily said.

"Forgive me for not believing you," Sienna said, dryly. "You two are in love."

Chapter Twenty-Five

E MILY SLEPT BADLY.

The wards kept Justice's influence out, she thought, but she still felt *something* at the edge of her dreams. A presence, perhaps...or just random flickers from the depths of her mind. She drifted in and out of sleep for what felt like hours before a knock at the door awakened her. Frieda sat up as Emily dragged herself out of bed and walked over to open the door. Karan stood outside, carrying two mugs of steaming Kava.

"Drink this, then get dressed and come downstairs," she said. "We might have to go out soon."

Emily took the mugs, passed one to Frieda and turned back to Karan. But she was already heading down the stairs...Emily shook her head, closed the door and walked over to the window. It was dark outside, but she saw faint glimmers in the distance. They were on the very edge of dawn.

"I slept poorly," Frieda said.

"You owe Caleb an apology," Emily said, without looking back. She looked out the window as she sipped her drink. People were gathering in the darkened street, but the wards made it hard for her to see them clearly. "You were very unpleasant to him."

"He deserved it," Frieda said, unrepentantly.

Emily sighed. She knew Frieda didn't like Caleb much – and she was fairly sure Caleb felt the same way – but there were limits. Insulting Caleb in front of his younger siblings would probably have led to a real fight, if Sienna hadn't returned. Lady Barb had warned her against humiliating a man in public unless she was prepared to deal with the consequences.

She turned to face the younger girl. "Apologize to him, *please*. He doesn't deserve *that* sort of treatment."

Frieda sniffed. "Should I prostrate myself, or will getting down on my knees suffice?"

"Just say you're sorry," Emily snapped, as she yanked the curtains closed. She wasn't sure if it was the lack of sleep or the grim awareness that they might be attacked at any moment, but her head was starting to pound again. "And *do* try to sound convincing."

"I hope Marian is going to apologize too," Frieda said. "She was *very* unpleasant to you."

"I'll live," Emily said. She pulled off her nightgown and reached for her shirt. "And so will you."

"So will Caleb," Frieda said.

Emily finished dressing, then splashed water on her face as Frieda climbed out of bed. She looked a little unsteady, although she tried hard to put a brave face on it as she removed her nightshirt. No one had ever accused Frieda of lacking determination, whatever else she lacked. And yet, she remained alarmingly short for her age. Her childhood had stunted the rest of her life.

At least she's put some meat on her bones, Emily thought. *She doesn't look like she's starving now.*

She met Frieda's eyes. "How's your magic?"

"Recovering," Frieda said. "I should be back to normal tomorrow."

Emily nodded. Her one experience with Berserker had left her feeling tired and drained for far too long. She would have died if Jade hadn't been there. Frieda had learned the spell later in life, after entering Martial Magic in Third Year. She'd had more reserves to draw on than Emily, but the spell had still drained her.

"Come on," she said, once Frieda was dressed. "Let's go face the music."

There was no sign of Marian when they reached the bottom of the stairs and entered the living room. Caleb and his father stood in one corner, having a quiet discussion that broke off as soon as Emily and Frieda appeared. Emily felt her cheeks heat, noting how Caleb couldn't quite meet her eyes. He looked dreadfully embarrassed. No doubt his father had given him a lecture on behaving himself too.

"Caleb." Frieda's voice was clipped. "I apologize for my conduct."

Emily resisted the urge to sigh out loud. Frieda didn't *sound* convincing, even if she *hadn't* thrown herself to her knees and begged for forgiveness. She certainly didn't want to admit she might have been wrong.

"Thank you," Caleb said. He didn't sound as though he believed her, but he appeared willing to accept the apology at face value. Emily reminded herself, wryly, that he had younger sisters. "I accept your apology."

Sienna entered, followed by Karan. "A messenger visited the street thirty minutes ago," she said. She sounded cross. "We are to present ourselves at Crossroads Corner at sunrise, so we can hear a formal announcement, or face punishment."

"That was all he said," Caleb added. "He just made his announcement and vanished."

"It could be a trap," Emily pointed out. General Pollack might be the only member of the city's government left alive, even if he *hadn't* held a seat on the council. The Hands of Justice would certainly want to arrest him. And then there was Sienna and Emily herself...turning up for the announcement might be a mistake. "Do they want *all* of us?"

"Apparently so," Sienna said. "We'll be going under glamours, of course."

General Pollack cleared his throat. "The younger children will be staying here," he said, firmly. "Karan, Croce and Marian will not leave the house."

"Father," Karan said, "I..."

"Have to stay home," General Pollack said. "I'm not going to take you into a dangerous situation."

Emily forced herself to think as Caleb passed her a cheese sandwich. The Hands of Justice would know where General Pollack lived. His address was a matter of public record. But arresting him, if he stayed in Sorcerers Row, would be difficult. The sorcerers would defend their territory...unless, of course, Justice came into play. If the entity absorbed spells, she asked herself, what would happen if it brushed against a ward?

We might want to reprogram the wards, she thought, as she started to eat the sandwich. It tasted stale. *Perhaps we could feed it too much magic...*

She shook her head, grimly. Justice was too powerful, she suspected, to be overloaded...and if the entity *was* overloaded, the resulting explosion might destroy the city. Even a necromancer didn't wield so much power...nothing short of a nexus point *did*. The combined power of every magician on Sorcerers Row couldn't hope to match *that*...

"Caleb," she said slowly, "is there a concealed nexus point within the city?"

Sienna gave her an odd look. "There were always old legends about catacombs under the castle," she said, "but there was never any suggestion of a nexus point. The closest one is several hundred miles away."

Emily and Frieda exchanged glances. There had been an entire network of catacombs under Mountaintop, concealing the school's greatest secret. If Aurelius had managed to drain hundreds of students to power the school's wards, why couldn't Janus and his sect do the same with willing volunteers? Given enough time, they might even be able to match a nexus point...until they ran out of victims.

But by then, they might have secured their grip on the city, she thought, as she took her cloak and wrapped it around her shoulders. *They might not need Justice any longer.*

The *presence* struck her as soon as they opened the door and stepped out onto the street, an icy pulse of *something* drawing her towards the square. She gritted her teeth against the compulsion, knowing it would keep wearing away at her defenses until they collapsed. The handful of others on the streets, heading northwards themselves, looked as though they were struggling against an invisible force.

"Put up a glamour, then keep it in place," Sienna ordered. She cast one over her husband as she spoke. "Do *not* let it slip."

Emily nodded, casting the spell as they reached the end of the street. The wards remained in place, yet the outer edges were starting to fray. Emily couldn't tell if the entity had tried to break them or if a more conventional sorcerer had, but either way it was a grim warning that Sorcerers Row couldn't hold out indefinitely. The sheer difficulty of convincing a dozen sorcerers to work together would make any more active defense impossible.

She took Caleb's hand, feeling a little odd as she looked up at him. His glamour made him look like a merchant, a man twenty years older than her. She *knew* it was a glamour, she saw flickers of his real face below the mask, but it still felt as if she were being unfaithful. Perhaps it was just an effect of using a glamour. The spell was more than just an illusion. It convinced anyone looking at it to believe the illusion. Even a person who *knew* it was a glamour might be fooled...

And it isn't that different to the spell Justice used, she told herself. *It pushes everyone to believe in it.*

There was no sign of the City Guard. The streets were patrolled by the Hands of Justice, all wearing red robes and silver runic armor, all carrying swords and whips.

She couldn't help noticing that they also wore the same clenched-fist icon, clearly visible on their shoulders. Their expressions were so identical – so cold and hard – that she wondered if they'd been enchanted...

And yet, they snapped at people, seemingly at random. A young woman was told off for wearing a colorful dress, a young man was reprimanded for showing too much leg...an older woman had her necklace torn away and smashed to the ground, for no reason Emily could see. She braced herself, readying a spell as the fanatics peered at her, but they moved on without comment. Clearly, she was modest enough not to draw their attention.

That young man would have looked modest in King Randor's Court, she thought. The absurd outfits the king's young blades wore had always struck her as silly. *And what was wrong with the woman's dress?*

She winced as they reached the crossroad at the foot of Temple Row. The entire street was sealed off...a low mummer of...*something*...ran through the crowd as they saw the piles of scorched rubble where a dozen temples had once stood. Emily felt it too, even though she'd never believed. The temples – and the statues – had been labors of love, pieces of art crafted by those who truly believed. Now, a number of temples were gone, along with all of the statues. She didn't blame the crowd for being angry...

"We saw them burning," Caleb whispered. "We just didn't know what we were seeing."

Emily nodded, stiffly. The anger grew, murmurs of rage running through the growing crowd, but there was also fear. If Justice was truly real, should he be worshipped exclusively...she shivered at the thought, wondering just how big a shock it would be if they came face to face with a real god. And then she sensed the presence – again – as a middle-aged man floated up into the air. He carried a golden staff in one hand, holding it above his head. The presence grew stronger and stronger until the entire crowd fell silent. Some of them even fell on their knees.

But not many, Emily thought. *The ones who were easy to overwhelm have already fallen.*

"This is the Time of Judgement," the man's said. His voice sounded quiet, but it echoed with overwhelming force. Emily felt the rune on her chest grow warmer, warning her of subtle magic. "This city will become the Throne of Justice Himself! His eyes will see all and judge all!"

There was a long chilling pause. Emily wondered, morbidly, how many people had secrets they would rather stay hidden. A *real* god, walking the world, would be able to see those secrets easily, wherever they lurked. Everyone had something to feel guilty about, even if it was something as minor as not returning an overdue library book. And even something minor could turn into a far greater sin if the sinner never came to terms with it.

No hiding place down here, she thought.

"This city will be prepared for his assumption," the speaker continued. "You, his chosen people, will be prepared for his judgement. Us, his brave followers who maintained the spark when all was dark, will serve you as we cleanse you and ready you for your life in a truly just world."

Emily held Caleb's hand and listened, wondering when the speaker would get to the point. She'd known quite a few men who'd acted as though they'd fallen in love with their own voices, but the speaker seemed different. He was so consumed with his own certainty that he wanted to share it with everyone. But then, coming face to face with his god must have seemed like proof he'd been right all along. If she'd been a worshipper who'd met her god, she suspected she would have felt vindicated too.

"This city belongs to Justice and Justice alone," the speaker said. Emily straightened. It felt as though it had taken hours, but they were finally getting to the meat of the matter. "The worship of all other gods is now forbidden--" a rustle ran through the crowd, hastily dimmed by the presence "--and all temples, statues and idols are to be destroyed. Your Household Gods are to be smashed--" another rustle, angrier this time "--and your holy books burnt."

Bastards, Emily thought. She couldn't help a hot flicker of anger. Burning books was the closest thing to blasphemy she knew, even though the local religions hadn't been too keen on the idea of printing presses. *And yet, letting everyone read their texts won them more converts.*

"Everyone is expected to present themselves for religious instruction at sunrise and sunset," the speaker continued. "Those who do not receive instruction will be whipped. All shops are to be supervised, with prices fixed to ensure that everyone can afford to eat. Shopkeepers who attempt to evade the rules will be executed. All banks are to be closed, as sources of evil..."

Emily listened in numb horror as the speaker read out a long series of rules. The price-fixing alone would lead to disaster, but it was hardly the worst. Young women were not to be on the streets unaccompanied...and not at all after dark; young men were to present themselves for additional religious instruction before being absorbed into the Fists – not Hands – of Justice. The priests of every other religion were to surrender themselves at once; anyone who'd been part of the government was to report for duty by the end of the day...

And anyone who disobeyed, they were told over and over again, would be whipped – or executed.

They're building a theocracy, she thought. *This is not going to end well.*

"No one is to leave the city," the speaker finished. Emily's heart sank. The presence was strong enough to make teleporting dangerous. It reminded her of the haze she'd sensed at Farrakhan. "All will serve Justice."

The Fists of Justice stamped their feet, brandishing their swords. "Justice, Justice!"

The crowd muttered angrily. Emily glanced at Caleb, then at Sienna. If the crowd rioted, with so many armed men watching them, there would be a bloodbath. She didn't know what to do, if all hell broke loose. Fight to help the crowd or run, knowing the riot would quickly turn into a slaughter ?

She sensed the presence grow stronger and looked back at the speaker. The tip of his staff glowed with an eerie white light, a flare that was – somehow – *wrong*. She couldn't look directly at it, even as he cast a spell. A portly man was yanked into the air and suspended upside down, hanging over the crowd. The speaker's face tightened with disdain as the man screamed and begged for help, denying everything. And yet, it sounded as though he didn't know *why* he'd been targeted.

"This is a banker," the speaker said. He couldn't have put more disdain into his voice if he tried. "He invited credulous fools to put money in his bank, then used their gold to purchase more and more imaginary loans. He forgot the simplest principle of all – you can't spend more than you earn. And then his loans caught up with him and his bank evaporated.

"We promise you justice." There was nothing less than absolute conviction in his voice. "And we swear to you that you will *have* justice."

He waved his staff. Emily sensed a sudden flow of magic, guided by something that felt oddly familiar, an instant before the banker's body glowed with blinding light. She looked away, instinctively, as the banker screamed in pain. There was nothing she could do. When she looked back, the body was nothing more than stone. She didn't have to look at his face to know he'd died in screaming agony.

And he might not even have been a real banker, her thoughts reminded her. The only banker she actually *knew* was Markus. Was he in danger? The Bank of Silence was heavily warded, but it was also an obvious target. *They might just have scooped someone off the street to serve as an example.*

She forced herself to think as the crowd recoiled, panic starting to spread. The magic felt familiar, yet…she couldn't quite place it. A spell she hadn't used, but one she'd seen…seen where? The memory seemed lost within the shadows of her mind. What was it?

The speaker made a gesture. The petrified man dropped from the air…

…And shattered into a thousand pieces when he hit the ground.

Chapter Twenty-Six

FOR A LONG MOMENT, THERE WAS ABSOLUTE SILENCE.

"Go home," the speaker said. "And spread the word of Justice!"

Emily glanced sharply at Sienna, who nodded. The Fists of Justice were already advancing, waving their swords and cracking their whips at anyone who didn't look as though they were moving fast enough to suit them. She took one last look at the speaker, who was lowering himself back to the ground, then hurried after Sienna as the Fists moved closer. The crowd seemed too stunned to fight.

They just saw someone killed in front of them, Emily thought. Her own thoughts seemed to have trouble catching up with what had happened. *And they thought they sensed a real god.*

She glanced at the ruined temples as they walked past Temple Row. The Fists of Justice were everywhere, sifting through the rubble and ruthlessly extracting anything of religious value. Others were readying the next set of temples for destruction, carting out books and parchments and piling them up in the center of the street, ready for burning. She felt shock and dismay run through the crowd as the pile of irreplaceable parchments caught fire.

A priest in a red robe stood at the corner of the street, handing out pamphlets to everyone as they passed. His gaze flickered over Emily, then landed on Caleb; Emily tensed, expecting trouble, but he merely passed Caleb two copies of the pamphlets instead. Emily was torn between relief and annoyance at being so casually dismissed, simply for being female. The priests didn't seem to be handing *anything* to women, even women who were clearly alone. She knew she should be relieved – she didn't want to attract attention until she figured out how to beat the entity – but it was still annoying. It was the first step in dehumanizing women. She couldn't help noticing that all the priests were male.

The streets seemed colder, somehow. She kept hold of Caleb's hand, glancing from side to side as they hurried home. The shops were closed, streets were barricaded; Emily wondered, grimly, how long it would be until the Fists of Justice knocked their way through the makeshift barriers and started to patrol the streets. They wouldn't want to allow anyone to defy their rule, not in the early days. A hint of weakness might prove disastrous. She suspected it wouldn't be long before the Fists came for Sorcerers Row, even though most sane city councils ignored magic-users as much as possible. The street might prove a haven for the disbelievers and discontented.

And they have...something...on their side, Emily thought. *If Justice drew energy from the spells hurled at him, the wards protecting the street will be an all-you-can-eat buffet. The sorcerers won't stand a chance.*

Hundreds of wards drifted through the air as they turned into Sorcerers Row. Emily sensed a dozen sorcerers looking at her – looking at everyone – through the wards; she shivered, helplessly, as the wards drifted over her skin. They felt formidable, but they might prove worse than useless against Justice. She hoped the wardcrafters had enough sense not to hook themselves directly to the wards. The feedback from one or more of them breaking would be enough to kill their creators.

Sienna stopped to speak to one of the sorcerers on the barricade. Emily glanced at Caleb, then took one of the pamphlets and tested it for hidden surprises. The rune on her chest warmed as soon as she opened it, warning her of subtle magic. She tested the paper carefully, trying to find the rune. Someone had drawn the pattern out so carefully that it only formed when the pamphlet was opened. It was a very low-power rune, so subtle that it might pass unnoticed, but given time it would have an effect on anyone close by.

"Clever," she muttered.

"Whoever designed this was disgustingly inventive," Caleb agreed. "That's *nasty*."

Emily nodded. On one hand, it was reassuring. The Hands of Justice – the *Fists*, now – seemed to think they *needed* to force people to convert to their faith. They weren't confident enough to believe otherwise. But on the other hand…most of the city's population, even the strong-willed, wouldn't realize the rune existed, let alone what it did. They might not convert immediately, but their resistance would slowly wear down to a nub. Just leaving the pamphlet open in the wrong place might prove disastrous.

"We can destroy the rune," she said. She silently cursed the unknown designer under her breath. She'd seen her fair share of charmed or cursed books, including one that was supposed to drive its readers insane, but this was *obnoxious*. Even an experienced sorcerer might miss the rune unless he had special protections. "And we can warn others to destroy it too."

"Unless it's charmed to react badly when the rune is broken," Caleb said. He cast a series of spells over the pamphlet. "It doesn't *look* to be charmed, but there could be something else hidden between the pages."

"Keep an eye on me," Emily ordered. She peered down at the pamphlet, carefully. "And don't let me do anything stupid."

"That's a full-time job," Caleb teased.

Emily ignored him as she read the pamphlet. The writer had used the New Learning – a combination of English letters and phonic spelling – to make a simple case for justice. And Justice. An indictment of the guildmasters and their rule, a condemnation of the other religions and their gods, a simple statement that Justice was the sole god of Beneficence…and a set of rules and regulations intended to keep the population in line. If anything, it was worse than she'd feared. The entire population would be re-educated until resistance was not only futile, but inconceivable.

"Crap," she muttered.

Frieda hurried over to join them. "What now?"

"Good question," Emily said. The Fists of Justice had to be stopped. Once they had the city in an iron grip, they'd start advancing into Zangaria. She had no doubt that advance parties of priests were already preparing the true believers for the next step. King Randor would not react calmly when he heard the news. "I don't know."

She contemplated possibilities as Sienna led them back to the house. Attacking Justice directly would be futile, at least until they devised a way to defeat the entity.

It would just get them killed. Starving the entity of magic might work – she'd defeated the Manavores using something similar – but Justice might be able to break free of any traps before he ran out of power. The Mimic had lasted for quite some time between feeding sessions...

"This cannot go on," General Pollack said, once they were inside. His glamour had been removed. "I'll have to find out just how many councillors are actually left."

"The guildmasters were killed," Caleb said.

"There will be others who survived," General Pollack told him. "Even if the standing guildmasters are dead, they will have successors."

"Who will think that there is a real live god walking the streets," Sienna said. "We might be alone."

"We need help," General Pollack said. "If no one tries to resist, they'll have all the time in the world to tighten their grip on the city."

Emily nodded. She'd been in Alexis when King Randor had nearly been overthrown by a coup. The plotters would have won if they'd had a chance to take control of the rest of the city, crushing resistance before it could take shape. But they hadn't...

Her lips twitched. *They would have gotten away with it, too, if it wasn't for us meddlesome kids.*

"The moment you step outside the street, you'll be challenged," Sienna pointed out. "They already have men watching Sorcerers Row."

"I'll sneak through the gap." General Pollack sounded enthused by the chance for real action, despite the risks. He hadn't led from the front during the last war against the necromancers. "I have plenty of experience in sneaking around."

He looked at Caleb. "I'll take Caleb with me. His magic can help us avoid detection."

"Be careful." Sienna shared a long look with her husband. "And make sure you trust the people you find."

Emily winced. The sheer power of the entity was terrifying. Someone who might be trustworthy at one point might be converted into an implacable enemy, just by constant exposure to the presence. She looked at the pamphlet in her hand and cursed the unknown writer under her breath. There was so much subtle magic involved that it would be *very* difficult to muster resistance.

And they have had plenty of time to plant spies everywhere, she thought, grimly. *The general might walk into a trap.*

"Be *very* careful," she said to Caleb. She held up the pamphlet. "And make sure you warn them to burn these."

Sienna glowered down at hers. "Nasty. Very nasty."

Emily dropped hers in the fire and watched it burn. "Here's a different question," she said, slowly. "How much food do we have?"

Karan muttered a word, just loudly enough to be heard. "Not much. We have preservation spells on the cooler, but...we'll be running out of food within the week, assuming we go on short rations."

Sienna gave her eldest daughter a sharp look. "Start filling bottles and buckets with water before it occurs to them to turn off the pipes," she ordered. "Take Marian with you – she can do something useful."

Emily glanced at her in surprise. She hadn't seen Marian all day. But then, Sienna had probably told her to stay in her room until she felt like apologizing. Emily felt a moment's pity for the younger girl, mixed with annoyance. Marian had every right to mourn her brother, but...

She's grieving, Emily told herself, firmly. *And I won't let it get to me.*

"She's still sulking," Karan said. "But I'll try to get her to work."

"See that you do," Sienna said.

Emily looked at the table, thinking hard. If no food was coming into the city – if even the fishing boats were forbidden to leave – the entire population would starve. Sienna and her family could hold out for a week, if Karan was right, but what about the poorer families, the ones without magic? It wouldn't be long before the poorer parts of the city began to starve, forcing them to beg for food. And the Fists of Justice would be right there, ready to offer food with one hand and religious instruction with the other. Starving people would be in no condition to resist.

Caleb caught her eye. "Do you have any other thoughts?"

"They'll come after us, sooner rather than later," Emily said. The coup plotters had tried to hunt Alassa down, after all. They'd succeeded too. If General Pollack truly was the last living – or at least free – member of the former government, he'd be hunted too. The Fists of Justice would want to convert or eliminate him before he could cause trouble. "I don't know how long Sorcerers Row can hold out."

"It's safe," Karan protested.

"It might not be for long," Caleb warned. "You didn't see that...that *thing*."

"We have to assume the worst," Sienna said. "And plan for a hasty departure."

Karan didn't look as though she believed her mother. Emily didn't blame her for having doubts. Sorcerers Row was the safest place in the city...if one happened to be a sorcerer or had magical relatives. No one would have dared lay a finger on Karan – or any of her siblings – for fear of Sienna's revenge. And few people would linger in Sorcerers Row. Outsiders came in, did their business, and then hurried out before a sorcerer decided to use them for target practice.

But the wards won't stand indefinitely, she thought, numbly. *Not now.*

"We can fight," Croce said. "We have weapons."

"Only a fool fights in a burning house, son." General Pollack said, warningly. He waved a hand at the wall. "We'd be surrounded, trapped in our own house. Even if they couldn't break in, they could keep us from breaking out."

Emily caught the expression on Caleb's face and winced in sympathy. General Pollack had pushed Casper hard, but he'd also made no secret of the fact he favored his eldest son. Caleb had never quite clicked with his father. He was brave, and a skillful magician, but he was no fighter. Croce, on the other hand, was doing well at Stronghold. She wondered, grimly, if General Pollack saw his youngest son as a replacement for his eldest.

I'm sorry, she thought.

"Perhaps we should move now," Sienna said. "There are places in Fishing Plaice we could stay."

Karan smirked. "I thought Fishing Plaice was not safe."

"Nowhere is safe now," Sienna said.

"Better to wait for darkness before we move." General Pollack reached for his cloak. "Caleb, you're with me."

Caleb's face was unreadable as he followed his father to the door, but Emily knew he was dismayed. She didn't blame him. Caleb wanted his father's approval, but he couldn't do what he needed to do to get it. Casper had suffered the same problem, yet...she shook her head, wishing she could give Caleb some reassurance. She didn't want him to die too.

"I need to contact Alassa," she said, once Caleb was gone. "She has to know what's happening here."

"Tell her that we will try to deal with the problem ourselves," Sienna said. "The last thing we want is an invasion force crossing the bridges."

"And getting slaughtered by Justice," Frieda put in.

Emily nodded. "I'll tell her," she said, although she didn't know what King Randor could or would do. He had sorcerers under his command, including Jade. Maybe he'd order them to do something stupid. "And I'll warn Lady Barb too."

"Make sure she knows not to teleport into the city," Sienna warned. "The *presence* makes teleporting dangerous."

"Just like the haze in Farrakhan," Emily said, as she headed for the door. The technique was different, she was sure, but the results were similar. "Do you know if Janus or any of his fellows came from Heart's Eye?"

Sienna's eyes narrowed. "To the best of my knowledge, Janus does not have any actual magic. But the Fists of Justice probably have a few sorcerers working for them."

Emily nodded and hurried up the stairs. Frieda followed her into the bedroom, then sat and watched as Emily wrote a message to Alassa on the chat parchment. She'd hoped her friend – or her husband – were close enough to the parchment to see it glow and write a reply, but there was no response. Scowling, she put the parchment on the dressing table and wrote a long letter, explaining what was going on. Her wrist hurt after she'd finished, but she forced herself to write a second note to Lady Barb. She should be able to see the note and respond quickly.

She might not be able to come, Emily mused. She ran her fingers over the chat parchment, thoughtfully. Something was nagging at the back of her mind, but what? *She might be deep in the Blighted Lands...*

Her mouth dropped open as the pieces fell into place. The speaker had used an odd spell to petrify the banker, but it was similar – very similar – to the spell Aloha had used to make the first set of chat parchments. Emily was *sure* of it. The chat parchments *did* carry magic from one piece of parchment to the others...indeed, in some ways, they were all the *same* piece of parchment. It was a simple spell, on the surface, but it became far more complicated when someone tried to write it down. And someone had warped it into a nightmare...

She looked down at the parchment, not seeing anything. The secret behind Aloha's spell had leaked quickly, unsurprisingly. Magicians could be relied upon to try to duplicate spells, once they knew something was possible. It was no surprise that someone had managed to improve on the original piece of work. Using it to transfer magic was really nothing more than scaling up the chat spellwork.

And then they channel it into a spell concealed in the staff, she thought. She couldn't help feeling a flicker of admiration. Whoever had modified the spell was brilliant. *They must have been using the staff to boost the presence too.*

She sobered. *And they're using their talents to support a theocratic state.*

"Shit," she muttered.

Frieda looked up. "Emily?"

"There are spells to shatter wands," Emily mused. "Aren't there?"

"Yeah." Frieda's right arm twitched. She'd been forced to use a wand at Mountaintop. It would have stunted her magic if Emily hadn't taught her how to use her powers without it. "I've had them used on me."

"We can use them against the speakers," Emily said. She felt better than she had for a long time, just putting the pieces together. "I wonder if they have amplifiers scattered through the city."

Frieda frowned. "Amplifiers of what?"

"Magic." Emily scowled. The last time she'd seen anything like it had been at Whitehall. "But we still have the problem of just how to deal with Justice."

She rose. "We need to talk to an expert. And Markus is the only expert we have."

"And so you're sneaking out to see him," Frieda said. "You *are* going to tell Sienna, aren't you?"

"I'll have to," Emily had no idea if Markus was still alive, but she needed to find out. Aloha had taken up an apprenticeship somewhere and wouldn't thank anyone who disturbed her. "And you'd better come with me."

"With pleasure," Frieda said. Her smile widened. "It isn't safe out there."

Chapter Twenty-Seven

"Y OU LOOK FUNNY," FRIEDA SAID.

"So do you," Emily countered. The glamour was definitely in place – Frieda looked like a normal young man – but there was something odd about the way she moved. "Try to walk more like a man."

"So I should swing my shoulders and thrust out my chest?" Frieda stuck out her tongue, mischievously. "And stick my head so high in the air that I bang my chin into the nearest wall, which I didn't see because my eyes were looking up..."

"Just walk normally," Emily said. "And try not to make eye contact."

She sighed as she tested her own spell. It was easy enough to use a glamour to look like a different woman – she'd done it often enough – but passing for a grown man was a great deal harder. Anyone who didn't know the glamour was there might not notice it, yet they might realize – at some point – that there was something odd about the two young men. And once they got suspicious, they might look closer and eventually peer through the glamour.

"Ready," she said. "Let's go."

The glamour flickered the moment they stepped out of the house and brushed against the network of wards and sensing spells. Emily had to smile, even though it wasn't really funny. Trying to break through a glamour was considered bad manners, particularly if the glamour covered up some minor blemish rather than anything more serious. But once they walked out of Sorcerers Row, the glamour settled back into place. She allowed herself a moment of relief as they headed down the streets, making sure to steer well away from Temple Row. The Fists of Justice would take an interest in anyone who went there.

Beneficence wasn't *her* city, but she still felt a pang at seeing just how much the city had changed in less than a week. The shops were closed, homes barricaded and the streets almost deserted, save for a handful of men scurrying to and fro. There were no women at all, not even prostitutes. But then, the Fists of Justice had made it clear that whores were sinners too.

And it doesn't matter to them if the women had a real choice or not, she thought, darkly. *All that matters is that they sold their bodies for money.*

She gritted her teeth as they walked past a row of closed shops. She didn't understand how a woman could willingly sell her body, giving herself to a dozen different men in a day, but she understood that choices were sometimes limited. If someone had to choose between prostitution or starvation and death, which choice should they make? Which choice would *she* make? She liked to think she would sooner die than sell herself, but she knew it wasn't that easy. And if she'd had children, the choice would be even harder. Could she leave them to starve too?

But the Fists of Justice don't care about circumstances, she thought. *That* had shone through their words. They didn't care *why* someone had made a bad choice, they didn't care that all the other alternatives were worse...only punishment mattered. *All they want is power.*

She shook her head. She could see their point — once someone started accepting excuses, where did they stop? But she could also see they were taking it too far. She'd heard similar arguments back on Earth, with religious leaders convinced they were in the right and that the other side was pure evil. There was a difference between murder and killing someone in self-defense, but the Fists of Justice had long since lost perspective. All they wanted to do now was impose their will on the entire city.

A loud noise up ahead brought her out of her thoughts. She looked down the street and swore, inwardly, as she saw the crowd gathered outside Bankers Row. They hurled abuse at the bankers, promising to tear them limb from limb as soon as they stepped outside the wards. A couple of banks on the edge of the street had been burned to the ground, while others were so heavily protected that the rioters didn't have a hope of setting them on fire. But it hadn't helped some of their staff. A dozen men and five women hung from makeshift gallows, their bodies swinging in the breeze. It looked as though they'd been beaten to death first, *then* hung. She knew it wouldn't have been quick.

"We'll have to use the tunnel," she muttered. The Fists of Justice were patrolling the edge of the crowd, sometimes flicking their whips at protesters who weren't enthusiastic enough to suit them. "Come on."

She half-expected trouble outside the tunnel entrance, but the house looked completely untouched. The wards opened as soon as she touched the doorknob, allowing her to slip inside the house and down a short flight of stairs to the tunnel entrance. She braced herself as she opened the hatch, then cast a pair of light globes as they hurried down the tunnel. Nothing barred their way until they reached the far end, where an iron door was firmly shut. She pressed her fingers against it, reaching out with her magic. The unlocking spell was so carefully hidden that it took her nearly ten minutes to find.

"Neat," Frieda said. She sounded impressed as more protective wards shimmered into existence. Emily felt her glamour flicker, then fail completely. "If you'd tried to blast the door open, Emily, the blowback would have killed us both."

"Glad you like it." Markus stood just inside the door, looking grim. "It took weeks to put it together."

Emily eyed him, concerned. Markus looked as though he hadn't slept for a week. His face was pale, there were dark rings around his eyes and his hands wouldn't stop twitching. He could have left the bank at any moment, she knew, but he might not have been able to get back inside. And yet, who knew when the mob would discover the tunnel? Would Markus be able to escape if they blocked his way?

"You need to sleep," she said, bluntly.

"I'll sleep when I'm dead." Markus turned, motioning them to follow him. "I took the precaution of laying in a stockpile of food and arranging for some of my staff to sleep here, but I didn't expect…"

He waved a hand towards the doors as they entered the lobby. The air crawled with protective wards, but Emily could still hear the braying of the crowd. A couple dozen children, ranging from three to ten, kicked a ball around the room, watched by their parents and older siblings. The men were armed, she saw, and some of the women carried wands, but they couldn't hope to defend themselves if the wards shattered. And, she saw in their hopeless eyes, everyone knew it was just a matter of time.

"They're safer in here," Frieda said.

"Until we run out of food," Markus said. "I designed this place as a fortress, and the wards will keep out any conventional threat, but we're short on food. We may have to evacuate in a couple of weeks or so."

"And then get caught," Emily said.

Markus led them up to his office and closed the door. "I assume you know what's going on outside," he said, as he waved them to seats. "What's happening?"

"Trouble," Emily said.

She ran through the whole story, starting with Justice's appearance and ending with the charmed pamphlets. Markus listened carefully, not saying a word, as she outlined her belief that the 'god' was nothing more than a magic trick. But, trick or no trick, Justice was immensely powerful. The spells that had created the entity – and allowed it to channel power to its followers – had to be handled carefully.

Markus chuckled, humorlessly, when she'd finished. "I was still working my way through the papers." His chuckle became a giggle. "I was wasting my time, wasn't I?"

"Yeah," Frieda said. "It looks that way."

Emily shot her a sharp look. "You have to be careful," she said to Markus. "The wards are blocking out its influence, but they won't last forever."

"A god could snap my wards easily." Markus jabbed a finger towards the window and the crowd below. "That they haven't come to crush me suggests they *can't*."

"Unless they want a scapegoat," Frieda said. Emily looked at her in surprise. "There *has* to be someone to blame for their failures."

"And then someone *else* will ask why they haven't punished Markus already," Emily countered, although she knew Frieda had a point. Tyrants found scapegoats useful when it came to avoiding blame for their own failures. And if the scapegoats were powerless, there was no danger of them turning on their enemies. "What answer will they give?"

"Not a good one." Markus shook his head. "The real joke is that I think I figured out a solution to the mess Vesperian created."

Emily snorted. "I wish you'd found it a week ago."

"So do I." Markus shrugged. "We can't replace the money Vesperian lost, but we can buy back the notes. Not at face value, I admit…we don't have that sort of money, even if we pool all of our remaining funds. But we can make sure that some of the investors get some of their cash back."

Emily considered it. "And it will give you a claim on the railway," she said. "And its stockpile of goods."

"Assuming it survives," Markus said. "There were people talking about burning the station to the ground, before…before Justice made his appearance. We could recover the iron, if someone melted the engines, but it wouldn't be so useful. There would be a glut on the market."

"The law of supply and demand strikes again," Emily said, dryly.

Frieda cleared her throat. "The *problem* is rather more serious," she pointed out. She turned and walked to the windows. "The Fists of Justice are in firm control."

"And bent on making us pay for our sins," Markus said. "Literally."

Emily frowned. There was something in his voice…"Do you know them?"

"I had an uncle who was a devotee," Markus said. "He would…he wasn't a very important man, so no one really cared what he did. He was forty and he acted like he was twenty, holding wild parties and drinking from dusk till dawn. He never had any trouble getting friends to come, either. They knew he was good for wine, women and song."

"I know the type," Emily said.

"Everyone thought he was mad," Markus added. "He partied in the night, then scourged himself in the day. He'd hurt himself, curse himself…he'd fast for long hours, pushing his body to the limits. He went on and on about how he was a sinner, about how he deserved to be punished for his crimes…he just never stopped. And then one day his heart gave out and that was that."

Emily shuddered. "What did he *do*?"

"Nothing, as far as anyone knew," Markus said. "He was a lesser son of a lesser branch on the family tree. Not important enough to be considered worthy marriage material, but too attached to the family wealth to cut ties and set off on his own. Maybe it was just the heavy drinking. Most sorcerers know better than to drink heavily."

He shook his head. "But my uncle embraced their beliefs willingly. What happens when someone tries to impose such rules on an entire city?"

"They have something that looks like a god," Emily said. "They might succeed."

"They *are* succeeding," Markus pointed out.

Emily felt cold. Once, years ago, she'd read a story where divine laws were divinely enforced. It had struck her as utterly horrific – the world had been bad for everyone, particularly women – even though the creature in charge hadn't been a *real* god. But she knew there were people who would consider such a world to be ideal, especially if they were the ones on top. The Fists of Justice were already well on the way to turning Beneficence into a nightmare.

"Then we will have to stop them," Emily said. She wondered if Alassa had seen the message yet. King Randor had been keeping her hopping over the last months, moving from castle to castle in hopes of tightening her ties to her nobility. "Whatever it takes."

"Good luck," Markus said. "How do you intend to proceed?"

"I wanted to consult with you about magic," Emily said. She outlined what she'd sensed in the morning and how it linked to the chat parchments. "Is there any way to disrupt the link?"

Markus frowned. "I don't believe so." He stroked his chin thoughtfully. "Allowing magic to flow from...from the entity to a staff might be more complicated than merely sending words, but it's still magic. As long as the staffs were linked, magic would be able to run between them."

"And then it flows into the spellwork." Frieda turned and walked back to join them, her face grim. "Overpowering a wand-spell can be disastrous."

"Perhaps we should concentrate on disrupting the spellware instead," Emily mused. "And then the magic would flow in all directions."

"Or explode," Markus said. "We could even try to drain the power."

"Only if we lured Justice into a prepared battleground," Emily said. A necromancer could drain another magician of power, but it would cost them their sanity... if they survived the experience. Justice was powerful enough to overload and kill anyone stupid enough to try to drain him. "They would see the trap, wouldn't they?"

"Perhaps," Markus said. "We could use runes to steer magic away from him, if his spells started coming apart."

Emily frowned. A normal spell would leak power until it finally collapsed, although that could take some time. But if Justice was something akin to a Mimic, and she suspected he had a lot in common with them, she was fairly sure he would recycle power rather than lose it. Perhaps, given enough time, they could set up a trap, but it wouldn't work unless the entity was careless. And she knew they couldn't count on anything of the sort.

"We need more information." She silently promised herself that she would try to dispel Justice, the next time she faced the entity. It was worth trying. Few magicians would consider using such a simple spell against a god. "And we need to lay our plans carefully."

"I'll start rigging a trap here," Markus said. "If he decides to break in, we can at least try to delay him."

Emily nodded, although she suspected it would be pointless. Justice was simply too powerful to be stopped easily. If there was something physical to him...they could steal gunpowder from the powder mills and try to blow him up. She didn't think that would work either – she knew it wouldn't stop a Mimic – but it might slow him down. Besides, better to secure the gunpowder before the Fists of Justice put it to use. Sienna and the other sorcerers might not recognize it as a potential threat.

General Pollack will, she told herself. *He's seen firearms in action.*

"We have to get back," she said. "Do you have a spare chat parchment?"

"I have several pieces," Markus said. "You know how to activate them?"

"Yes," Emily said. She'd done it before, once. "Have you told Melissa about...about this?"

"She urged me to run." Markus looked up at Melissa's portrait. "But...you know...I couldn't leave."

Emily understood. Markus wasn't anything special, without his family. There were plenty of other talented magicians out there. But the bank was something *new*, the first of its kind...something that could change the world. Markus could no more abandon the Bank of Silence than Emily could abandon Heart's Eye and the nexus point.

"Getting out of the city might prove difficult," Emily agreed. "Don't try to teleport."

"I might have to swim," Markus said. "Or turn into a bird and fly."

"Good luck," Frieda said sarcastically. "They'll probably have archers on the walls by now."

Emily replaced her glamour, then followed Frieda back through the tunnel and out onto the streets. The racket from the mob was growing louder, shouting and screaming for Justice to come and teach the bankers a lesson. Emily shuddered, despite herself, at the waves of emotion roiling through the sound. The people wanted someone to blame for everything, and they'd chosen the bankers. It never seemed to occur to them that everyone who'd fallen for Vesperian's prattle had played a role in their own downfall.

And some of them are just out to cause trouble, she thought, as they hurried away from Bankers Row. *They want to tear the place to the ground.*

She stopped, dead, as she saw the Fists of Justice gathered around a midsized house. A small crowd watched, hooting and hollering, as a man, a woman and four children were marched out of the building, their hands trapped in solid wooden boards placed around their necks. They were helpless, utterly defenseless...

Emily felt sick as the jeers grew louder. She didn't know what the family had done, or what they were supposed to have done, but she wanted to help them. She *needed* to help them. But the Fists of Justice were carrying staffs and wearing charmed breastplates. She couldn't stop them without revealing her presence, drawing the entity to her. She'd give up every hope of stopping them for good.

Damn you, she thought. She turned and led Frieda away, cursing herself. *And damn me too.*

Chapter Twenty-Eight

CALEB MET THEM AS SOON AS THEY WERE INSIDE THE HOUSE. "ARE YOU ALL RIGHT?"
Emily groaned as she dispelled the remainder of the glamour. "I've been better," she said, softly. She'd walked away, leaving a family to their fate. "How about you?"

"We just got back," Caleb said. He helped her remove her cloak and hung it on a peg. "They're in the living room, waiting for you."

"Good." Emily glanced at Frieda. "Shall we go?"

General Pollack had placed a large map on the table, Emily saw when she walked into the living room. Beneficence was probably not drawn to scale, she noted as she surveyed the odd design, but it was fairly usable. Someone had scribbled a series of notes on the paper, using red ink to designate enemy positions. She hoped the map wasn't particularly valuable.

"Lady Emily," a voice said. "I am pleased to see that you have returned home."

Emily looked up and blinked. Harman sat on the far side of the table, next to three men Emily didn't recognize. One looked like a fisherman; the other two were either soldiers or craftsmen. There was an air of dignity about them that reminded her of some of the other craftsmen she'd met.

"I'm glad you survived," Emily managed. She'd assumed Harman had been killed during the massacre. "How did you get out of the square?"

Harman looked pained. "I survived for the very simple reason I wasn't there," he said. "The Grand Guildmaster believed that my presence would not be welcomed, so I spent the day supervising the accountants who were dismantling Vesperian's web of lies. And then I hid when...when they came for me."

"I found him in the Mirthful Mermaid," General Pollack said, briskly. "Our emergency plans called for using the bar as a rendezvous point, if the city was attacked."

"Because of all the booze," Sienna said, dryly.

"*And* because it is far enough from the Guildhall to be off anyone's target list," Harman said, quickly. He glanced at Emily. "Should I be talking about that to you?"

"She's not going to tell King Randor," Caleb said, hotly.

Emily nodded in agreement. King Randor was the only significant outside threat, as far as Beneficence was concerned. The other kingdoms would be unable to get an army into the city without marching over Zangaria, not when Beneficence controlled the waters around its territory. King Randor would be interested to know where the guildmasters would assemble if all hell broke loose, but right now it didn't matter. The *real* problem was defeating the Fists of Justice before it was too late.

Besides, they'll change the plan after I leave, she thought. *They won't want to take the risk that I might tell King Randor.*

"I beg your pardon, Lady Emily," Harman said. "It is my duty as a guildmaster to protect the city."

"A guildmaster who only kept his position on sufferance." The fisherman sneered. "You wouldn't have been allowed to stay away if you were actually *important.*"

"Dagmar, *my* guild could have prevented this crisis," Harman snapped. "If you'd listened to me…"

"Your guild thought it was a fun idea to cheat us out of our money," Dagmar said. "You were lucky to be allowed to *live*."

"And you do not speak for all of us," one of the others insisted. "We do not have a quorum!"

"We won't," Harman snapped. "The other guildmasters are dead! I'm the last survivor and…"

"And you are worthless," Dagmar snapped back. "Do you think you can lead us to victory?"

"The guildmasters themselves are corrupt," the third man said. "They need to be replaced completely."

"Blasphemy," Harman insisted. "Ambrose, you are nothing more than a traitor!"

General Pollack slapped the table, hard. "This is not the time to fight." His voice was frigid. "Need I remind you that most of the City Guard has been captured or subverted or killed? Need I remind you that our city, our *home*, is being steadily reshaped while we sit here and bicker like *children*? Need I remind you that *we* – yes, *we* – represent the remnants of the government? Need I remind you…?"

He looked from face to face. "This is not the time to fight," he repeated. "After we win, we will elect new guildmasters and rebuild the government."

"Or replace it," Ambrose said.

"We will decide how best to proceed after we win," General Pollack said. "We do not have much time. Sorcerers Row is the safest place in the city, but it won't remain safe for long."

"There have been a series of probes against the wards, looking for weak points," Sienna said, coolly. "Someone is readying themselves to break into the street."

Harman looked as though he wanted to say something, but General Pollack glared him into silence. Emily eyed him, thoughtfully. She didn't pretend to understand the politics, but Harman was definitely unpopular. Did he really think he could boss everyone else around, just because he was the last guildmaster? Or was he desperately trying to cling to *something* he'd once owned? It wasn't as if the Fists of Justice would have any use for him either.

General Pollack ran his fingers over the map. "I managed to speak to a number of old friends," he said. "We put together this outline. As you can see, the Fists have established patrol bases around the city and are currently running patrols through the major streets. So far, they've left the alleyways, Fishing Plaice and the Lower Depths alone, but I expect that to change as they build their numbers. Starry Light and Temple Row, by contrast, have a strong presence."

"Makes sense," Harman said. "The wealthiest part of the city."

"Correct," General Pollack said. "They've already arrested a number of prominent citizens and their families, taking them to the Iron Cage. I don't know what they've done to the former occupants, but I don't think it was anything good."

Emily glanced at Caleb. "The Iron Cage?"

"The city jail," Caleb explained. "One of the strongest buildings in the city."

"Getting them out will be impossible," Harman said. "That building is *tough*."

"Correct," General Pollack said. "We would probably be able to get inside if we were uninterrupted, but they'll respond at once to any challenge to their power. We'd be knee-deep in Fists before we got through the first set of wards."

"And they have a *god*," Harman said. "How do we fight *that*?"

"It's a trick," General Pollack said. "*Justice* is nothing more than a complex set of spells."

Emily winced, inwardly. If she was right, that was *far* too close to the truth for her peace of mind. They might defeat Justice only to discover the birth of a dozen other entities within the year.

"That's no spell," Dagmar said.

"It can be beaten," Sienna said. "It's just a matter of figuring out *how*."

Harman frowned. "And if you're wrong?"

"Then it's a god." Dagmar sounded oddly amused. "It can still be beaten."

Emily gave him a surprised look. How could someone believe that a creature was a god and yet, at the same time, believe it could be beaten? But then, the Norse, Roman and Greek gods hadn't been invincible either. Justice might be powerful – there was no doubt about that, she knew all too well – but not unstoppable. God or no god, the entity could be stopped.

And we have to keep believing that, she told herself, firmly. *If we believe we cannot defeat him, we may as well surrender now.*

"It is neither all-seeing nor all-powerful." Sienna crossed her arms under her breasts as Emily glanced at her. "It would have crushed us all by now if it were a *true* god."

General Pollack nodded. "For the moment, we will do our best to evade Justice while we undermine their control over the city," he said. "We do not have the time, unfortunately, to gather the information we need before taking the offensive. The longer we wait, the stronger their position will be."

"But that would mean risking exposure," Harman pointed out. "Shouldn't we build up our strength first?"

"They'll be doing the same," General Pollack said. "And they already have a big head start."

"They also have a god – all right, a powerful entity," Harman insisted. "We'd be drawing their attention!"

"You're already at the top of their list of targets," General Pollack said. "You are, after all, the last surviving guildmaster."

Harman looked pale. "Fine. How do you want to proceed?"

"We'll wait until nightfall," General Pollack said. "At that point, we'll gather our forces and launch a set of hit and run attacks against their positions. If we hit here" – he tapped a street on the map, only a short distance from Sorcerers Row – "they will dispatch reinforcements, of course, from Temple Row. It's their closest strongpoint."

"It's too close," Harman said.

Dagmar frowned. "Or do you have something else in mind?"

"It's a diversion," General Pollack said. "We need to sneak someone into the temple. Janus, the bastard, does not appear to have moved into the Guildhall. Nor has he gone to the castle. He's staying in the temple and rarely showing himself."

Emily frowned. If Janus wasn't showing himself...what did it mean? Was he the one pulling Justice's strings? It would make sense, although Janus had been at the square when Justice had made his big appearance. Her tired mind produced a dozen possibilities, each one more complex than the last. Janus might even *be* Justice...

"He might just be consolidating his power," Croce said. "It's only been a day since the coup."

True, Emily thought.

"We have to find out what he's really doing before we can figure out how to counter it," General Pollack said. "And that means getting into the temple and finding out." He looked at Emily. "Lady Emily, will you attempt to sneak into the temple?"

Emily blinked in surprise, then glanced at Caleb. Her boyfriend looked as surprised as Emily felt. He hadn't known his father planned to ask Emily to undertake a dangerous, perhaps suicidal, mission. Emily wondered, vaguely, if he'd expected to be asked first...it made sense, she supposed. But then, General Pollack *had* watched her walk into Heart's Eye and kill a necromancer. He might hope she could do the same again.

But we're not facing a necromancer, Emily thought. She'd killed a Mimic, but she'd had help. *This might be far more dangerous.*

She hesitated, just long enough to see a sneer drift onto Harman's face. Sienna was better-trained and more experienced, but she would be needed on the front lines. She didn't know how many other combat sorcerers were in the city, yet some of them would be needed with Sienna and others would refuse to cooperate. Caleb would be needed too, while the rest of his siblings were too young. And *none* of them had any real experience with Mimics. She *was* the best choice.

"I'll go," she said, quietly.

"I'll come with you," Caleb said.

"You're going to be here," General Pollack said. "I need you to start putting together a set of wands."

Caleb stared at him. "Father, she's going to need help..."

"I can go with her." Frieda's voice was silky-smooth. "Caleb, you *are* going to be needed here."

Emily looked at General Pollack. He was right, she knew; Caleb *would* be more useful on the streets. But had the general made that decision because it was the practical solution...or because he didn't want to send a second son into danger by her side? Casper had died because he'd followed her into Heart's Eye. Might General Pollack wonder if Caleb would go the same way? She hoped, deep inside, that she would never know.

"Frieda can help me," she murmured. The thought of walking into the temple – and perhaps confronting Justice for the second time – scared her more than she cared to admit. But at least they were doing *something*. "I'll be fine."

General Pollack looked at his watch. "We'll move out after sunset," he said. "That gives us five hours to assemble the troops."

"Most of whom have no training," Harman warned. "And the ones who do haven't been in the military for years."

"You never forget," General Pollack said. "Emily, Frieda; get some rest."

"Understood," Emily said.

"I'll come with you." Caleb ignored his mother clearing her throat. "We need to talk."

Emily nodded, not trusting herself to look at Sienna. They walked out of the room and up the stairs. Marian was coming out of her bedroom as they approached, looking murderous. The expression on her face was nasty enough to make Emily ready a spell to defend herself, just in case. It didn't *look* as though Marian wanted to apologize for anything. The younger girl walked down the stairs and through the bottom door, never looking back.

"Give us some privacy," Caleb said to Frieda. "Please."

Frieda glanced at Emily, then hurried into the bedroom. Emily couldn't help noticing that she'd left the door open, just a crack. Caleb cast a privacy ward, then two more, blurring them together to defeat any listening ears. Emily hoped it wouldn't bring Frieda running out of the bedroom to discover why everything had gone quiet.

"He didn't tell me," Caleb said. "I didn't know he was going to ask you to do *that*. Emily…you could get *killed* in the temple!"

"I know," Emily said. She was scared, but…she boxed the fear away in her mind, refusing to allow it to dominate her. "I understand the risks."

Caleb stared at her. "You could be killed – or worse. What will happen when that…that *creature* focuses on you?"

Emily shivered. Justice had been powerful, powerful enough to make her waver despite all her defenses. She had more experience with mind-manipulation than the average student at Whitehall, but still…Justice had nearly overwhelmed her. And she'd been quite some distance from the entity. Who knew *what* would happen if she was right next to it? Or if it focused all its power on her?

"I'm the best-qualified person to walk into the temple," Emily said, pushing her doubts and fears aside. "Everyone else is needed back here."

"Sarnia could go," Caleb snapped. "*She's* got the power and experience…"

"No, she doesn't," Emily said. She had no idea if Sarnia had even *joined* the resistance. The older woman had a family she wouldn't care to see threatened. "I'm better qualified than almost anyone else."

Caleb shook his head slowly. "I don't want to lose you," he said. He looked into her eyes. "This…"

Emily wished, suddenly, that she could *promise* she'd survive. But she knew Caleb was right. Entering the temple would be dangerous, very dangerous. If she was caught, she would be killed…or brainwashed. Her defenses were tough, but they wouldn't stand up to sustained attack. No defense was perfect. Lady Barb had hammered that into her time and time again.

She reached out and took his hand. "I'll be fine," she said. "You'll be fine too."

"You might not be," Caleb said. "Emily…"

He sighed. "I'm sorry."

Emily blinked. "What for?"

"All of this." Caleb waved a hand at the wall. "My family…everything."

"Don't worry about it," Emily said.

She pulled him close and hugged him, despite the risk. It had been easy at Whitehall, where they'd just been students…it had been easy to be themselves. But here, Caleb's family was watching them, judging them…it wasn't easy to relax. She hugged him tighter, unsure if she envied or pitied him. On one hand, Caleb had a family that genuinely loved him; on the other, that family restricted him in ways Emily could barely comprehend.

You're not just marrying him, Lady Barb had said, two years ago. *You're marrying his entire family.*

Caleb returned her hug, slowly. "I'm sorry," he whispered. "I wish…"

Emily heard something at the bottom of the stairs and peered down. Marian stood there, looking up at them. Caleb pulled himself free and glared at his younger sister, magic sparking around his fingertips. Emily glanced at him in surprise, wondering if he would actually hex the younger girl. And yet, as Marian stamped up the stairs, she felt Caleb's magic fading back into nothingness.

"I'm sorry about her too," Caleb said, once Marian had walked into her room and slammed the door. Emily could hear love and affection in his voice. "She isn't normally like this."

"She's not having a good time," Emily said. "And she's too young to understand."

She shook her head. Marian was probably having problems coping now all of her siblings were away at school, leaving her alone with her parents. On one hand, someone would be looking after her; on the other, she'd have her mother's undivided attention. And she was growing up, watching helplessly as her body changed…Emily remembered going through puberty herself and shivered. *That* had not been a pleasant experience.

At least Marian has a mother who will help her through it, she thought, darkly. Her mother had shouted at her, when she'd tried to talk about female matters. There was no way in hell she'd ask her stepfather for advice. Marian didn't know how lucky she was. *She has a family who loves her.*

"After this, we'll go back to Whitehall," she promised. "We can go up the mountain and…"

"If we have time," Caleb said. He didn't sound enthusiastic. "We're going to have to work hard to catch up with everyone else."

"I know." Emily lifted her head, parting her lips. "But we can do it."

Caleb leaned down and kissed her gently. "I hope so," he said, as he pulled back. "But we have to survive the next few days first."

"We will," Emily promised.

Chapter Twenty-Nine

I T WAS DARK, VERY DARK.

Emily slipped through the backstreets, silently cursing the Fists of Justice as she kept a careful lookout for spies. Frieda followed, watching her back. Beneficence had once been the most well-lit city on the Nameless World, illuminated with gaslights that wouldn't have been out of place in Victorian London; now, the city was as dark and silent as the grave. Even the footpads and other criminals seemed to have removed themselves from the streets. The only people she'd seen, since they'd slipped out of Sorcerers Row, were a couple of patrols prowling the streets. They'd walked past Emily and Frieda without noticing them.

She tested the glamour as they picked their way towards Temple Row. The night-vision spell made everything look eerie, creating pools of shadow that seemed to move the moment she looked away. She was relieved, despite herself, that most of the statues had been destroyed, even though she knew two-thirds of the city considered the feeling blasphemy. The statues would have looked far too creepy in the grey haze. She spotted a handful of blankets, clearly concealing something positioned against the wall; she eyed them for a long moment before deciding that whoever owned them was trying to hide. The Fists of Justice, if the reports were to be believed, hadn't been kind to anyone they'd caught on the streets after dark.

The presence grew stronger as they neared their destination, a pulsing heartbeat that echoed through the air and brushed against her magic. Even mundanes could sense it, according to General Pollack. Emily had no idea how that worked, but she didn't blame the resistance for feeling scared. They wanted – they *needed* – more data before they did anything more than attacking patrols and raiding isolated outposts. She took a breath, bracing herself as the presence seemed to grow stronger for a moment. Her attention seemed to draw *its* attention.

Don't think about it, she told herself. Justice would worm its way through the gaps in her defenses if she gave it a chance. She wished, grimly, that there had been a chance to get the children out of the city. They'd be the most vulnerable to a constant subtle whispering at the back of their minds. *Keep your eyes on the ball.*

Frieda touched her hand as they reached the end of the alleyway. A dozen Fists stood at the edge of Temple Row, their eyes flickering from side to side as they watched the streets; beyond them, workmen and slaves carted away the debris from the other temples, even though night had fallen two hours ago. Emily glanced back at the Fists and shivered, remembering the guards who'd defended Farrakhan. *They'd* been smoking, chatting quietly to keep themselves awake, but the Fists seemed utterly intent on their work. There was something oddly inhuman about them, as if all their humanity had been leeched away.

She glanced at Frieda, who held up her fingers in a sign Emily remembered from Mountaintop. *Proctors.*

Emily looked at the Fists. Proctors? The Mountaintop Proctors had been dead bodies animated by the wards; they'd been drained of life force to feed the wards, then put to work as enforcers to keep the students in line. She didn't think the Hands of Justice would have done the same…would they? They'd be in real trouble if the secret had leaked out before the coup. But now…they *could* turn their fanatics into zombies, if they wished. They were already committed to victory or extinction.

And they might have drained them to feed Justice, Emily thought. She reached out with her senses as carefully as she could, trying to detect a glamour that might have hidden a dead face, but there was too much interference for her to be sure of anything. *That might be where he's getting his power…*

She inched back into the alleyway before any of the fanatics caught a glimpse of them. The glamour *should* hide them from unwary eyes, but she had no idea how well it would hold up against the fanatics. An alert set of guards might just investigate something they glimpsed out of the corner of their eyes, even though it might have been nothing. And if they had sorcerers – or merely a handful of magic-users – the glamour wouldn't last long at all.

Frieda held up her hands again. "Five minutes," she signalled. "Then we will see."

Emily nodded. General Pollack had planned a series of attacks, all designed to get in, land a punch and then get out again before the enemy had a chance to respond. He'd admitted, openly, that the best they could do was give the Fists a bloody nose, but it might buy time for Emily and Frieda to slip into Temple Row. If, of course, the watching guards were distracted. Emily bit her lip, concerned. The fanatics didn't look as though they would be distracted easily.

But the slaves might try to escape, she thought, peering out of the alleyway. *I would, if I'd been given the chance.*

She shuddered. She'd been told that some slaves were merely working off debts – a concept she found sickening, even if people insisted such slaves were treated well – but *these* slaves were definitely working against their will. A number even wore the tattered remains of priestly garb, when they'd been allowed to wear anything at all. They were being forced to rip their own temples to shreds. She gritted her teeth as she pulled her head back, knowing there was nothing she could do to help them. She'd just have to hope they defeated the Fists of Justice as quickly as possible.

A brilliant flash of light came from Sorcerers Row. Emily braced herself as the guards looked around, apparently confused. Two more flashes of light followed, both marking attacks on enemy patrols. Sienna and her fellows spent power freely, making it clear that they were going on the offensive, while their mundane counterparts launched more subtle attacks. The Fists of Justice would have to react quickly, General Pollack insisted, if they wanted to retake control of the streets. And their nearest reinforcements were at Temple Row.

Unless they're more intent on preserving the temple than retaking the streets, Emily thought, grimly. The plan had seemed workable, when they'd been going through the final aspects after a brief nap, but now it struck her as being more than a little chancy. They'd underestimated the sheer level of activity around the building. *They may think they can retake control in the morning.*

She tensed as she heard the sound of running footsteps. A trio of men in red robes, one carrying a staff that blazed with power, ran out of the Temple of Justice and straight towards the guards. There was a brief exchange of orders, then the guards followed the priests onto the streets, away from Temple Row. Emily inched forward, noting where the other guards were watching the slaves. The temple hadn't been left completely unguarded. She could knock them down with magic, but that would reveal her presence...

We need a distraction, she thought, as she peered down the street. *Something that will keep them busy...*

She braced herself, then shaped an unlocking spell in her mind and cast it with all the power she could muster. The slaves jerked upright as their chains unlocked, coming free and falling to the ground with a mighty clatter. They broke free a moment later; some attacking their captors with tools or their bare hands, others running in all directions. Emily caught Frieda's hand and pulled her onto the street, hurrying down Temple Row towards the Temple of Justice as the riot swelled out of control. The guards didn't seem to notice them. They had too many other problems to worry about.

So do we, Emily thought, as they reached the temple. Another group of guards stood just inside the building, looking altogether more serious. Two were definitely magic-users, although she didn't think they were full sorcerers. Their magic fields seemed a little unfocused. *Those guards aren't distracted...*

Frieda tapped her arm, motioned for Emily to stay put, then ran forward, dispelling the glamour as she moved. The guards noticed her, an instant before she threw a string of fireballs, brilliant lights and blinding spells into the temple, then ran down the street. Emily watched, torn between horror and relief, as the guards either clutched their eyes or gave chase, hurling hexes and curses after Frieda. It was easy, terrifyingly easy, to slip past the guards and into the temple. They didn't have a hope of noticing she was there.

She tensed as she felt magic pervading the temple, streams of power that led underground. It *was* very much like Mountaintop, although she didn't think Mountaintop had harvested enough power to create a god. Maybe *that* was why Justice hadn't made many appearances, before all hell broke loose. The Hands of Justice hadn't had the power to manifest him on a regular basis.

And now they do, she thought, inching forward. *But where are they getting the power?*

The temple felt spooky. It was brightly lit, yet empty. Her footsteps echoed through cavernous chambers that should have been filled with worshippers. Statues of Justice were everywhere, all following the same theme of resolute certainty. Justice was an implacable judge, an entity who could not be questioned. She caught sight of a statue holding a set of scales and winced. The scales of justice, it seemed, always had to be balanced.

She allowed the magic to lead her to a set of stairs, disappearing down into the darkness; carefully, she walked down them, keeping her magic at the ready. The rune on her chest started to heat, warning her of subtle magic; her skin crawled as she felt it reaching out to touch her, plucking at her mind. Anyone who found the stairs without proper preparation, she realized as she reached the bottom, would not only find themselves walking out again, but also lose all memory of having discovered the stairs in the first place. They'd never know what they'd found once they left the temple. And yet, it was a strikingly *passive* defense for such a secret.

The lower levels appeared as deserted as the temple itself, but she kept the glamour around her as she made her way down the corridors. A handful of doors lay in front of her, all closed and locked, secured by powerful wards. She studied the closest door for a long moment, then inched forward to test the defenses. It didn't *look* as though they were keyed to a particular mind, but a mistake in breaking them down would prove disastrous. And yet ... she didn't think she had a choice. The Fists of Justice would eventually return for morning prayers...

And if they catch me, she mused as she pushed her magic against the defenses, *I will be in real trouble.*

The defenses snapped and snarled at her as she forced her spells into the gaps and broke them, one by one. It was tough, the defenses easily enough to keep out the average student, but Lady Barb and Sergeant Miles had forced Emily to practice breaking *far* more complex protections. She'd broken into a dozen offices in Whitehall, just to prove she could. She tried not to think about the times she'd been *caught* by her tutors as she snapped the final set of wards and carefully turned the knob. No one would speak for her if she was caught *here*.

She opened the door carefully, watching for unpleasant surprises. She'd been caught, twice, because the tutors had hidden spells within the doorknob itself, spells that she hadn't been able to pick up because they'd been lost in the haze. But here, there were no spells. There didn't even seem to be any alarm bells. She lifted her gaze as she inched into the room, watching for trouble. But there was none...

The room was a large office, she realized, as she looked around. It was surprisingly simple: a wooden desk, a pair of chairs and a bookcase crammed with old manuscripts. And yet, there was a glass window at the far end of the room. She checked her glamour as she walked up to it, ready to duck at any moment. It opened over a large chamber, allowing her to look down at a set of altars. She shivered, remembering the day Shadye had tried to sacrifice her to the Harrowing. The altars looked eerily similar.

She forced herself to look away and walk to the desk, keeping a wary eye out for other booby traps. She'd known tutors who'd trapped their desks, even when they couldn't be bothered warding the entire classroom. But there was nothing, as far as she could tell. The only magic on the desk revolved around a small collection of parchment scrolls, piled up in front of the chair. They were so old that Emily felt herself drawn to them, even though she knew they could be dangerous to touch. The spells were designed to protect the scrolls against the passing of time.

And stealing them might set off an alarm, she thought, as she opened the first scroll. *I can't take them out of here.*

The parchment crackled at her touch, but opened without resistance. She peered down at the writing and froze. The writing was incredibly old, the words and spell notations horrendously anachronistic, but there was something *familiar* about it. She leaned closer, her mind refusing to accept what it was seeing. The spell diagram, fantastically complex, was a Mimic, but *not* a Mimic. She peered down at the writing, feeling her head starting to pound with shock. She'd seen the writing before, nearly a thousand years in the past.

Master Wolfe, she thought, numbly. She sat down in shock. *But I saw him die.*

She forced herself to work her way through the parchment. She'd been there when Master Wolfe had designed the first Mimics. He'd needed her help and insights to get started, although he'd taken the idea and run with it. Master Wolfe had been a genius beyond compare, even if he *had* been seen as a low-power magician. And yet, he'd died before he had a chance to improve on his work. She'd always assumed someone else had found his notes and brought the Mimics to life.

But this...this was his handwriting, his personal sigil. It made no sense. She'd seen him die, his head caved in by a treacherous magician. He couldn't have written the parchment scrolls before he'd met her, because he hadn't been that advanced at the time. But he couldn't have written them afterwards because he'd been dead! Unless...

He wanted to make himself immortal, she thought, numbly. *What if he succeeded?*

She pushed her feelings aside as she studied the scrolls. The Hands of Justice had stumbled across a way to *build* a god. It was a very complex spell – all the more so because the 'god' wouldn't be drawing its core from a living being – but doable. And yet, the more Justice grew and developed, the greater the chance of something going badly wrong. Justice might wind up questioning its existence...

...Or developing the intellect to judge its creators.

She felt sick as the implications started to sink in. The Mimic, for all of its power and the terror that had followed in its wake, had been a limited entity. It had killed its victims, then replaced them, burying its true nature until the time had come to feed again. Justice, by contrast, was a growing entity. Sooner or later, no matter how many layers of control the priests wove into the spellwork, it would break free.

They're sacrificing countless people to make it work, Emily thought. *And yet, the power requirements are steadily increasing.*

She resisted the urge to giggle. Vesperian's Ponzi scheme had fallen apart when the inflow of money had come to an end. The Hands of Justice might also fall apart when they ran out of people to kill...

Gritting her teeth, Emily read through the rest of the parchments. Most were part of the god-creation spell, but a handful seemed to be part of something greater. She looked at the bookcase, wishing she had the time to go through it more carefully. The spell in front of her was so huge that she couldn't tell what it was actually meant to do. All she could say for sure was that the power requirements were astronomical...

They couldn't muster so much power without a nexus point, she thought. *But why?*

Emily looked up as she heard a scream, echoing through the window. Something was happening down there, but what? She had a feeling she knew the answer. She rose, knowing she'd have to be careful. If she was seen, the Fists of Justice would come looking for her and *they* wouldn't be distracted by a glamour...

She slipped over to the window and peered down. Four red-robed priests, all carrying staffs, stood around an altar. A young man – still a boy – lay on the stone, his eyes wide with terror. Emily stared in horror as the priests lifted their staffs and brought them down on the boy's head, killing him instantly. The surge of magic flowed into a cobweb of spellware that flared into existence, channeling the power through the building...

...And then it was gone, as quickly as it had appeared.

Necromancy, Emily thought. *Shit.*

She hurried back to the desk. If she glanced at the scrolls, just for a moment, she would be able to use memory charms to reproduce them later...

...And then a spell slammed into her back.

Chapter Thirty

E MILY FROZE.

She thought, fast, as the spell sliced its way through her wards. It was unusual, not configured like any freeze spell she knew; it was actually a handful of spells, rather than a single enchantment. The combination allowed it to get through her wards, freezing everything below her neck. And it…it wasn't very secure. She tested it, readying a spell to break free.

"Lady Emily," a calm voice said. "It is a great pleasure to meet you at last."

Emily kept her face expressionless as Janus stepped into view. He wore a golden robe and carried a staff in his hand, a staff glowing with magic. His eyes were bright with something Emily didn't care to study too closely, a *vindication* that allowed him to overcome any setbacks and keep going. She met his eyes for a second, looking for a red taint, but saw nothing. He wasn't a necromancer…

I can break out, she thought. It wasn't easy to escape a spell that froze her entire body, but she'd mastered it. *But if he thinks I'm trapped, he might talk too much.*

"I have followed your career with great interest," Janus said. "It's clear that you too are a believer in Justice. I salute you."

Oddly, Emily had the feeling that he meant it. There *was* genuine respect in his voice. And yet…she reminded herself, sharply, that one didn't have to use subtle magic to sound convincing. One just needed to be an excellent liar. Nothing she'd seen, before or after crossing worlds, had given her any faith in priests or their religions. They were mortal men who sinned as much as their flock.

"I was very pleased when I heard that you were coming." His lips quirked in a thin smile. "But you could have just announced yourself instead of sneaking into the temple."

Emily shivered. She'd been betrayed? They'd known she was coming? In hindsight, had her path been carefully cleared? Or was Janus bluffing, trying to force her to reveal something she didn't want to reveal? She was fairly sure he knew she was part of the resistance.

Unless he thought I fled the city after Justice revealed himself, she thought. *He hasn't seen me since then, has he?*

"I doubted my welcome," she managed, finally. She nodded at the scrolls on the desk, cursing his spell under her breath. The longer it remained in place, the harder it would be to recover after she broke it. "What are you doing?"

Janus cocked his head. "We are building a truly *just* society. All will pay for their sins, Lady Emily. All will know that there *is* justice. I would have thought you would support our goals."

He went on before she could answer. "The court cases you handled personally in Cockatrice showed a genuine interest in justice," he added. "You were *just*. You didn't allow personal feelings or aristocratic connections to sway your judgements. You spoke of all being equal before the law. Why do you not support us?"

Emily indicated the scrolls. "You're sacrificing hundreds of people to feed your god," she said, slowly. "How can that be *just?*"

Janus showed no reaction to her words. "They volunteered. It was clear that summoning Justice back into the mortal world would require a sacrifice. Decent men, god-fearing men, would have to offer themselves to him. And they did – they chose to give their lives so our god could live."

"You drained their life force and used it to feed your god." Emily met his eyes, seeing utter certainty looking back. "You're mad!"

"The *world* is mad," Janus said. "There is no *justice.*"

He paced, moving in and out of Emily's field of vision as he walked around the room. "I have seen court cases decided by who paid the largest bribe. I have seen crooks allowed to walk free because they were noblemen while their victims were commoners. I have seen magicians hex and curse innocent civilians, yet were left untouched because of their power. I have seen fathers sell their children into slavery to pay their debts; I have seen mothers fleeing their wifely duties; I have seen children treat their parents with disrespect. I have seen priests turn their temples into rackets and guildmasters turn their guilds into weapons.

"And now, an entire *city* is brought to its knees because a lone man managed to take all the money!"

His voice rose. "Where is the *justice?*"

Emily gritted her teeth, testing the spell holding her in place. She could break free, but he'd know in an instant what she'd done. Perhaps if she weakened it gingerly, she'd find it easier to snap when the time came to run. Janus seemed to want to talk, but she had no doubt he'd try to kill her as soon as it became necessary. Or, worse, throw her to his god.

"Your god never came," Emily said. "And so you *built* a god."

Janus rounded on her. "We *summoned* a god," he hissed. "The rites and rituals said we had to prove our worth, so we did! We solved the puzzles, made the prayers, offered the sacrifices...and our god appeared!"

Emily looked down at the scrolls. Master Wolfe had created something wondrous and terrible, a series of spells designed to create a powerful entity...*without*, perhaps, needing powerful and experienced sorcerers to start the ball rolling. Someone from Whitehall would have had more sense, she suspected, than to cast the spells without working out *precisely* what they did first. Janus and his comrades lacked even a basic magical education.

The warnings aren't at the back of the scrolls, she thought. *There weren't any warnings at all!*

She forced herself to think. "So you summoned a god," she said. She might as well humor him, for the moment. "And then...what?"

Janus smiled. "Vesperian's project was doomed," he said. "It was easy to calculate that he would eventually run out of money. And yet, more and more people were being drawn into the whirlpool. All that imaginary money--" he laughed, briefly

"--looked so tempting that people chose to ignore the warning signs. They should have stayed with gold and silver. I did try to warn my guild, you know."

Emily blinked. "You did?"

"I saw trouble coming," Janus said. "It was obvious. I didn't get a chance to look at the books, of course, but I could pick up enough of the wider picture to see disaster looming. It wasn't really anything *new*, you see. Only the scale was far larger than anyone would have believed possible, Lady Emily."

"I know," Emily said, quietly.

Something clicked in her mind. "Your guild," she repeated. "You were an accountant, weren't you?"

"I trusted my guildmaster," Janus said. "I didn't realize just how badly he'd exploited his position until we were being spat at in the streets. No one had time to worry about Vesperian when we were fighting for our survival."

Harman is an accountant, Emily thought, numbly. *And he was right next to us when we made our plans.*

She gritted her teeth. She'd have to warn General Pollack, once she got out...if, of course, it wasn't already too late. Sienna's spells should have revealed any spell-controlled traitors who entered her house, but if Harman had betrayed them willingly...

"You made the disaster worse," she realized. She'd worry about Harman later, if she had time. The real problem was still Justice. "You *encouraged* people to buy his notes."

"We didn't need to," Janus said. "We just watched and waited."

"Until the bubble finally started to burst," Emily said. "And when you knew it was going to happen, you used your god to kill people who were connected with the project."

"Justice passed judgement on them," Janus said.

"But he didn't," Emily pointed out. "Antony wasn't his father."

"Justice passed judgement on Antony," Janus said. "It was what he deserved."

And whatever you used to target Emil wasn't perfect, Emily thought. She wished that she had a few hours to go through the scrolls. Choosing the entity's target – one man in a large city – wouldn't be easy. A blood connection? Or something more subtle? *You got his son instead.*

She gritted her teeth. A mistake? Fathers and sons were definitely linked by ties of blood – Antony wouldn't be Emil, but he'd be close enough to be affected by blood-bound magic aimed at his father. Or were the Hands of Justice already losing control of their creation?

"He was a young man," she said. "He didn't deserve to die."

Janus laughed. "Clearly, *you've* never been a young man."

Emily rolled her eyes in annoyance. She'd never been particularly well-endowed, but still...no one would mistake her for a man unless she used a glamour. She opened her mouth to point out that Janus had been a young man himself once, but she knew it would be futile. Janus had convinced himself that the entity was a real god, therefore nothing it did could be wrong by definition. Justice could slaughter children in their cradles and Janus would rationalize it away, somehow. And the other true believers would follow him.

"And then you killed Vesperian," Emily said. "And when the bubble exploded, you were ready to take over."

"And build a truly just world," Janus finished. He leaned forward. "Lady Emily, surely you can see that we should be on the same side."

Emily shook her head. She could see their point — she'd seen too much of what passed for justice in the Nameless World — but they'd gone too far. Their creation would eventually consume the entire city, even if they didn't lose control sooner or later. And even if they somehow overcame *that* problem — a dispelling spell *might* stop Justice before the entity could do any more damage — they'd still be crushing anyone who disagreed with them. One nightmare would be replaced by another.

The Shah of Iran wasn't a very nice man, she recalled. *But the Mullahs weren't an improvement.*

"You're not about justice," she said, quietly. "You're about power."

"Power to set things *right*," Janus said.

"No," Emily said. A dozen arguments rose up in her mind, but she knew none of them would make a difference. Janus was a fanatic. He wouldn't listen to logic and reason. "You might have started out with good intentions, but you'll wind up twisting them into a nightmare."

"We have a *god*," Janus insisted.

"A creature who is incapable of telling the difference between a man and his father," Emily said, sharply. Justice, if she'd reasoned the scrolls out correctly, wouldn't be particularly intelligent. That would come, in time, but for the moment he'd be no smarter than the average dog. "A creature who is incapable of understanding subtle points…"

"There are *no* subtle points." Janus darted to his feet, glaring down at her. The affable pose was gone. "There are no *excuses*."

"There is a difference between a man who steals because he wants gold and a man who steals because he needs to feed his children," Emily pointed out. Janus was far too close to her for comfort. "One is a criminal…"

"It makes no difference," Janus insisted. His eyes bored into hers. Emily could sense, again, something peering at her *though* his eyes. "Both of them are thieves!"

He stepped back, his face twisting as if he'd smelled something vile. "That's how it always starts," he hissed. "Excuses! He needed to steal because he has a family to feed! He beat his wife bloody because she nagged! She killed her husband because he beat her! Excuses, excuses, excuses…they're nothing more than ways to escape responsibility for their actions! And yet, the goods are stolen or a person is dead…"

Emily winced, inwardly. On one hand, she knew he had a point. An excuse was nothing more than an excuse. But, on the other hand, some excuses were valid. She would have felt sorry for a man who needed to steal to feed his family or for the woman who killed her abusive husband. And yet, that didn't excuse their crimes…

did it? She knew people who would have supported the husband for beating his wife, if the woman was a nag. They would have happily accepted the husband's shitty excuse.

And that's why we want to believe in an omniscient judge, she thought. *God, who sees everything, would be able to weigh the excuses in the balance and come to a perfect judgement.*

She closed her eyes for a long moment. She could see Janus's point. The Nameless World had never been a just place. She'd seen countless people abused because they were peasants, because they lacked magic, because they'd been in the wrong place at the wrong time...

...But she also knew Janus was wrong. His theocracy could no more create a perfect state than anyone else. And the entity he'd created would turn into a monster.

"I understand how you feel," she said, opening her eyes. It was true. "But this is utter madness."

"You punished a couple for abusing their servant," Janus said. He stepped back into view, his eyes quizzical. "How is this different?"

Emily shuddered. A young girl, younger than Frieda, had risked everything in coming to her baroness for justice. Emily knew, all too well, that her predecessor would have kicked the girl out of his castle – if she'd been lucky. But Emily had heard the case and passed judgement in the girl's favor. And yet, she knew people had muttered that she'd taken matters too far. Paying for the girl's medical treatment was one thing – and organizing that had been tricky – but turning her former master and mistress into serfs was quite another.

"You can't judge everyone." Emily flinched as she heard another scream echoing through the walls. "And you can't see *everything*. You cannot determine if an excuse is valid or not..."

"*Justice* can make those judgements," Janus insisted.

Emily shook her head. Justice couldn't even *begin* to judge fairly. Janus might *think* he was asking a god to pass judgement, but instead he was sending a monstrous entity out to kill. No doubt he thought everyone was guilty of something. In hindsight, Alba had been amazingly lucky. Justice could have killed her as easily as it had killed Antony.

She felt a twang of regret, mingled with a grim determination to stop Janus – whatever the cost. He didn't know what he was doing. How could he? He'd found the scrolls, but it was clear he lacked the background to do anything beyond taking them for granted...

"He can't," she said.

Janus lunged at her. His hand was wrapped around her neck before she could react.

"Justice is a god," he snarled. Emily had to fight to avoid panic. "And he will pass judgement on you!"

Emily gasped for breath as he released her. "Where...where did you find the scrolls?"

"They were hidden under the temple," Janus started to pace again. "We uncovered them two years ago, when we expanded the lower levels. The note on the scrolls said they would only be discovered when we needed them."

And if Master Wolfe managed to turn himself into a Mimic, Emily thought, *he might have come up here after escaping the castle.*

She considered it, briefly. A Mimic would never grow tired, as long as it had a constant supply of magic. She shivered as the implications sank in. Master Wolfe had been a skilled magician, yet even *he* would have had to resort to necromancy to live if he'd become a Mimic. His sanity would have eventually slipped completely, even though he no longer had a human brain to warp. But, before then, he could have founded the city. Beneficence was old, yet there were no reliable stories from the days before the Empire. God alone knew what might have happened between Master Wolfe's apparent death and the rise of the Empire.

A thought struck her. *Were those notes left for me?*

Janus turned back to face her. "You will join us," he said. "Surrender your will. Embrace Justice."

Emily snapped the freeze spell, then hurled a freeze charm of her own at him. Janus looked surprised, but somehow managed to use his staff to block the spell. Emily sensed a wave of magic surrounding the wood, pulsing out in all directions... Janus might not be a magician in his own right, but he'd somehow learned to manipulate magic in ways no mundane should be able to match. She promised herself that she'd figure out how he did it afterwards.

Janus snapped out a word. A wave of force struck Emily, throwing her back. She barely had a moment to wrap protections around herself before she smashed through the glass and plummeted to the chamber below. Someone shouted, loudly, as she drew on her magic to land as gently as she could. The shock of the impact still hurt...

"Justice," Janus shouted. "Come!"

Emily cursed as a red-robed man leapt at her, his face twisted with hatred. She slammed a force punch into his chest, tossing him through the air and into the far wall. Another appeared, his staff blazing with light; Emily threw a wand-cracking spell at him, and had the satisfaction of watching the staff shatter into dust. Moments later, raw magic tore the priest apart...

"Justice," Janus repeated. His staff glowed brightly. Magic flared through the chamber. She launched a fireball at him; it flickered out of existence an instant before it struck its target. "Come!"

And then Emily felt the presence all around her.

Chapter Thirty-One

EMILY GRITTED HER TEETH AS THE PRESENCE TORE INTO HER, A WAVE OF ENERGY THAT threatened to bring her to her knees. It whispered to her, promising a world of stability, of security, of *justice*, if she only let it into her heart. The torrent of power was so strong that her resolution buckled, nearly breaking once and for all. The rune on her chest heated, keeping her focused. She still had to fight to get out of the way as Justice coalesced in front of her. The entity looked more godlike than ever before.

"Justice!" Janus shouted. "Justice!"

Emily focused her mind, trying to think. She had to get out, she had to run... she felt the creature tugging at her magic, trying to drain her. Her wards, already damaged by Janus, started to break completely. No wonder Alba had been so badly drained, she noted as she hastily reinforced them. Alba had lacked the control to rebuild her protections – or her mother's protections – as Justice stripped them away.

She looked at Justice. The entity flowed so brightly that it was impossible to see details, but her mind filled in the blanks. She felt a moment of sour admiration for the person who'd designed the entity – Master Wolfe or one of his students, perhaps – as she realized how well it went together. They'd taken one of the nastiest mind-control spells she knew – that anyone knew – and melded it into the entity. Any attempt to break the spell ran the risk of speeding up the end.

"You're not real." She took a step backwards, then another. "You're not real."

The magic *surged*. She forced herself to jump to the side as a lightning bolt snapped through the air, passing through the space she'd been and slamming into the wall. It wasn't just a lightning bolt, she noted, as she threw herself over an altar and ducked behind it. A second bolt crackled over her head. Justice – or his creator – had wrapped a number of spells into each bolt. If one of them didn't get her, the others would.

Justice *kicked* the altar. It shattered, pieces of rock flying everywhere. Sparks of raw magic tore at Emily's wards, screams of pain echoing through her mind. She stumbled to her knees, her defenses starting to buckle under the onslaught. A volley of impressions - screams - stuck her as she brushed against the altar, a mark left behind by the dead. The early sacrifices might have been volunteers – she wondered if Janus had tried to sacrifice magic-users or people with undiscovered magic potential – but their successors had been held down and drained for the good of society. Janus, like all fanatics, would build his utopia on a pile of dead bodies.

Damn him, she thought.

She forced herself to crawl as the entity loomed over her. It was *playing* with her, inching forward to make her think she had a chance to escape. Or was it? Did it have more in common with a Manavore than she'd thought? Could it *see* her as long as she didn't use magic? She looked up at Janus, still standing in what remained of his office, and knew it wouldn't matter. He'd direct his god to her if she tried to escape without using magic.

Gritting her teeth, she pulled herself to her feet. Looking at Justice with her senses was like looking into a blinding light, but the more she looked the more she saw the complex chain of spells that held him together. Master Wolfe had *definitely* been a genius. And yet...

She braced herself, then cast the single most powerful dispelling spell she could. Justice flickered, just for an instant. Beyond him, darkness fell as light globes flickered out of existence and wards failed. Emily thought, for a second, that she'd actually won. And then the god lunged forward, power billowing around him. Emily had to throw herself right across the room, drawing on her magic, to escape its reach.

"There is no escape," Janus shouted. She couldn't see him any longer – her eyes were starting to hurt – but she could hear him all too well. "Judgement is coming!"

The dispelling charm didn't work, Emily thought. *He's too complex to be easily banished.*

Justice walked – or glided – towards her, his appearance blurring into a mass of lights and raw power. She wasn't sure if he'd switched off the glamour or if it no longer affected her, but it hardly mattered. Janus still ranted, behind his god. She tuned him out as she tried to think of another option. Direct attack was futile. But there were other possibilities.

She launched a fireball at the nearest altar, then picked up the pieces with magic and threw them at the entity. Justice didn't react as the chunks of stone flew towards him, but staggered when the rocks passed through his chest. Emily felt a flicker of surprise – she hadn't been sure what she'd expected to happen, but clearly *something* had – and launched more pieces of debris at him. Justice slowed, yet he wasn't stopped. And that meant...

I could thrust my mind into the maelstrom, she thought. *But I'd never get out alive.*

She looked up. Justice was backing her up against the wall. His power beat against her, pushing her back until she could retreat no more. But there were still options... she gathered her magic, then slammed a powerful hex into the ceiling. It shattered, dust and rocks raining down on the entity. Justice staggered, again, under the weight of the assault, distracting him for a moment. Emily yanked her wards around her, then hurled herself up and through the hole. The spell started to fail a moment later, as Justice started to drain the mana, but it was enough to get her to the top.

Not enough to stop him, she told herself, as she landed on the temple floor. *I need something bigger.*

A line of young men – boys, really – knelt at the front of the room, watched by a grim-faced man with a switch in one hand. He lifted his hand as soon as he saw Emily and started to chant a spell; she froze him in place, hoping the boys weren't fanatics. She didn't want to hurt them, even though they might not feel the same way about her. But, from the shock in their eyes, they hadn't wanted to be there either.

"Run," she shouted. "Now!"

The boys scattered as the presence grew stronger, faint lights flickering around the hole in the floor as Justice glided up to continue the pursuit. Emily gritted her teeth, then started to transfigure the pieces of debris to gunpowder. Justice might not be stopped by an explosion, but she hoped it would make him reconsider his options. She turned and ran, hurling a fireball behind her, as the entity hovered into view. The blast from the explosion picked her up and threw her into the wall. She barely had a moment to put up her arms and catch herself before it was too late.

She hit the ground, gasping in pain. The entire temple shook violently, pieces of debris crashing to the floor. She staggered to her feet and turned, blood trickling down her arms and legs. Justice stood in the middle of the crater, unhurt. He had his back to her, but the cobweb of magic around him was growing stronger. Two of the boys stumbled towards him, their heads bowed. Emily opened her mouth to shout a warning, but it was too late. He touched their foreheads gently, almost reverently...

...And both boys crumbled into dust.

Shit, Emily thought.

She could barely move as the entity slowly turned to face her. Its expression blurred, then coalesced into a stern face that peered down at her from an impossible height. A judge, she thought, a stern judge handing down judgements that could never be questioned. She heard a statue toppling to the ground behind her, but she couldn't break free. Justice had her in its power. It was all she could do not to fall to her knees and beg for a forgiveness she knew wouldn't come.

A hanging judge, she told herself. Her aches and pains faded into a dull haze as it advanced towards her. *Everyone is guilty of something.*

Her magic faded as the cobwebs grew stronger, brushing against her wards. She *felt* them, stroking her magic...she felt as though she was on the verge of some great insight, but it refused to materialize. There was something about them...

And then she heard a voice. "Emily!"

Emily's magic sparked as *something* wrapped itself around her, yanking her through the air at terrifying speed. For a second, she felt utterly helpless as the cobwebs grew stronger, trying to pull her back. And then the cobwebs tore, releasing her. Magic flared around her as she flew through a hole in the wall and landed on the ground. Frieda stood over her, looking grim.

"Emily," she said. "What happened?"

"Help me up," Emily's managed. Her magic felt drained. She hadn't felt so bad since her duel with Master Grey. Her throat was so dry she was sure she could taste dust. "Hurry!"

Frieda helped her up. Emily leaned against her, peering into the darkened temple. The entity stood within the shadows, looking back at her. It had her scent, she knew; she could barely move, let alone run. Justice could finish the job at any moment, if it wished. It could kill Frieda too...

...And yet, it wasn't moving.

It can't leave the temple without permission, Emily guessed. *Or perhaps without proper preparation.*

She tore her gaze away from the entity to look up and down the street. Dead bodies lay everywhere, slaves killed by their former owners and priests torn limb from limb by their former slaves. Fires burned in the darkness, suggesting many of the original attacks had been successful. And yet, she knew she'd failed. She'd learned a great deal about Justice, but not enough to kill him.

And Janus will be up here at any moment, she thought, grimly. She would have liked to think that Janus had been squashed by falling debris, but she knew she didn't dare count on it. *He can give Justice permission to come after us.*

"We need to move," she muttered. She drew on what remained of her magic to regenerate her energy, although she knew she'd pay for it later. "That thing is going to be released soon."

She leaned against Frieda as they stumbled down Temple Row. Someone shouted in the distance, but she couldn't make out the words. The guards who should have been on duty were either dead or gone – she hoped, in a moment of savage fury, that they were dead. Janus and his comrades might have started out with good intentions, but they'd jumped off the slippery slope long ago.

"Hurry," Frieda hissed. "They're coming back."

"Get us into the alley," Emily ordered. It hurt to talk. She suspected she'd pushed her magic too far in the last couple of hours. "But don't try to glamour us unless there's no other choice."

She could hear running footsteps as Frieda pulled them both into the alleyway. The Fists of Justice chanted prayers as they ran past the entrance, heading down to the damaged temple. Emily wondered, absently, how many of them would start to question their own doctrines before deciding the answer was probably *none*. The Fists of Justice would have been exposed to the entity for so long that it was unlikely any of them could even *begin* to question it.

Janus must have gone the same way too, she thought, as she sagged against a stone wall. It smelled of garbage and worse, but she was glad it was there. *The longer he spent with his god, the more he came to believe in its divinity.*

She resisted the urge to close her eyes as the shouting grew louder. Frieda could probably get her back to Sorcerers Row – if nothing else, Frieda could turn her into something lighter and *carry* her – but she didn't dare sleep. This close to the presence, this close to its endless whispers…she knew it would leech its way into her mind. She knew it had already come far too close to crushing her.

Frieda caught her arm. Emily jerked. She'd been closer to sleep than she'd realized.

"They're starting to probe the alleys," Frieda hissed. "We have to move!"

Emily forced herself upright. Her entire body felt drained, but somehow she managed to stumble down the alley. She heard doors being knocked down and windows smashed, men shouting and women screaming as the Fists of Justice tore the block apart looking for them. Emily prayed, silently, that they wouldn't abuse the innocent civilians, but she knew that prayer was unlikely to be granted. The Fists had been humiliated, first by General Pollack and then by Emily herself. They'd be out for revenge.

The noise grew louder as they reached a crossroads and stopped, trying to determine which way would take them further away from the hunters. Frieda wanted to go down the south passage, but Emily stopped her. She'd never liked hunting, but

Alassa had talked enough about it for Emily to know the basics. One group of hunt-ers would drive the animals forward while the other group lay in wait, knowing the animals would eventually run into their trap. The Fists of Justice would know they had to make their way back to Sorcerers Row. They'd be lying in wait.

Which is why we meant to drive them away from Sorcerers Row, she thought. General Pollack had accounted for that, hadn't he? *But what if that part of the plan didn't work?*

She leaned against Frieda as they headed east, trying not to disturb the handful of people sleeping rough. Some of them woke up, looking around blearily. Emily tried to warn them to run as she and Frieda stumbled past, but it didn't look as if they believed her. Besides, they probably didn't have anywhere to go. She felt magic flick-ering over her head and gritted her teeth, hiding their presence as much as possible. The Fists of Justice were using magic to hunt for them.

They won't be able to get a solid look at us without a blood sample, she thought. *And I don't think I left any blood behind.*

She cursed under her breath. She'd been bleeding after the explosion...had she dripped some blood on the temple floor? Would they think to look for it? She didn't *think* Justice could suggest it to his creators. She'd been too dazed to check before Frieda had yanked her out of the temple...

Keep the defenses up, she told herself, sharply. Blood magic was dangerous – and more for her than anyone else – but it could be beaten. She knew how to defend herself, if she had a chance to focus. *And...*

"Stop," a voice bellowed.

Emily turned. Five men ran towards them, carrying swords. Frieda stepped for-ward, lashing out with her magic. The first spells flashed out of existence against their armor, but the second set – picking up and throwing cobblestones – were grue-somely effective. Their victims were smashed to bloody paste.

"Back to Sorcerers Row," Frieda insisted.

Emily nodded as they started to run. She could hear more shouts behind them as the other Fists caught the scent, following their dead comrades...in hindsight, she should have tried to make a diversion to give them a chance to sneak away. Too late for that now...she closed her eyes for a moment as they turned the corner, passing yet another smashed statue. The sight tore at her heart, even though she didn't believe. No matter what happened, Beneficence would never be the same again.

She glanced at Frieda. Did *she* believe? She'd never talked about religion with any of her friends, save for Caleb and Alassa. Did she think the destroyed temples and statues were blasphemous? Or did she think the money could have been better spent on something else?

Frieda staggered to a halt. "Emily, look!"

Emily lifted her weary eyes and stared in horror. Sorcerers Row was burning. A dozen houses had caught fire, eerie-looking flames spreading from house to house as the remaining wards struggled to contain them. The stench was overpowering, warning her that hundreds of dangerous potions and their ingredients were burning. She covered her nose and forced herself to *look*. Caleb's house was completely gone, nothing more than a roaring blaze...as she watched, the roof fell in, the entire house collapsing into a pile of burning debris. She'd never liked the ramshackle house, but she knew Sienna and General Pollack had loved it. It was their home...

She peered down the street. The barricade had been destroyed, smashed to rubble. A number of bodies were clearly visible, but so badly mutilated that she didn't have a hope of identifying them. Was one of them Caleb? Her heart skipped a beat as she realized her lover might be dead. Or General Pollack? She didn't *think* there were any women among the dead, but several of the bodies were so badly battered she couldn't tell if they were male or female. Sienna and her daughters might be dead too...

They struck back, Emily thought. *Harman betrayed us. We marched out to attack them, and they struck while we were gone.*

Frieda caught her arm. "What now?"

Emily stared at her. "I don't know." Caleb couldn't be dead, could he? She didn't want to even *consider* the possibility. "I just don't know."

Chapter Thirty-Two

F RIEDA LED HER INTO A SIDE-STREET. EMILY LEANED AGAINST THE WALL, AS SOON AS THEY were out of sight, and forced herself to think. Her body *ached*, but there was no time to sit and sleep. The shouting grew closer as more and more Fists swarmed the area, searching for them. They couldn't stay still for long...

I don't know where to go, she thought, frantically. If Caleb and his family were dead, she had nowhere to go. She also didn't have any *money* on her. Even if she somehow convinced an innkeeper to give them a bed for the night, she'd be running a terrible risk. The innkeeper might betray them to their enemies. She didn't know anyone else in the city...

She kicked herself, mentally. She *did* know someone else in the city. Markus.

"We have to get to the bank," she muttered. She drew on the last of her energy, forcing herself to stand on her own two feet. "It's the only place we might be safe."

Unless it's been attacked too, she thought, as they stumbled down the street. *If the Fists managed to break into Sorcerers Row, they might have managed to smash the banks too.*

She gritted her teeth, forcing her body to *move*. She'd faced necromancers and demons and powerful sorcerers...she was damned if she was allowing a bunch of religious fanatics to get the better of her. Their power was based on a *trick*, although it was a terrifyingly *effective* trick. The magical haze they'd unleashed made it impossible for her to risk sleeping in the open, let alone teleporting out of the city. She told herself, firmly, not to give in. Despair was a worse enemy than anything.

The streets grew quieter as they made their way towards the banks. A handful of buildings were nothing more than piles of ashes, marking – she hoped – places where the resistance had struck at their enemies. There were no bodies, as far as she could see. Thankfully, there were no guards either. The Fists of Justice had too many other problems to worry about guarding the remains of their patrol bases.

They got a bloody nose, she thought, vengefully. *But will it be enough to stop them?*

"There's a patrol outside the tunnel entrance," Frieda whispered. "Stay here."

Emily wanted to argue, but everything was catching up with her again. Her vision was starting to go hazy. She could only watch as Frieda slipped out of the alley and headed towards the guards, then slumped against the wall and prayed. It was all she could do to keep herself awake as she sensed flickers of magic, magic that had a hard and nasty edge to it. She hoped Frieda had cast it, rather than one of the guards. If the Fists of Justice had found the tunnel, they'd definitely assign a sorcerer to the guards...

Frieda reappeared, looking grim. "Got them," she said. "Come on."

She helped Emily to her feet, then half-carried her down towards the house. It crossed Emily's mind that the banks might have already fallen, that they might be walking into a trap, but she knew there was nothing she could do about it. If Markus was alive and well, he'd help them; if he was dead or imprisoned, they would soon be dead too. Janus might have wanted to convince her to join him, but she suspected that ship had sailed. She'd blasphemed against his god...

"Hurry," Frieda muttered. They reached the house and opened the door. It looked as though someone had tried to break down the wards, but lacked the skill to make it work. Emily frowned, trying to understand why something was wrong. "Emily..."

Emily's legs collapsed under her, the moment they were inside the house. The floor suddenly felt very comfortable. She closed her eyes, just for a second...

...And opened them again, in shock.

She jerked upright, panic flashing through her mind. She lay on a bed, completely naked. A black woman – only a year or two older than herself – held a wand over Emily's body, casting some kind of spell. Emily tried to lift a hand – she wasn't sure if she wanted to defend herself or cast a spell – but her head swam and she fell back to the bed. She could barely move.

"Lie still," the woman said. "You're very badly drained."

"I know," Emily managed. Her throat felt dry, very dry. She could barely talk. Melissa had once cast a tongue-twisting hex on her, back before they'd come to a truce, but *that* hadn't been as bad as this. "What...what happened? Who are you?"

"My name is Pandora," the woman said. She withdrew the wand, then produced a small gourd and held it to Emily's lips. "How much do you remember?"

Emily forced herself to concentrate as she sipped the warm liquid. It tasted of chicken, mingled with herbs and spices. She was in a bad way, then. She'd been told, time and time again, that potions were meant to taste dreadful, if only to prevent addiction. A Healer wouldn't want her to drink something that tasted nice unless she *had* to drink it. She felt the liquid sliding down her throat, warming her chest... magic pulsed through her, healing the damage. It was a surprisingly comfortable sensation.

"I'm not sure," she admitted. Her memories got hazy after escaping the temple. She remembered that Sorcerers Row had been burning – she felt a stab of pain at the thought of losing Caleb – but little else. "What happened?"

"You collapsed inside the safe house," Pandora said. "Your companion managed to get you down the tunnel and call for help. We carried you into the bank and settled you down. And then you slept."

Emily nodded, curtly. "How bad is it?"

"Better than you had any right to expect," Pandora told her. "You pushed your body to the breaking point, but luckily we got some potions into you before your internal organs started to collapse. I've fixed most of the damage, Lady Emily; the remainder will heal by the end of the day. Your magic was drained quite badly, but I think it will recover within the next day or so. I advise you to avoid using magic for the next few hours, at the very least. I'd recommend longer, but I don't think that will be possible."

Emily carefully tested her defenses. They were gone. The network of wards and protections she'd built up over the last few weeks were gone. She shivered, feeling vulnerable. She'd known her defenses could be broken, if someone had the power and experience to crack their way through her protections, but this was different. A prank spell designed to turn her into a frog would work, if someone cast it on her. She might as well be naked.

She scowled as she looked down. She *was* naked.

"I'll have food served in a few minutes," Pandora informed her. Emily's stomach rumbled at the thought of food. "I expect you to eat every last morsel. I'll force it down your throat personally if you refuse to eat."

"I'll eat," Emily said, hastily. She knew Pandora wasn't joking. "Can I have something to wear?"

"If you can stand up," Pandora said. "Your clothes were beyond repair, I'm afraid, but there is a nightgown in the cabinet."

Emily sat up and swung her legs over the side of the bed. The room was windowless, but otherwise it could have passed for her bedroom at Whitehall. A bedside cabinet, a desk, a pair of chairs...she wondered, as she forced herself to stand on wobbly legs, why Markus had bothered to install a bedroom in the bank. It didn't seem large enough for a married couple, yet it was too large for a bank clerk...she shook her head, dismissing the question. She'd worry about it later, if there was a later. The nightgown, thankfully, was long enough to cover everything. She pulled it over her head, wincing as it scratched her skin. The door opened a moment later, revealing Frieda. She was carrying a large tray of food.

"Eat," Pandora said. "Or do I have to compel you?"

"No," Emily said, hastily.

Frieda put the food down on the table, then gave Emily a hug. "I thought...I thought..."

"It's all right." Emily held the younger girl for a long moment, then looked down at where her watch should be. "How long was I out?"

"Twelve hours." Pandora lifted her wand, meaningfully. "Eat."

Emily sat back on the bed, taking a deep breath. It smelled nice, although there was an edge to it that made her stomach churn. Someone had probably laced the dinner with potions to help speed her recovery. She braced herself, then took a bite. Beef stew, mixed with mashed potatoes and chopped vegetables. She wondered, as she took another bite, just why Markus had installed a kitchen in his bank too. But then, he *had* expected trouble.

"I have good news," Frieda said, as Emily finished her meal. One of the potions must have been an appetite enhancer. She hadn't been able to keep herself from eating, once she'd had a few bites. "Caleb is alive and on his way."

Emily sagged in relief. "What...what happened?"

"The message didn't have any useful details," Frieda said. "Markus said he would summon Caleb as soon as you were awake."

Emily let out a breath she hadn't realized she'd been holding. She'd been too tired – and then too drugged-up – to dwell on the fact Caleb was missing, yet...she looked at her fingers, feeling relieved. Caleb was alive! And his family...she hoped his family had survived. They'd already lost one son in the last few weeks.

"Good," she said. She looked at Pandora. "Can you show him in when he arrives?"

"If you wish." Pandora's voice tightened. "But make sure he does all the work."

Emily felt her cheeks heat as Frieda giggled. "I didn't mean it like that," she protested. "I…"

"Markus also wants to speak to you," Frieda said. "Should I go fetch him now?"

"Maybe," Emily said. Her stomach felt satisfied, for the moment. She knew that wouldn't last. She'd been so drained that she'd need to eat again soon, as the potions worked their magic on her body. "Do I look reasonably decent?"

"You look like a woman who donned a burlap sack instead of a dress," Frieda said, mischievously. "Why, I recall a story about a happy couple who accidentally swapped clothes when they had to get dressed in a hurry…"

"I don't want to know," Emily said. She'd never liked wearing revealing clothes, even for Caleb. The nightgown she'd worn to Alassa's hen party had *technically* covered everything, but it had been so revealing that she'd blushed when she'd worn it. "As long as I'm not showing off anything important."

"It was funny," Frieda said.

"The aftermath probably wasn't," Pandora said. She tapped Emily's shoulder, passing her a potions bottle. "When you feel hungry again, eat. Take two spoonfuls of this potion every hour until the bottle runs dry. You" – she looked at Frieda – "make sure she eats, when she's hungry."

"Understood," Frieda said.

Pandora nodded, giving Emily a sharp look. "You pushed yourself to the limit," she warned, firmly. "I won't hesitate to put you to sleep if I think you're risking your health again."

Emily nodded, keeping her face expressionless. *Every* Healer – everyone she'd met with some medical training – seemed to have the same bedside manner. The Healers at Whitehall were strict, often threatening to tie students down if they didn't stay in bed until they were fully healed. Lady Barb had even told her class, a couple of years ago, that hardly anyone could be trusted to take care of themselves. Her patients always thought they knew better than their healers.

Pandora slipped out of the room, leaving Emily and Frieda alone. Emily looked at Frieda, seeing the strain on the younger girl's face. Frieda had done well, very well; she needed to rest herself, not stay up to watch Emily. And yet…Emily felt a sudden rush of affection that surprised her more than she cared to admit. Frieda had risked everything to save her.

She looked up as Markus entered the room. "Emily." He sounded tired. "I'm glad you recovered."

"Thank you," Emily said. "Are we safe here?"

"For the moment." Markus gestured towards the wall. "The mob is still out there, but so far they haven't done more than tickle the wards. I imagine that will change soon."

"Probably." Emily frowned as his words sank in. The Fists of Justice had smashed Sorcerers Row, but not the banks? It was odd. Taking out the resistance made sense, she supposed, but the banks were their scapegoats for the whole crisis. They'd have to smash them sooner or later. "They have an incredibly powerful entity on their side."

Markus eyed her. "What happened?"

"It's a long story." Emily sighed. She wasn't sure how much she wanted to tell him. Markus was innovative, as were his friends. They might start trying to build Mimics of their own, if they knew it was possible. But she had to tell them *something*. They had to understand that the 'god' was nothing more than a powerful spell. "Can I tell everyone at once? That'll save some time."

"If you must," Markus said.

Emily groaned. "Janus was an accountant," she said. "Harman was – is – an accountant too."

Frieda swore. "You think he betrayed us?"

"Someone had to," Emily said. She was sure she was right. "Janus was very well informed, right from the start. Harman could have betrayed us…"

And he wasn't at the square when all hell broke loose, she added, mentally. *Did someone warn him to stay away?*

"Harman is an ass," Markus said. "But that doesn't make him a traitor."

Emily frowned. They had no *proof*. But there were truth spells and truth potions and plenty of other ways to get information out of an unwilling donor. She doubted Sienna would hesitate to *use* the spells, if she was still alive. Her family had nearly been killed. And yet…

It made sense, she told herself again. Harman had been a guildmaster. He was, as he'd said himself, the last surviving guildmaster. Perhaps Janus had hoped Harman would join any resistance to the new theocracy, just so he could betray it from the inside. Or maybe he'd even been intended to *lead* the resistance, covertly keeping it powerless until the time came to drop the hammer. General Pollack certainly hadn't been *intended* to survive.

"We'll figure it out," she said. "And if he *is* the traitor, we can use him."

"I have no doubt of it." Markus cocked his head. "Caleb just passed through the wards. Jo is bringing him up now. Should I give the two of you some privacy?"

"No," Frieda said, quickly. "She's in no shape for anything."

Markus gave her a sharp look. "I'm sure she'll be fine." He winked at Emily as she flushed. "Although I wouldn't take Pandora's advice lightly. If she's told you to be careful, be careful."

"I'll be very careful," Emily said. She didn't feel up to doing more than holding hands. Her stomach felt queasy. "Frieda, why don't you get some rest?"

"Because someone has to look after you," Frieda said. "Emily…"

"Come with me," Markus said, firmly. He reached out and took Frieda by the arm. Emily saw Frieda flinch and sighed, inwardly. Frieda had problems being touched too. "You can tell me what happened to you while Emily and Caleb have their emotional reunion."

Frieda scowled. "I need to be with her…"

"I'll be fine," Emily promised. Caleb wasn't going to hurt her. She trusted him not to hurt her, trusted him to kiss her…"You go take some rest."

"Emily." Frieda sounded almost as though she were pleading. "Be careful, *please*."

The door opened. Caleb stepped in. Emily's eyes went wide. Caleb looked… *stricken*. It crossed her mind, suddenly, that she didn't *know* the rest of his family had survived. They could be dead. Caleb could be the last survivor. Or…her imagination provided too many possibilities, each one worse than the last. General Pollack and Sienna might have been captured and brainwashed by now…

"Emily." Caleb sounded worried. He hurried over to the bed and gave her a hug. "She didn't make it out in time."

Emily stared at him as he pulled back. "*Who* didn't make it out in time?"

"Marian," Caleb said. She could hear panic and fear in his voice. "They caught her! They *took* her!"

Emily swallowed, hard. The Fists of Justice were sacrificing children – and young adults – to power their god. Marian – a young woman with magic, but only limited training – would be an ideal sacrifice. They'd put her on one of the altars, stab her with their staffs…she shuddered at the thought. Marian had been rude and unpleasant, but she didn't deserve to die like that. No one did.

"Then we have to get her back," she said, standing up. Her legs still felt wobbly. "Where is everyone?"

"Fishing Plaice," Caleb said. "I said I'd bring you back with me."

Frieda cleared her throat, loudly. "Emily isn't fit to travel. Bring your family here."

"I have to go," Emily said. She could make it, if she tried. "Someone has to explain what's actually happening."

She took a breath. "And someone also has to deal with Harman. He might have betrayed us."

"I'll kill him," Caleb vowed. "If he hurt my sister…I'll kill him!"

"I know." Emily felt a sudden stab of envy. Marian was lucky to have siblings who cared about her. "And I'll help you."

Chapter Thirty-Three

"SHE'S STILL ALIVE," SIENNA SAID. "I PERFORMED A BLOOD RITE. SHE'S STILL ALIVE, BUT I can't find her."

Emily nodded, trying to breathe through her mouth as she stood in the kitchen. The tiny house in Fishing Plaice stank of rotting fish, along with other things she didn't care to think about. Caleb had said, as they'd slipped through the streets, that it was a dosshouse for new immigrants, although most of them apparently moved on as soon as they found a decent job and better lodgings. It had been empty, apparently, until the resistance had turned it into a base. She could see why.

Sienna paced the room. "I'll kill him. I swear...I'll kill him."

Emily kept her face expressionless. General Pollack had been utterly furious when Caleb had told him about Harman. Emily knew he could accept political differences, even outright enmity, but not betrayal. And it hadn't just been General Pollack who'd been betrayed. His children had been lucky to escape the blaze...

And one of them didn't escape, Emily thought. *Marian was taken by the Fists.*

She gritted her teeth in helpless frustration. Caleb's description of the raid on Sorcerers Row had been confused, but the attack had clearly come without warning. Marian should have jumped into the escape shaft as soon as all hell broke loose, as her mother had told her to do. Instead, when they'd reached the meeting point, they'd discovered her missing. There had been no way to go back for her before it was too late.

And God alone knows what they're doing to her, Emily thought. The Fists could use a blood rite themselves, she supposed, but they'd still have problems localizing Sienna and the rest of her family. *They might just have decided to sacrifice her.*

Sienna swung around to face her. "You said you had something important to tell us." Her eyes burned into Emily's. "What?"

"I need to discuss it with everyone," Emily said, firmly. She didn't want to tell Sienna everything either, but...she sighed, inwardly. It looked as though the secret of the Mimics was on the verge of getting out too. "Were my chat parchments destroyed?"

"Caleb didn't have time to grab anything," Sienna said. "They were probably lost in the flames."

Emily cursed under her breath. The chat parchments could be replaced, the next time she met up with her friends, but when would *that* be? Alassa and Imaiqah were in Zangaria, Frieda and the Gorgon were at Whitehall...she had no idea where *Aloha* was. Maybe she'd have to organize a reunion in Dragon's Den. She'd meant to show off her house at some point. A sleepover would be fun, perhaps...

She rubbed her eyes as Sienna turned away, pacing the room like a caged tiger. Emily felt sorry for her. Sienna wanted to go rescue her daughter, but the older woman's training told her it was better to wait and make preparations instead of rushing into what was probably a trap. The Fists of Justice presumably knew who they'd caught. They had to know Marian would make excellent bait.

"It doesn't matter," Emily said. "There are some other chat parchments in the bank."

"Getting word out may help," Sienna said. "But probably not in time to be useful."

Emily nodded, slowly. Someone on the outside – perhaps with only a vague idea of what was going on – would be slow to send help. King Randor would be more worried about the theocracy spreading to Zangaria than anything else, while the White Council would need to seek political consensus before dispatching an army of sorcerers and soldiers. And neither of them would know *precisely* what they were facing. Justice would rip them to shreds.

I might need to get out of the city, Emily thought. *Someone has to tell the outside world what's going on.*

She knew that wouldn't be easy. Hell, she wasn't sure if escape was *possible* any longer. The bridges were guarded, she'd been told, and the Gap was sealed. Teleporting wasn't a possibility as long as Justice's presence dominated the city. Sienna had warded the dosshouse thoroughly and yet Emily could *still* feel the presence at the back of her mind. The resistance was already struggling to maintain its numbers with Justice slowly wearing them down. Given time, the Fists would become invincible.

"I'm sorry," she said, quietly.

"Don't be," Sienna said. "This wasn't your fault."

The door opened. General Pollack entered, followed by Caleb. They both looked grim.

"It wasn't him," he said, shortly.

Emily blinked. "What?"

"Harman didn't betray us," General Pollack said. "I poured various potions down his throat and Caleb cast a number of spells. He couldn't resist us. The questions we asked…"

He sat down, heavily. "He confessed to a number of accounting irregularities," he added, as he reached for a bottle of wine. "Some voting fraud, some embezzlement… enough to get him a few years in slavery, if he'd been caught a week or so ago. But he wasn't the one who betrayed us. He was doing what he'd been told to do before I nabbed him."

"Oh," Emily said. She'd had been so *sure*. And yet, in hindsight, *she'd* known that trouble was coming even without seeing Vesperian's books. "What…what happens to him now?"

"Right now, he's throwing up the potions we gave him," General Pollack said. "He'll feel like he's been on a three-day bender for several days to come. And after that…he'll probably want a little revenge."

"Blame it on me," Emily said. Had Janus *intended* her to draw the wrong conclusion? Or had he merely had a stroke of luck? "I made a mistake."

"It wasn't a bad guess." Caleb looked down at the floor. "You just happened to be wrong."

"I'll speak for you, if he does make a fuss," General Pollack said.

"We have other things to worry about right now." Sienna sat down at the table, resting her elbows on the hard wooden surface as Markus and Frieda entered the kitchen. They both looked as tired as Emily felt. "Emily, I believe you wish to share some explanations with us...?"

Emily sat down at the table, taking a moment to gather herself. Caleb already knew some of it – although she hadn't told him everything – but the others didn't, not yet. She wondered if she dared ask for an oath, yet...she shook her head. They had a right to know what was going on, without her trying to impose rules. Hopefully, they'd understand the need for secrecy.

"It's a trick," she said, flatly. "That entity is no god."

"So it's a trick," Sienna repeated. "What *is* it?"

"It's...something akin to a Mimic," Emily said.

She launched into a long explanation, trying to get the idea across without giving too much away. It was probably pointless – her audience was composed of magicians – but she had to try. She told them about the Mimic in Whitehall, about how she'd worked out that it was actually an advanced spell...and how Justice had been designed along the same lines, although with a number of differences. They had to understand what the fanatics had done.

"The Mimics are *spells*," Sienna said, when she'd finished. "At what point, Emily, were you going to tell the *rest* of us?"

Emily winced at the cold anger in Sienna's tone. "The Grandmaster – the *previous* Grandmaster – believed the information was better kept secret. He feared that sorcerers would start trying to duplicate the spells if they knew it was possible."

"And yet, you also found a way to stop them," Sienna added. She still didn't seem happy. "Didn't you?"

"Yes," Emily said. "A simple dispelling charm should work against a Mimic."

Master Wolfe had *definitely* been a genius, she thought, as Sienna reeled. It had shocked her too, when she'd first realized the truth. Hardly anyone would reach for one of the simplest charms in the spellbook when confronted by a Mimic, let alone think to use it. But if one already knew the secret, dealing with a Mimic was easy.

"I tried to dispel Justice," she said, outlining everything that had happened in the temple. "It didn't work."

"It might not be possible to stop it," Sienna said, slowly. "If it absorbs magic and it's largely immune to physical attacks..."

"They'll run out of people to sacrifice, sooner or later." Emily grimaced as a nasty thought occurred to her. "They didn't create an *entirely* autonomous creature, either. Justice seems to have limits. I think they need to make some preparations before they let him go out to hunt."

"Those staffs," Caleb said.

"I think so." Emily kicked herself, silently, for not thinking of it first. In hindsight, scaling up the chat parchments so they could channel power was an obvious trick. Aloha was going to be furious when she found out. She'd invented the chat parchments, but she hadn't taken them any further. "I think they use Justice as a source of power for spells, channeled through the staffs."

"So we force them to drain their power," Sienna said. "Just like facing a necromancer."

"Justice has a *lot* of power." Emily paused. "He's also not particularly intelligent."

"You *think*," Sienna warned.

Emily nodded, curtly. Given time, Justice *would* grow into an intelligent being... or, at least, that was what she'd taken from the scrolls. Janus and his comrades really *hadn't* known what they were doing. And when Justice *did* develop intelligence, all hell would break out. He'd know what he'd have to do to survive and he'd want to do it. Beneficence might simply be the first city to be sacrificed to keep him alive.

"Perhaps you didn't use enough power when you tried to dispel him," Caleb suggested. "We could *all* try."

"It's possible," Emily said. "But the notes suggested that dispelling him would be very difficult."

She wished, suddenly, that she had a battery. She could have used it to power a dispelling charm and aimed it at Justice. It *might* have been enough to counter any protections built into the spell matrix. But his magic-absorbing aura would make focusing the charm difficult. She might accidentally feed him instead. Perhaps, if she pushed the charm a little further...

I need time to think, she thought. Sienna was talking, but Emily barely heard her. *And perhaps some more rest.*

Frieda nudged her. "Emily?"

Emily looked up. "I'm sorry, I was miles away."

"I said that I will not leave my daughter in their hands," Sienna said. "And we do not have time to waste. We have to take the offensive."

"I must agree," General Pollack said. "The longer we delay, the stronger they get."

Emily glanced at Markus, who nodded. She agreed. Justice *was* steadily tightening his grip on the city. More and more people were surrendering to him as his constant presence wore down their will to resist. And there was no way to evacuate the city in the hopes that Justice would starve. He'd just cross the bridges and walk into Swanhaven or Cockatrice.

We could blow up the entire city, she thought. The nuke-spell glimmered in her mind, a mocking reminder of a power she didn't dare use. *But would even that produce enough power to destroy him?*

"We might be able to limit his reach," she said, remembering the cobwebs she'd sensed in the temple. "Cutting him off from his supporters and warding him might be enough to limit his power intake. He'd start to starve."

And if you're wrong, her thoughts mocked her, *you'll lead everyone to their doom.*

Frieda cleared her throat. "We attacked them once," she said. "Will it be so easy to attack them a second time?"

"It wasn't *easy*," General Pollack said. "We lost fifty men in the attacks."

"And Marian," Sienna said, quietly.

"They knew we were coming," Frieda reminded him. "General...getting close to the temple a second time might be impossible."

Emily nodded in grim agreement. It hadn't been easy to slip through the guards the first time, even though Janus had implied she'd been *allowed* to enter the temple. She supposed he *could* have been bluffing, but he'd had no reason to lie. Now, with their temple damaged and their reputation tarnished, the Fists of Justice were unlikely to let anyone anywhere near their god. Getting close enough to do some damage might be impossible.

We'll have to think of something, she thought.

"We could try to lure Justice out of the temple," Markus said. "Perhaps we could start pushing the protesters back from the banks. They'd have to do *something* to remind everyone they're in charge."

"We could go after the staffs," Frieda offered. She winked at Emily. "They break as easily as wands."

"That would work." Emily glanced at Sienna. "Can you get a rough idea of Marian's location?"

"Very rough." Sienna shot an odd look at her husband. "Everything is a blur."

General Pollack looked worried. "I've never heard of anything that can cut a blood tie completely," he said. "You should be able to find her."

"There are some forms of disownment that would cut all the ties," Sienna said. "But I'd have to do the rituals to make them work. Marian couldn't do it, let alone an outsider."

"And you might kill her," Caleb said, quietly.

"I might," Sienna agreed. "There's a *reason* they're rarely used."

There was a long silence. Emily looked from Sienna to Caleb and back again, feeling an odd flicker of...something she didn't care to name. Family...she *liked* Caleb's family, but did she want to marry them? And yet, she wasn't seeing them at their best. They'd lost one child to a necromancer, while another had been kidnapped... their house had been destroyed, leaving them homeless.

"I think it's time to start working on a plan," General Pollack said. "I'll gather the remaining forces, with the intention of luring the enemy out of place. Markus, I want you to try and find a way into the temple that won't be risky. We *could* go through the drains."

Emily had to smile. That was a good thought, if it was workable. If nothing else, Janus and his ilk might not notice until it was too late. She might have an opportunity to take the cobwebs apart before they noticed her, trapping Justice in one place.

"I'll see what I can find." Markus shrugged. "They might have sealed the drains, of course."

"They might," General Pollack agreed. "Dear--" he looked at Sienna "--start working on ways to break their staffs."

"Or drain them," Frieda said. "What happens if you cancel the spellware they use to focus the magic?"

Emily glanced at Markus. "What happens if you use a cancellation charm on a chat parchment?"

"I don't know," Markus said. "The magic is linked to blood, so it's quite resistant..."

He stroked his chin. "We *do* know that burning the parchment renders it useless," he added, after a moment. "But smaller charms might not work."

"They won't have used linking charms for their spellwork." Sienna's voice was cold. "I'll see what I can do."

General Pollack nodded. "Emily, you know these creatures best," he said. "See what you can come up with..."

"I will," Emily said. An idea was already at the back of her mind. The Hands of Justice had taken one idea and scaled it up a little. What would happen if Emily took *their* idea and scaled it up still further? "Can I borrow Caleb to help me? We do work well together."

"I bet you do," Markus teased.

Sienna gave Emily a long, hard look. "Yes, provided you keep Frieda with you as well," she said, firmly. "That is *not* negotiable."

Emily clamped down – hard – on the urge to make any number of sarcastic remarks. Caleb's sister was missing. He wasn't going to waste time making out with her when his talents were needed elsewhere. Caleb had his flaws, but he wasn't *that* sort of person...

"I understand," she said. No doubt Sienna would have insisted on leaving the door open, if Frieda hadn't been there to play chaperone. "Frieda will be helpful too."

"Good," Sienna said. "We need to move as soon as possible."

"They'll expect us to move at night," Caleb pointed out. He jabbed a finger towards the stained window. It wouldn't be long until darkness fell over the city. "They'll be ready."

"We'll see if we can get into the sewers," General Pollack said. "And we'll see what other problems we can give them too."

Emily rubbed her forehead. She was starting to feel hungry again. Her head ached...she gritted her teeth, remembering Pandora's words. She'd have to find something to eat quickly before she got to work.

"We have to stop them," she said. Hurting the Fists of Justice wouldn't be enough. Janus had to be stopped. "I don't think they knew what they were doing."

Sienna's eyebrows crawled up. "Are you sure?"

"The scrolls were very basic in many ways," Emily said. Whoever had written them – she was sure it had been Master Wolfe – had been a genius, but there had been a startling lack of explanation. Most sorcerers would know better than to cast a spell when they didn't know what it was intended to do. "And Janus talked about *summoning* a god, not *creating* one. I think they don't even begin to grasp the underlying theory."

She sighed. Janus had effectively hypnotized himself. "And when they lose control," she added, "they might not even notice."

Chapter Thirty-Four

"NICE ROOM," FRIEDA SAID, SARCASTICALLY. SHE SENT A LIGHT-GLOBE AHEAD OF HER AS she hurried into the room. "I can't imagine any monkey-business here."

Emily had to admit she had a point. The room had been stripped bare of everything apart from a table so rickety she was afraid to breathe on it and a framework in the corner that might – might – have been part of a bed. The wooden floor was sticky, her feet making odd sounds as she walked over to the table and dropped her notebook on top. She didn't want to know what caused the smell, but it was everywhere. It was probably the least romantic place she'd ever seen.

"They would have stuffed an entire family in here, if they were lucky," Caleb said, from the door. "This would have been all they'd had."

"Ouch." Emily had never quite grown used to the limited privacy at Whitehall, but this room was far worse. No one would have had *any* privacy. "Can you find us some chairs?"

"Sure," Caleb said. "Just give me a moment."

Frieda caught Emily's eye as Caleb hurried back out of the room. "Make sure you eat something," she said. "I can hear your stomach from over here."

Emily nodded, tiredly, as she opened the notebook. Markus had given it to her, explaining that he'd started producing them to promote the bank. Emily doubted the notebooks helped to bring in new customers, but it would be useful. She needed to write down everything she could remember from the scrolls, then try to draw it into a coherent whole.

"Here," Caleb said, dragging a pair of chairs into the room. "I'll just go pick up the third chair."

Emily took one of the chairs, sat down and started to write. The spell notation was ancient, but thankfully she'd had plenty of time in Old Whitehall to get used to reading it. She translated it mentally as she went along, noting where the designer had cunningly buried aspects that would only come into play when the entire spell was created. Justice would develop intelligence – of a sort – fairly quickly, intelligence that would be focused around his core principles. Emily wondered, as she sketched out each set of spells, just what the original designer had been thinking. The entity didn't seem *designed* to serve as a weapon.

Maybe he just wanted an implacable judge too, Emily mused. Justice – at first – would not be able to break his own rules. But, as he grew more and more intelligent, she had no doubt he'd be able to spot loopholes and take advantage of them. *Or maybe he was setting a booby trap for future generations.*

"I think we might be able to copy the trick they used," she mused. Getting a spell through Justice's magic-absorbing field would be tricky – perhaps that was why the dispelling charm hadn't worked – but she'd had an idea. Linking charms weren't affected by wards. "We'd just have to get something else through the haze."

"I hit him with rocks," Frieda said. "It had *some* effect."

Emily nodded. Justice might have been surprised – if he was *capable* of being surprised – when the rocks hadn't fallen out of the air as soon as they'd entered his field. Most magicians didn't think to use spells to *throw* objects rather than propel them through the air. It was a weakness she'd taken advantage of more than once. But, lacking any real physical component, flying rocks were unlikely to rip him apart.

"They were inside his field," she said, as she sketched out a set of notes. Sorcerers Row might be in ruins, but Markus had enough supplies – in the bank – to give them a chance to build their own weapons. It wasn't as if a staff was anything more than a carefully-primed piece of wood. "That gives us an *in*."

She frowned. Something was nagging at the back of her mind, something she'd missed.

"You're talking about putting a charm on the end of a staff and thrusting it into him," Caleb mused. "How do you know the charm will survive the field?"

Frieda snickered.

Caleb glared at her. "Shut up!"

Emily rubbed her forehead, tiredly. "I don't," she said, choosing to ignore Frieda's unsubtle joke. "We might have to launch several staffs at him."

"Risky," Frieda said. "We don't have any way to measure the potency of his field."

"Even the most powerful wards barely notice chat parchments," Emily pointed out. She could do a couple of experiments. It wouldn't be too hard. "And if we could get a modified spell through the haze, we could take Justice apart before he has a chance to kill us all."

"It might work." Caleb stroked his chin as he stared down at her notes. "What if we set up a link between Heart's Eye and here? You'd be able to overfeed him instead."

"We could try," Emily mused. She didn't think it was a good idea. Overfeeding the entity might be disastrous. Either Justice would become *more* powerful, or there would be an explosion. "But I don't think there'd be much of a city afterwards."

She sighed. "I don't think we could even *get* to Heart's Eye to set up the other end of the link. It's a very long way away."

"True," Frieda agreed.

Emily looked down at her parchment. She was missing something, something obvious. But what?

A nasty thought struck her. "Caleb," she said, slowly. "Where are Karan and Croce?"

"Croce's teaching some of the young men how to fight," Caleb said. "Karan was brewing potions…why?"

Emily wasn't sure she wanted to follow the chain of logic to its ultimate destination, but she didn't have a choice.

"Caleb," she said. "The attack on your house…how did they get inside the wards so quickly?"

Caleb looked back at her, puzzled. "They must have hit them with staggering force. Those staffs they use channel vast amounts of magic…"

"Your mother did a very good job," Emily pointed out. There were too many oddities about the whole story for her to take it at face value. The Fists of Justice hadn't just punched through Sienna's wards. They'd devastated Sorcerers Row itself. "The wards were designed to deflect magic, not absorb it. You should have had ample warning to grab what you needed and run before it was too late."

She closed her eyes, unwilling to say the next words. "The attack must have started from *inside* the wards. Caleb, I think Marian betrayed us."

Caleb stared at her in shock. "Emily..."

"She never liked Emily," Frieda put in. "And she was obsessed with Justice..."

"Shut up," Caleb snapped. Emily sensed ragged magic sparkling around him and winced, inwardly. Caleb was as tired as she. They were *all* tired. "Emily, Marian wouldn't have betrayed us!"

"Someone told the Fists of Justice that I was going to the temple," Emily said. She could see the pain on his face. She damned herself, silently, for making him suffer. "Someone let them into the wards. All she needed was a chat parchment and a staff of her very own."

"They didn't capture her," Frieda put in. "She went with them willingly."

"Shut up," Caleb hissed. "Shut up, or you will never speak again."

Emily groaned, inwardly, as Caleb started to pace the room. She was too tired... she should have talked to him in private. Or, perhaps, talked to his parents. He was going to hate her for this, even if she was right. And if she was wrong...

"It might not have been her fault," she said. Janus had known that General Pollack had been appointed to command the City Guard. He'd had ample opportunity to prepare a few contingency plans. "If she'd seen Justice, she might have been overwhelmed..."

"Marian would not have betrayed us," Caleb said. "She..."

His voice trailed off. Emily understood, all too well. Marian had loved Casper, mourned his death...blamed *Emily* for his death. She'd had good reason to want to follow Justice even before the entity had begun making appearances. And once Justice had gotten his hooks into Marian's mind, she would no longer have known right from wrong. She'd been so focused on avenging Casper that she hadn't realized what she was doing.

And what, her own thoughts asked her, *if she* did *know what she was doing?*

"Emily." Caleb breathed rapidly, clenching and unclenching his fists. "Emily, if you're wrong about this..."

Emily silently filled in the blanks. The end of their relationship, certainly. A new enemy, one who knew too much about her. And...perhaps Caleb would try to kill her. She wouldn't even blame him if he wanted to take a swing at her, not after what she'd told him. He valued his family, *loved* his family. The thought of losing them hurt him more than he could say.

And if he had to choose between me and them, she thought bitterly, *he'd choose them.*

She closed her eyes in pain. She'd never had siblings. She'd never really understood, not at an emotional level, just what it meant to have siblings. Or, perhaps, what it meant to be betrayed by someone so close to her. Caleb would never recover from the blow, even if Marian turned out to be innocent. He'd still have to cope with *Emily* hurting him...

"I'm sorry," she said. She didn't open her eyes. "Someone had to have betrayed us..."

Emily heard footsteps echoing across the room, followed by the door slamming. She opened her eyes. Caleb was gone. She wondered if he'd gone to tell his parents... to tell his parents what? That their youngest daughter might have betrayed them? Or to formally end the courtship. Or...

They'd had fights before, Emily remembered. There had been friendly arguments over magic techniques and a nastier argument over more intimate matters. They'd hurt, more than she cared to admit, but they'd kissed and made up. She hoped, deep inside, that they could put this argument behind them too...

"He's never been a younger sister," Frieda said. "He can't understand what it's like."

Emily gave her a sharp look. "Explain."

Frieda looked...tired. "The first two or three children are treated like...like valuable children." Her lips twitched, as if she wanted to smile humorlessly. "After that, they become a drain on resources. The older siblings know they're wanted; the younger siblings aren't so sure. All the bitter resentments start to pile up..."

"Marian was loved," Emily said. Frieda had grown up in the Cairngorms, where families lived close to the edge. She'd known, from the moment she was old enough to think, that her family considered her expendable, that she might be killed one day so the rest of the family might live. Marian had lived a very different life. "Marian *is loved*."

"She may not have seen it that way," Frieda said, quietly.

Emily looked down at the table. They had to stop Justice. She *knew* they had to stop Justice before the entire city was consumed. And yet, part of her wanted to stay in the room and hide. She'd hurt Caleb badly, even if she was right. And if she was wrong...

She shook her head. It didn't bear thinking about.

"Fuck it." She looked up at the younger girl. "Do *any* of us have a happy family?"

"Imaiqah," Frieda said, after a moment. "And Jade."

Emily nodded, tiredly. Jade was an only child. So was Alassa. Frieda had no intention of ever going home, any more than Emily herself. Emily had no idea about the Gorgon or Aloha. Imaiqah was the only one with a large *and* happy family.

And even her family has secrets, Emily thought. *What will happen when some of them get out?*

She rose, feeling her joints starting to ache. Her body was tired and her soul...she felt dead, as if her thoughts and feelings were wrapped in a grey haze. She wanted to climb into bed and forget the world, forget everything...she knew, intellectually, that she was being stupid, but it was hard to *believe* it. She didn't *want* to believe it.

"Sit down," Frieda said. "I'll get you some food."

She rose and gently pushed Emily back into her chair. "I know how you feel," she said, briskly. "But you're in no state to talk to anyone at the moment."

Emily closed her eyes, again. Perhaps a little nap...she heard Frieda walking across the room and leaving, closing the door behind her. A little nap...the door opened again, seconds later. Or had she fallen asleep? She couldn't swear to anything. And yet...the footsteps echoing towards her were not Frieda's.

She turned. Sienna stood behind her, carrying a tray of food and a mug of water. Emily cringed, inwardly. Sienna was the last person she wanted to talk to right now, even though they *had* to work together. If Caleb had been mad at her, Sienna would be even worse. Perhaps she should save time and insult the rest of the family.

"Eat," Sienna ordered, putting the tray on the table. "Please."

Emily hesitated.

Sienna snorted. "You would hardly be the first young woman to have emotional problems at the worst possible time." She sounded more annoyed than angry. "Or to put your foot in your mouth when no one has any patience or tolerance at all. You need to eat, so you will eat."

She tapped the table, meaningfully. "Eat."

Emily gritted her teeth and took the spoon. Sienna – or someone – had cooked another fish stew. It smelled vaguely *off*, but her spells insisted it was safe to eat. The people who lived in Fishing Plaice probably didn't get the best food, she thought, as she took a bite. It was so bland and favorless that she wished for spices, or even salt and pepper. The potato was just as favorless as the stew.

They probably cooked it for hours, just to make sure it was safe to eat, she thought. Sergeant Harkin's lessons on outdoor survival hadn't been remotely fun. She suspected the boys had gotten more out of them than any of the girls. *At least I can eat it*.

Sienna sat down, facing her. "Now, do you want something to drown your sorrows or are you up to being sensible?"

Emily took another bite of the food. "Sensible."

"Glad to hear it," Sienna said. She met Emily's eyes. "We have one problem at the moment – Janus and his pet creature. I expect you and Caleb to work together *without* letting your emotions get in the way. Can I rely on you to do that?"

"I think so." Emily looked down at the table. "I don't..."

"He told me." Sienna sounded as though she'd bitten into a lemon. "I don't want to admit the possibility, but it does exist."

Emily refused to look up. If she was right, Sienna's daughter had – willingly or unwillingly – betrayed her family. And if she was wrong...she hoped, for Sienna's sake, that she *was* wrong. The prospect of having to face an outraged mother across a dueling circle was terrifying, but so too was the thought of Sienna's life being torn apart. She didn't want to hurt any of them.

"We will hope it isn't true," Sienna said. "And yet, we will have to consider the possibility that it *might* be true."

"Caleb hates me," Emily said, miserably.

"He's certainly not very *pleased* with you," Sienna agreed. She sounded oddly amused. "Do you think you're the *first* person to have romantic problems?"

Emily looked up. "No."

"I've been a young woman, as much as my children might wish to disbelieve it," Sienna said, wryly. "I have a mother, sisters, even aunties and female friends. And I happen to know more about Karan's relationships than she'd be happy about me knowing. Fights between couples are not unique."

She snorted. "After this whole...affair...is finished, you and Caleb can sit down and decide how you want to proceed. Believe me, I have had many arguments with my husband. We have often thrown things at each other."

Emily sighed. "That isn't reassuring."

"I suppose not," Sienna said. She rose. "You have work to do. I expect you and Caleb to concentrate on your problems afterwards, when the entire city is not in danger. If your relationship is strong, you'll get through this and be all the stronger for it; if not, you're better off finding out now than when you're married and have three children."

"I know," Emily said.

"And if you decide not to continue with the relationship, cut it off cleanly," Sienna said, firmly. "You'll just make yourself and Caleb miserable if you prolong the agony."

Emily looked up at her. "Did you ever accuse your husband's sister of treachery?"

"No," Sienna said. She smiled, rather dryly. "But, as disagreeable as that woman is, I never had reason to suspect her of being a traitor."

Her voice hardened. "If Marian betrayed us of her own free will, I will take steps," she said, coldly. Emily shivered, helplessly. She had no doubt, suddenly, that Sienna would kill her own daughter, if necessary. "And if she was enchanted into betraying us, I will do everything in my power to free her from the taint. She *will* be free, even if it costs me everything."

She looked down at Emily. "And if you are wrong, Emily, I will know it wasn't through malice," she added. "I won't hold it against you. The world would be a happier place, perhaps, if more people remembered that some mistakes are just *mistakes*."

"I know," Emily whispered. "Thank you."

Chapter Thirty-Five

"T HAT'S THE PLAN," GENERAL POLLACK SAID. "DO YOU HAVE ANY QUESTIONS?"

Emily shook her head. The plan was simple enough, but she was all too aware of its weaknesses. If Janus knew more about sorcery – and the forces he'd unleashed – than she thought, he'd be able to deduce their plan. Indeed, it was the *only* plan that had a hope of both destroying Justice and rescuing Marian.

She glanced at Caleb. Her lover – her ex, perhaps – resolutely did not look back at her. His younger brother wasn't so restrained. The nasty look he gave Emily would have scared her to death, five years ago. Now, after facing necromancers and dark wizards and all manner of strange creatures, it was no longer so intimidating. She resisted the urge to sneer back at him as General Pollack fielded a couple of questions. Markus and Harman were laying plans to take control of the city after Justice was destroyed.

And they're being a little premature, Emily thought, as she glanced down at the staff in her hand. *We haven't won yet.*

She tested the staff, remembering lessons she'd taken with Sergeant Harkin. Staff-fighting wasn't her forte – she'd reluctantly come to admit that she had no talent for weapons at all – but the staff felt right, like the staves she'd trained to use. Hopefully, Janus and his comrades would overlook it. They'd assume the resistance would resort to non-magical weapons, knowing magic was unreliable near Justice. And yet...she reached out mentally and felt the spell embedded in the wood. It had taken nearly three hours to make staves for everyone, even though – technically – any piece of wood should have sufficed. The charm at the end of the staff alone had taken nearly two hours.

It would have been completely impossible without Sienna and her contacts, Emily thought, sourly. Too many secrets had leaked out over the last few days. Someone with an imagination could probably put the pieces together and work out how to create their own entity, if they were foolish enough to try. *And even with the staves, this is still a gamble.*

She shivered as General Pollack dismissed the first group of resistance fighters. She'd worked through the equations, using what she'd learned from the Mimic to understand how Justice worked, but she knew there was no guarantee of success. Whoever had designed the Mimic she'd killed had been careful to leave a safeguard, a simple trick that could be used to destroy the creature. But the Fists of Justice hadn't even *known* they needed a safeguard, let alone possessed the skill to implant one. No trained sorcerer would have risked casting so many spells without a solid idea of what they *did*.

Frieda nudged her. "You sure you're all right?"

"Yes," Emily said, crossly. She'd eaten enough to keep her going. "I'll survive."

She ran her hand through her hair as General Pollack dismissed the second group of fighters, sending them out to wreak havoc. The Fists of Justice would know, of course, that the attacks were diversions, but they'd still have to deal with them. Large parts of the city were already starting to starve, something General Pollack insisted would undermine the new government. Emily hoped he was right. The Fists of Justice had banned fishing boats from leaving the Caldron, but they'd presumably stockpiled food in anticipation of having thousands of hungry mouths to feed.

Unless they planned to feed the starving to their god, she thought, grimly. *They might have planned to purge everyone who wasn't already committed to them.*

"Karan and I will be leaving in ten." General Pollack glanced at his watch, although Emily was sure he could *feel* time ticking away. "Dear, a word?"

Sienna nodded, tight-lipped. She followed her husband into the next room, leaving the youngsters alone. Emily found herself torn between speaking to Caleb, even though his siblings were *also* in the room, and keeping her mouth closed. She didn't know what to say – or even if she *should* say anything. Frieda hadn't helped by insisting everything was Caleb's fault...

She closed her eyes for a long moment, centering herself. There would be problems...of course there would be problems. But she'd survive. If worse came to worst, she could put their plans into action herself, without him. The University didn't *need* Caleb, did it? But she didn't want to shut him out of his dream...she shook her head, silently promising herself that she would talk to Lady Barb as soon as possible. She needed advice from someone she trusted to be helpful, but detached.

Sienna returned, tapping her staff on the ground. "Let's move. Time is not on our side."

Croce rose, looking pleased to be finally doing something. Emily looked at Caleb, feeling another pang, then stood and followed them to the door. Frieda slipped up next to her as Sienna checked the wards and opened the wooden door. The stench of poverty flowed into the room.

"Make sure we have everything," Sienna said. "We won't be coming back."

Outside, the streets were even darker than the previous night. Justice's presence seemed ever more powerful, whispers filling the air whenever Emily allowed her mental defenses to slip. Sienna's wards had done an effective job at shutting out the entity's influence, but now...Emily glanced at Caleb, feeling a flicker of genuine concern. Caleb was hurting, just like her. Who knew what Justice's influence would do to him?

Or to me, Emily thought, as she cast a night-vision spell. *Or to any of us.*

She resisted the urge to cover her ears as they hurried down the darkened streets. The whispers couldn't be shut out so easily. She gritted her teeth, raising more defenses as she looked around. Fishing Plaice was a nightmare, stone and wooden buildings piled on buildings until the entire complex had become a maze. She forced herself to breathe through her mouth as the smell of rotting fish – and too many unwashed humans in close proximity – grew stronger. Sienna had banned her young daughters from visiting Fishing Plaice, Emily recalled. Emily didn't blame her for a second.

"The streets are not normally this quiet." Caleb slipped up beside her, his face pale in the darkness. He sounded as though he was trying to carry on, despite everything. "This place never sleeps."

Emily nodded. General Pollack had told her that a bunch of Fists had tried to enter Fishing Plaice, only to be driven out by the locals. Surprisingly, Janus hadn't launched an all-out attack...or, perhaps, it wasn't *that* surprising. Fishing Plaice would be an absolute nightmare for any hostile force, a place where the defenders knew the region intimately and could turn it against the invaders. Better to leave them to starve than to risk an offensive.

Or maybe they're preparing to send Justice into Fishing Plaice, Emily mused. *Or do they think we can push him out?*

She glanced at Caleb. Was he trying to pretend their argument had never happened? Or was he trying to put his emotions behind him, during the mission? Or... she shook her head in annoyance. Boys were so hard to understand, sometimes. But then, she'd heard boys saying that *girls* were hard to understand too. It wasn't that hard, was it? But then, she'd often found her fellow girls hard to understand too... and she *was* a girl. The boys didn't even have *that* advantage.

"They must be hiding," Emily said. She doubted the locals were *sleeping.* "Are they going to get in our way?"

"Probably not," Caleb said. "We're not a threat."

Emily looked at the darkened houses as they slipped down a narrow street. They looked...shabby, as if the owners couldn't be bothered to maintain them properly. Small piles of garbage were everywhere, adding to the stench. There was no rubbish collection service here. The remainder of the city might be reasonably clean, by local standards, but Fishing Plaice was a mess. She doubted any of the permanent residents gave much of a damn about hygiene.

The ones who have the drive to get out do, she thought, as they halted on the edge of the district. *And those who don't are trapped until they die.*

Emily sucked in her breath. A large building lay ahead of them, wrapped in shadow. Beyond it, Emily saw the sea...they were right on the edge of the island. The stench was stronger, somehow, sinking into her very bones. She had no idea how the locals managed to tolerate it, day in and day out. She'd have to burn her clothes and bathe for hours when she finally managed to leave the city.

"Stay here," Sienna hissed. "I'll beckon you when the time comes."

Caleb reached for Emily's hand as Sienna hurried into the darkness. Emily hesitated, then pulled her hand back. They couldn't hit the reset button, no matter how much she might wish they could. Afterwards, if they survived, they would have to sit down and have a proper chat about the future. And decide what – exactly – they wanted from each other.

Alassa knew she was working towards marriage, Emily thought, numbly. *And Imaiqah knew she just wanted to have fun.*

Frieda popped up behind them, leaning forward and peering towards the sewage plant. Emily was almost relieved. Frieda would save her from having to have that conversation until they were safe. She pushed her emotions out of her head as Sienna returned, looking pleased with herself.

"The original guards were gone," she said. She motioned for them to follow her back to the building. "I dealt with the newcomers."

Emily glanced around with interest as they walked up to the doors and into the building, trying to ignore the seven dead bodies on the ground. She'd never grown used to seeing death, even though it had been a constant companion since Shadye had kidnapped her for the first time. She didn't even want to *think* about how many people had died, directly or indirectly, because of her. Vesperian would never have been able to lure so many investors into his web without her innovations. And she'd heard that some of his investors had committed suicide after his death.

"This place stinks," Frieda said, wryly. "What *is* it?"

"A wonder of the world." Sienna sounded oddly amused as she opened a hatch and motioned for them to climb down. "The Sewers of Beneficence."

Emily nodded in agreement when Frieda shot her a questioning look. The sewers *were* a wonder of the world, all the more so for not using any magic at all. Beneficence had cold running water piped to every home – at least, every home connected to the water pipes – and a web of sewers to take away the waste. And now, with manure being sifted for saltpetre and other chemical compounds, the sewers were profitable. She groaned as Sienna launched a light globe into the air, casting an eerie radiance over the scene. It was somehow not a surprise to spot the 'V' emblazoned into the wall.

Emily scrambled down the ladder into a chamber that looked like a giant swimming pool, only one crammed with liquid waste rather than water. Emily felt her stomach churn as the stench somehow managed to grow even worse…she forced herself to look away as Sienna led them towards a giant tunnel heading into the darkness. There would be all sorts of bacteria breeding in the pool, she knew, as well as methane. Striking a match might cause an explosion. Or was that right? There was a way to get methane from manure, if she recalled correctly. She just couldn't remember *how*.

Something to think about, she told herself. The ledge felt dangerously narrow, given the risk of falling into the slop. *If we can make methane, what can we do with it?*

It didn't get any better as they made their way down the tunnel. The ceiling was too low for comfort, even though she *knew* it was safe. Sienna and Caleb had to keep their heads down as they walked to avoid bumping them into the ceiling; Emily was shorter, but she still kept her head down, fearing contact with the roof. She clearly saw a faint slime lining the walls, droplets of water dripping down and plopping into the sewer. The sewage itself seemed to ripple, although there was no wind. Emily kept a wary eye on the liquid as they headed further down the tunnel. The stories she'd heard about alligators in the sewers suddenly seemed creditable.

Frieda coughed, suddenly. The noise was so loud that Emily jumped.

"Quiet," Sienna hissed.

"Sorry," Frieda said. "But how do we know we're heading in the right direction?"

"I have a blood tie to Marian," Sienna snapped. "We're heading straight towards her."

Or as close to straight as possible, Emily thought, as they passed a crossroads and crawled over a bridge barely wide enough for a child. She had no idea how much the sewage workers were paid, but it wasn't enough. Maintaining the network had to be an absolute nightmare. *We should come up in Temple Row, but what if we can't get all the way up?*

She felt her magic tingle and knew the answer. *We'll have to blast our way through the roof.*

"They keep talking about monsters down here," Croce said. He was bringing up the rear. "All the sorcerers who flush their experiments down the drain…"

"That practice was banned years ago." Sienna glanced back, annoyed. "Although the giant spiders ate up the giant cockroaches."

Emily swallowed, hard. She hoped Sienna was joking.

Pouring potions down the drain would be dangerous, she reminded herself. Professor Thande had cautioned them, time and time again, to be careful when disposing of alchemical brews…even ones that had seemingly failed. Putting a dozen failed potions in the same place was asking for trouble. *Most sorcerers and alchemists would know better, wouldn't they?*

She pushed the thought aside as Sienna reached a ladder, leading up into the darkness. A reddish liquid dripped down into the sewage. Emily turned away, revolted. It looked like blood. She didn't think she wanted to know for sure. If someone had died up there…

"Keep back," Sienna ordered. "I'm going up."

Emily felt her skin crawl as Caleb's mother scrambled up the ladder. The sense of something being wrong, very wrong, was growing stronger. And yet…she flinched as she heard a clanging sound, followed by a flash of magic. The trickle of blood turned into a stream.

"Come on up," Sienna hissed.

Emily glanced at Caleb, who shrugged and started to climb the ladder. Emily followed him, trying to keep her mouth firmly closed. The blood splashed over her fingers and stained her clothes, making the ladder slippery as she inched her way upwards. Caleb helped her out when she reached the top, allowing her to look around. The floor was awash in blood, slowly flowing to the hatch and pouring down into the sewer. She looked up and stared in disgusted horror. Bodies, countless bodies, hung from meathooks, blood dripping to the floor. They had suffered the death of a thousand cuts.

They must have used something to keep the blood from clotting, she thought, numbly. She felt as though she'd gone beyond horror, beyond feeling anything. *Then they hung them up here to die.*

"Fuck," Frieda muttered.

Emily glanced at her. Frieda was covered in blood. They were *all* covered in blood, their clothes clinging to their bodies as blood pooled in their boots. Emily wanted a bath, but she knew she didn't have time. They had to find Marian and destroy Justice. There was no other choice.

"It beats falling in the sewage," Croce said.

Frieda smiled. Emily glanced from one to the other, then dismissed the thought. She'd been taught not to treat blood lightly, to do everything in her power to make sure none of her blood ever fell into enemy hands. And even a dead man's blood could be used in a potion or turned against his relatives...she looked up at the bodies again and shivered. This wasn't part of a dark rite or a ritual, not as far as she could tell. It was savagery, plain and simple.

"This way," Sienna said.

Emily had a flicker of *déjà vu* as they made their slow way out of the chamber and up the steps. The temple was as dark and silent as the grave, yet she could feel Justice's presence all around her. There were no guards, no one trying to block their way...she wondered, darkly, what it meant. Had General Pollack drawn off everyone? Or did Janus feel his god could protect itself? She wouldn't have bet against it. Janus truly *believed* he'd summoned a god.

That might work against him, she mused. They reached the top of the stairs and headed down the corridor. *Perhaps we can break his faith.*

She tested the staff, carefully. The spell *should* work...she thought. But if it didn't...

"We're on the ground floor." Sienna touched her hand to her heart, then moved it around until she was pointing at a pair of stone doors. "She's in the hall."

Croce moved forward, staff at the ready. "On three?"

"On three," Sienna confirmed. "Get ready."

Emily braced herself as Sienna counted down to zero, then cast a powerful blasting spell at the doors. They shattered, pieces of rock flying in all directions as Croce and Caleb ran forward. Sienna, Emily and Frieda followed them into the room...and stopped. Justice stood in front of the altar, his presence so overwhelming that it was like running into a brick wall. Behind him, Emily barely made out Marian lying on the altar. She was wrapped in powerful magic...

"Welcome," a mocking voice said. Emily glanced around. Janus stood by the wall, leaning on his staff. A thin smile played over his face. "You will be judged."

Chapter Thirty-Six

*S*HIT, EMILY THOUGHT.

She forced herself to think as Justice's presence beat against her wards. She'd reworked them over the last few hours, using everything she'd learned to block the entity's influence, but it was still wearing them down. The rune on her chest burned, as if the entire room was supercharged with subtle magic. It felt like overkill. Anyone who spent more than a few minutes in Justice's presence would be drawn to him, subtle magic or not.

"You're mad." Sienna's voice sounded faint, as though she were a very long way away. "This...this *thing* is not a god."

"And yet, he will pass judgement on you." Janus didn't sound angry. He didn't sound as though he had anything to defend. He sounded...as though he was so absolutely sure of himself that he didn't *need* to crush dissent. "He is a god!"

Emily looked at Justice, trying to see through the haze. The entity had definitely grown stronger, its presence more substantial...it was hard, so hard, to make out a face, but she was sure there was *intelligence* looking back at her. It wasn't a Mimic, she reminded herself, sharply. The sole Mimic she'd encountered had been driven by hunger and malevolence, but Justice was different. He − it, perhaps − felt like a stern father, peering down at her from on high. She wasn't sure she wanted to look any closer. The entity's sheer presence might infect her mind.

It's an idea, she thought, numbly. *And ideas spread from mind to mind.*

She looked past the entity, trying to see Marian. Caleb's sister was wrapped in magic, yet...she was clearly being prepared for sacrifice. It was hard to tell if Marian was awake and aware or not, but...she'd clearly bitten off a bit more than she could chew. Emily wanted to walk around the entity and check Marian personally, yet her legs refused to move. The entity had them in its clutches.

"Let my daughter go," Sienna snapped. "She's an innocent!"

"No one is innocent," Janus informed her. "All must be judged."

Emily felt a hot flash of envy. Marian had betrayed them, willingly or not. And yet, Sienna was still prepared to fight for her daughter, even if the fight seemed hopeless. Marian didn't know how lucky she was...

Sienna raised her staff. "Name me one person who is completely without sin," she challenged. "Your monster will destroy everyone!"

"There must be balance." Janus's voice was calm. "All must pay for their sins."

Balance, Emily thought. Something was nagging at her mind, but...she couldn't put her finger on it. The Hands of Justice fought for balance, complete balance. Murderers must be killed, arsonists were to be burnt, criminals were to be stripped of their goods...she knew, all too well, that they couldn't hope to achieve *true* balance. All they could do was make criminals suffer for their crimes. *They want balance...*

"You cannot make those judgements." Sienna moved forward, slowly. Her sheer force of will was astonishing. "How can *anyone* make those judgements?"

"*He* can make those judgements." Janus nodded to Justice, still standing in front of the altar. "I am merely his Speaker."

He's stalling, Emily thought, dully. It felt odd, but it made sense. Janus was playing for time, hoping that Justice would eventually convert them to his cause. And it might work, she conceded. The pressure against her defenses was growing stronger. *He wants us to join him.*

"And yet, he kills the people you ask him to judge," Sienna said. She took another step towards him. "He shows no mercy."

"He shows no mercy when none is deserved." Janus still sounded very certain. "He sees all, hears all, knows all. And so he can pass judgement."

He believes every word he's saying, Emily thought, grimly. She glanced at Caleb. He stared at Marian, fighting to walk to her. Beside him, Croce eyed Janus with open hatred. *There's no way we'll get through to him.*

She swallowed, hard. How long would it be, she asked herself, before Justice decided that life *itself* was a crime? All crime *was* committed by the living, after all. She recalled a quartet of comic book characters who'd argued just that. And in his current state, Janus might decide such a piece of insane troll logic actually made sense. Justice would unleash a slaughter that would drown the whole world in blood. Janus…might even turn himself into a lich, just to honor his god.

Sienna's eyes hardened. "What did you do to my daughter?"

"We merely introduced her to the truth," Janus said. "She was one of many who saw the manifestations of Justice. And she pledged herself to us."

"You didn't give her a free choice," Sienna charged. "Your…pet monster warped her mind."

Janus showed a flash of anger. "You *dare* to question her faith?"

Sienna looked back at him. "She would hardly be the first youngster to join a cult!"

"She saw a *god*," Janus snapped. "Do you question it?"

His face darkened with rage. The presence grew stronger, billowing around the staff in his hand. Emily followed the surge of magic as best she could. It was a complex series of spells, but the more it moved, the more she saw of it. Perhaps, if she could muster the energy to move, she could ram her staff through the haze and into the god. And then cast the spell, knowing it would be projected through the staff…

"I do," Sienna said.

"She saw a god," Janus repeated. "How is worship *not* a valid choice?"

Emily winced. If a choice was the *right* choice by default, then…well, it *was* the right choice. It couldn't be disputed. Anyone who argued against it was either ignorant or wilfully evil. She recalled a whole string of religious arguments from Earth that had revolved around the same premise – the truth was the truth, therefore anyone who disputed it was a liar by definition. And once you accepted that a religion was true, you could use it to justify anything.

No religion is ever as good as its god, she reminded herself. Something still nagged at the back of her mind. *It's only ever as good as its followers.*

"I could cast a spell on someone that would make them believe every word I said," Sienna said. "I could make them say or do or believe *anything*. That wouldn't make it a valid choice."

"You're human," Janus said. "Justice is a *god*."

And that makes it okay, Emily thought. She shivered. *You'd do anything if god told you to do it.*

Sienna managed another step forward. "Release my daughter," she said. "Take me instead."

Emily stared at her. A trick? Or was Sienna giving up? Her mental defenses were strong, but she hadn't faced Justice before, not at such close quarters. Justice might be wearing Sienna down, exploiting flaws in her defenses to break through and warp her perception of reality. Or maybe she was trying to get Marian off the altar before anything else happened to her. Emily could sense the cobweb of magic growing stronger...

They're draining her power, she realized. *But slowly, very slowly...*

"Your daughter submitted herself to us," Janus said. "She came of her own free will."

"You want to believe that," Sienna said. "Justice warped her mind."

"Justice is a god," Janus said. "He has no reason to lie..."

Sienna threw herself forward, snapping out a pair of spells. Janus caught the first on his staff, deflecting it into the ceiling; the other struck the staff and blasted it into sawdust. Emily sensed the sudden shift in magic and reached out for the cobwebs, hoping to tear them apart while Justice was distracted. Instead, the magic surged and slammed into Sienna, picking her up and hurling her through the air. Croce lunged toward Justice, waving his staff wildly; Justice backhanded him, casually. The force of the blow smacked him against the far wall.

Marian screamed, her entire body shuddering. Her wrists and ankles were tied to the altar, keeping her trapped. Caleb shouted something, but Justice caught his eye and he froze, helplessly. Emily saw him trembling with rage as she tried to undo the spell...but there was *no* spell. Justice wielded raw magic like a hammer.

We need a Manavore, Emily thought. *Or something else to soak up the excess magic.*

"Justice protects me," Janus said. "They have been judged."

Emily glanced at Frieda, then back at Janus. "Please, will you let me check on them?"

"Of course," Janus said. He sounded unbearably smug. "They have been judged."

The presence seemed to grow weaker, just for a moment, as Emily checked on Sienna as best as she could. Both of Sienna's legs were broken, as far as she could tell; her left arm looked as though it was broken or twisted out of shape too. Sienna was fighting to remain aware, knowing – all too well – that falling asleep so close to Justice might prove fatal. Emily didn't even dare give her a painkilling spell. It would have weakened her defenses at the worst possible time.

"Croce's been knocked cold," Frieda said. She sounded as though she was fighting to keep her voice under control. "His right arm is a mess."

Emily nodded, wincing in sympathy as she walked over and knelt beside Croce. Judging from the state of his arm – it felt as though his bone had been smashed into powder – Croce was incredibly lucky his neck hadn't snapped, killing him instantly. His right ribs felt broken too. Putting them back together would require a trained Healer and a great deal of luck. She tried to cast a freeze spell, intending to put Croce in stasis until they could get him somewhere safe, but the magic refused to form. Justice was steadily sucking all of the magic out of the chamber.

She looked up. Janus looked back at her, his eyes...composed. He wouldn't help her, she was sure. He was so convinced Justice was *real* that he would believe Croce's suffering was precisely what he deserved. There were no arguments that would get through such fanaticism. Everything that happened – that had ever happened – had happened because it was the will of god. A fanatic who believed so strongly could ignore all contradictions in his faith.

Of course God can change his mind, she thought, as she picked up her staff. She hadn't even noticed when she'd dropped it. *He's God. He can do whatever he likes.*

She forced herself to think clearly as she looked at Justice, leaning on her staff. The entity seemed more human – no, *humanoid* – now. A stern judge, a stern father... she was appalled to find herself drawn to him...to *it*. There was something about the implacable, yet *just* entity that appealed to her more than she cared to admit. A judge who would not be swayed, a judge who would not be bribed or intimidated, a judge whose only interest was judging and upholding the law...

It's a trap, she told herself, firmly. *And it's trying to get into my wards.*

Caleb stumbled as the presence pulled back. He turned, his eyes streaming with tears. Emily understood, all too well. He'd been unable to look away from Justice, forced to stare into the blinding light. He was lucky he hadn't been blinded – or drained. Justice was warping the magic within the chamber, trying to drain all of them. Somehow, she found it a little reassuring. A god who *needed* human sacrifice – or even human prayers – was nothing more than an immensely powerful entity.

"I'm sorry," Caleb managed. He took her hand. This time, she let him hold it. "I..."

"It's all right," Emily whispered. She fought to come up with a plan, but her brain refused to function. Were they going to die together? Or be converted into the next generation of Fists of Justice? "I..."

A thought struck her. It was a gamble, a desperate gamble, but they *were* desperate.

"Speaker," she said, fighting to keep her voice stable. "I ask for judgement."

Janus smiled. "You ask for judgement?"

"I ask for a judgement from Justice," Emily said, carefully. Caleb's hand suddenly tightened on hers. "I ask to put my plea to him in person."

"That is your honor," Janus said. He gestured towards the entity. "You may speak to your lord and master."

Emily pulled her hand free, then forced herself to step towards Justice. The whispering grew louder until it deafened her. Caleb said something, but his words were so faint that she couldn't make them out. She hoped he understood she was trying something desperate, something that might easily get all five of them killed. Hell, she hoped Frieda understood it too.

Up close, the presence was overwhelmingly powerful. The urge to go down on her knees was so strong she had to fight to remain standing. She knew she had to kneel, to offer proper respect, but she wanted – she *needed* – to do it on her own terms. Justice's sheer power was pushing her defenses so hard that the slightest chink would be enough to allow the entity to rip her mind to shreds.

She knelt, carefully. Justice loomed over her, a presence thousands of miles tall... she knew it was an illusion, she *knew* it was a trick, yet it gnawed at her mind. She tightened her defenses, marshalling her arguments. Justice had been created to uphold an ideal. She just had to convince the entity there was a better way to fulfil its function...

"My Lord," she said. It was hard to keep her voice stable. "I ask you for judgement."

"YOU MAY SPEAK," Justice boomed. The words seemed to come from all around her, a deafening chorus that tore at her mind. "SPEAK."

"There is a man who has killed many children," Emily said. The presence was growing stronger and stronger. "He has killed many who will never have the chance to face judgement. He has done this in the belief that he is right, that their deaths are just. But how can the death of a child, of those who have not been judged, be right?"

There was a chilling pause. "IT IS NOT. THIS MAN MUST BE JUDGED."

Emily allowed herself a tiny moment of relief. The Hands of Justice had never encouraged vigilantism, even though they'd patrolled the streets with whips and canes. They'd always wanted to be sure they were punishing the right people. A person could not be condemned to *anything* without being properly judged. And Justice had been wired to *believe* in the tenets of his creator's faith. He couldn't look away from them.

"This man believes that he is doing the right thing," Emily said. She didn't dare try to lie to the entity, not now. It was so powerful that she wasn't even sure she *could* lie. Putting a string of words together was suddenly the hardest thing in the universe. "Does that make his actions *just?*"

"NO," Justice boomed. The odd sense of *intelligence* looking back at her grew stronger. She wondered, suddenly, how long it would be until Justice slipped his leash. The whispers were already fading. "I MUST RESTORE THE BALANCE."

Emily swallowed, hard. Either this worked or...

"Janus has killed hundreds of children," she said, carefully. It had to work. Surely, it would work. There was no question of guilt. "And hundreds more who will never be judged."

Janus let out a squawk of pure rage. "Everything I have done, I have done for Justice. I fear no judgement!"

"Then be judged now," Emily said. Sweat poured down her back as the presence shifted around her. Justice was moving, heading directly for Janus. "Accept his judgement."

She braced herself, unsure of what to expect. A man who doubted his religion might have run, or tried to fight; a fanatic who knew where he stood with the lord would stand his ground. Emily gritted her teeth, her fingers curving around the staff as Justice focused all of its attention on Janus. She hadn't had time to study *all* the texts, but she was fairly sure the deaths of so many innocent children would upset the balance. One didn't behead children for being cheeky...

"YOU HAVE BEEN JUDGED," Justice said. There was no doubt at all in its voice. "AND YOU ARE GUILTY."

Janus's mouth opened, in shock or anger or merely to argue...Emily didn't know. It was too late. His body blazed with white light, so bright that Emily had to throw up a hand to protect her eyes. He screamed in pain and terror, then fell silent. Darkness fell so rapidly that Emily found herself blinking frantically, half-convinced she was blind. And when her vision cleared, she saw a stone statue looking back at her. Janus had died in screaming agony...

"JUDGEMENT," Justice said. The cobwebs seemed to be fraying. Marian screamed, thrashing against her restraints. "I SHALL JUDGE ALL..."

Emily cursed under her breath. They'd killed Janus, but they'd also freed Justice from his restraints. She grabbed the staff, braced herself and then thrust it into the entity's back. The shock of contact threw her back, but the staff remained in place... if Sienna was right, the entity shouldn't be able to dislodge it. It might not even know it was there.

Grabbing for the parchment in her pocket, she began the spell.

Nothing happened.

Chapter Thirty-Seven

F OR A LONG MOMENT, ALL EMILY COULD DO WAS STARE.

The plan had been so simple. Use the staffs to get one half of a charm into the entity, then use the other half of the charm to channel a dispelling charm into its soul. It should have worked. They'd certainly tested the charm repeatedly between crafting the staffs and setting off to the temple. And yet...

She looked at Caleb. He looked back at her, equally stunned. Their secret weapon had failed, leaving them with nothing. Magic wouldn't work; physical force wouldn't work...she glanced at Frieda, motioning for her to slip back. Perhaps they could escape before Justice broke free completely.

"We have to get Marian," Caleb said. "Help me!"

"ALL WILL BE JUDGED," Justice said. The entity didn't seem to have *noticed* the attack. "I WILL WALK OUT AND PASS JUDGEMENT ON ALL."

Frieda held up a second staff. Emily took it, but hesitated. If the second charm failed too, they'd only provoke the entity. It was immensely powerful and now it was free of all restraints. She had to think of something, but what? Thrusting herself into the entity would almost certainly get her killed or brainwashed. Her defenses were already threatening to splinter as the entity grew in power.

Marian screamed, again. Caleb hurried over to her side and started to free her, but the bonds refused to break. Emily cursed under her breath as the entity slowly turned to face Caleb, its power rising steadily. She forced herself to look, realizing that the cobweb spells were breaking one by one. And yet, it still drew power from Marian.

It'll need another source of power soon, she thought, numbly. There were five people in the chamber, just waiting for the entity to dine on them. And beyond the temple, there was an entire city. *But it'll run out of victims soon.*

She gritted her teeth. Justice's power demands would keep rising until they simply *couldn't* be met. The entire city – and Zangaria beyond – wouldn't be enough to power the entity, not unless it found a way to lower its power requirements. But she doubted it could, not without a great deal of help. And who could help it?

Me, she thought. *But it would be foolish to trust me.*

"YOU WILL BE JUDGED," the entity said.

"Caleb," Emily shouted, as the entity jabbed a finger at Caleb. "Get down!"

She felt the power levels rising, a moment before Justice cast his spell. Marian screamed, once again. A blast of white light shot over Caleb's head and splashed harmlessly against the far wall. Justice advanced, moving his arm as though it was were a gun. The moment it caught sight of Caleb, it cast another spell...

"Wait," Emily shouted, as Caleb rolled out of the way of another blast. "We have to talk."

Justice turned to face her. "ALL MUST BE JUDGED."

Emily fought for words. The entity's presence was starting to feel a little ragged. Perhaps the trick to defeating it was to force it to expend power faster than it could drain it...but that would almost certainly kill Marian too. What would happen if *she* killed Marian? Would the girl's death spell the end of Justice? Or would Justice merely turn one or all of them into a source of power?

She focused her mind. *Keep it talking*, she thought. Perhaps Frieda and Caleb could get Croce and Sienna out of the chamber before it was too late. Limiting the number of available power sources would force Justice to burn energy trying to catch some power. *Perhaps we can find a way to trick it.*

"Tell me," she said. "What gives you the right to pass judgement?"

"I AM JUSTICE," the entity said.

Emily forced herself to meet its eyes. Something looked back at her, an oddly inhuman intelligence. She'd met demons and fairies, but this was something else. She wanted to look away, but somehow she held its gaze. The entity had to believe her if she was to chip away at its faith in itself.

"Tell me," she managed. "How do you know you're Justice?"

The entity seemed surprised by the question. "I WAS THE LORD OF JUDGEMENT WHEN BALOK THE MANY-HUED WAGED WAR AGAINST SOLARIS, KING OF THE GODS. I HAVE PASSED JUDGEMENT SINCE I WAS BROUGHT INTO THE WORLD. I REMEMBER EVERY JUDGEMENT. I AM JUSTICE"

Emily frowned, wishing she knew more about the gods. She'd never paid enough attention to the myths and legends of her new world. She certainly didn't know enough about the stories, particularly the ones Janus and his comrades would have believed, to argue with Justice. And yet, there were options...

She pushed her mind out, trying to sense the ebb and flow of power. "Do you remember every last detail of every last judgement?"

"YES."

"Then tell me," she said. "What did Balok *look* like?"

Justice hesitated. "BALOK THE MANY-HUED WAS JUDGED FOR WAGING WAR AGAINST SOLARIS, KING OF THE GODS. HE WAS CONDEMNED TO A MILLION ETERNITIES IN THE PITS OF..."

"You said," Emily agreed. "But what did he look like? What was he wearing? Who watched the trial? Who cheered your judgement?"

She reached out with her mind again, carefully touching the magic. Justice drew power directly from Marian now, his last true link to anything outside the spell nexus that had created him. Emily gritted her teeth as she parsed the lines of power, realizing that killing Marian would solve nothing. Justice wouldn't run out of power and die quickly enough to save the city, let alone the rest of them.

"I...DO...NOT...RECALL," Justice said.

Emily felt a hot flash of triumph, mingled with fear. Lady Barb had talked about subtle magic and how it could warp a person's mind...and how a victim could respond with fear and anger, if the mental framework started to crack. They'd lash out at the people trying to help them, just to avoid the pain of breaking free. Justice wasn't human, but he might easily go the same way.

Marian screamed. Caleb hurried back to her and started to fiddle with her bonds, but it was starting to look as though she couldn't be freed in a hurry. Justice had a direct link to her magic, to her very soul...Emily paused as a thought struck her. Perhaps, just perhaps, the link went both ways.

"Tell me about another judgement," Emily said. It would keep the entity talking while she thought. "Who else have you judged?"

"I DESTROYED THE CITY OF GRAYREN FOR SIN AND DEPRAVITY," Justice informed her. "THE INHABITANTS WERE EXECUTED FOR THEIR CRIMES AGAINST THE NATURAL ORDER."

Emily nodded. "And what *were* those sins?"

There was another pause. "I...DO...NOT...RECALL. I PASSED JUDGEMENT ON THEM..."

"What did they do to deserve it?" Emily asked. "Did you find all of them guilty? Was there not a single innocent man, woman or child in the entire city?"

The entity said nothing. Emily pressed her advantage.

"How could a child have committed a crime worthy of death?" she asked. "How could you destroy them all?"

Justice peered at her. "THEIR PARENTS WOULD HAVE TAUGHT THEM TO SIN. THEY WOULD HAVE SINNED IN TIME."

"But they would not be guilty themselves." Emily risked a glance at Caleb, still struggling with Marian's bonds. "How can executing them be *just?*"

She felt the presence grow stronger, again. Logically, Justice stood condemned by its own rules. It could *not* execute children because they *might* grow up into criminals. But if it was learning to think, it might manage to evade that argument by reasoning that the children *would* grow into criminals and it was merely executing them before they committed a crime...a crime they certainly *would* commit. It made no logical sense, but if Justice needed to believe it to survive...

"THEY WOULD HAVE SINNED. I EXECUTED THEM FOR SIN."

"But they never had the chance to sin," Emily pointed out. "How can that be just?"

Justice made no answer. She tested the power again, then carefully strode around the entity and walked to the altar. Marian looked weak, her strength slowly draining into the creature's insatiable maw. She didn't have long to live, Emily realized. At some point, she'd be too far gone to recover, whatever happened. Caleb looked at her, his eyes despairing.

"Get your mother and brother out of here," she whispered. She didn't want Caleb to see what she might have to do. "Hurry."

She looked up at the entity. "How did their parents sin? Why do you not remember?"

"I...DO...NOT...KNOW," the entity said.

"You should know," Emily said. She studied the threads of power, trying to work out how they fit into the spell matrix. Justice was changing even as she watched, the spellwork growing more and more complicated. She hadn't seen anything like it since she'd created the wards at Heart's Eye. "If you don't know your own history, how do you know you are Justice?"

The entity glared at her. "YOU ARE TRYING TO MAKE ME DOUBT."

"An unquestioned belief is not worth having," Emily quoted. "In fact, it is positively dangerous."

"IT IS WOMEN WHO LURE MEN FROM THE PATH OF RIGHTEOUSNESS. IT IS WOMEN WHO MAKE MEN DOUBT."

Emily lifted her eyebrows. Justice wasn't *human*. Why would it embrace a misogynist attitude? Janus hadn't struck her as particularly misogynistic – she'd met far more unpleasant people in the past, when women had been second-class at best, property at worst. Perhaps the doctrines Janus had used to shape Justice were twisting the entity, now that it was thinking for itself. Or perhaps it was merely grasping at straws to keep her arguments from forcing it to question itself.

"And if a woman says something," she said, "does that make it automatically wrong?"

Justice said nothing. Emily watched, wondering just how far the entity could question itself before it had an existential crisis. If it *was* Justice, it should remember everything; if it *wasn't* Justice, then how did it know it was doing the right thing? She had no idea just how advanced – how intelligent – Justice's spell matrix had become, but it might figure out a way to justify its memory gaps to itself.

Marian screamed, again. Her fingers twitched. Emily looked down at her. The bonds were made of something that looked like plastic, but couldn't be. There was no plastic on the Nameless World...she tested one and discovered it was practically unbreakable. Breaking the altar itself might be quicker, if she wanted to get Marian away from Justice. But the entity was connected to her.

"And if you can't answer that question," she said, carefully resting her fingers on Marian's chest, "how do you know you're a god?"

Justice howled in rage – and doubt. Marian screamed...Emily hesitated, then thrust her mind into the spellware linking Marian to Justice. It was strange, an elaborate mixture of advanced spells and crude incantations that should never have held together for more than a few seconds, but they worked. Marian twisted, trying to push Emily away, as Emily forced her way up the link. Justice was powerful, but vulnerable. She could see his weaknesses now, see all the places where the spellwork was fraying...

He's trying to evolve, she thought, numbly. *And it's working.*

She was tempted to watch, even though she knew she shouldn't. It was *very* much like Whitehall's wards, but they'd had nearly a thousand years to grow. *And* they had an unlimited power source to draw on. Justice was evolving so rapidly that he might not make it out of the temple before he collapsed, even if he *did* manage to drain everyone else. She took a moment of grim relief in knowing that Janus's madness probably wouldn't get any further, then reached for the matrix. Here, inside his core, Justice was defenseless. The pressure on her mind was gone.

Goodbye, she thought.

Marian screamed. A hand caught her and yanked her back. Emily recoiled, her mind struggling to cope with the sudden transition. Her legs buckled...someone was holding her, holding her back. She tried to kick out, but her body was weak...

"You'll kill her," Caleb said.

Emily's head spun. Caleb had grabbed her...was he a Fist? Had Justice overwhelmed his mind? Or...she looked at him and knew the truth. He was terrified for his sister...Marian was screaming in pain...pain Emily had caused.

"Let go of me," she snapped. Something was trickling down her nose. It took her a moment to realize it was blood. "I have to stop him."

"You'll kill her," Caleb shouted. "Let her go!"

Emily stared at him. "I won't kill her," she said, although she wasn't sure if that was actually true or not. Justice might drain Marian completely before Emily managed to stop him...coming to think of it, if he did she'd lose her chance to reach inside his defenses. "Let go of me."

Caleb held her, tightly. She'd always known he was stronger than her, physically, but it had never mattered before. Now, she didn't have the strength to resist. Her body felt weak and frail. She tried to knock her head back to strike his nose, but it didn't have any effect at all. Frustration bubbled up within her, mingled with rage and terror. Caleb wouldn't save anyone, not even his sister. They were all doomed...

She fell forward, suddenly. Caleb gasped in pain. Emily managed to turn, just in time to see Frieda clinging to Caleb's back. As Frieda's hands clawed at his throat, Caleb stumbled back, trying to stop her before it was too late. Emily stared at them for a long moment, then forced herself back to Marian. She'd just have to hope that Frieda could distract Caleb long enough to let her finish the job.

I'm sorry, she thought. She knew Caleb would never forgive her for risking his sister, even if Marian had betrayed them. He'd do whatever it took to stop her. *I'm so sorry.*

Justice loomed over Marian, his dark eyes growing larger. "I AM JUSTICE. AND I SHALL JUDGE YOU ALL."

"This girl is an innocent," Emily said. "And you are killing her."

"SHE CAME TO ME OF HER OWN FREE WILL," Justice informed her. The entity didn't seem to notice — or care — when Emily touched Marian's chest again. "SHE IS MINE."

"You cannot explain the gaps in your memory," Emily said. If she could distract it for a few more seconds, she might just be able to put an end to it. "Can you...?"

"THEY ARE OF NO CONCERN. I AM JUSTICE."

He's decided to deal with the problem by ignoring it, Emily thought, as she reached for the threads. *How very human.*

"No," Caleb shouted. "Emily, *stop!*"

Emily ignored him as she plunged her mind back into the maelstrom. Justice was growing ever more powerful, yet his spellwork was simplifying as she watched. Maybe he could make it out of the temple after all. He would become a god-king, she realized, if he managed to gain more power. And he would be unchallengeable.

No sword could harm him, no spell could hurt him…his followers would spend the rest of eternity under the rule of an utterly inhuman entity. A computer ruler could hardly be worse.

Enough, she thought.

She reached for her magic, for the last scraps of power. Justice was draining her, even now…but it gave her access to his core. The spells were resilient, designed to cope with vast influxes of power, yet not to cope with an attack from the inside. Emily noted, as she took hold of the spells and *pulled*, that the staffs *should* have worked. Quite why they hadn't was a mystery.

Or maybe the drain went through the link too, she thought. Justice was fragmenting, pieces of spellware splintering off in all directions. Its presence rose one final time, then collapsed completely. *The parchments were drained before they could be triggered.*

Justice screamed, a sound that tore at her ears…and exploded with light. The spellware flared with power, collapsing in on itself. Emily fell backwards, her mind falling back into her body…she landed on the floor hard enough to hurt. Her body ached, her head throbbed…she forced herself up, just in time to see Justice shatter into thousands of luminescent pieces.

And then, they were gone.

Marian was crying, soft hopeless sobs that tore at Emily's heart. But she was alive…the spells were gone completely. Emily tugged at the bonds, somehow unsurprised when they came free easily. The power that had been holding them together was gone forever. Marian felt light in Emily's arms, flopping around as though she was too tired to move. And yet, she was alive.

Frieda coughed. Emily turned to look at her. Frieda's face was bruised – Caleb didn't look in any better shape – but she was alive. They were both alive.

"Is that it?" Frieda stumbled to her feet. "Is it over?"

"Yeah." Emily leaned against the remains of the altar, trying to gather what remained of her strength. The headache was already fading, but she was exhausted. And yet … given time, they'd all get back to normal. "It's over."

And the horror in Caleb's eyes told her that *they*, too, were over.

Chapter Thirty-Eight

"WHAT A MESS," MARKUS SAID.

Emily nodded in agreement as they stood on the roof, looking down over the city. The streets were slowly returning to normal, but it would be a long time before Beneficence recovered completely. Hundreds of people had collapsed, badly shocked, after Justice's death; thousands more were starving, searching desperately for something to eat. The last two days had been nightmarish, even after the fishing boats had started plying their trade again. She was surprised that so many citizens had worked together to save their city.

Community isn't an empty word here, she thought. *People do spend their lives with their neighbors.*

She looked down towards the makeshift gallows, feeling sick. Some of the surviving Fists of Justice had managed to shed their uniforms and escape, but most had been caught by outraged citizens and killed, either beaten to death or hung in the streets. Emily knew, all too well, that some of them had been innocent, that they'd been sucked into something they didn't understand or overwhelmed by Justice, but she hadn't been able to do anything to save them. The citizens had demanded their piece of flesh. And really, how could she blame them?

Markus gave her a sidelong look. "What happened to the scrolls you found?"

Emily shrugged. Sienna had insisted on searching the remains of the Temple of Justice for the scrolls – and anything else the Hands of Justice might have hidden away – but they'd found nothing. The scrolls might have been destroyed, during Emily's first encounter with Justice, or they might have been taken before the entity was killed. She hoped they'd been destroyed, but she had no way to know for sure. The secret was out and spreading. It was sheer luck that most people believed Justice had been nothing more than an illusion.

And Janus an incredibly powerful sorcerer, she thought. *But better they believe that than the truth.*

"I wish I knew," she said, reluctantly. The thought distracted her from the dull ache in her heart. "If they were taken, they could be out of the city by now."

"Some of Janus's comrades were never found," Markus said. "They might try again."

"They might," Emily agreed. "But we know how to stop them now, if they do."

She shook her head, tiredly. Beneficence would never be the same again.

Markus cleared his throat. "I heard about you and Caleb," he said. "Are you all right?"

Emily snorted. "I've been better," she said. She'd never felt *quite* so rotten before, even after the Grandmaster's death. "I don't...sometimes I think I should never have started to court him, and sometimes I think I should never have come to his city."

"Perhaps not," Markus agreed. "I suspect he reasoned that he could go with you, if necessary, and his family would be fine. It was a little different when *he* became the Heir."

"*You* were the Heir," Emily pointed out. "And you gave it up for Melissa."

"I knew my brother would take my place," Markus said. He shrugged. "They were teaching me how to be Patriarch from the day I was old enough to string two words together. I knew what the job entailed before I went to Mountaintop. Caleb, on the other hand…I think he was probably a little overwhelmed. It isn't easy to cope when you find that you're suddenly expected to be the family's next head."

"Ouch," Emily said. She didn't really want to talk about it. "Is it that hard?"

"Think about it," Markus said. "Caleb and you met at Whitehall, right? You spent most of your time in an environment where you could both be yourselves. Here… before Casper's death, Caleb could come and go as he pleased. No one really expected him to be anything more significant than just another magician on the family tree. Now…Caleb has all sorts of new responsibilities…"

He sighed. "It would have been harder for us, perhaps, if we hadn't made a clean break. Caleb…didn't want to give up his family."

He didn't want to give up his family for me, Emily thought. It was a bitter thought. But how could she ask him to give up his family? *And I didn't really want to marry into the family.*

Markus looked pensive. "You outgrew him."

Emily glanced at him. "What?"

"When you met him, you were seventeen," Markus said.

"Eighteen," Emily corrected. She wasn't entirely sure of her *precise* age, but she *had* been sixteen when Shadye had kidnapped her and she'd spent somewhere between four and five years on the Nameless World. "It was at Cockatrice."

"And you were ready for him, at the time," Markus added. "But as you grew older, you started to see his flaws too. Maybe you could have overcome them, if things had been different, but one of you would have had to give up something important."

Emily scowled. "You seem to be good at giving advice."

Markus stuck out his tongue. "I was Head Boy. Do you have any idea how many youngsters I consoled after emotional break-ups? How many young men and women I helped to come to terms with their relationship issues? How many gifted magicians I helped to steer their way through betrothal and marriage contracts?"

"No," Emily said.

"A lot," Markus told her. "And let me tell you, Emily, that you and Caleb have been very lucky, compared to some of the others. You can end your relationship without fear of familial repercussions."

"I know," Emily said, quietly.

She shook her head, slowly. Marriage was a holy state, as far as the magical families were concerned. Divorce was almost unthinkable, particularly if children were involved. A couple might choose to live separately, perhaps on opposite sides of the Allied Lands, rather than endure the condemnation of both families. A married couple would be expected to work through their problems rather than split up at the slightest provocation.

And Melissa chose to leave rather than accept her family's choice of husband, Emily thought, grimly. *Who can blame her?*

Markus cocked his head. "Harman has arrived." He held out a hand. "Coming?"

Emily nodded as she followed him down the stairs and into the office. Harman, wearing the bright robes of Grand Guildmaster, stood by the window, peering at the streets below. The other guilds were currently electing new guildmasters – if nothing else, the crisis had loosened up the requirements a little – but it would be at least a week, according to Sienna, before the city council was reconstituted. Harman might even lose his seat when the newcomers took theirs.

But at least that will make him want to listen, Emily thought. *Vesperian's black hole isn't going to go away. He needs to present the council with a plan to save the city if he wants to stay in power.*

"Lady Emily," Harman said. His voice was unfailingly polite, but there was an undertone of resentment. Emily didn't blame him. She'd fingered him as a traitor and he'd suffered for it. "I understand that you have a plan?"

"I do," Emily said. It was actually Markus's plan, but her name might help in convincing the city council to adopt it. "Please, take a seat."

She sat and smoothed down her skirt. Harman eyed her for a long moment, then sat down facing her. Markus ordered drinks and then sat himself. Emily couldn't help thinking that he looked tired and yet, at the same time, enthusiastic. But then, he had to look supremely confident. Harman would expect her to have discussed the plan with her allies first. If she couldn't sell it to them, who *could* she sell it to?

"The problem is simple," she said. "Thousands of people poured money into Vesperian's scheme. Vesperian then used that money to buy supplies for his ongoing project, gambling on recouping the money when the extended track went into service."

"Yes," Harman said. "And now the money has vanished."

"I propose to buy back the notes at a third of their face value," Emily said. Markus had spoken to the other surviving bankers. They'd be investing chunks of their own money in the recovery scheme. "We'll start with the smaller investors, but hopefully we should be able to buy back a majority of the notes within the next week or so."

"The note-holders will not recover all of their money," Harmon noted.

Emily nodded. "That cannot be helped," she said. The combined investment from both her and the bankers wouldn't be enough to replace *all* the losses. All they could do was cushion the blow. "However, each of the investors will get *something* back."

"A large number of suits have already been filed against Vesperian's estate," Harman said, coolly. "How do you propose to deal with those?"

"This will be their only real chance to recover *anything*," Markus pointed out. "There is no way the entire estate, even putting aside the argument over who owns what, can meet the demands for repayment. I believe that most of his creditors will see reason."

"You may be right," Harmon said. He looked directly at Emily. "I assume you want something in return, Lady Emily?"

"I want the railway," Emily said, flatly.

Harman raised his eyebrows. "You think you can make it work?"

"I believe that the line between Beneficence and Cockatrice was already profitable," Emily countered. "Putting a line between Cockatrice and Swanhaven – or the Iron Hills – is a little harder at the moment, but the original railway is solid. Given time, the network can be gradually extended further into Zangaria without requiring such a vast investment."

She leaned forward. "However, this only works if the railway remains intact. I have no interest in a pile of scrap metal."

"The railway station was burned to the ground a week ago," Harman said.

"The damage is mainly cosmetic," Emily countered. "Vesperian's staff had the sense to send most of the engines and rolling stock to Cockatrice before all hell broke loose. The railway lines themselves are largely untouched. Rebuilding the station and replacing the handful of damaged rails won't take *that* long, given how many people have an interest in reopening the line. The engineers agree that a week or so is all they require to restart a basic service."

"I see," Harman said. "And, given what else is involved, why should the city itself not run the railway?"

Emily glanced at Markus, who shrugged. "In that case, the city would also become liable for the original investment," he said. "You'll have to sue yourselves to recover the investment, then satisfy your creditors. I don't think the guilds will appreciate it."

"Particularly as they'll be dipping into their own funds to repay the debt," Emily said. She shrugged, trying to sound as though she didn't care. "Naturally, *us* buying back the notes will be contingent on an agreement you *won't* try to requisition the railway or attempt to recover the rest of the money."

She watched Harman for a long moment. The crisis hadn't happened on his watch. Of all the old guildmasters, he was the only one who could claim any innocence at all. And yet, he might well wind up being the scapegoat if the money was never recovered. He had to know it, too. The Accountants had never been popular, even before their corruption had been exposed by the New Learning. It was easy to imagine the new council throwing him to the wolves to escape blame themselves.

"I believe the council would go for it," Harman said, finally. He glanced at Markus. "I assume you will be handling the details?"

Markus bowed his head. "Of course."

"I should have an answer for you by the end of the day." Harman made a show of preparing to rise. "Is there anything else we have to discuss?"

"You'll need to rewrite the laws to prevent something like this from happening again," Emily said. "Something, perhaps, that will keep the next Vesperian from running his own disastrous scheme."

"We're already looking at options." Harman shrugged, expressively. "The real problem is encouraging investment while discouraging over-investment."

"Perhaps insist on openness," Emily said. Earth had had rules, but she didn't know how they'd worked. Markus and his fellow bankers would have to reinvent them. "A business that wants investors should be able to disclose its current position, if only to make sure potential investors know what they're getting into."

"And make sure that promises are not *too* exaggerated," Harman added. "*That's* not going to be easy."

Emily nodded in agreement. Vesperian was hardly the first person who'd made grandiose promises, although *his* project had been several orders of magnitude greater than any she'd seen in Cockatrice. She'd met any number of businessmen who'd promised her unimaginable sums, if she invested in their plans. Some of them had even managed to turn a profit.

"It will be a while before another such scheme gets off the ground," she said. "You should be able to lay the ground rules before then."

"We'll certainly try," Harman said. He gave her a sharp look. "What actually happened?"

Emily raised her eyebrows. "I beg your pardon?"

"Janus was no sorcerer," Harman said. "I knew him. He was always a devoted little prick, but he was no sorcerer. Where did he get his power?"

"Magic," Emily said. She groaned, inwardly. The secret was definitely spreading. "He did something unprecedented and...and it allowed him to create a false god."

"Ah," Harman said. "And will it happen again?"

"I hope not," Emily said. She wished for a chance to examine the scrolls again, although she knew she should be glad they'd been destroyed. If, of course, they *were* destroyed. Master Wolfe's secrets might have vanished back into the past. "I don't think what he did would be easy to replicate."

"I hope you're right," Harman said. "The city is fragile, Lady Emily. We could not endure another...another fake god."

"I don't think that will be a problem," Emily said. Sienna knew the truth, as did a couple of her friends. They'd keep an eye out for the scrolls. Perhaps they *had* been destroyed after all. "Janus was unique."

"In many ways," Harman agreed. "The pressure of his job drove him insane."

Emily kept her thoughts to herself. The Accountants – and she counted Harman among them – had been corrupt. She hated to think what it must have been like, for an honest man, to watch as his fellows embezzled from their clients, praising them openly while stealing and using the account books to conceal their crimes. Janus must have found it a relief, she suspected, when double-entry bookkeeping had changed the world. He could watch his former guild collapse with a clear conscience.

But he could have left earlier, she thought. *What kept him in his job?*

She shrugged. She'd probably never know.

"It won't happen again," she said, instead. "I'm sure of it."

"Good," Harman said. "And that leads neatly to the final point."

He met her eyes. "The city council would prefer you left the city today, Lady Emily. Your presence is...disruptive."

"She saved you all," Markus pointed out, sharply.

"Yes," Harman said. "But she's also disruptive."

Emily held up a hand before Markus could say or do something Harman would regret. In truth, she'd expected to be asked to leave days ago. Too many people were muttering about how *her* innovations had allowed Vesperian to thrive, how *her* innovations had brought the city to its knees. And while she *had* defeated Justice, most of the city didn't know what had really happened. They didn't know they should be grateful...

"I understand," she said. She rather doubted she was expected to attend the rest of Casper's funeral, let alone Caleb's confirmation as Heir. God alone knew what had happened to Casper's casket. Sienna hadn't said anything, but...If nothing else, it was an excuse for her and Frieda to leave the city. "I'll be gone by the end of the day."

"Thank you." Harman rose. "And I hope we will meet again."

Emily concealed her amusement as Harman left the room. She didn't think *anyone* had told her anything *quite* so insincere...

"I'm sorry," Markus said. "I can petition the council, if you wish. They cannot send you into exile without a proper hearing."

"Don't worry about it," Emily said. "Just send a message to Frieda, telling her to meet me on the bridge. She won't want to stay either."

"Probably for the best." Markus rose and held out a hand. "Good luck with resuming your studies, Emily."

"I'll need it," Emily said. She rubbed her forehead. She'd have to work hard – very hard – to catch up. *And* she would have to do some of that with Caleb. It was going to be awkward as hell. "I'll be sure to give Melissa your love."

"She said she would come visit at half-term," Markus said. "By then, hopefully everything will be back to normal."

"Or as normal as it gets around here," Emily said. Beneficence had been changing – for better and for worse – even before Vesperian's death. "Don't forget to send the message."

"I won't." Markus paused. "Caleb is waiting for you downstairs. Do you want me to sneak you out the back?"

Emily hesitated. She didn't want to face Caleb, not now. But she didn't have a choice. They *had* to talk...

"I'll meet him downstairs," she said. She knew she was being silly, but she couldn't help feeling that facing a necromancer would be easier. "I'll walk with him to the bridge."

"Good luck." Markus waved a hand. "See you next time."

Chapter Thirty-Nine

CALEB STOOD BY THE DOOR WHEN EMILY ENTERED THE LOBBY, LOOKING AS IF HE HAD AGED several years in the last few months. His face was scarred – Frieda *had* caught him a nasty blow, during their brief fight – although Emily was surprised he hadn't asked his mother to heal it. But then, there were far more injured people on the streets, people who could never live a normal life without magical healing. He'd just have to live with his scars until he returned to Whitehall.

"Emily." Caleb sounded nervous. "I...how are you?"

Emily looked back at him for a long moment, unable or unwilling to put a name to any of her emotions. She'd liked Caleb, even *loved* him. He'd been a decent man, for all of his faults; she'd trusted him enough to lower the barriers completely, to allow him to enter her and take her virginity...she thought, though she didn't *know*, that he'd been a virgin too. Were they both still virgins if they'd swapped virginities?

Her lips twisted at the absurd thought. Caleb looked alarmed, then offended; Emily sighed inwardly, realizing he thought she'd been laughing at him. But she hadn't laughed...she closed her eyes for a long moment, centering herself. The dull heartache felt worse when she looked at him...

"I'm fine," she lied. She nodded to the door. "I have to walk to the bridge."

Caleb's expression tightened. "They're kicking you out? After everything you did for them?"

"Someone has to take the blame." Emily pushed open the door. A gust of warm air struck her. It smelled faintly of fish from the market down the street. "And I'm leaving the city anyway."

She cast a privacy ward as they started to walk down the street, heading to the bridge. She'd meet Frieda there, hopefully, and then teleport back to Dragon's Den. Or all the way back to Whitehall, perhaps. A night in her own bed felt like a very good idea, but the sooner she was back at school the better. She had a lot of work to do.

"Mother said you probably wouldn't want to stay," Caleb said. "She had a lot of sharp things to say to me."

Emily nodded. Having a mother like Sienna was a two-edged sword. She would fight for her children, defend them...but she'd also keep them firmly in line. Caleb hadn't lived up to the standards she expected from her children. Emily was grimly sure that Sienna would make him pay for it.

"But Marian wanted to apologize to you," Caleb added, after a moment. "She was...she was overwhelmed."

"I don't blame her," Emily said, tartly. *She'd* been overwhelmed by blood magic, four years ago. "Is she recovering?"

"Slowly," Caleb said. "Mother thinks she'll be going to Whitehall next year."

Emily glanced at him. "Is that a good idea?"

"She's too fragile for Stronghold, after...after...well, everything," Caleb said. "Mother actually thought about keeping Marian at home and teaching her personally, but she doesn't know everything Marian will need to learn. I have strict orders to look after her when she arrives."

"Ouch," Emily said. She wondered if Sienna was doing Marian any favors. An overprotective brother dogging her heels would make it harder for her to establish herself at school. But she didn't blame Sienna for wanting to protect her child. "Don't be *too* overbearing."

"I learned from Casper." Caleb smiled, his face lighting up. "Mostly, I learned what *not* to do…"

"True," Emily agreed. "But…"

She shook her head. Casper had followed her to Heart's Eye. Caleb, she knew now, wouldn't do the same. He wasn't a fighter, not at heart. He was a researcher…

"But nothing," Emily said. She touched his arm, lightly. "Take care of her."

They walked in silence for a long moment, unspoken words hovering between them like a shroud. Emily missed, with a pang that almost brought tears to her eyes, the times when they'd walked hand in hand. She'd liked that…had she ever *told* him she'd liked that? And there had been the kissing and…she wondered, suddenly, how Imaiqah could move from boyfriend to boyfriend so easily. Part of her wanted to kiss him again, despite everything that had happened…

Caleb reached out and touched her shoulder. "I…I need to tell you something," he said, slowly. She stopped, turning to look at him. "I…I thought Marian was going to die."

Marian would have died, if Justice hadn't been stopped, Emily thought. *She…*

She bit off that thought, hard. There was nothing to be gained by making Caleb – or herself – feel worse. She wanted to scream at him, to lash out with her magic… and at the same time, she wanted to wrap her arms around him and feel *safe*. But she knew she couldn't do either.

"I thought you would kill her." Caleb's voice was quiet. "I thought…"

"I understand," Emily said. She felt a pang, mingled with bitter understanding. When the chips were down, Caleb had put his family ahead of her. "You thought your sister was going to die."

"Yes," Caleb said. "I should have trusted you. I…"

He looked away, one hand playing with his hair. "I didn't want to consider the possibility that she might have betrayed us. Casper was a jerk, at times, but he wouldn't have betrayed the family. When you suggested it, I got so angry…"

And Frieda didn't help, Emily thought.

Caleb fell silent for a long moment. "Marian was a brat to you," he said. "She was having problems coping with Casper's death. She…"

"I don't blame her," Emily said. "I never knew what it was like to have siblings."

"Lucky you." Caleb looked back at her. "I always imagined that I would leave the family, one day. There was little for me here--" he waved a hand at the surrounding buildings "--and Casper was the Heir. I would complete my studies and get my mastery, then open a university or maybe a small research lab. I'd see my family every so often, and that would be that."

He waited. Emily said nothing.

"I liked you from the moment we met," he added. "I..."

Caleb broke off. "I was free to court you, I believed. No one would object to the courtship, nothing would be at stake. If we married, I would be your consort. I..."

Emily closed her eyes in pain. She'd been on the Nameless World for years and yet, sometimes, the differences in *culture* still caught her by surprise. Caleb hadn't been interested in a pointless fling, any more than she was. Of *course* he'd considered all the implications of a successful courtship and marriage. He'd understood all the implications she'd chosen to ignore...

There's a difference between courting a nobleman and the heir to a throne, Emily thought, recalling Alassa's patient lectures. *Whoever you marry will shape your life.*

She opened her eyes, looking up at him. "But things are different now." She felt her patience snap. "You're the Heir to your family – and, prospectively, the Heir to House Waterfall. Right?"

"I don't *think* I'll be *the* Waterfall," Caleb said. "We're probably not close enough to the main line to be considered..."

And you would have had a shot at the family title if you'd married me, Emily thought. She knew Caleb probably considered it a relief. Could a candidate refuse the post if they were elected? She didn't know. *Now...they may blame you for losing me.*

"Things are different now," Emily repeated. "The implications of our relationship are different too."

She met his eyes. "And you didn't trust me, when the crunch came," she added. That hurt more than anything else. "You thought..."

Caleb looked back at her, evenly. "Mother drilled my failings into me. She...she told me that the entire city was at stake."

"It was," Emily confirmed.

"I couldn't let her die," Caleb said. "I..."

"And so you let her be drained further," Emily snapped, irritated. "She nearly died because you didn't trust me!"

Caleb turned away, angrily. "I should have trusted you. But I didn't."

Emily felt magic tingling at her fingertips, demanding release. She fought it down, despite her frustration. They were dancing around a simple point, as if neither was willing to say what had to be said. And all the apologies in the world wouldn't make it better – or easier. They...their relationship had died in the Temple of Justice.

Lady Barb would be direct, Emily thought. *And I have to be direct, too.*

She cleared her throat. Caleb turned back to her.

"When we started this courtship," she said, "we agreed that we – that either of us – could call it off at any moment. And now..."

Caleb looked pale, but unsurprised. "You want to call it off."

"So do you," Emily snapped. She wondered, suddenly, just *what* Sienna had said to her middle son. "In the temple...you didn't trust me."

She felt another pang of grief, mixed with anger. She'd trusted *him*. She'd trusted him enough to let him kiss her, to touch her, to go inside her...it hadn't been easy to make that decision, to let him have her...

...And yet, she'd kept secrets from him, too.

Men desire physical intimacy to prove there will be physical intimacy, Lady Barb had said, during one of her brutally frank lectures. *Women desire emotional intimacy to prove there will be emotional intimacy. And neither gender really understands what the other wants.*

Caleb looked oddly relieved. "I'm sorry," he said. "I thought..."

"Courtships fail," Emily said, sharply. Lady Barb had had a failed courtship, although Emily didn't know the details. "It happens."

She controlled her anger with an effort. "Inform your mother that we are no longer courting," she said, stiffly. No doubt Sienna would start looking at eligible young women for her oldest surviving son. She told herself, firmly, that she wasn't going to be jealous when Caleb finally found a wife. "And that we are still friends."

Caleb blinked. "Friends?"

Emily hid her amusement. She didn't want him to think she was laughing at him. "We have a project to finish," she reminded him. "And a university to build."

He gaped at her. "You still want me to help?"

"We can't get out of doing the project," Emily pointed out. They'd both be in trouble if they failed to scrape a passing grade. "I'm not explaining to Lady Barb why I had to repeat Fifth and Sixth Year."

"I suppose it would be an awkward explanation," Caleb said. "Mother would not be pleased, either."

Emily smiled, despite herself. "No, she wouldn't," she agreed. It would have been nice to have a parent who cared about her grades, but she could see the downside. "She'd be much more likely to lock you in your room and force you to study."

"She would." Caleb looked pensive. "She was always furious when we came home with poor grades or bad reports. Casper couldn't sit down for a week after his teacher tattled on him for some silly prank."

"Ouch," Emily said. She believed him. "And afterwards, we *do* have to open a university."

She smiled. Caleb wouldn't be happy running his family, but he'd have time to work on Heart's Eye before his parents died. Hell, perhaps Sienna would be interested in helping with the university. She knew a *lot* of magicians who might be willing to share what they knew...

"If we can," Caleb said.

Emily held out a hand. "Friends?"

Caleb took her hand and shook it, gravely. "Friends."

It wasn't going to be easy, Emily knew, as they resumed their walk towards the northern bridge. They'd been lovers, with all that implied...their relationship would never be *simple*, no matter what they did. Part of her still wanted to kiss him, even though she knew she could never go back. The girl who'd courted Caleb had died in the Temple of Justice, too.

"I heard that Annabel Vesperian and her son were sighted in Zangaria," Caleb said. "Do you think King Randor intends to use them?"

Emily shrugged. Vesperian *had* owned property in Zangaria. No doubt Markus and the rest of the bankers would lay claim to it eventually, once they collected the notes and sorted out what they were owed. Vesperian's heirs would be wise to run further, if King Randor wasn't keeping them in custody. They'd have enemies in Beneficence until the day they died.

"I imagine they're of little use," she said. She knew next to nothing about Vesperian's wife and son, but she was fairly sure they wouldn't be much use to Randor. Unless he held them until they could be traded back to the city for concessions…perhaps he'd send them back anyway, as a gesture of good will. It would get *some* use out of the hapless pair. "I don't know what he'll do with them, if he *has* them."

They stopped, for a moment, at the foot of Temple Row. A small army of priests, and builders were already at work, trying to rebuild the destroyed temples. The original statues seemed beyond repair, but a number of smaller statues of household gods had been put up in their place. Emily wondered, as she watched a team of builders carrying a golden relic out of one of the temples, what the destruction would mean for the city's religions. Who knew *what* they would come to believe?

"They're not planning to rebuild the Temple of Justice," Caleb commented. "Mother was saying that most of the worshippers are dead or gone."

Emily winced. "*That* will go down well."

"Probably," Caleb agreed, equally sardonically. "But then, there *is* a gash in the floor that leads down to the sewers, so workmen have to be paid danger money to work there."

"And wind up swimming in sludge if they're not careful," Emily said. They started to walk on. "Has…has your mother started talking about other girls for you?"

Caleb shook his head. "By tradition, there's supposed to be a three-month gap between the end of one courtship and the start of another. We were careful, but still…"

Emily nodded, curtly. They'd taken precautions against pregnancy, precautions that were supposed to be infallible, but tradition had its uses. Three months was more than long enough for them to come to terms with the end of their relationship. Maybe she wouldn't be upset when she saw Caleb with another girl…

Her heart clenched. She knew it wouldn't be easy.

But you'll have to get used to it, she told herself, firmly. *Cursing his future bride is not acceptable behavior.*

Caleb gave her an odd look. "And you?"

Emily shook her head. She didn't have anyone who would try to arrange a marriage for her, no close family who'd start the negotiating process without even bothering to check with her first. Void was the closest thing she had to a father, and he'd made it clear that he wouldn't arrange anything for her without her permission. He'd also told her that he'd received a number of requests for her hand, but he hadn't bothered to reply. Emily couldn't help feeling grateful. The idea that complete strangers, some of them easily old enough to be her father or grandfather, would want to marry her...

Her lips twisted in disgust, then annoyance. She wouldn't date again for a while, perhaps not until after she'd left Whitehall. And who knew what would happen then?

"I'm sure mother would be willing to help," Caleb said. "She knows people..."

Emily elbowed him. Sienna probably *did* know people, but Emily had no intention of asking Sienna to help her find a partner. Besides, it would probably lead to a set of etiquette landmines she didn't want to detonate. Better to see what happened at Whitehall and afterwards, she told herself firmly. It wasn't as if she found anyone else particularly attractive.

And you have plenty of money, despite it all, she thought, wryly. *That'll make you very attractive indeed.*

She smiled as the northern bridge came into view. A stream of people flowed in and out of the city; merchants from Cockatrice and Swanhaven rubbing shoulders with magicians and emissaries from across the Allied Lands. Frieda stood at the south end, next to a tall blonde woman. Emily felt her heart skip a beat as she recognized Lady Barb. The older woman hadn't said she'd come...

My chat parchments were destroyed, Emily thought, as she hurried forward. *She couldn't tell me she was coming.*

"Emily," Frieda said. She shot Caleb a nasty look. "Are you all right?"

"Yes." Emily glanced at the guards in the gatehouse, wondering if they had orders to make sure she crossed the bridge. She didn't envy them if they did. "I'm fine."

"Good," Frieda said, crossly. Her black eye hadn't quite healed, giving her a menacing appearance. "Because if you weren't..."

Emily gave Lady Barb a hug, then turned back to Caleb. "I'll see you back at Whitehall," she said. "And tell your family..."

She broke off. She wasn't sure what she wanted to tell them.

"Thank them for their hospitality," she said, finally. Sienna and her family *had* hosted her, after all. "And for everything else."

"Of course," Caleb said, seriously. He looked as though he wanted to hug her too, but didn't quite dare. Emily didn't blame him. The situation was already awkward enough. "I'll see you at Whitehall."

He turned and walked off, not looking back.

Chapter Forty

UNDER OTHER CIRCUMSTANCES, EMILY WOULD HAVE ENJOYED HER WALK ACROSS THE bridge. The stone structure spanned the Tribune River, a churning torrent that roared down the gorge and poured into the sea. Water crashed over jagged rocks that stabbed skywards, daring anyone to clamber down to the river and then climb up to the city. She'd heard that some people did try to ride the rapids in kayaks, but most of them died in the attempt. Only a handful of experienced canoeists made it to the sea.

But now, she just felt cold.

"I'm sorry it didn't work out," Lady Barb said, briskly.

She walked beside Emily, her long, blonde hair glinting in the sun. Frieda ran ahead of them, looking – for a moment – like the child she should have been. But she'd never had a chance at a real childhood, much like Emily herself. Emily wanted to reach out and hug her, hug both of them. And yet, she knew it wouldn't help.

"Me too." She looked up at Lady Barb. "Did you know...?"

"That it would fail?" Lady Barb shrugged. "You never really know how strong a relationship is until it runs into rocky waters. Either the happy couple manages to overcome their difficulties – and the relationship survives – or they are torn apart. In your case...I hoped you'd overcome your problems."

Emily nodded, looking down at the river. "I wish..."

"Don't wish," Lady Barb said, firmly. "What happened, happened. Concentrate on the future."

Emily sighed. "What happened to you? I mean...to your courtship?"

"There was a young man – still a boy, really – who wanted to court me," Lady Barb said. "I was older than you at the time, twenty-two...just young enough to be flattered, but old enough to be careful. It turned out that we had very different ideas of our role in a relationship and we parted on bad terms."

"Caleb and I are still friends," Emily said, although she wasn't sure if that was true. "What happened to him?"

"He married, had kids...he's still alive, as far as I know," Lady Barb said. "I haven't bothered to keep tabs on him."

She gave Emily a sidelong look. "Be careful," she said, seriously. "Caleb was your first, wasn't he? You'll always be entangled with him, as much as you might wish to deny it. He may feel the same way too. Being friends again might not be an option."

"It has to be an option," Emily said.

"You were *sleeping* with him," Lady Barb said. "There is no way you can avoid an emotional tie."

Emily touched her heart. It ached. "Why...why is it so difficult?"

"Because men are men and women are women and immature members of both genders have problems relating to the other." Lady Barb's lips quirked up. "Women are nervous, and understandably so, of having something put inside them; men, too, are nervous about putting something *in* something. The risk of being violated is matched by the risk of losing something very important to you."

"Oh." Emily *knew* she was blushing. Her cheeks felt warm. "I never thought about it like that."

"Few people your age do," Lady Barb told her. "And five years from now, you'll look back on your youth and wonder just what you were thinking."

Emily rubbed her cheek. "How much did Frieda tell you?"

"She didn't say much," Lady Barb said. "Sienna's letter was a little more detailed."

"Yeah," Emily said. She hadn't expected Sienna to contact Lady Barb, but in hindsight she should have. Lady Barb had accompanied her when she'd first visited Beneficence. She and Void were the closest thing Emily had to parents. "What did *she* tell you?"

"Just that you and Caleb had broken up," Lady Barb said. "*And* that you'd fought a god."

"It was a Mimic," Emily told her. Lady Barb's eyes went wide. "Or something related to one, anyway."

She sighed, wishing – again – that some of the scrolls had survived. If Master Wolfe had written them...she wondered, grimly, how long he'd lived. Theoretically, a Mimic could survive indefinitely with enough power. But if he'd been eating other humans and consuming their souls, he might have started to lose his identity. Or gone mad. Or...

I fought a Mimic at Whitehall, she thought. *Did I kill all that remained of him then?*
She shook her head. She'd never know.

"We'll discuss it later," Lady Barb said.

Emily nodded in agreement as they reached the end of the bridge. There were no guards on this side, merely a customs post. The officers took one look at them and waved them on, without even bothering to ask for papers. But then, they'd be used to magicians crossing the bridge and walking to the nearby portal. They'd probably be more concerned about someone who intended to stay in Zangaria.

And they presumably don't know who I am, Emily thought, as they walked down the cobbled road. *King Randor ordered me never to return without permission.*

She sucked in her breath as she saw a plume of steam in the distance. There *was* a station on the north side of the city, if she recalled correctly. A steam train could still run from Cockatrice to the station, even if the bridge hadn't yet been cleared. Or maybe the driver hoped to cross the line and get into the city, where the train could be unloaded easily.

"I'll be taking you back to Whitehall this evening," Lady Barb said. "But first... there's someone who wants a word with you."

She nodded towards a man, standing by a tree. Emily felt her heart start to race as she recognized Void. He'd been with Lady Barb, the last time she'd seen him; she'd thought they were both heading into the Blighted Lands. Had he come back to see her too?

"Frieda and I will wait here," Lady Barb said, firmly. "Come back here when you're done."

Emily nodded and walked towards Void. It was hard, so hard, to resist the temptation to run. The Lone Power looked to have aged in the last couple of weeks, although she knew that was probably an illusion. His long, dark hair spilled out over a face too patrician to be called feminine, even though she knew some male magicians disdained long hair. But then, Void was too old and too powerful to care what his peers thought of him. Indeed, he had very few peers.

"Emily." Void's voice was calm, composed. "What happened between Caleb and yourself?"

"It's a long story," Emily said. She didn't really want to discuss it with anyone. "Do you really want to know?"

"Yes," Void said. "Please, talk."

Emily sighed and started to explain. Void listened, sometimes asking a thoughtful question, as the whole story spilled out. He didn't seem surprised, she noted; he seemed more concerned about her than anything else. She clung to that feeling, even though she knew it could be deceptive. The thought that someone cared about her was important. She *needed* it more than she cared to admit.

"I expected as much," Void said, when she had finished. "I didn't think he would be able to cope with you."

Emily blinked, wiping a tear out of her eye. "With me?"

Void turned to watch the train as it puffed its way back along the line. "I destroyed a village, once," he said. "The entire place was…was hag-ridden. I couldn't save the inhabitants without spreading the contamination across the country. My partner was already dead. There was no time to send for help, Emily, so I took care of it. I stood at the edge of the village and summoned fire, lots of fire. The entire village burned to the ground. Fifty-seven men, women and children died in the blaze I unleashed."

Emily shivered, helplessly.

"I knew some of them," Void added, after a moment. "I'd spoken to them during my investigation. The innkeeper who knew everything, the village hedge-witch who was searching for an apprentice, the young lady who wanted to make a life in the big city, the young man who wanted to marry her…"

He turned to face Emily. "I killed them all, because it was the only way to prevent a greater catastrophe," he told her. "I made that choice. I was the only one who *could* make that choice. I heard some of them begging for mercy, promising anything, as the flames washed around their hovels. I burned them to the ground anyway, then sifted through the ash to be *sure*.

"Not everyone can make those choices, Emily. Caleb couldn't, it would seem."

Emily scowled at him. "Should he have risked letting his sister die?"

Void shrugged. "To save the rest of the city?"

"It isn't a fair choice," Emily said. She understood Caleb's feelings more than she wanted to admit. Marian hadn't deserved to die. But the cold equations might well have dictated her death. She wasn't sure she could have made the deliberate choice to murder the girl, even if it would save countless more lives. "He didn't have to make it."

"The world isn't fair," Void said. "And yes, he *did* have to make it."

He glanced towards Lady Barb, then back at Emily. "You'll have to make those choices yourself, in the future," he warned. "And close connections will only get in the way."

"Maybe," Emily said, stubbornly.

Void shrugged and reached into his robes, producing a parchment scroll. "This is for the Grandmaster. Don't try to open it."

Emily felt the charm on the seal as she took it and nodded, once. "What *is* it?"

"An apprenticeship offer, if you still want it," Void said. Emily stared at him. "An *unconditional* apprenticeship offer. You could come with me now, if you liked."

"I want to finish my schooling first," Emily said. She held the parchment gingerly. In the right hands, it was worth hundreds of crowns. "After that…"

"You'll be ready to learn from me," Void said.

He stepped backwards. "You did well. I would be proud to have you as my apprentice."

Emily blushed. "Thank you."

Void raised a hand in salute. "You're welcome."

He vanished in a flash of light. Emily stared at where he'd been for a moment, then tucked the scroll into her pouch and hurried to join her friends.

Lady Barb gave her a sharp look when she arrived. "Back to Whitehall?"

"Yes," Emily said. "Back to Whitehall."

End of Book Twelve

Emily Will Return In:

The Gordian Knot

Appendix: The Financial Crisis of Beneficence

The roots of what became known, alternately, as the Railway Crash, the Banking Crisis and Vesperian's Folly rested in three factors, all introduced – deliberately or otherwise – by Emily.

First, the spread of the New Learning (everything from abacuses to steam engines) encouraged a rapid growth in craftsmanship and opened up whole new vistas for technological advancement and profit. As a free city, situated close to the Barony of Cockatrice, Beneficence was well-placed to take advantage of these developments without interference from a jealous monarch. Steam engineers and artificers, for example, were happy to move to the city and start training apprentices, who would in turn train others.

Second, the issuing of microloans from various banks, particularly the Bank of Silence, ensured a thriving commercial sector. Anyone with a dream – and a semi-workable proposal – could apply for a loan and most of them would be granted. (And most of them would repay the loans.) This fueled the growth of an investment infrastructure and, eventually, the first true stock market.

Third, the collapse of the Accountants Guild – a direct consequence of the spread of new forms of bookkeeping and cheap paper – ensured that there were few old-style professional financiers within the city. Of those who remained, only a handful were savvy enough to see the danger signs and issue warnings, none of which were actually heeded. Like financial bubbles on Earth, everything looked good until it suddenly wasn't.

Vesperian, a wealthy merchant who had made his first fortune through trade, was ideally placed to take advantage of the industrial boom. His first investments in steam technology produced an improved steam engine that opened up whole new vistas for both steam-powered ships and railway engines. The opening of the Beneficence-Cockatrice Railway – a direct link between Beneficence and Cockatrice City – suggested that tying the remainder of Zangaria and even parts beyond would be a relatively simple task. Accordingly, Vesperian started work on the Beneficence-Zangaria Railway. It would rapidly become known as Vesperian's Track.

He did not, however, have the cash reserves to fund the project himself. Reluctant to approach his peers or King Randor for a loan, Vesperian solved the problem by selling shares in the railway to all and sundry. These investments, which rapidly became known as 'notes,' promised repayment within two years, at (originally) a rate of ten-to-twelve. If someone were to invest, for example, ten crowns in the railway, they would receive twelve crowns at the end of the two-year period. Through a great deal of marketing, aided by the success of the Beneficence-Cockatrice Railway, Vesperian managed to raise a staggering sum and work began.

Problems appeared, however, almost at once. The task of gaining permission to construct even the first stage of the line (Beneficence-Cockatrice-Swanhaven) ran into political problems within Swanhaven. Vesperian switched to another barony, but the ruling aristocracy required a great deal of expensive soothing before they would grant the necessary permissions to start construction. Worse, the sudden demand for everything involved in producing railway track and steam engines drove up prices all across Beneficence, sending the costs of even the first stretch of track into the stratosphere.

Unable to repay his first set of loans, with the first set of creditors baying at his heels, Vesperian struggled desperately to raise more money. This forced him to up the promised repayment rate (at the height of the bubble, he was issuing notes promising repayment at ten-to-twenty) and, while he was successful in paying off most of his early creditors, this created the impression that the line was already earning money. Bizarrely, Vesperian's early success only ensured that the eventual – inevitable – collapse was a great deal worse.

By this point, it seemed the entire city had caught railway fever. Thousands of investors poured money into the project, from children offering their pocket money to bankers and wealthy guildsmen offering vast sums. The few dissenting voices – mainly people who had been priced out of the market by the rising costs of iron products – were roundly ignored or mocked. No one wanted to believe that the whole affair was about to end in tears.

Complicating matters was the simple fact that Vesperian was not a very good bookkeeper, let alone an accountant. He wasn't keeping close track of the number of notes he was issuing, and his estimates of how much money he owed were off by at least an order of magnitude. By the time he realized how badly he was on the hook for literally tens of *thousands* of crowns it was far too late. Rumors were leaking out and some of his older creditors were demanding repayment. His attempt to convince Emily to invest in the project was a final desperate bid to repay his debts. When it failed, he knew he was done for. His death, seemingly at the hands of a god, marked the moment the bubble burst.

The results were disastrous. Vesperian had left behind a great deal of material, but as prices plummeted there was no way it could be sold to recoup more than a fraction of the debts he owed. The notes investors had collected so carefully, blood-bound or not, were suddenly worthless. Thousands of people who had planned their financial affairs on the assumption they would be repaid discovered that they wouldn't be. Even people who hadn't invested in the railway were affected; shop-keepers, for example, discovered that their debtors couldn't repay them (because their money had vanished) while their creditors were hungry for cash and willing to use whatever force was necessary to extract it. Vesperian's Track was merely the first business to collapse into rubble, countless thousands of workers suddenly finding themselves unemployed. As more businesses followed it, the city's poor relief found itself utterly overwhelmed.

The Guildmasters were utterly overwhelmed, unable to come to grips with each wave of disaster before the next one hit. There was no way to repay the investors, let alone allow them to repay their own creditors. This led to outbreaks of rioting as investors and creditors alike realized that there was a real risk of starving in the streets or simply being enslaved for non-payment of debts. (Perversely, some debtors calculated that slavery was a better option than remaining free and hungry.) The City Guard simply wasn't strong enough to control the rioters (and a number of the guardsmen owned notes themselves.) Even as the Guildmasters tried to parse out just how much money Vesperian owed his creditors, events had already slipped beyond their control.

It shouldn't have surprised anyone, really, that economic collapse was followed by a political shockwave that nearly tore the city apart.

Appendix: Religion in the Nameless World

The Nameless World is quite definitely pagan in how it approaches religion. Instead of a monotheistic religion, it is generally believed that there are entire multitudes of gods and godly families. Indeed, it is agreed that certain gods are actually the *same* god, but called by different names. (Like Mars and Aries, both Gods of War.) Therefore, despite the vast number of religions and sects, there is surprisingly little religious conflict.

Gods are generally divided into three categories. The Great Gods represent aspects of the physical and spiritual worlds, such as health, war and farming. The Loci Gods represent particular locations and are rarely worshipped outside it. The Household Gods represent a specific household. It is generally considered polite, when entering a city or a home, to visit the temple and pay your respects to the city's god, even if you are not staying.

(There is some debate over the exact nature of the Household Gods. Some people believe they're the souls of the family's ancestors, while others believe they're actually newborn gods.)

It is important to realize that the vast majority of worshippers *believe* in the gods, even if they don't worship them. One is not expected to worship any god – or worship at all, if one chooses – but it is generally considered unwise to deliberately insult a god. Another person's rites or rituals may seem odd, yet that doesn't make them invalid. Tolerating other rites is considered good manners.

The vast majority of people will pay their respects to a multitude of gods throughout their lives. However, a number choose to dedicate themselves to one particular god – almost always one of the Great Gods – and never worship any other. These people are devotees (dedicated followers), initiates (junior cultists) and priests (senior cultists).

Unsurprisingly, the majority of religions are effectively cults and operate accordingly. Most of them try to find something unique, something exclusive – and often secret – to draw in new and significant worshippers. A small cult may be quite sincere; a larger cult, which may draw in thousands of worshippers, may be run more as a racket than anything else. Devotees are expected to make contributions, for example; initiates often turn over their possessions to the cult. (A number of cults are astonishingly rich.) Cults also find ways to fleece outsiders – a number of cults operate a sacred prostitution service disguised as a fertility rite, for example; others sell prayers and blessings to those who are prepared to pay.

The general attitudes of outsiders towards specific cults can vary widely. Some cults – the Harvest Goddess followers – are regarded as largely harmless. Others, including the Blood Worshippers or the Crone's followers, are regarded with considerable suspicion. There are no shortage of rumors surrounding their innermost mysteries and rituals, most of which are exaggerated. Parents tend to get annoyed when their adolescent children rebel by joining some of the more harmful cults. They feel that the rites and rituals serve as an excuse to engage in forbidden practices. They are not wrong.

It is unusual for a government to interfere in religious matters, provided that religious teachings do not threaten public order. Most religious cults don't attempt to encourage their worshippers to question authority, let alone stand up to their rulers. Those that do are targeted for extermination. Rumors of their presence can unleash a — sometimes literal — witch-hunt.

About the author

Christopher G. Nuttall was born in Edinburgh, studied in Manchester, married in Malaysia and currently living in Scotland, United Kingdom with his wife and baby son. He is the author of twenty-six novels from various publishers and fifty self-published novels.

Current and forthcoming titles published by Twilight Times Books

Schooled in Magic YA fantasy series
     Schooled in Magic — book 1
     Lessons in Etiquette — book 2
     A Study in Slaughter — book 3
     Work Experience — book 4
     The School of Hard Knocks — book 5
     Love's Labor's Won — book 6
     Trial By Fire — book 7
     Wedding Hells — book 8
     Infinite Regress — book 9
     Past Tense — book 10
     The Sergeant's Apprentice — book 11
     Fists of Justice – book 12
     The Gordian Knot – book 13

The Decline and Fall of the Galactic Empire military SF series
     Barbarians at the Gates — book 1
     The Shadow of Cincinnatus — book 2
     The Barbarian Bride — book 3

Chris has also produced *The Empire's Corps* series, the *Outside Context Problem* series and many others. He is also responsible for two fan-made Posleen novels, both set in John Ringo's famous Posleen universe. They can both be downloaded from his site.
     Website: http://www.chrishanger.net
     Blog: http://chrishanger.wordpress.com
     Facebook: http://www.facebook.com/ChristopherGNuttall